The Cavalier's Woman

by

JOAN HUNTER

A KANGAROO BOOK
PUBLISHED BY POCKET BOOKS NEW YORK

THE CAVALIER'S WOMAN

POCKET BOOK edition published June, 1977

This POCKET BOOK edition includes every word contained in
the original, higher-priced edition. It is printed from brand-
new plates made from completely reset, clear, easy-to-read type.
POCKET BOOK editions are published by
POCKET BOOKS,
a Simon & Schuster Division of
GULF & WESTERN CORPORATION
1230 Avenue of the Americas,
New York, N.Y. 10020.
Trademarks registered in the United States
and other countries.

ISBN: 0-671-81085-5.
Cover illustration by Hector Garrido.

Printed in the U.S.A.

For Steve (Winkle)

Place me as a signet upon thy heart,
   as a signet upon thine arm,
for Love is as strong as death.
                —Canticles, viii, 6. The Secret Lore
                of Magic. Idries Shah.

She looked at him, as one who awakes:
The past was a sleep, and her life began.
                —Robert Browning.

Rupert
the Devil

ONE

As dawn slid under the curtains, rising like mist to creep across the panelled room, Venetia Denby awoke and could not sleep again.

She rolled over onto her back, aware of the unfamiliar mattress beneath, the alien pillow under her head, staring into the shadows of the tester, seeing the black solidity of the bulbous posts at the foot, the watery sheen of the silken drapes, finer than the serge ones on her own bed at home.

A shiver ran through her, but she stayed quiet, unwilling to rouse her sister Ella, who slept soundly beside her. In that still hour, when even the birds had not started to call, she wanted no harsh discord; happy to be alone with her thoughts to relish the delight of being in Oxford, at last.

For a while she hugged this tremendous fact to herself, then she slipped out of bed, padding across the polished wooden floor with its Turkey rugs resembling colorful islands on a brown sea. The casement was tightly shut against the night air, and Venetia flung it wide, inhaling the exhilarating dewy freshness, leaning far out and gazing enraptured, at the city spread below. Oxford, the Royalist headquarters from almost the beginning of the war, was the place which had become Venetia's lodestar—and now, she was really there.

Her mind was still dazed with the speed of events of the past days—the sudden flight from their home in the Cotswolds which had been threatened by advancing Roundhed troops. It had been a last minute rush; servants jostling each other as they ran, emerging from doorways carrying their own or their masters private possessions. In the courtyard had been a confusion of neighing horses, sweating grooms, carriages and wagons into which refugees and goods were hastily piled. Venetia's stepmother, youngest child in her arms, big-bellied with the next due at any time, had frantically tried to round up the toddlers, who were wilfully running about, getting in everyone's way, while their nurses distractedly attempted to control them.

Samuel Denby, big and floridly handsome, looking much more the jovial country squire than a fighting man, had stamped about giving orders. Dogs had barked, while children cried, mingling this uproar with that of arguing, tearful female voices, but eventually the cavalcade had creaked into motion, beginning its journey to Oxford.

On arrival the previous night, it had been too late to do anything except pack the little ones off and fall, exhausted, into bed. But now it was a glorious sparkling morning and Venetia stretched her arms wide in a transport of joy. It was good to be alive on this 15th day of July, 1643—to be eighteen years old, and part of this bustling city, crowded with troops and Courtiers, noblemen and their ladies, instead of stuck in some dull backwater, missing all the excitement. Soon her betrothed, Michael Haywood, would be calling, and, in a matter of hours, her dearest ambition would be fulfilled when he took her to meet his commander, Prince Rupert.

Her heart thudded at the thought—chin cupped in her hand, she leaned on the window-ledge, dreaming. It was as if the Fates had conspired to bring about this war especially for her, answering her prayers and her longing, when she had spun that strong web of want, its threads reaching out over time and space to draw him toward her.

She had heard his name long before the war—back in 1636, when her father had returned from a rare visit to Whitehall Palace, and regaled his children with stories of the Court and news of the arrival of the King's nephews, two German Princes, Charles Louis and his brother, Rupert. It was their first time in England, the homeland of their mother—she was Elizabeth, only sister of Charles I, and had been married young to Frederick V, Elector Palatine and Duke of Bavaria.

Venetia's father had enthused about Rupert—an adventurous youngster, already an experinced soldier.

Rupert—it had appeared very strange to her English ears then, foreign, exotic, variant, so they told her, of "Robert." She was ten and impressionable, repeating it

3

to herself—Rupert—Rupert. The sort of name to whisper into her pillow, tossing all night to the rhythm of it.

Locked away in the peaceful village, occupied with her studies, domestic duties and the perplexities of growing up, Venetia forgot the Prince, yet, somewhere at the back of consciousness, there remained the image built up by her father's words. Then, suddenly, the political seesaw tilted and he went home to help Charles Louis form an army to try and win back the Palatinate. Their father had lost it along with Bohemia, long ago when he had set himself up in opposition to the powerful Catholic, Ferdinand of Austria.

England raised money to back them. Young men seeking adventure offered their swords in the service of the widowed Queen Elizabeth and her gallant sons. In Venetia's own family, Mallory, her eldest brother and fledgling soldier, volunteered to go. She ached to be a boy, to fight beside him and for him! The Queen and her cause were but gray shapes, meaning little to her— it was Rupert who was real! Rupert whom she longed to serve!

Mallory marched away, full of high hopes and ambition, and Michael went with him. Weeks passed, and they arrived home unexpectedly full of stories of the battle of Vlotho in Westphalia, and how the Palatine army had been vastly outnumbered by the Austrians. Prince Rupert, a Colonel at eighteen, had led the cavalry with reckless bravery, but they were beaten and he was captured and shut up in the grim castle of Lintz.

The months flowed by, as smoothly as the Danube beyond his prison walls. Venetia performed the daily round learning the housewifely skills which it was appropriate that she should know in anticipation of being a bride. She was maturing quickly; there was a glow now in Michael's eyes when he came on his decorous visits. An answering response stirred her blood, filling her with unrest, making her wish that he was not quite so circumspect in his treatment of her.

But now, in England, trouble was brewing. There was a strife in London between King Charles and his Parliament, its ripples spreading wide over the country. In their mellow Tudor manor on the borders of a snug village, the Denbys found their own lives disrupted. Venetia understood little of the principles involved, but she was upset by the loud dissenting voices of her father, backed up by his sons, Mallory and Jonathan, as they argued with friends who could not share their support of the King.

Their closest neighbors, Tobias Fletcher and his boy, Giles, questioned the concept of absolute monarchy, the tax demands and foreign policy, the management of the Irish affairs and, most of all, the behavior of his French Queen. They shared the general alarm at her popish agents in Court, the freedom of priests and Jesuits, the virtual suspension of anti-Catholic laws.

The Fletchers visited the Denby house no more, and Venetia was forbidden to speak with them. The clouds were gathering ominously, and the storm broke while people were still trying to convince themselves that Civil War could never happen.

Although their father's face was serious, Mallory and Jonathan were unable to conceal their delight when, one morning in August, Michael came fresh from the courier, waving letters and shouting:

"Prince Rupert has landed at Tynemouth with his brother, Maurice. They have come to fight for King Charles!"

Venetia had been half way down the wide staircase when she heard him. The name broke like the blare of trumpets in her ears, as the men shouted it below. It swelled on a surge of sound—Rupert of the Rhine!

That stormy petrel had been released at the pleas of his Uncle Charles, who needed him by his side in the coming conflict and nothing could stop Venetia's brothers from riding to Nottingham to join him.

The village settled back into its usual somnolence after the flurry of departure, but now its serenity was ruffled by the backwash of events shattering the world beyond the softly rolling hills which sheltered the valley. A post-boy bearing news, a sudden influx of troops moving through the area, and Squire Denby's lads coming home on leave.

Because of their service at Vlotho, Mallory and Michael offered themselves as volunteers in Rupert's Lifeguard. Samuel Denby, unable to resist the call, rode with them, leaving Venetia to support her stepmother, Catherine. His first wife had died in childbirth, and he had married again, this delicate, pretty woman, not a great deal older than Venetia. A new family of brothers and sisters had arrived with depressing regularity, rendering

5

her even more helpless. Venetia found that with her father absent, the steward, bailiff and tenant farmers were turning to herself for guidance.

It was hard to have to sit, listening to complaints, trying to balance accounts, while the weeks slipped by and her head was reeling with stirring tales sent home in letters by Michael or the brothers. Venetia was able to glut herself on news of the Prince, no man in England was given more flamboyant publicity by both sides. The King favored him above all his advisers, granting him his own command, General of the Horse, with special permission to take orders from no one except His Majesty. His shock tactics of the headlong cavalry charge rocked the Roundheads. His daring excursions behind the enemy lines in a variety of disguises, his dramatic appearances where least expected, his phenomenal luck in coming out of the most desperate scraps unscathed, all added to the legend. The Roundheads began to look on him with superstitious dread, circulating stories of brutality and devilish practices.

At first, the Royalists had been confident of an early victory, for their army consisted, in the main, of aristocrats, officered by gentry whose education had involved swordsmanship. They had fully expected to put in their places the tapesters and tradesmen who were generally thought to fill the ranks of the enemy.

Lately, however, Venetia had been aware of a change in attitude; it was not going to be so simple.

A shaft of bright sunlight cut into Venetia's eyes, rousing her. Birds were whistling cheerily in the trees level with her window, and Oxford was beginning to stir into life.

She launched herself across the room, jumping on the bed, pummeling her sister. "Ella! Wake up! Lord, what a sluggard you are!"

Ella grumbled crossly, tucking down under the quilt. "Go away!" And it was not until Venetia shouted that there were half a dozen young officers clamoring outside the bedroom door, that her china-blue eyes snapped open.

While she dressed, Venetia reflected that no doubt the lie would be truth soon enough for Ella, just fifteen, was man-mad, and there had been a distinct shortage in their village of late. Meg, her maid, rustled about, unpacking bags, shaking the creases from hastily folded

You are reading a book.
Do you know how lucky
you are? More than half
the people in the world
do not know how to read
or write.

UNICEF is trying to
change that by helping
to train teachers and
equip schools in many
countries.

UNICEF is also bringing
medicine, health services,
and better nutrition to
needy children in poor
countries.

Whenever you help UNICEF,
you make a big difference
in the lives of many
children, in many very important ways.

U. S. Committee for UNICEF
331 East 38th Street
New York, NY 10016

gowns and getting them on to hangers in the cupboards. She chattered breezily, hoping to convince the young ladies, and herself, that everything was normal and that they had not just been uprooted and flung upon the mercies of a strange town!

There was a hesitant tap, and the door opened wide enough to admit Aunt Hortense, all whispering black taffeta and clicking strings of pearls. She reminded Venetia of an agitated bat.

"My dears," she smiled and bobbed, wisps of hair escaping from under her lace cap. "Poor little lambs! I trust you managed to sleep. And your sweet stepmother, so near her time—and your father already departed to rejoin his regiment, such a conscientious spirit!"

Venetia thought it more likely that he had had quite enough of squalling brats and hysterical women.

"Oh, this war—this terrible war!" Hortense fluttered to the window. "Oxford was once so peaceful, and now 'tis full of soldiers. You've no idea how disorderly they are! The tales I could tell you, were it not for the tenderness of your years! Why, not long ago, the Prince himself separated two quarrelling drunken troopers with a pole-axe!"

Venetia, washing at the pewter basin which stood on the flat top of the carved oak chest, managed to ask casually "Prince Rupert? Have you seen him, aunt?"

"I have caught a glimpse, once or twice, when he clattered by on that great black horse of his. A most restless person, I understand, always off on some skirmish with his troopers, spends little time at Court and practically none with the society of the town!"

"He's a soldier, aunt, and there is a war on." Venetia stood still while Meg fastened the strings of the finely-pleated damask skirt which had gone on after the linen shift and a couple of petticoats.

"I know, dear, but he is also Royal, and people expect decorous behavior from someone so eminent." There was no doubt that Hortense was enjoying the war, it gave her endless topics for gossip. "He has made himself mighty unpopular with the Courtiers. I hear that he is so proud and domineering, so hot-tempered and rude at the Council-table."

Venetia eased her arms into the full sleeves of her bodice, turning to the mirror on the dressing table to fasten the front. "That is not what Mallory says."

7

"Oh, Mallory!" Her aunt threw up her hands and eyes in mock despair. "He will not hear a word against his chief. He is a typical of the wild young men who positively idolize Prince Rupert."

A commotion below in the courtyard announced the arrival of the Denby brothers and Michael, come to greet the newcomers. Excitement dried Venetia's mouth; though she romanticized about the Prince, it was Michael who had awakened her senses, rousing her body to passion. A desperate urgency thrust aside convention to their rare meetings; he had stopped treating her as if she were some untouchable holy relic, and they were both fully aware of his continual danger.

She quickly put the finishing touches to her toilet, and within minutes the room was filled with loud male voices, the glint of steel, flashy clothing and big boots. She was swept into Michael's arms, breathing in the sharp smell of outdoors while his mouth closed on hers, stabbing her with an instant reminder of stolen hours of love.

He released her and held her away, at arms' length, grinning with delight; "Sweetheart! Here, let me look at you. Jesus! You grow more fair every time I see you."

Sometimes his adoration worried her; she knew that she could not return it. They had been betrothed when she was still in her cradle, and the marriage had been arranged, as was customary, with lands, property and religion of prime consideration. They had played together as children, and he was always rather patronizing, provoking her into attempting to equal him in acts of daring; climbing a higher tree, swimming a more turbulent stretch of river, enjoying hearing the fear in his voice as her horse gathered his limbs for that spring over a more formidable obstacle than Michael thought it prudent to tackle. "Don't, Venetia! You will get hurt!"

When he had come back from Vlotho, a toughened suntanned soldier, he had seemed even more superior, but had been packed off to London and the study of Law. He kicked his heels at the Inns of Court, chewed his pen, plagued his tutors and racketed around with the other students, glad when finally the call to arms released him. He came to say goodbye to Venetia before leaving for Nottingham and found that she had developed from a scrawny tomboy into a very beautiful woman. He had fallen in love completely and for ever.

She knew that she was very lucky for he was a pleas-

8

ant person to be with; handsome, slightly built but sinewy, surprisingly strong, with a thin, sensitive face, shy hazel eyes under thick brown lashes, and quizzical brows over which fell untidy strands of pale hair. There was something endearingly vague and rumpled about his whole appearance, and he had a hesitant way of glancing across, as if for approval of what he said, and of laughing in mock dismay when anybody outwitted him.

Aunt Hortense was flustered by this sudden influx of hearty warriors, rattling their swords and scuffing her rugs. "La, I don't know what things are coming to these days. Really, sirs, this is a young girl's bedchamber! Not one of your parade grounds or rude soldier's quarters!"

"Nor the tents of the camp-followers, eh?" Mallory put in gleefully.

"Hush, sir!" she chided, mouth turned down reprovingly. "Don't mention such loose wantons before gentlewomen! And surely Jonathan is too young even to know of their presence."

Mallory threw back his tawny mane of hair and yelped with laughter. "God dammit, he's seventeen! He's not confined himself to purely military activities, I can assure you!"

Michael's arm was around Venetia's waist again, pressing her to him while the Denbys engaged their aunt in conversation, their broad shoulders between her and the lovers.

"God, I must see you alone," Michael whispered into the curls on her temple. "It has been so long——"

Three months since she had lain in his arms, deep in the night when the whole household was asleep, on his last, snatched leave. Those thrilling, tormenting, unsatisfying embraces, marred because he was so afraid of making her pregnant; kind and thoughtful of him, of course, but she longed to be swept away by an impetuous passion which tossed caution to the wind. She was tempted to urge for permission to marry quickly, but there was a strange reluctance within her.

"I don't see how we can arrange it, with Aunt Hortense so watchful over my morals," she teased him, twining her fingers in his hair.

"The evenings are balmy in the fields by the river. Come there tonight with me," he urged.

She prevaricated, while her mouth smiled and her mind boiled with the thought uppermost in it. "You must first of all take me to see your Prince. This 'Rupert' that you praise to the skies."

Because she felt guilty, she twisted away from him with a provocative rustle of skirts, leaning forward at the looking-glass to adjust the fine linen collar with its trim of point-lace, which draped the low neckline of her tight, high-waisted bodice. Sometimes she marveled at her ability to be so two-faced, wishing Michael were not so easily duped, telling herself, crossly, that it was all partly his fault; he was forever talking about Rupert, whom he admired so much.

He frowned, his prime objective to make love to her as soon as possible, "I'll see what can be arranged."

"That is of no use!" Caution fled, and her voice betrayed her before she controlled herself, adding, more reasonably; "I would like to see him today." She gave a little laugh, slipping her arm through his. "Really, Michael, you have stirred up an almighty curiosity in me to set eyes on this paragon."

TWO

Oxford had welcomed the King when he moved in to make it his headquarters in the winter of 1642. Undergraduates gladly forsook their books to join with the townsfolk in throwing up earthworks and digging trenches to strengthen the fortifications.

The more sober members of the community might deplore the fact that the University languished with so many scholars abandoning their studies, and complain about the drunkenness and brawling, but the tradesmen rubbed their hands in delight. Never had they been able to charge such high prices for food, drink and beds.

Now, in the place of gownsmen, it was a more common sight to see a gang of high-spirited horsemen, covered in dust, swirling their drover's whips and herding plundered cattle through the streets to the quadrangles where they were slaughtered to supplement army rations.

Recruits were drilled in every available square, troopers and Courtiers billeted in spare rooms, and the whole exciting, colorful disruption worked its magic on the female population as it always will, when a sleepy city suddenly erupts into a garrison town.

The sight of so many virile males far from home, loved ones and restraining influences, expending their splendid energy on marching, training and learning how to kill, drove them mad. It was an irresistible challenge and the most demure damsel acted the harlot, while mature matrons behaved as if this was their last chance of youth, before old age set in!

Venetia needed no second bidding to snatch up a shawl and ride out with Michael through the wide, busy streets, in the direction of the meadows by the river where recruits were mustering for the Prince's inspection. Halfway there, they were met by two riders who hailed her brothers noisily and with much doffing of plumed hats and bowing when Venetia was introduced. They were as gaily dressed as for a party, one in green silk with gold swagging, the other in rose velvet, and they wafted a gust of musky perfume.

The green-clad beau was French with an impressive title which Venetia did not quite catch, but the others called him "Etienne." His slim companion, Adrian Carey, was given to graceful gestures and posturing, when he was not engaged in watching Etienne with shining eyes. He reminded Venetia of a rather pretty girl. He lost no time in acquainting her with the fact that he was an actor, which surprised her for she had not imagined that there would be players among the King's troopers.

"My dear, why not?" he said, toying with his red-brown ringlets. "I don't say that I actually take sword and engaged the enemy, but there are other ways in which one can assist. I was on the London stage, but since those confounded Roundheads closed the theaters, I have been on the road, following our armies, giving them entertainment."

"Where is Madame d'Auvergne this morning?" Mallory asked the Frenchman, who heaved his elegant shoulders in a shrug.

"*Mon Dieu!* I defy anyone to get my wife out of bed at an early hour," and he gave Mallory an odd smile as he added: "You should know that, Monsieur."

They were blocking the road, starting an argument

with a carter who wanted to get past. After a brisk exchange of insults they moved on, still laughing, while Etienne waved and kissed his fingers to women who had come to the upper windows attracted by the noise. Venetia felt unreasonably irritated at the way in which Ella was goggling at him in open-mouthed admiration. She did not want to be bothered with her; as it was, her ears were still ringing with Aunt Hortense's reluctant goodbyes, after warning her for the twentieth time to be cautious, to be vigilant and to be sure to be home before dark!

The certainty that the outing was about to be blighted was increased by the sound of hooves behind her. It was the youngest member of Denby's first family, Timothy. He was spurring his fat pony after them, hair tousled, clothes flung on anyhow. Normally, Venetia felt very protective toward this boy at whose birth their mother had lost her life.

"Hey, wait for me!" He was shouting, making shop-keepers look around as they took down their shutters.

Ella tossed her head and scowled. "Who wants a baby like you with them?"

"Baby yourself!" retorted Timothy hotly, his chin setting in that obstinate way which meant trouble.

"You cried because you had to leave your rabbits behind." Ella delivered this home-thrust unmercifully, and Venetia's palm itched to slap her, well aware that Etienne and his friend were looking back with amused grins, while Mallory's expression grew dark. If they did not behave, he would wheel around and escort them home and her morning would be ruined.

Timothy had deliberately ridden his mount too close to his sister so that her beast swerved. "You are just a great ugly girl. I'm going to ask the Prince if I can join his Lifeguard!"

It was still cool in the meadow, purple clover and blaze of yellow buttercups starring the lush green, a few tenuous strands of mist clinging near the water, and there was that clarity over all which promised a hot day. The recruits were beginning to straggle in, a motley assortment, armed with a miscellany of pikes, rusty swords and unwieldy ancient muskets. Their reasons for enlisting were as varied as their weapons, mostly in the expectation of action, looting and pay.

"Although there will be little likelihood of money,"

12

remarked Mallory, casting an eye over them. "I haven't had much since I joined. We mostly supply our own needs. The army is hopelessly in arrears and they'll have to 'live on the country,' like the rest of us."

"Plundering, d'you mean?" Venetia glanced at him, shocked.

Etienne was watching her in pleased contemplation as a man might look at a work of art, smoothing his thin line of dark mustache thoughtfully. "Madame, if the Cavaliers take what they consider to be the spoils of war, remember that they are branded as Delinquents by Parliament and their own estates delivered up to swell the exchequer of the enemy. I am paying for the troop I brought over from France myself, and many are doing the same, providing equipment and meeting the running costs."

"Of course, His Highness is used to this kind of thing," Adrian's tone had the edge of malice. "This is the way they do it in Germany. He will not think twice about leaving plundered country behind him, saying that it is the need of war."

Unhappily, they dwelt for a moment on every grizzly tale they had ever heard about the armies which ravaged Europe, while the sun shone from a cloudless sky on this typically English scene, where the windmills turned lazily on the horizon, and across the far side of the silver bank of the Cherwell, milkmaids approached the patient cows, armed with yoke and pail.

Beneath a clump of elm trees on the opposite end of the field stood a group of men, their horses cropping the grass in the shade. Their clothing and demeanor, the sound of their voices, cultured and confident, denoted that they were officers.

Venetia dismounted and, with her hand resting lightly on Michael's arm, walked over the sward. As they drew closer, one of those well-bred voices was drawling, "Such wonderful news, Your Highness, that of Prince Maurice so soundly beating Sir William Waller at Roundaway Down."

She did not need to ask which of the men was Prince Rupert; as soon as she saw him she knew who it would be. The flood of intuition and excitement stopped her voice for a second, then the words to Michael flowed on, glad of something to say, so that she need not just stand struck dumb by the impact of the wonderful and in-

13

credible fact that he existed. He was only a few feet away from her, deep in conversation with his adjutants, different somehow from anything she had expected, her dream-picture instantly forgotten by the overpowering reality.

She had not realized his immense height. Mallory was six foot one, but Rupert topped him by at least four inches. He was lean and lithe, moving with an unself-conscious grace, and Venetia could not drag her gaze from his strikingly handsome face; that olive skin, those dark flashing eyes, the high cheekbones and aquiline nose which gave him a hawk-like appearance. His mouth was beautiful; the upper lip finely cut with a curl which hinted at contempt for incompetence, while the lower was full and firm adding to the strength of his jaw with the slight cleft in the chin.

His hair was dark brown with highlights of rich chestnut where the sun played over his head and it fell from a center parting, curling across his shoulders and chest. His manner was reserved, austere even, and yet, beneath this apparent control, lay a thinly concealed temper relentless and fierce. Venetia wanted to break through the veneer, to be caught up in the fury, the power, which lay just under the surface, not dormant but held in check.

He was dressed simply, in a well-worn leather doublet thonged down the front, a lace-edged kerchief knotted around his neck, plain burgundy velvet breeches, and boots pulled high up his legs, not rolled over into bucket-tops as were those of some of the other officers. A red silk sash spanned his narrow waist, and a serviceable baldrick carried the swept-hilt rapier which hung at his left hip. A page hovered nearby, holding his feather-loaded hat, his scarlet cloak, and a brace of pistols. At his feet lay a white dog of an unusual breed, shaggy and large, head resting on its paws while it panted in the heat, its black beady eyes fixed on its master through a thick mane of fur.

Mallory presented the members of his family, and he hissed in the ear of the stunned Venetia; "Curtsey, you fool! He is of the Blood Royal!"

There was no need to remind her; every inch of him shouted the fact aloud. She obeyed her brother, dipping down, skirts spread gracefully then she rose, daring to look up into his face as if he were a god to be worshipped. This was the instant truth of the situation but

14

she did not want it to be known to him; not yet. A brief smile lifted his haughty mouth, the somber gaze met hers for a second, and when he spoke it was with an accent just strong enough to render the deep cadences of his voice even more fascinating. Its timbre scraped down her spine into her belly and she suddenly needed to sit.

Normally she was noted for witty remarks, well able to give a pert answer to any man. Now, infuriatingly, when she most wanted to make an impression, her mind went blank.

Timothy pushed rudely in front of her, gazing up at his idol. "Sir, Your Highness . . . ," he blurted, red to the ears, aware of Ella behind him, arming herself with taunts to goad him later. "Will you take me into your horse?"

The men laughed but Rupert looked at him seriously. "A very young recruit, eh? How old are you?"

Timothy drew himself up proudly. "Eleven, sir."

"So . . . when I was your age, I wanted to be a trooper too, but they would not let me. You will have to wait, I fear. But you can study war, just as I did. There are many books which will make you a better soldier when the time comes." He rested a hand on the shoulder of the crestfallen child. "And what would your sister say if I took you from her? I already have two of her brothers."

Venetia felt the meadow and everyone there melt away as he looked at her in that way he had, when he really concentrated, as if she was the only person of importance in the world. She was seized by a driving physical longing which astonished her by its force; she had never felt this desperate hunger for Michael, deprived, angry and jealous when the Prince turned away.

A groom was holding the fine stallion, ready for him, ebony coat glistening, leather trappings polished and immaculate. He put his foot in the stirrup and swung up easily, still talking to Timothy.

"I'm sorry to disappoint you, but get on your pony and come with me to review these new men. Then you can at least say that you have ridden with Rupert."

"By God, he has a very high opinion of himself!" thought Venetia, furious because he had not spoken to her like that. He wheeled his horse, turning on a couple of subalterns, all lovelocks, laces, braid and flash, loung-

15

ing against a tree-trunk, chatting to an entranced Ella.

"You there!" His stentorian voice brought them to attention. "Enough of the fallals! We've work to do. To horse, Lieutenant!"

Venetia shivered at the sight of the black scowl on his stern young face. "He is insufferably conceited!" she remarked to Etienne who was at her elbow, missing nothing of her reactions, raising his peaked, satyr brows quizzically. Everything seemed to amuse him and he laughed aloud when she added, "I would hate to anger him!"

Rupert rode out into the brilliant sunshine, his eyes raking over the raw material before him and, more than anything on earth, Venetia yearned to be the horse between his velvet-covered thighs, or the reins under his sunburned hand.

" 'Sdeath! He's in the devil of a mood this morning." Mallory shaded his eyes against the glare. "Those poor bastards are in for a rough time!"

"Perhaps the Duchess of Richmond said 'no' last night." Adrian had disposed his shapely limbs in the grassy shade and was engaged in nothing more taxing than stringing together a daisy-chain.

Michael was spreading out his cloak for Venetia to sit on and frowned disapprovingly at him. "He probably did not even ask her. Don't forget, she is the wife of his best friend, and Rupert is the soul of honor!"

He refused to elaborate on this tantalizing bit of information, sitting beside Venetia, elbows on his knees, watching the officers trying to make headway with the clumsy, inept levies. His face darkened as Etienne showed no such compunction, leaning on one elbow, looking up into her face, grinning puckishly, and gossiping.

"A mighty fine woman, Mary Lennox, Richmond's wife. They call her 'Butterfly' and this sums her up."

Mallory had gone to help the Prince. They were riding slowly down the lines, studying the shuffling men who fidgeted nervously under Rupert's eagle eye and Etienne told her some of the problems connected with turning them into competent fighters. The majority had never even heard the ordinary words of command, and were quite without any sense of military discipline. If they were needed urgently for an engagement, the most that the officers could teach would be the basic rules of taking their place in the line of battle, keeping their horses straight in the ranks and advancing to the charge without losing their order. Fortunately, most of the yeomen were used to riding as a matter of course, picking up sword-play as they went along. The foot were a more difficult problem, and the sergeants were sweating it out under the hot sun, struggling to pound a modicum of drill instruction into these confused amateurs.

Etienne watched Venetia watching the unusual beauty and regal bearing of the General of Horse, and mur-mured, close to her ear, *"Chérie,* your heart is in your eyes! Be more careful, lest Michael note it too."

There was something about the Chevalier which en-couraged confidences, it was almost as if he had been a close friend of long standing and she did not bother to disguise the savage note in her voice, speaking low, "I want him!"

Etienne chuckled. "So do many women, but they find him maddeningly elusive. He is dedicated to winning the war and thinks of little else. For one thing, he hasn't the time, and is forever in the saddle, so short on rest that bed, for him, means sleep. You must meet my wife, Damaris. If anyone can help you she will. Your brother Mallory, is very fond of her, by the by. Hasn't he told you?"

Venetia was nonplussed. "Don't you mind?"

Adrian was on his knees arranging the completed flower wreath on her hair, head to one side, studying the effect. "Mind?" he butted in. "Why should Etienne mind? He has me."

Etienne had been followed at a discreet distance, by two smartly-liveried servants who now brought over a picnic hamper, spreading refreshment on a damask cloth. Venetia was still digesting Adrian's remark and its implications when Rupert cantered up, waving aside the wineglass which the Chevalier proffered and taking a swig from a battered canteen handed by his page. He mopped the sweat on his face with his sleeve, speaking a few words to his dog who leaped high, trying to reach him. Venetia wanted to attract his attention, but she might not have existed as far as he was concerned and this nettled her; she liked to exist, most emphatically, and for men to recognize that she did.

The Chevalier had known Rupert since boyhood days at the Hague. Venetia could hardly have met anyone more informed and the morning slid away while she completely forgot Michael sitting beside her, growing ever more silent as her eager questions tumbled out and she drank in the replies.

Etienne soon had her laughing at his wicked impersonations of the commanders who had been offended by Rupert's position of seniority, calling him "The German," and hinting darkly, that if he took London he would send it up in flames.

"Ah, the quarrels and intrigues within our own ranks," Etienne was finishing a dish of raspberries as a dessert to hard-boiled eggs. "Sometimes, I think that the settlement of their personal disputes is of more importance to many of them than beating the Roundheads! Not to the *Pfalzgraf*, of course, he merely wants to get on with his job, but he is hamstrung by the Courtiers."

It was noon; the sun, a white-hot disc, glared against the azure expanse. A halt was called, and the men relaxed, glad to leave the ranks, knotting into little grumbling groups, seeking shade and rest. Venetia was making automatic responses to everyone in her circle, while her whole attention was focused on the Prince.

He turned his horse over to the groom, then got rid of his sash, stripping off his buff coat, jerking his cravat loose, opening the front of his shirt down to the ribbon-looped fastenings of his breeches. Sweat made great dark arcs on the fine linen under the armpits, across the back and up from the waist. His hair was plastered to his forehead, and he rubbed over his face and neck with a towel before stretching his arms, giving a wide-mouthed yawn and flinging himself down full length at the base of a tree.

The servants brought food which he shared with several troopers who had been given permission to sit with him. These tough, experienced veterans, their skin tanned by exposure to the elements, eyes crinkled at the corners with continually peering into the distance in search of an enemy, treated their chief with an enviable familiarity tempered with admiration and respect. He seemed to be at ease with them, and while not talking a lot himself, he occasionally made some remark which evoked a burst of laughter. At one point, through the hum of conversation which dipped and soared, Venetia could hear him, using some strange-sounding tongue, guttural and harsh, when he spoke to a blond, bearded, leather-clad man who was spreading out charts for him to study.

The wine was strong and it made Venetia drowsy, fogging all thought but the one growing desire to lie at Rupert's side as his dog did; that fortunate animal who had the Prince's fingers fondling his ears and stroking over his fur. Etienne had told her that it had been given to Rupert to alleviate the boredom in prison and had been his constant companion ever since. It was called Boye.

The meadow had become very quiet, only the clink of harness broke across the subdued murmur of voices. Bees droned, filling the fragrant stillness with their soothing sound, and some instinct made Venetia raise her lids to find Rupert staring at her, his eyes slightly narrowed. Her face flamed. Though she knew that this was a God-sent opportunity which any sensible woman would use to give him a returning glance of bold invitation, she could do nothing but hope that he might recognize the adoration in her eyes, before she was forced to look down, nervously folding the pleats of her skirt one over the other, in an agony of longing, fear and embarrassment.

Etienne made Michael promise to bring Venetia to a supper-party which his wife was giving that evening. Venetia wanted to ask if Rupert would be there, but a warning spark in Michael's eyes silenced her. The Chevalier insisted on sending one of his own coaches to fetch her and she spent a couple of flustered hours tyring to decide which gown to wear.

The Frenchman had rented a handsome, red-brick house set in spacious gardens, with outbuildings at the back for the complicated work of his servants. Inside, it was given to solid comfort rather than fashionable furnishings, with big chimney-pieces, ribbed plaster ceilings, heavily-carved staircase and polished floors.

The drawing-room was already crowded when Venetia entered on Michael's arm, feeling her inexperience keenly. Mallory snatched a couple of goblets from a loaded tray carried by a passing servant, and Michael introduced her to some of his friends, young scions of good families, accompanied by girlfriends from every station. Venetia began to relax as she realized that she was being accepted, initially for the sakes of Mallory

19

and Michael, and then very much on her own behalf as the gentlemen bowed over her hand.

A new world was unfolding before her, wholly different from anything she had encountered in the country, and she guessed that Mallory would not have brought her along had it not been that Michael had her in his care. It took a while to adjust to the uninhibited tenor of the talk which flowed around her, and the oaths which appeared to be high fashion. The accepted views of morality were changing fast, replaced by an indifference, cynicism and selfishness, which was worrying the older generation who blamed the war for it.

In the adjoining *salon* musicians had arrived, and couples wandered off to listen, applaud and commence dancing. Mallory's party weaved their way through the throng to where glass doors led out onto a terrace and the evening breeze fanned away the smell of stale perfume, tobacco and sweat. Etienne was lounging with his elbows on the stone balustrade by the side of a splendidly-built woman, who disengaged herself from him to reach up and kiss Mallory in an open, proprietorial manner.

"Mallory, my darling. So you are back in Oxford at last. I've missed you."

He was grinning down at her. "You are a very charming liar, Damaris. Come and meet my sister, and do not corrupt her."

This worldly, laughing woman, stunningly beautiful with that unusual combination of raven hair and violet eyes, could have been intimidating, for she exuded all the confidence which Venetia was painfully conscious of lacking. But this certainty, this security in her own identity, made Damaris an extremely kind person so that she adroitly ignored Venetia's shyness. She was a talkative, outgoing, inquisitive creature, who was soon in possession of the relevant facts of her life and history, putting her at ease.

Damaris had been educated on the Continent and married to the Chevalier at fourteen, the alliance arranged by their respective families.

"And I think I was very fortunate." She patted her husband's cheek affectionately. "We get on mighty well. When he told me that he was volunteering to serve King Charles, I insisted on coming too. I've left the babies with my mother-in-law who has borne them off to her *château* in the heart of rural France."

"How many children have you?" Venetia could never imagine Catherine abandoning her brood in such a light-hearted manner.

"Three—two girls came first, and I could see myself going on trying every year until we produced an heir, but, fortunately, the next was a boy."

"Thank God!" interjected Etienne, who was listening to her with an indulgent smile.

"Oh, come, Etienne, you are so ungallant!" She tapped him lightly with her closed fan. "You know that you don't really mind if we bed together every so often to make a baby and keep your parents happy."

There were strange undertones in their relationship. It was not until later, when the men had wandered over to the tables where the ivory game chips and playing cards were strewn, that Venetia began to comprehend the life-style of the Chevalier and his Lady.

Damaris was sipping the wine in her goblet, regarding her over the rim. "Mallory tells me you are but lately come to Oxford from the country. No doubt you wonder if your brother is my lover, eh? Don't blush, child—of course the thought has occurred to you. Yes, he is, and you need lose no sleep on Etienne's account. I have my friends and he has his, an excellent arrangement and I am very fond of him. The only point at which there is any disagreement between us is our rivalry over the junior officers. But even then, we usually compromise and share them, each of us, in our individual way, giving them a new experience."

Several times during the evening, Venetia had heard Prince Rupert mentioned as the men discussed his latest successs and the women sighed over his good looks and his inaccessibility. At last, she found courage to broach the subject to Damaris.

"Ah, I wondered when you were going to speak of him." Her hostess had taken her to the buffet table, keeping up a light flow of banter with her other guests as she passed among them. "Etienne tells me that you have fallen madly in love with him, and who could blame you? But an amour will not be easy to arrange; he spends his time with his mercenaries, and has few close friends, perhaps only Will Legge and the Duke of Richmond. He is not easy to know, very aloof. If it were

Maurice, now, that would be different. I'm sure he'd be only too happy to oblige you, but Rupert—he is certainly no squire of dames."

The room was swaying for Damaris had been keeping Venetia's glass brimming, and she was glad to sink into a deep chair, filled with soft cushions covered in plushing velvet. She muttered something about Richmond's wife.

Mallory had left the gaming-tables and now he and Damaris were eating from the same plate, and she licked her fingers clean from the grease of a chicken-bone before replying. "Well, yes, there is talk. Mary is one of the Queen's ladies. The Prince seems to be somewhat smitten since he first met her a few days ago. I doubt that it will come to anything. He will value Richmond's friendship far beyond the enjoyment of any woman. He won't betray him, so don't worry your head about that.

Useless advice, when he was still as far above Venetia as the moon and stars, and his name was being shouted across the room, for the company had reached the stage of pledging everyone; the King, the Queen and each member of the Royal family. It was expected that gentlemen should honor every toast to the full; not a mere sip, but with glass or tankard drained to the bottom in one draught. Several weaklings had already succumbed and lay prone in corners whence they had been dragged by considerate comrades, so that people would not keep tripping over them.

A bustle in the hallway heralded the approach of Damaris, leading forward a new arrival, their progress halted until he could disengage himself from a group of girls in billowing satin dresses who descended on him with little welcoming shrieks and kisses, while fellow soldiers gathered to pound him on the back in vigorous congratulation.

"Come, Harry," Damaris was saying. "Here is someone I want you to meet." Her firm fingers were on Venetia's arm as she introduced him. "General Harry Wilmot, fresh from triumphs over the rebels in Wiltshire."

Wilmot's reputation had reached Venetia. Gay, witty, dissolute, one of the King's top commanders, he fought boldly and well, when he was in the mood. He was about thirty, handsome enough in a raffish way, wearing all the exaggerated points of fashion so detested by the

22

Puritans, his blue velvet sleeves slashed with white satin and frothing with lace, a great plumed hat cocked at an angle on his flowing brown hair, his mustache twirled up in a mocking flourish.

"This is Venetia," Damaris was beaming. "Isn't she lovely, Harry?"

"Charming, quite charming." The sly, teasing eyes were going over her with relish, and he managed to imprison her hand in his free one; the other was clamped around the handle of a pewter tankard. "Fit solace indeed for the weary warrior home from the toils of battle."

With the practiced skill of the experienced seducer, he soon had her penned in a corner. Venetia tried nervously to edge around him, sorry to give this cool reception to such a noted General. Wilmot did not budge an inch, taking a deep swallow before putting his drink down. He wiped his full lips on the back of his hand.

"Well, now, moon-flower of my middle years, I assume that you will want the conventional chatter to start with, though I can think of one or two things I'd rather we did. What shall we talk about?"

"Prince Rupert," she said instantly.

Wilmot looked pained at this turn of events. "The Prince? I' faith, why is it that every pretty wench I have a mind to lie with wants to discuss him?"

"You know him?" Venetia could not keep the eagerness from her voice.

"I have that doubtful privilege." Wilmot pulled a face.

"You don't like him?" Her tone was accusing.

His eyebrows shot up. "'Tis nearer the truth to say that he does not like me!"

There seemed to be so many people with whom Rupert had quarrelled. Was he indeed such a very difficult person to get on with?

"Difficult! He's deuced impossible!" Wilmot answered emphatically. "I fought beside him in the Dutch Army, back in '35, and even then he looked down that long nose of his at George Goring and myself. Didn't approve of our drinking habits, and haughtily declined all invitations to join us! Dammit, he still does! He's not altered much, though I would say that his Austrian imprisonment did naught but aggravate his already hasty temper. Did you know that his nickname, home at the Hague, was Rupert the Devil?"

Two bumpers of wine later they were ensconced on a

settee, half concealed in an alcove. A foolish move, Venetia knew, with this dangerous individual, but caution had fled before her obsession with Rupert. Here was a man who had spent many hours in his company, had been his comrade-at-arms, faced death with him, dared to argue, shout at, and oppose that passionate, determined will.

Laughing and exchanging bawdy jests and advice with his friends who had discovered their nook, Wilmot was well pleased with the situation, thinking that he was about to add Venetia's name to his list of easy conquests. He was prepared to indulge her a little longer by discussing his enemy.

"He demands his way on every issue," he continued, settling back comfortably, amusing himself by trying to inveigle a hand into her bodice. Venetia wriggled away, not as tipsy as he was hoping she would be. "My Lord Digby gave him the name of, 'His High Illustrious Arrogancy,' and the title has stuck! Very apt indeed!"

He was getting difficult to control and Venetia was thankful when Michael appeared, curtly informing him that she was his betrothed. The General eyed him up and down contemptuously.

"Don't ruffle your feathers at me, my game-cock! 'Tis not I who will endanger her virtue. You ride in Rupert's Lifeguard, do you not? My advice to you is to be negligent in your duty. Allow some Roundhead dragoon to shoot him in the back, if you want to keep her!"

At Michael's outraged expression, he suddenly roared with laughter, bawling to Damaris who had drifted across to see what all the noise was about. "These lads don't know how to take their liquor, Damaris, my sprite! Bring me another bottle, and get rid of that young buck whom you intend to swive before the night is out! Come upstairs with me first, and I'll show you what a real man can do!"

One of Damaris' cardinal principles was never to interfere in other people's lives, and she was liberal with her home, throwing it open to her friends. Later, Venetia stood at the window in one of the bedchambers, very much as she had done that morning, but now the steeples, the wide plazas, the quods, timbered houses and shops were shrouded in mystery under the wash of the sickle moon. Somewhere, beneath those dreaming spires, he lived and breathed. Did he too gaze out at the night from

24

a casement beneath the eaves? Or was he lying with his friend's wife clasped in his arms?

Michael was a tender presence in the darkness, undressing her as carefully as if she were a precious piece of china, knowing the intricacies of hooks and laces almost as well as her maid. In the spinning blackness of the canopied bed, Venetia very nearly convinced herself that it was Rupert's large, aristocratic hands which caressed her. With her face buried in Michael's hair, she pictured those saturnine, proud features, and at the end, roused to a peak of passion, it was all that she could do so not to cry his name aloud.

Michael knew, with that sixth sense developed by those deeply in love, that there was something wrong. "What is the matter, darling? Did I not please you?"

She was instantly contrite; he was so good to her. "Of course you did, Michael. I think that I have drunk too much wine. It makes me melancholy."

The nimble lies which sprang to her tongue surprised even herself. He said no more and she listened to his breathing, feeling the weight of his head on her breast. Silent tears spilled over, running back across her temples. Rupert's bravery, his Royal birth, his romantic history and personal beauty were deadly auxiliaries against any future peace of mind. And it was all so futile, she decided, with that desperate, small-hours finality; he could never love her.

THREE

Sunday turned Oxford into a city of bells. All day they had pealed, the noise vibrating in Venetia's aching head. In the evening, Damaris called for her and they rolled through the streets in her coach to join the crowds eager to catch a glimpse of the reunited Royal couple, as they took a stroll in the garden of Merton College after church.

Damaris had the effect of making every woman in her

vicinity feel more feminine, her finger on the pulse of fashion. The Queen too was famous for her poise and faultless chic. Venetia was anxious to give a good account of herself, and dressed with care.

It had not been hard to keep abreast with the current vogues even in the Cotswolds. Peddlers called regularly, bringing a breath of the outside world, packs bulging with samples of material, ribbons, furs and laces. On market-days there were stalls where a woman might browse happily for hours, bemused by the antics of the wily hucksters who cried their wares, temptingly holding up a dazzling array of shawls, cuffs and collars of Flemish lace, fans, muffs, colored hose, garters with sparkling paste buckles, and embroidered high-heeled slippers.

The country-bred girl learned the art of improvisation; Venetia had become an accomplished needlewoman, and had found a local seamstress almost as skilled in producing clothes economically, using materials to hand, or ordering them to be delivered with the next train of pack-horses. Damaris had been astonished to learn that the dress Venetia had worn the night before and now this outfit, had both been made at home. She commented approvingly on the way the green silk skirt was hooked up at one side for walking, displaying the contrasting tobacco-brown petticoat, admiring the cut of the bodice, with its basque and stomacher edged in the same shade of velvet braid, cunningly boned to fit Venetia's slender waist.

She had taught Meg how to help her copy the latest hair-style; her thick locks, the color of sun-ripened corn-sheaves, had been coiled into a bun, pinned high on her crown, while the side pieces were rolled into long, fat ringlets, the forehead line softened by a curling fringe.

"Faith, my dear, you show the same restrained elegance as His Highness," Damaris exclaimed, the bunch of purple feathers in her wide-brimmed hat nodding in agreement as the coach jolted over the cobbles. "He is most sparkish in his dress, and has a natural flare for rich dark colors set off against a somber background. And he is so maddeningly casual about it all—it happens without any apparent effort on his part. All the young bloods strive earnestly to imitate his style, which does nothing to endear him to Lord Percy and Wilmot, who rather fancy themselves as leaders of fashion."

A footman ran around to open the door, lower the

step, and hand the ladies out. Within minutes, as they made toward the spectators lining the gravel paths, Damaris had formed her own retinue of gallants, each vying for her favors. The shoulders of their escorts cleaved a way for them toward the neat avenue between the box-wood hedges.

"There they are," Damaris said on a sharp intake of breath, and all along the line men's hats were sweeping off, and women dropping into curtsies, like flowers bending before the wind. Erect and dignified, King Charles moved slowly past.

With almost superstitious awe, Venetia watched him; this was their King, the man they were fighting for, and there was a great regality about him, in spite of his lack of inches. His brown hair, beginning to streak with silver, brushed the shoulders of a beige satin doublet. His face was shaded by the rim of a black hat, and there were tight lines about his mouth which betrayed the nervous tension under which he now lived.

Henrietta Maria was a disappointment, thin and sallow, until one saw the vivacity of her black eyes, which changed constantly from sparkling merriment, flashes of anger and indignation, back to fun again. Today she was in a fine mood of triumph and optimism, as light-footed and dancing as the tiny spaniels bounding before her. She was exquisitely gowned, a flashing creature who reduced even the beautiful women who formed her train of ladies-in-waiting into cloddish lumps.

"That's Lord Jermyn, just behind the Queen," Damaris was saying. "He is her secretary, and some say her lover. She likes to think herself a fascinating spitfire." Venetia wished that Damaris had kept that piece of information to herself.

She wanted to retain her illusions about the Royal pair, to think of them as a fairy tale King and Queen, presiding over a chaste, decorous Court. But the comments continued, for in common with Etienne, Damaris seemed to know all things, and most people, nobles, Generals and ladies, a mine of gossip and information.

"Oh, look!" She gave Venetia a sharp poke with her elbow. "There's my Lord George Digby, Bristol's son. Mark him well, for he is no friend to your Prince."

He was a dandy, graceful of mien and gesture, his fair skin emphasized by black velvet, his expression that of an depraved choir boy. An exceedingly beautiful person indeed, slender and well-proportioned, with guileless blue eyes shadowed by feathery lashes, his oval face framed in golden curls, artlessly tumbling over his lace collar, adding to the cherubic appearance. His head was bent earnestly, reverently, toward the King, and his hands, smooth and dimpled, were in constant play as he talked.

Damaris was chattering about other notables, but Venetia was blind to everyone for she had caught sight of Rupert.

He was some way behind, slowing his impatient long-legged pace to match that of the woman walking with him. No one needed to tell her that it was Mary Lennox, the Duchess of Richmond. Venetia's eyes bored into her, trying to fault her beauty, miserably accepting that this was impossible.

Etienne was lolling on the day-bed when Damaris and Venetia returned, listening to Adrian who had abandoned his guitar for the spinet. The thin, plucked notes hung, clear-cut, on the evening air, the melancholy of the pavanne striking an echo in Venetia's soul.

Damaris shot her husband an annoyed glare. "Etienne, I do wish that you would not wear your spurs indoors!"

He raised his head an inch from the pillow, squinting down the length of his legs which were draped across the couch with such a fine show of careless ease, arching an ankle to survey one of the offending articles attached to his fawn doeskin boots.

"*Chérie,* you know perfectly well that this season it is almost *de rigueur* for any man of fashion to retain his spurs on almost -every occasion! Would you have me appear an uncultivated boor?"

"Thank God that these cushions are but rented and not our property," she retorted briskly. "And I hope for Adrian's sake, that you leave them on the bedside table at night, or he'll have the marks of rowels on that tender peaches-and-cream skin of his!'

"My dear, what a fascinating thought!" squeaked Adrian roguishly.

Etienne moved over, patting the place beside him when Damaris told him to be kind to Venetia because she was so unhappy about Mary Lennox.

"Oh, that bitch!" he remarked, filling her glass with splashing generosity. "She'll lead a fellow on, but she's so dammed faithful to her sobersided spouse that no one

28

else could get even a blade of grass between those buttocks."

Damaris kept a day by day journal of events and explained to Venetia, "When the King is back on his throne, and myself once more incarcerated in the country, I shall write a book—my 'Memoirs of the Great Rebellion!' "

"Not all of them, surely? It would never get an imprimatur!" Etienne gave a yawn, already acutely bored at the prospect of having to listen to her reading aloud extracts from her masterpiece. "Moreover, women don't write books!"

"Then it is high time they started!" Damaris was one of those advanced thinkers who considered the female every bit as capable as the male, questioning their lordly assumption of superiority. With her eye for detail, good memory and flair for expressing herself, she was busy amassing material; every tract which came out of London, each public declaration by some important personage, now found its way into her collection.

Rupert was the principal target of the gutter press. To the impressionable Puritans, the alarming vision of this unusually tall, dark foreign Prince, wrapped in a cloak of hellish scarlet, accompanied always by a weird dog, seemed the very personification of evil. They were convinced that Boye was his familiar, able to make himself invisible and spy on godly troops, taking intelligence of their movements back to his Prince of Darkness. They almost ran out of epithets for him, the most polite of which were "Prince Robber," "The Diabolical Cavalier," "Plunder-Master-General," and "Ravenous Vulture!" He was cast in the role of the villain, a slavering ogre whose fiery breath stank of butchery, blood and Continental warfare.

"Is he really the 'loose and wild gentleman' that they describe?" Venetia asked after reading an account of his hanging Roundheads at their own front doors and plundering wholesale. "They say that he has shown no more mercy to any that oppose him than to a dog."

Etienne shook his head impatiently, filled with indignation at the lies spread about the King's finest General. "The London newsmongers hate him because he is a hard-headed soldier and could see, after Edgehill, that the best way to finish the war quickly was to strike direct at the City. This stirred the merchants into a ferment, they feared for their property, so they put pressure on Parliament. A charge of High Treason has been drawn up against him and Prince Maurice, by the Commons."

"He doesn't look like a brute." Venetia visualized that sensitive face. "I've never seen a more handsome man."

Adrian was getting piqued by all this talk of Rupert, no one had even bothered to inquire about his latest performance.

"His nose is too big." He posed against the spinet, so that his delicate profile was shown to full advantage.

"Oh, I don't know about that." Etienne snatched at the small round handglasses which dangled from a ribbon attached to Venetia's waist, gazing at his own rather pronounced features. "I think that it lends a charming touch of dignity and strength."

An attendant had come in with a lighted taper and was going around the room holding it to every candle. Damaris began to gather up her souvenirs to free the table for the supper dishes. As she swept toward the bureau, her arms full of papers, something floated to the floor and Etienne picked it up.

It was a letter, addressed to "His Highness, Prince Rupert," and someone had been scribbling sketches over the back of it, as if to pass the time in an idle moment. There were heads and human figures; a man with a pike borne on one shoulder, a girl's face, a boy with curling hair and a detailed row of buttons running down his doublet.

"I begged them from the Prince for Damaris' scrapbook." The Chevalier informed Venetia. "Did you not know that he is a most considerable artist?"

A letter had come from the bailiff whom Denby had left in charge of his house. Shortly after they had left, it had been occupied by a Roundhead company.

Venetia found it strange to imagine strangers moving through the pleasant rooms, handling those personal belongings, rifling drawers, cupboards and chests. A crop-haired rebel Captain would now sit in her father's carver at the head of the table; some unknown person sleeps in the bed where she had dreamed her girlish fancies and, later, lain in Michael's arms. Another would occupy the chamber where all the Denby children had been born.

Venetia had little time to brood for Michael came next day, to tell her that the Prince was moving out of Oxford to attack the second most important city of England—Bristol.

Her reaction flattered him; he believed her distress to be on his account. "Don't worry, love. To know that you will be here, waiting for me, will give me a magic immunity from harm. We march at dawn tomorrow." He kissed her briefly and clattered away to his duties.

Venetia knew of one person only who could help her, and she found Damaris in the courtyard of her house, supervising the packing of her largest coach. It was a bright splash of sapphire, with gilt varnish and green leather trappings, and so heavy that six sturdy horses were required to pull it; especially with the added supplies of clothes, blankets, hatboxes, medicine chests, brandy-flasks, and cases of sack, which Damaris refused to trust to the covered carts. Two of these were coping with the overspill of luggage which a lackey was stowing inside with remarkable compactness to leave room for the personal servants.

"Are you going with him?" Venetia watched her helplessly; somehow she had not expected this.

Damaris was handing up a squat black liqueur bottle to her maid, Nancy, who tucked it away in a neat compartment under the seat. "But of course, dear. I travel everywhere with my Etienne. How else should I know if he is having the right food? He has a delicate stomach, you know. I'm a very experienced camp-follower—in every way."

"And this is permitted?" Venetia thought of the female riffraff who trailed behind the armies as a collection of common harlots, she had not realized that married women were included.

"It is encouraged." They sat on the coach step in the shade and let the lackeys finish loading. "The Generals say that the men are better fed and looked after if their wives go along. And we help with the wounded."

The yard was full of activity with ostlers, footmen and pert maids scurrying to do madam's bidding. Her spaniel yelped as someone gave it a sly kick, and the kitchen cat did not blink a golden eye, his paws folded neatly under him, indulging his love of sun-warmed stone, too indolent to take up the challenge thrown out by a row of saucy sparrows perched on the guttering. But already Venetia could feel that chill lonely stillness which would

31

descend on her when Rupert had gone. If she did not act now, the chance would be lost, never to come again, she could not afford to hesitate. Damaris had said that no rumor had reached her of the Prince either sending for one of the camp whores, or having affairs with the Court ladies, yet he was only human. There must come a time when his high standards relaxed and, when this happened, Venetia was determined to be available.

"You'll take me with you?" It was more of a demand than a request.

"My dear child, it is no picnic, I assure you." Damaris looked doubtful. "And His Highness will be far too busy to notice you, were you to run around his tent stark naked! De Gomme and La Roche, his engineers, will be his constant companions, they'll be poring over plans together, you'll see."

When she saw Venetia's desperation, and realized that if she did not aid her, she was likely to do something foolish, she relented. "I don't know how we are to achieve your aim. Mallory and Michael will never countenance your joining the leaguer. You know how ridiculously touchy men are about the honor of their sisters or the women they intend to marry, no matter how much whoring they do themselves. You can ride with me, once we have put a good distance between ourselves and Oxford, but till then I think we had better hide you with the players. Adrian will help, he loves intrigue, and Jonathan is friendy with one of the girls."

Early next morning she stole out to the stable calling softly to her horse, Orion, and he answered, whinnying gently while she patted his neck and harnessed him. Jonathan was waiting for her, and they rode to the fields beyond the town where a camp had been formed.

Jonathan gave the password to the pickets and they trotted within the circle of carts, toward one at the rear. At Jonathan's voice, a girl's tousled head came out between the flaps at the rear, and the flickering light of the flares played on a pale face and slim, fragile hands which gleamed against the dark woollen shawl flung over her shoulders.

The two women eyed one another suspiciously for a moment, the sister and the mistress, then they smiled simultaneously and Jonathan sighed with relief; they were going to be friends. Now he could leave them with

32

a contented mind, slipping back to rejoin his troop before it was discovered that he was missing.

The players had two wagons, and the largest was occupied by Meriel and her father, the actor who ran the show, Thomas Carter. It was not the time for introductions, for he and most of the other members were trying to snatch a little sleep. Meriel and Venetia conversed in whispers, peeping out at the smouldering fires, too excited to settle down.

As the sky lightened, a breath like a sigh stirred the waiting crowd as, sweet and high and far away, sounded the note of a trumpet, answered by another. From the West Port of the town came the noise of hooves and marching feet, and the rumble of heavy vehicles. This galvanized the leaguer into action; horses were backed between shafts, men cursing, bleary-eyed, fumbling with awkward strappings, while fires were stamped out, children rounded up, dogs whistled to heel, and a rough column formed under the direction of the wagon-masters.

Louder and nearer jogged the cavalry, and, beyond a curve in the hedge, the banner of the Palatine came into sight, in the lead was Rupert himself, magnificent on his powerful destrier, the first sun-rays glinting on his steel corselet while the wind tossed the crimson feathers in his black beaver. His Lifeguard kept close beside him, followed by the troopers, a brave array of plumes, swirling cloaks, lace collars and gilt-chastened swordhilts.

The dragoons and infantry, musketeers and pikemen formed clumps of color, the individual standard of each troop borne proudly, essential as a marker of headquarters when in billets, and as a rallying point in action. By the law of arms a company that lost its flag was barred from having another until they had redeemed their tarnished reputation by taking an enemy one.

After the soldiers came the Prince's sumpter-wagons and those of the principal officers, followed by lumbering vehicles carrying ironshot, match, barrels of gun powder, smiths' materials, the engineers equipment, and the tents.

Behind the military jolted the coaches carrying either the wives of the senior officers, or bejewelled and feathered ladies who could make no such legal claim. A group of women riding side-saddle, cloaked, sensibly booted and attired for hard weather, were married to those of lesser rank, and the motley collection among whom Venetia was numbered, fell in at the rear.

For time immemorial a wandering army attracted a conglomeration of hangers-on. There were victuallers, tinkers, hawkers and sharp-dealers, musicians and play-actors. All were out to make a quick penny, including whores less fortunate than those borne in their splendid conveyances, brash, strident-tongued slatterns who obliged the soldiery for a modest fee.

The *cortège* moved off along the dewy, shadowed hillside, and Venetia, perched up in the player's cart, could feel nothing but happiness because she was part of it; even the simple natural phenomenon of dawn was a miracle because the Prince was there.

At noon a halt was called, horses were fed and watered, weary troops chewing on bread, cheese, cold pies, slabs of beef, washed down with ale or cider. Venetia had brought food with her, packed in her valise along with a few simple necessities, and she shared what she had with the players. They were a convivial group, a dozen in all, living in the carts along with their costumes and properties, musical instruments, mummers masks, and thick bundles of scripts. Meriel was the only female, although several scruffy drabs hung around, attracted by the eloquent voices, the lordly airs affected by the actors. They were never short of stage-struck volunteers for crowd scenes. But all the roles, including those of women, were given to the men, although Thomas Carter, who had acted abroad, assured Venetia that this would not always be so.

At night the travel-stained caravan toiled upward toward a village. The Prince and his staff commandeered the largest house, the officers took over the inn and, in the fields, the leaguer settled in for the night. The carts were drawn into a protective ring, lads were sent to search for firewood, and soon fragrant smoke circled lazily heavenwards. The seasoned campaigners slung iron pots on tripods over the flames, and in no time little family groups were squatting around the fires having their supper.

Meriel took Venetia through the camp where people greeted them with easy friendliness, and it became very clear that the rank and file adored their Prince, no matter how much he might annoy the nobles.

"Reckless young devil he is," one grizzled battle-scarred warrior assured her, offering a slug of brandy from a blackjack. "A grand fighter! Shot-free, so they

34

say! D'you know he's never been wounded? He's ever foremost in the charge in the most exposed position that spur can drive to, chief object of the enemy's hatred, and yet he rides unharmed!"

"Not like poor Prince Maurice." A younger, broken-nosed rascal was rubbing his chin through the stubble, eyeing Venetia with unconcealed interest. "He gets hurt in almost every fight. Who are you with, sweetheart?"

Venetia ignored him, listening to the other man as he continued:

"Oh, yes, he knows what a soldier needs, by Christ! Worked his way up through the ranks himself, he did, in the German armies. He sees that we have food in our bellies, and something between us and the cold ground at night. Many's the time he's slept out in the open, along with us, and I've seen him, shirt stripped off, waist deep in mud, working in the trenches, digging under city walls to lay explosives. I was at Litchfield when he set off the first mine that had ever been used in England."

He gave a rumbling laugh, taking a pull at the bottle, then going on: "You should hear the lads yell when we storm through a city; 'Damn us! The town is Prince Rupert's!' "

Wrapped in her cloak, gazing out at the stars through the half open flap of the wagon, Venetia hugged these words to her, and marvelled at the odd statement made so positively by Meriel. Everyone else had told her that she was mad to love him, that nothing could possibly come of it. Meriel had merely said, with a strange, fey look in her eyes:

"You'll succeed, my dear. But I will not promise you happiness."

FOUR

It took five days for the straggling procession to wend its way through the countryside to Chipping Sodbury, where the Prince rendezvoused with his brother who was serving with the Western Army under Lord Hertford.

On the second day, Venetia rode up nearer to the van and joined Damaris. Then she had better quarters, for the Chevalier was usually able to procure a room for his wife and Venetia shared with her. Mallory was furious at the deception played on him, but Michael, after the first shock, expressed nothing but happiness at having Venetia near.

She found no opportunity to meet the Prince; as Damaris had warned he was a very busy person, and extremely uncommunicative, apart from his chosen intimates among the professional soldiers. One night, when they had been forced to bivouac in the open, she saw him seated at a trestle drawn close to the tent entrance to catch the fading light, deep in consultation with the Captain of his guards, Sir Richard Crane. His hair fell forward across his face as he bent over papers strewn about the table. Boye was at his knee, tail thumping the grass, and Rupert absently fondled the dog's silky ears.

He glanced up as Venetia passed through his field of vision, and his eyes were as she had seen them when he was angry with his lazy Lieutenants, with something alight, like a flame, in their black depths. It was a look which sucked out all her strength. She was so disturbed, so racked with longing to kiss his perfectly molded mouth, that she could not pretend to respond to Michael when later he pushed her back on the earth in the shadow of the wagon, twisting away, picking a quarrel with him to avoid contact.

The nights were short; His Highness's trumpeters had them up at three in the morning. Yawning, grumbling, shivering in the ground mists, they could do no more than snatch a hasty bite, bundle up their belongings, and be off as the first birds heralded the dawn.

Venetia was lucky to be with Damaris who was able to treat the march as an adventure, enjoying to the full the fun of living alfresco, while her servants performed the more unpleasant chores. It was impossible not to draw comparisons with the hardships that Meriel endured, forced to gather kindling, fetch water from the streams, and keep the cooking-pot well stocked. The actors had added poaching to their list of accomplishments, and there was usually a rabbit to be gutted, or a hen which had strayed from its own backyard.

It was Sunday, and the sound of church bells, ringing out from Bristol, was borne on the breeze to reach the

36

Cavaliers as they entered a hamlet on the north side of the city. Their arrival caused the usual pandemonium, with the cavalry pounding in first, then the infantry swinging down the single street where the locals gathered to gape, barefoot urchins falling into step beside the column, and the village sluts well to the fore, shouting.

"I'll 'ave that little 'un, at the back!"

"Ho there, General! Mind you don't wear 'em out, with all that marching."

"Uds Lud! Look at 'im! Cor, 'ee can come and quarter 'isself on me, any time 'ee likes!"

Prince Rupert requisitioned Westbury College, fanning all things into flame by the speed of his coming. Venetia found Meriel, on her knees by the brook, pounding linen on the broad, flat stones, her cheeks pink with the effort. Some of the other women had already finished, smocks and petticoats, shirts and drawers, baby clothes and diapers spread out on the bushes, bleaching under the blaze of midsummer.

"Damned war!" Meriel gave an extra hard slap with her father's hose against a slippery boulder. "I shall be glad when 'tis over. Just imagine laying abed late, and then rising to find this done." Meriel often spoke longingly of the kind of life that she had never known. She had been on the road since she was born, brought up by her actor-manager-adventurer father. Her mother had died young and from her, Meriel had inherited her appealing delicate appearance, and her psychic ability. Because she was not allowed to speak lines, though this was her ambition, she contributed to the show by telling fortunes; but they were cautious, choosing customers with care, for she had no desire to be accused of witchcraft.

"I cannot predict for myself," she told Venetia. "But one thing I do know I must love your brother Jonathan with every fiber of my being, while I am able."

They were completely absorbed in one another, oblivious to mockery, wandering hand in hand, gazing into each other's eyes, whispering imbecilities. Venetia wondered how the family would react if he suddenly appeared with her as his wife.

For all her fine-boned slender build, Venetia had a strong constitution, an ability to adapt speedily to situations, and an iron will which enabled her to complete any project on which she had set her heart. Brought up among boys, she had learned early to out-hunt and frequently outride them; with screams and tantrums, or, if these failed, storms of tears, she insisted on being allowed to join in when they had their fencing lessons. She had been the despair of her nurse, who deplored such hoydenish behavior, and strove to school her young charge to be ladylike. Later she had conformed, but now her old rebellion surged up. Resentfully, she watched the Prince gallop across Durdham Down toward the tower of Clifton Church spiking on a leafy rise.

The chaplains conducted a service in the open for the leaguer which was interrupted by the boom of cannon-fire blasting from the direction taken by the reconnaissance party. Venetia's heart plummeted, her thoughts fleeing into that wilderness of horror where she saw Rupert maimed or killed a hundred times over.

They clopped back unharmed, leaning against the cantles of their saddles, relaxed and laughing; Venetia could hear the Prince whistling to his dog; he sounded in high good humor. Michael said that while they were standing in the churchyard on the crest, the Roundhead gunners manning Brandon Hill Fort opposite, suddenly woke up to their presence. Two or three cannon-balls were sent crashing over, but no one was hurt and Rupert coolly continued to survey the city spread out in the hollow below. In answer to that challenging fire, he had put a battery there, leaving Colonel Washington in charge with his dragoons.

On Monday, the army deployed in full battaglia on the edge of Durdham Down. Maurice had gone back over the Avon to draw up the Western force in a similar manner on the south side. The sun sparked off breast-plates and helms, the forest of pikes, sixteen feet high, and the wicked gleam of musket-barrels. The Royalist army marched wide, looking larger than it really was, all the panoply of death flaunting its gayest colors, and the great standard of Prince Rupert rippling out against the smarting blue of the sky.

It was a formidable spectacle, calculated to shatter the nerve of the defenders; and the Prince paraded them there long enough for the full impact to be driven home. Then he sent in a trumpeter with a formal summons to the Governor, Colonel Nathaniel Fiennes, to surrender the town. This was refused, as was expected, and the skirmishing began in earnest.

The defences of Bristol were strong and well planned;

a wall and ditch protected it and there were four forts on the Downs side, with the River Avon making an awkward obstacle on the other. Royalist spies, busy within, sent cheering reports to Rupert. Optimism ran high among the besiegers, for Nat Fiennes was not the most valiant of men, and although Bristol was reputedly Puritan, many leading citizens were for the King.

Rupert moved his headquarters further into the suburbs; the surgeons and their assistants turned a large farm-building into a hospital and, in the nearby fields of Redland, the women camped, waiting events.

Mining and sapping were out of the question on this stony grounds, so every vantage point was seized, and the hedgerows lined with musketeers. The gunners sweated to get the artillery into position, and soon this deeper roar thundered across the sporadic rattle of small-arms, a vigorous duel which lasted into the dawn. Leaving his men to continue the bombardment, the Prince crossed the river for a Council of War with the Western Army at Knowle.

And with all this excitement seething around her, Venetia could do nothing but wander after Damaris in an agony of concern for Rupert, who, with his usual indifference to danger, hourly took the most appalling risks.

Damaris became really cross with her, "Oh, do stop fretting your bowels to fiddle-strings about him! Don't you know that the bullet isn't fashioned in hell yet, that can kill the Wizard Prince? What about your brothers and Michael, to say nothing of my own Etienne? Can you not spare a prayer for them?" She marched her to the surgeon's quarters. "Do something useful. Occupy yourself in tearing linen into bandages."

The Chevalier clanked into the big, stone-flagged kitchen, where several straw pallets were already occupied by groaning men. The scrubbed wooden table had been cleared for the use of the doctors, and on the hearth the fire roared beneath cauldrons of water.

Etienne wore his soldier's gear with considerable panache, although regretting that it was impracticable to don the full armor of a cuirassier for any other occasion than sitting for his portrait. Like most officers, he had compromised and settled for the more comfortable, if less safe, thick leather jacket which reached almost to the knee. While this would turn sword blows, it could not check bullets, so his gilded Milanese back- and breastplate were buckled on top. He made a splendid—almost heroic figure, and knew it.

Damaris beamed her approval, very practical of a sudden, with her curls tied back, sleeves rolled up and a plain twill apron fastened over the front of her gown.

"Dearest, you look just as if you've stepped down from some tapestry depicting the ancient days of Chivalry."

" 'Tis deuced hot!" Her husband eased his crested helmet from his sweat-drenched hair. "Rupert has returned, and a full-scale assault is planned for early tomorrow morning. The password is to be 'Oxford,' and we've to wear green tokens and no collars, so that we may recognize one another and not shoot our own fellows by mistake."

"He had no mind to sit it out and starve them into surrender?" Damaris drew off a mugful of ale from a barrel set on a bench in an airy corner, and passed it to him.

He gulped it back, perched on the edge of the table. "That is what Maurice and Hertford wanted to do. But you know the *Pfalzgraf*, he has not the temperament for a drawn-out siege, and seems certain that the breastwork, on this side, is so badly manned that it will be easily carried by storm."

Though worn out by bedtime, sleep did not come easily and Damaris got up at last, going over to join Venetia at the window where the military masquerades made a fine firework display against the purple darkness.

"Just listen to that racket!" she complained, as the crash of ordnance tortured the air of the summer night which should have been soft and mysterious, full of stars and love, the sound of owls, nightingales, and the rustle of tiny furry creatures.

They went back to bed, and Venetia lay taut, worrying about her family, wondering what they had made of her hastily scribbled note, and if Catherine had started labor yet. Timothy's freckled face and babyish mouth, rose behind her closed eyelids. She hoped that he would not follow her example and run away to join up, and Ella—how long would it be before some irresponsible member of the Oxford garrison got that flighty little minx into trouble?

The firing had died and the silence was eerie, stretching

40

endlessly so that sleep began to wash over Venetia, one face only filling her dreams—Rupert's, with its proud eagle lines and the dark fire of his glance.

Suddenly the staccato rattle of musketry, cries and cheering from the south, sent the Oxford commanders rushing from their billets, bawling orders as they ran. Drums were rolling, trumpets blaring out for "Boot and Saddle," and the Prince was shouting for the signal to be fired for the massed attack, before vaulting onto his horse and hurling like a thunderbolt toward the line between Brandon Hill and Windmill Fort.

Damaris fumbled for the flint and tinder to light the candle, consulting the enameled face of her watch. "It lacks two hours to the appointed time! I'll wager 'tis those fiery Cornish in Hertford's brigades wanting to snatch the glory of the first breach from Rupert's lads!"

Garbled reports of the battle came back to the leaguer with the injured. Venetia became numbed, unable to register shock, horror or pity, obeying the instructions of the surgeons, doing what was required of her. Now the hospital was very crowded, and the wives worked alongside the whores, enmities temporarily forgotten.

Jonathan limped in, his arm slung around the shoulders of a burly pikeman and his eyes were feverish with exaltation, his excitement so acute that he hardly felt the pain as the ugly gash in his thigh was sutured.

"We've broken in! And I was with them—Washington's men and Wentworth's almost quarreling for the honor!" He held Venetia's hand in a vice-like grip. "It was at the spur-work, just below Windmill Fort, where His Highness had said there was a weak point. He is always right! You should have seen Washington, driving us through that gap, yelling like a madman, 'Away, away with them!' as if he was out hunting!"

"What of the Prince?" Venetia gave Jonathan a shake.

Aglow with hero-worship, he described how Rupert had flown up and down the line. He seemed to be everywhere at once, instinctively knowing where his presence was most needed; directing, encouraging, rallying and rebuking, his voice as keen as a trumpet. He stopped a retreat at one point where a sally had been repulsed, leading the waverers back. They attacked again and won, inspired by this creature of fierce and desperate purpose.

"And his horse was shot under him. A musketeer got

41

it right in the eye, but he strolled off on foot, as cool as you please, till another was brought for him!"

Then Venetia looked at Meriel who had read her mind, and laid the exhausted boy back on the straw. He was trembling violently, his teeth chattering, and she tucked a blanket around him, bending to kiss his forehead, before following his sister. Only Meriel, who knew Venetia's inevitable destiny, helped her without comment as they went to the players' carts and found men's clothing in the property-boxes; and it was Meriel who laced her into the buff jacket, gave her a hat, discovered boots to fit, and fixed her up with a sword, remembering to pin on a green favor, and to rip the white collar from her shirt.

They saddled Orion, and Venetia found it strange to be riding astride, which she had not done in years. She bent toward Meriel, who kissed her solemnly, as if she were bestowing a benediction.

"The strength of your love will protect you—and him," she said.

Orion was eager to gallop, and Venetia kept him at full speed, rejoicing to feel the lift of his withers, the strong thighs which bunched up under him as he leaped the wall. She leaned over and patted the proud curve of his neck where the mane blew about, and his ears pricked at the sound of her voice. But he checked, scenting the carnage with flared nostrils, needing firm urging as they came closer to where the throbbing force of battle shook the earth.

Venetia rode over the broken track, coming out into the open, facing a hill, thick with brambles and furze, crested by a great fort which crouched sullenly, belching out flames and smoke. To her left loomed another, rising high over the meadow which dipped between, where a large body of troops and horsemen gathered. The round-shot from the enemy batteries passed clean over them, while their own artillery, more cunningly positioned, gave back destructive answer.

She paused for an instant, but she had already seen him despite the distance. The scarlet cloak which he wore in sheer defiance billowed out behind him as he flashed across the grass with controlled speed, straight as the bolt from a crossbow, up to the break in the defenses, where the activity was the thickest. Nothing mattered but her compulsion to be with him. She ground her spurs against Orion's flanks, shooting him forward so that his charge almost shocked up against Rupert's stallion.

This was too much for Orion. He snorted, plunged and kicked, hurling Venetia straight beneath the trampling hooves. The Prince reined in smartly; his big beast reared upright, missing her by inches. Orion's legs coiled like springs, ready to launch him into flight but Rupert's gauntleted hand grabbed the trailing bridle, pulling him up short with a jerk.

Venetia staggered to her feet and met the full blast of the Prince's rage, the dark brows curving beneath the peak of his helmet. Her hat had gone bouncing down the slope, and her hair glittered like bronze in the brilliant sunshine.

"God's wounds, a wench!" It was Sir Richard Crane, closing up beside his General, a wolfish grin on his craggily-handsome features.

Rupert did not find it amusing. "Denby's sister!" He snarled. "What the devil do you here?"

The moment had come but it was like a nightmare. She could not muster her thoughts, her head hurt, and her mouth tasted of blood where she had bitten her tongue at the impact.

"I seek to serve you," she blurted.

"More like, she lusts to serve *under* you, sir." Crane's smile widened. "Why, she had already fallen at Your Highness' feet!"

More members of the Lifeguard had moved in around the Palsgrave. They sat their mounts and laughed, looking her over with the casual arrogance of experts; Rupert's select gentleman volunteers who accompanied him everywhere. His angry, warning stare wiped the grins away.

"Get into the shelter of the wall and stay there!" The curt command scorched her ears. "Don't try to ride the beast! You'll break your neck!"

He was an awe-inspiring sight in black armor, looming over her on his destrier, the white plume of his headpiece adding to his size—almost superhuman.

His mouth was set in a stern line, the sweat trickling down his smoke-grimed face, and he wore that wild battle-air, which men, used to fighting with him, easily recognized. Venetia cowered back, dragging Orion with her. One does not bandy words with an avenging archangel.

He had already forgotten her as he swung around to

43

his staff. "A messenger to go to Prince Maurice." Hardly had he voiced the request, before a dozen men leaped forward. He selected one whose horse was fresh. "Tell him to come to me at once with a thousand of his Cornishmen!"

A galloper dashed up at full tilt with the news that a tertia had forced itself so near the quay that the shipping could be set alight. The town endangered by a blaze sweeping through its wooden structures would be easily subjugated.

"*Sacrément!* No!" The Prince thundered. "I have sworn that the King shall have Bristol, not a useless heap of ashes! If the town is fired, tell them that they shall have Rupert to reckon with! Ride man, ride!"

He turned and was gone himself with such speed that sparks flew up from the stones beneath the hoofs of his charger.

Maurice could not spare that number of men, but he came in person with five hundred, and the Royalists surged through, past the inner defenses, toward College Green and the Cathedral. The crooked alleys screwed down toward the sluggish River Frome and, in the din and reek, the sky rained shot from the tall gray gables which gave cover to the defenders. The afternoon heat grilled the tangle of men, locked in vicious combat on the blood-slippery steps.

At Frome Gate, they found themselves facing an army of two hundred screaming harpies, egged on by a forbidding Puritan lady, who had imbued them with her own fanatical determination that Bristol should not be crushed beneath the heel of the debauched Papist Cavaliers and their Devil Prince! They had blocked the gate with woolsacks and earth, putting up a hot fight against the swearing attackers who were half proud, half furious, at the vigor of these stubborn English wenches who put heart into their failing menfolk, yelling at them to go tell the Governor that they would stand firm and face the besiegers with their babies in their arms to keep off shot, if he was afraid!

With the clash of the striving city rising to join the defiant volley from the forts, Venetia crouched beside Orion. She gentled him as he shied and fretted every time a shot burst on the escarpment, and laid her face against his white forelock, wishing that a stray bullet would put an end to her misery.

44

There was a lull, and the commanders measured the work still to do, detailed their men and posted detachments to hold the outworks already gained. The mortars fell silent, and the forts waited in a stillness not at first apparent to those stunned by the bombardment. Rupert and his guard came sweeping back through the breach. He took up a position close by, where he could best receive intelligence and send directions, giving his adjutants orders to prepare to attack Brandon Fort. The fighting had dwindled; a drum sounded in the distance, and excited voices were shouting:

"A parley! They seek a parley!"

Rupert's trumpets brayed and the town was suspended in a weird hush as two Cavalier officers went in toward the castle to talk terms with Nat Fiennes.

Michael fetched Venetia, saying coldly that the Prince had sent him, and his silence, as they rode, hurt her more than the sternest rebuke. In the camp, women were weeping and preparing to bury their dead.

As the sun set, tired, hungry men returned to the camp, each with an exploit to recount. Venetia listened, and yet did not hear the talk which encompassed her, so absorbed in her own unhappiness that the tales of feats of arms, miraculous rescues and heart-rending agonies were like the outer ripples of a dream.

Damaris was folding gowns neatly, passing them to Nancy who packed them into a valise; they would be moving to Bristol in the morning. Like a mother whose first reaction to her child's narrow escape from danger in a burst of anger, so she lectured Venetia.

"What madness possessed you? You could have been killed!"

"I wish that I had!" Venetia answered between hiccuping sobs. "He will despise me for ever. And Michael and Mallory are so cross."

"Of course they are, and rightly so." Damaris could be hard at times. "You have exposed them to mockery. Their comrades lose no opportunity to exercise their wit at someone else's expense."

The victorious troops were already celebrating, and filling their pockets with loot as soon as an officer's back was turned. Singing and hallooing, arm in arm with the recruits who had deserted over to their side, they barged into the houses of noted Roundhead supporters, pointed out by their new companions eager to please. A mob

45

swept on to Bristol Bridge where the shopkeepers were notoriously Parliamentarian in sympathies.

Mallory had been among those striving to keep order, knocking sense into the thick heads of some of the ringleaders. Rupert had told his Lifeguard that he hoped the soldiers would take the city without pillaging it, and they knew that it was not so much a point of honor as a religion to him, to make good his word.

Mallory trudged into Damaris' apartment weary enough to drop. He was not overjoyed to see the object of his angry concern sitting there. His mistress, glancing at his glum face, sent her servants scurrying for refreshment, and opened one of her bottles of sack. Mallory unfastened his sword-belt, letting it jangle to the floor, while Damaris fussed with the buckles of his corselet, getting him out of it.

The food revived him, but the wine made him argumentative and he quarreled with Venetia, who hotly resented his overbearing attitude. As Damaris had surmised, the Lifeguard had lost no time in chaffing him.

"Leaving aside the raillery which I have suffered, you have succeeded in making Michael a laughing-stock! Why, only just now, I had to rebuke a couple of subalterns whom I overheard saying that Prince Rupert will put a pair of horns on Captain Haywood as high as a stag's antlers!"

Venetia was seething with rage. "You talk as if we are already wed!"

He jerked back his chair and stood up to cheat her of the satisfaction of being able to look down at him. "Dammit, you are as good as married. D'you think I don't know that he lies with you? Forget the Prince! He is not for you!"

The mob was already scattering before the soldiers arrived to complete the dispersal.

FIVE

"Bristol taken, Exeter shaking, Gloucester quaking." crowed the Royalist newspaper *Mercurius Aulicus,* showering Rupert with fulsome praises, and enlarging upon the difficulties which now beset gloomy London.

Fiennes was severely censured and very nearly court-martialed. The morale of the Parliamentarians was low and the leaders were quarreling. Robert Devereux, third Earl of Essex was their Captain-General, a sober God-fearing nobleman. But he was lethargic and overcautious, a very strange heir for the dashing, turbulent Earl, whom the elderly Queen Elizabeth had loved, yet sent to the scaffold forty years before. The Cavaliers amused themselves with his foibles. They made up ribald songs about his wife who had left him for another man, calling him "The Great Cuckold!"

Sir Thomas Fairfax and his father in the North, and Oliver Cromwell in the East, were more stirring names. Sir William Waller was a favorite of the eager partisans who fretted at the dullness of Essex. But even he had gone back to the Capital under a cloud and was not on speaking terms with Lord Essex.

Bristol had been a tremendous fillip to the Royalist party, and all agreed that it could not have been stormed by any one except the King's nephew. Meanwhile, the object of this acclaim was very busy squeezing contributions from the tight-fisted burghers, who found him unnervingly canny at driving a hard bargain, drilling the recruits who flocked in, strengthening the fortifications, and falling out with Lord Hertford.

"He and Maurice are a tactless pair!" Damaris was sitting with Venetia in a room at the *Bear and Staff* tavern, watching the actors rehearse. "They were so pleased to be fighting together again, that they practically ran the siege between them, just as if Hertford were not

47

there at all! I hear that the King is coming to settle their differences."

"Rupert will get his way, no doubt," drawled Etienne lazily, his voice coming from beneath the brim of his hat which was tipped forward over his face. He was slouched low in his chair, legs propped up on another.

"Oh, these soldiers!" Damaris, while acknowledging the Prince's capabilities, was fully aware of how his authoritative actions often exacerbated a situation. "Rupert, so quick to criticize others, is only too compliant in his dealings with Maurice."

"Ah, well," put on the Chevalier, pushing back his hat and regarding them with a smile. "Maurice is his brother, and not to be called to account!"

"My dear, we all know that he can do no wrong in Rupert's eyes." Damaris would most probably have said just the same had the Prince been present. "Was it not ever thus even when you were at Leyden University? He is really very naughty, and makes no attempt to get on well with the Council of War, dismissing with a 'Pish!' anything with which he does not agree. It is not the spirit calculated to endear him to the nobles who consider themselves every bit as good as the son of a dethroned King."

"That is half the trouble." Etienne sat up, reaching for the brandy bottle and applying himself to it with extreme diligence. "It is their poverty which makes the Princes so cursed touchy. Royal they may be, but they are also exiles, and penniless, dependent on their swords and the generosity of their relatives."

"Could you please stop talking, over there?" It was Thomas Carter, in a ferment because the rehearsal was not going too well. "We shall never be ready. Adrian— do concentrate, there's a dear! Stop looking at the Chevalier! Come, let us try that passage again."

The landlord of *The Bear* cared little who was victorious, providing the conquering heroes were hard drinkers, and he welcomed Etienne's recommendation that the players would provide an added attraction. The inn was the finest in town, Etienne would never settle for less than the best, if it were humanly possible. An archway led into the courtyard where the building enclosed it on either side, and galleries ran all the way around each story with flights of steps leading to them. It was very old with steep gables under a covering of

48

age-sooted slates, its wooden struts elaborate with heraldic devices and grotesques.

Venetia shared, with Damaris, a parlor panelled in oak, very dark, shiny and rich, with a massive chimney-piece heavily carved with biblical figures. Her bedroom was dominated by an enormous four-poster with faded brocade curtains, and there were cupboard, velvet-cushioned chairs, a mirror and dressing table, and a closed stool with padded seat and chamber-pot; a civilized touch, so much more pleasant than having to use the communal privy in the yard.

The actors had been given much less grand lodgings at the back of the stables, but this suited them well; there was room to rehearse, and it was convenient for reaching the temporary stage which they had erected at one side of the courtyard. There was no scenery so, as was customary, they incorporated the galley which became the upper windows of a house, the battlements of a castle, or a balcony for lovers, as the action of their play dictated.

Meriel, with Venetia's interests well to the fore, had suggested to Carter that they present a performance of "The Tempest," hinting that it might encourage some of the more wealthy citizens and officers to attend, if he could secure the patronage of the Palatine Princess.

"Excellent, my daughter! What a good idea! It will be a compliment to their Highnesses, for Will Shakespeare was dragged out of retirement to produce it as part of the wedding celebrations of their mother."

The day had arrived at last. "D'you think he will come?" Venetia asked Damaris for the hundredth time. She kept running to the windows which faced out onto the yard, but there was no sign of him.

"Maurice has promised to do what he can." Damaris was fixing a star-shaped black patch in a provocative position near the corner of her mouth, while Nancy brushed and coiled, pinned and ornamented her thick hair, little threads of steam wisping up from the curling-tongs.

Since the day of Bristol's capitulation, Venetia had glimpsed the Prince only from a distance. Her body still carried the bruises of her undignified tossing, but this was nothing to her mental hurt. Helplessness washed over her. It now lay in the power of those stars which Meriel said controlled their destinies to make him yield to the

49

persuasion of Maurice, and his own curiosity to witness the play written for his mother.

With an unreal sense of ritual Venetia began to dress, her mind drugged with portents. Her gown was of soft, rustling shot-silk which shimmered with rose and green. Damaris advised her not to overdo the demure effect.

"Try a little of my paint," she suggested, beckoning her to the mirror. "Pull your collar lower, and don't forget to lean over when he speaks to you, so that he can look down into your bodice. It never fails! You do not want to give him the impression you are untouchable. I have already hinted to Maurice of your feelings; no doubt he will have related them to his brother. And yet, my dear, you do not want to appear a wanton. There are quite enough of those as it is, only too eager to warm his bed."

Venetia nodded and listened to her friend whose advice was so sound; telling her that the Prince was a man, not a saint, and to treat him as such.

Nancy worked with the skill of an artist, enhancing Venetia's features with the subtle application of cosmetics. At home she had used some beauty aids, skin lotions brewed in their own still-rooms, creams for keeping the hands white, perfume distilled from rose leaves, but never paints. Nancy emphasized her good points, brushing her cheeks with a hare's foot dipped in rouge powder, reddening her lips with carmine, pressing a touch of blue shadow on her eyelids and blackening the tips of her lashes.

Etienne whistled wordlessly when he came in, turning her around slowly so that he could view her from all angles. *"Mon Dieu!* If this doesn't move him, then the *Pfalzgraf* must be gelt!"

Playbills had been pasted all over town in prominent places and had attracted a large crowd. The landlord kept his staff on the trot, bearing trays of foaming tankards, hot meat-pasties, crusty bread and fresh cheese to serve the customers crowding the benches in front of the stage. Bristol had been starved of entertainment during the dismal Roundhead occupation. Now trade was booming again. The Royalist soldiery spent their money freely; shopkeepers, warehouses and taverns benefited hugely, even if it was at the expense of those citizens who complained that they had been pillaged.

Carter was wearing the gray beard and flowing robes

of "Prospero," and leaned out of the window of the dressing room, raising an anxious eye heavenward; "Pray God that it keeps fine!"

The courtyard was open, and a sudden deluge, making patrons dash for shelter before the hat had been passed around, could be disastrous to their erratic fortunes.

Meriel, hooking the back of Adrian's gown, answered him cheerily. "There's not a cloud in the sky, father. We shall do well today."

The actors were suffering from their usual jitters before the show, but Venetia felt that no one could be as nervous as she, sure that she would never survive if he did not put in an appearance. Even the fact that she caused a minor sensation when Michael took her across to their seats, was of very little consequence compared with this huge emotion which was shaking her to pieces. Afterward, she never knew how she kept up that inane chatter, talking about nothing of any importance, while within her resounded one prayer, "Oh God! Let him come!"

She had never felt herself to be on particularly close terms with the Almighty, but it seemed that He heard, for there was a sudden commotion at the archway leading into the street, and Rupert strode abruptly out into the sunlight, his head rising high above his gentlemen; only Maurice was nearly tall enough to look directly into his eyes as they talked.

A spontaneous cheer rose from the crowd of troops and tradesmen, apprentices, and citizens on a spree. Hats came off, the men bowed while the women curtsied, peeking up to catch a glimpse of him. He uncovered and acknowledged the homage with a solemn returning bow, and the throng parted to let him through.

The Royal brothers took their seats on the other side of Mallory who occupied the place next to Venetia. Rupert's eyes were on her, his lips curving faintly in greeting. She could hear his voice with that foreign intonation, and Maurice's halting English, and she wanted to leap to her feet, thrust Mallory out of her way, hang on to Rupert's sleeve and tell him that she adored him.

Damaris, leaning across Etienne, was making some remark to Maurice, tapping him on the arm with intimate fingers. Behind them sat Rupert's friends, Richard Crane, Major Will Legge and Charles Gerard, in that privileged position of knowing him well enough to bend across his shoulder and address him. There were a bunch of his mercenaries near at hand, lean and war-worn, throwing their weight around, with bearded jaws, manes of unruly hair, and flashy weapons, laughing and joking and ogling the women.

Michael had grown very quiet, his fingers still laced with hers.

"He knows," she thought sadly. And how could anyone not be aware of the current pulsing through her, directed toward the Prince?

The noise died down as the play began. The actors were good, and held the interest of the audience. Venetia had seen them rehearse so often that she knew precisely where each well timed piece of business was worked into the plot. She was glad that everyone's attention was on them and ventured a glance sideways to Rupert's profile.

It was perfectly true that, as Adrian had remarked, his nose was large, curved like one of his falcons, but this fierce aspect was softened by the sweep of black lashes. Although they sat on the shady side, there were beads of sweat on his upper lip which was already darkening; because he was so swarthy, his beard showed quickly, giving him the predatory look of a brigand.

He sat with elbows resting on the arms of the landlord's best chair which had been dusted and put in the place of honor, and he was bareheaded, his hair rolling into thick rings past his shoulder-blades. He was wearing burgundy-colored plush, and his jacket was richly laced, with the top buttons fastened and the rest left undone in that casual, careless way so fashionable at the moment, displaying an amount of puffy lawn shirt. The sleeves were slashed to the shoulders with more shirt bulging through, ending at the wrists in wide, tight cuffs. His breeches were straight and decorated with tiny velvet buttons running down the outer seams from the thigh, meeting his supple leather boots which had the tops flopping over below his knees.

He was listening attentively to the play, smiling occasionally, making comments to Maurice and, without taking his eyes from the stage, reaching down a hand to silence Boye who was getting fidgety. Between scenes, he accepted a glass of sack, unfolded seemingly endless legs and stood up. And, with every heartbeat, Venetia was becoming more spellbound, the whole sequence of events taking on the ramifications of a dream.

The shadows were lengthening when, amidst wild bursts of applause, the actors took their bows. They were presented to the Prince who discussed the performance with Carter. Maurice was grinning at Damaris in a way which made Mallory bridle. She was playing them off against one another, languid and cynical, regarding all men with a kind of amused contempt. She was fond of Mallory, but the ease with which he usually cleared the field of rivals, piqued and provoked her; she fancied the younger Prince.

Michael wanted Venetia to go with him; he had booked a private room in another tavern, but she impatiently tugged him across to join the Chevalier and his wife, determined to be introduced to Maurice, and through him, to contact Rupert.

It was a daunting experience to be stared down on by the two hawk-faced Princes, so alike, and yet so different in personality. Maurice had the same type of over-pronounced good looks, but Rupert had a double share of strength and beauty. Maurice was a year younger than he, and in him that inner fire was damped down; Rupert, when annoyed, smoldered, whereas Maurice only succeeded in looking sullen. It was significant that one of his nick-names was "Twin," and that he was known as Rupert's faithful "Shadow." His men had affectionately dubbed him "the good come-off," because of his adroit management of retreats.

Damaris had told Venetia that Maurice was very popular with his troops, easy-going, not a particularly brilliant commander, but having a staunch reliability and the will to fight very stoutly when the occasion arose. Some people found him rather a boor and a little uncouth because he was not familiar with English manners and customs. But he had many attractive qualities, not the least of which was his gallantry in action, and his unquestioning devotion to his brother.

His warm brown eyes followed Damaris, bedazzled, like a rabbit before a stoat, and he alternated between speechless shyness and coltish confidence, stumbling over difficult English words.

The Chevalier, that wonderful friend to all lovers, prevailed upon Rupert to be his guest at supper. At first he had wanted to return to headquarters but, seeing Maurice's regretful face, he shrugged and relented.

Damaris organized the seating arrangements to suit her own plans. Rupert stood back so that Venetia might pass through the narrow space between the tables and himself to take her place further alone the settle. As her hips brushed his thighs, she felt his sudden startled flinch, followed immediately by an involuntary returning pressure. Trembling, she was glad to sit down. The possessive Michael put an arm around her and she wished him miles away.

She toyed with her food, appetite gone, trying to catch what Rupert was saying to Maurice, but they spoke in French; a curious French, interpolated with Dutch and German phrases, and this gave them ample opportunity for sharing private remarks and jokes which made them laugh, shutting everyone else out. This was a rude habit, which even Venetia had to admit was irritating, well understanding how it must madden the Courtiers if they did it at the Council-table.

At Etienne's end of the board, the subject had come around to General George Goring, who had been captured by the Roundheads at Wakefield. It was natural that such a convivial atmosphere, coupled with flowing ale and the company of pretty women, should bring him to mind.

"No one enjoys parties more than Roaring George," said Damaris, adding with a sigh, "Such a shame that he cannot be here."

"Will you be able to exhange him for a Roundhead prisoner, sir?" Richard Crane enquired of Rupert. " 'Tis a pity to have him cooped up in captivity when we could use his services."

A frown darkened the Prince's brow, he remembered him from pre-war days, though he had not yet met him in this conflict, "I shall see what can be done when we get some equally important officer to barter. He is a good soldier, when he's not as drunk as a fiddler's bitch!"

With a quirk of his humorous eyebrows, Crane tried to draw Venetia into conversation, winking at her when Michael was not looking. Damaris was flirting outrageously with Charles Gerard, whom Venetia had not met before, though Damaris assured her that he was one of Rupert's favorites and a valiant fighter.

Cards appeared as soon as the supper dishes had been

removed. Goblets were kept replenished, and clay pipes sent up fragrant smoke to coil around the low, crooked beams. Some of the Cavaliers still wore their soldiers' garb, smirched by rough usage, others had changed into a blaze of velvets and damasks. Their cloaks, slung over the back of chairs, sent out flashes of gold and silver lace as the tapesters brought in candles. In the background, Adrian was playing his guitar, and they started roaring out the chorus of "The Whore of Babylon," beating time with tankards and sword-hilts.

Taking advantage of Mallory's interest in the gaming, Damaris slipped out and, as if drawn by invisible threads, Maurice rose and followed her. They were not gone for long and when they returned, she seated herself demurely by her husband. Mallory glared at her, and she smiled sweetly back at him. Presently she came across and whispered to Venetia:

"He desires you. I've been talking to Maurice. Why else do you suppose we went up to my room?" Her violet eyes slanted with laughter; a delicious wanton, opulent and gamey, completely incorrigible. She assured Venetia that Rupert was defiantly attracted, and a woman like Damaris was not apt to misread a man's signals.

Venetia could not imagine how the objective was to be reached; Michael was glued to her side like a limpet, while the Prince ignored her, talking to Boye who had jumped up onto a chair beside him and was being fed with the tastiest morsels. But, in his misery, Michael had been gloomily drinking a large quantity of ale and was forced at last to seek the privy. Maurice stood up, with the faintest flick of a wink at his brother. Crane and Gerard, grinning, scraped back their stools and accompanied him on his mission to make sure that Michael was detained. And Will Legge, that solid, dependable friend to all, puffed at his pipe and watched these elaborate courtship dances with mature tolerance from behind a screen of smoke.

Then Rupert turned to Venetia; their elbows touched, eyes met and conversation began. It was so easy that she could hardly believe it. His shoulders obliterated the rest of the company and her heart was thudding so hard that she was sure it might leap into her throat and choke her.

"How does the little she-soldier find herself?" he

55

inquired seriously. "I hope that your fall did you no harm."

Venetia was thankful that someone, probably Damaris, had kept topping up her glass. She was full of alcoholic *savior faire*. "A few bruises, nothing more, Your Highness."

She sat at his side and shook at the thought of her own boldness. Something in common; bricks on which to build an affinity; a lifeline. She asked him if he had enjoyed the play.

He shrugged. " 'Twas pleasing enough, though I have seen my sisters act as cleverly."

Her ears pricked. Sisters? She wished that he would talk about his family, but he had fallen silent, looking at her in a most disconcerting way. She stabbed about for something stunningly deep and clever to say, knowing full well that when it was too late, she would be brimming with wise and witty remarks. Nothing came.

Boye pushed a damp nose into her hand, his bright watchful eyes going from the Prince's face to her own. The dog and Lintz. Her words rushed out and she was asking him about his imprisonment. He expressed surprise that she knew of it, and told her what it had been like to be shut up for three years.

"Boye was a present from Lord Arundel, the English Ambassador in Vienna. A small, woolly puppy, weren't you, old fellow?" He ruffled his pet's fur and was licked by a pink tongue. "Someone else gave me a wild hare, and I trained them to live together in harmony. But I let it go, it found captivity as irksome as I. God, it was so boring! They let me have books, and I studied the technical side of warfare. I drew a lot, played tennis, walked about the castle grounds, dined with Graf Kuffstein, who was the Governor and by gaoler. My confinement was close. I think they feared rescue bids. Kuffstein had been instructed to try and convert me to the Catholic Faith."

His brown fingers played with the stem of his goblet, watching the swirling golden liquid as he brooded on the frustrations of Lintz.

"I suppose it was good for the character. It taught me how to endure celibacy when necessary." His eyes were on her face and there were tiny sparks, jets of amber, in his blackly-dilated pupils.

56

With admirable aplomb, Venetia managed to say, "Were there no women in the castle?"

A faint smile tugged at the corners of his mouth. "There was a girl—you remind me of her—she too was fair, and had the same color eyes. Her name was Suzanne and she was Kuffstein's daughter."

"Did you make love to her?" The impertinent question burst out, and Venetia was too drunk to care.

His smile was mocking. "How eager women are to know that! When I finally went home, it was one of the first things my sisters asked. 'We've heard about you and Suzanne Kuffstein! Did you make love to her?' My mother was more concerned as to whether she had managed to convert me to Catholicism. To both queries I could answer, quite truthfully, no!"

It was foolish to feel this uprush of relief. Why should it matter to her that he may have loved some girl out of boredom and despair?

"In any case," he added, "her father had been kind to me. It would have been ill repayment, on my part, to have seduced his daughter."

Venetia did not want to think about Suzanne any more, so she asked him if the Elector Palatine had been captured also.

Rupert gave a sharp bark of sardonic laughter. "Charles Louis? Not he! He always manages to save his own skin. He escaped, fleeing from the battle, and fell into the river Weser on the way. Yet even so, our mother made it known that she was much relieved that 'he whom she loved best' was safe. She has always preferred him—he is a true Courtier. Now he spends his time flitting between the Hague and Essex House, currying favor with Parliament, apologizing to them because his wild brothers are traversing the country like freebooters!"

He was so furious that Venetia sobered, afraid that she had gone too far and that it would cross his mind that it was time this forward hussy took herself off and left him to his comrades.

"He is not for the Roundheads, surely?" she ventured.

"Charles Louis is for no one but himself!" He bit off the words with a savage snap. "He lingers about his friends in Westminster, begging that they will not stop his pension because of me! I hope he dies of ennui, listening to the long-winded Puritan sermons! I'll wager that mother still dotes on him, although he is betraying the King. I was never a *beau garcon*, as he is, to make her easy with me—she was forever telling me this. No doubt she corresponds regularly with him, and she hasn't written me a single letter since I came over!"

He spoke so passionately, mouth so sulky, eyes so reproachful, that Venetia suddenly realized that this untamable creature could be very capable of jealousy over precedence, position and power, childishly furious because his mother dared to prefer the suave, unprincipled Charles Louis, to himself. Elizabeth of Bohemia must be a remarkable woman indeed, to rouse resentment in her stubborn, willful son. Etienne had hinted of trouble between them; the Queen had borne thirteen children, nine of whom still lived, and Rupert was the one with whom she quarreled most frequently. They were too much alike, so the Chevalier insisted.

Venetia attempted to put this into words, and Rupert glowered, muttering something irritably surly in one or two languages. She was afraid that he was going to retreat into himself.

But he spoke again, giving a low laugh with an edge of bitterness. "She cared little for any of us when we were children. As soon as we were old enough to travel we were packed off to Leyden, some three days journey from her house at the Hague. She much preferred the company of her monkeys and dogs, and those friends who adored her so faithfully, squandering their fortunes to keep us all. Sometimes she would send for us and parade us before some notable person, like a herd of stud horses! Best of all, she loves to hunt. I have yet to meet the woman who can ride like my mother!"

The roisterers were bawling toasts, and some of the young bucks, with bared blades held aloft, had their feet on the table, sending the goblets crashing. The Prince swung around.

One dapper gallant, with a blue ribbon in the lovelock which swung over his left shoulder, pedged him, and added:

"We'll drink to His Highness's dog too! Glasses raised, gentlemen—to Sergeant-Major-General Boye! Who puts the fear of God, or the Devil, into those canting, sniveling rebels!"

The cheering made Boye leap against Rupert, barking indignantly. He patted him reassuringly, eyeing his men, none too pleased. "Hush, my Boye. 'Tis only your comrades, few of whom will be fit for duty in the morning."

Venetia laid a hand on his arm, emboldened by wine and the fear that he would leave. "Don't you ever forget the army?"

He was instantly guarded, experienced enough to recognize the worship in her eyes which he had become accustomed to seeing so often since the war began.

"I have no time." The well-worn excuse sprang to his lips.

"You had time enough to dally with Mary Lennox!" She was angry and desperate. Very well. Let it hurt his damnable pride to know that he and Richmond's wife were gossiped about! She would sting him to rage, if nothing else.

A dark flush spread up under his bronzed cheeks, astounding her by the sudden revelation that beneath his apparent confidence he was uneasy with women.

Rupert shot her a wrathful glare. " 'Sblood! What time did I spend in dalliance at Oxford? Three days, that's all! Much good did it do me!"

Elation surged through her. Mary had roused but not satisfied him. She began to feel her own power; the Prince and she were both becoming equals in this struggle to hide feelings and put up a sensible front. His face had set into moody lines with pouting mouth and heavy eyelids. Venetia wanted to run her fingers through his hair and kiss away the look of baffled anger.

He was talking again and she had not the faintest idea what it was about. She reached out and covered his hand with hers. In the candle-lit dimness, she could not tell his reaction, but he did not withdraw from her touch, and his eyes slid from her face, past the line of her throat to her high rounded breasts, and they narrowed, in a way which she recognized, hard and wary.

He drank down the last of his ale. She could smell the faint odor of it as he breathed, combined with the heavy masculine sweat on his clothes, the scent of leather and horses.

Rupert stretched and lounged to his feet. "It is very hot in here. Nightingale Valley would be refreshingly cool. Shall we go for a ride?"

Cool would hardly describe her feelings when in some secluded leafy glade with him, but the hope in his words dizzied Venetia beyond speech. Walking on soft billowy clouds of intoxication, she was carried safely past the eyes which marked their progress to the door, amused, mocking or envious; and there was Mallory, dice-box in mid-shake, registering shocked alarm.

In the stable, Rupert's page appeared, catching the hat which he tossed over and receiving his order:

"Take Boye back to headquarters, Holmes: I shan't need you any more tonight."

In a swift movement, the Prince put his hands around Venetia's waist and lifted her up onto Orion's back. It was the first time that he had touched her and she was sure that the air about them crackled. He said nothing, but mounted his own horse and together they rode out under the archway.

SIX

When they reached Durdham Down, the Prince spurred to a gallop, his hair streaming in the wind. Venetia suspected that he was doing it out of devilry, and also to test her ability against some yardstick of his own, most probably that Diana of the chase, his mother.

She flicked Orion with her whip, giving him the rein, determined to prove that she was no novice. His winged speed, the rush and whistle of the air, cleared the wine fumes from her brain. But the stocky pony was no match for the stride of Rupert's big animal, and he reached the rim of trees first, checking the courser, drawing him into a walk.

The view was wild, forest and cliffs intersected by the winding River Avon which had carved a deep gorge. Out toward the estuary, a ship, with sails spread before the breeze, was carried on the night-tide. It was a still evening. Faint and far away, the bell-ringers were practicing for Sunday.

Rupert helped Venetia dismount, standing for a moment with his hands at her elbows.

"You ride well," he said. Praise indeed from the finest horseman in Europe.

They led their mounts along a narrow path where the soil of the dusky forest floor was dotted with flowers which, when crushed by the hooves, sent up a sharp odor of wood-vetch and leek. As they passed through open spaces in the woods, they came across several late picnic parties, people resting, reading, playing with their children, and, in the seclusion of the undergrowth, couples were making love.

Curious stares followed the aristocratic young man and his beautiful companion. They were a striking couple, more richly dressed than most people who frequented Nightingale Valley, and their beasts were well fed and glossy. It could have been dangerous to come there alone, for there were footpads, working in gangs, ever on the look-out for victims, but the sword swinging at Rupert's hip, and the pistols in holsters each side of his saddle, would prove protection enough. It was not a healthy place to be in after dark, and some of the holiday-makers began to stir and gather up their belongings, casting speculative glances at the sky. Sunset-edged evening was throwing mysterious shadows, filling the gully with blackness.

The Prince tethered the horses in a glade, and they pushed on further among the trees, where he had to hold back brambles which threatened to tangle her hair. He hardly spoke and she found herself gushing information, about her home-life, her family, the people she had met in Oxford, and she listened to the words falling over themselves and thought, "Who is this fool?"

The branches arching somberly over his head reminded her of the fan vaulting of a great cathedral—the correct, magnificent setting for the pomp which would attend the nuptial of such a renowned Palsgrave, and there would later be a great State marriage-bed, with a fortunate Princess waiting for him among satin pillows. Venetia felt cheated because she could never be that bride: but even so, she would not have him take her casually like any back-street trollop. She needed time to develop the relationship so that friendship overlapped passion, affection blended with lust. Their first mating must not be done in stealth with the constant threat of interruption; a hurried groping, quickly over for him and as soon forgotten, and completely unsatisfying for her.

If she did not please him, he would not bother with her again.

All the time, she was seeing the light dappling over Rupert's face, running into his eyes, slanting across them spilling out again down to his mouth, and she gave up the struggle, unable to stop staring at his lips, so finely-chiseled, cruel yet sensitive, rarely smiling. He took her hand to help her down a difficult bit and they both stopped. He smelled of heat, and of the spicy perfume which he used on his cheeks after shaving. The combined effect was so overwhelming that she put her hands behind her, seeking the rock-steadiness of a tree-trunk and leaning against it for support.

The Prince rested an arm on either side of her, so that she was enclosed, and bent his head to kiss her. His mouth was unexpectedly gentle, almost hesitant, as if he were not too sure of her acceptance. This moved her deeply; she yearned for, and sorrowed over him. He should not feel uncertain ever, not Prince Rupert, and she slid her arms about him, her lips parting, tongue seeking his in welcome and celebration.

Venetia could feel herself dissolving, wanting only to be devoured; she rejoiced that she was no inexperienced virgin. Michael had schooled her well. Rupert pressed her back against the tree, his body hard and demanding, his kisses hot on her face, neck and shoulders where he had pushed her bodice aside. He was fully roused, desperate for relief, as if he had not had a woman for a long time. This was what she had wanted since the first moment that she had seen him, towering and godlike, in the meadow; his wildness, his roughness, and his need, were so exciting that she was sliding rapidly toward surrender and had no inclination to stop. But it must not happen there.

She heard herself saying "No!" several times. He ignored it and she broke away to stand, panting, on the other side of the path.

He looked down at her with the blackest scowl that she had ever seen on a man's face. "What's the matter? D'you expect me to woo you with soft words? Find a silken Court fop, if that's what you need. Don't play games with me!" His hands shot out like talons, ready to rend and tear at this woman who was frustrating him, fingers biting into her shoulders as he shook her. "Answer me! Do you want it or don't you?"

He was hurting her, forgetting his own strength, but she stood her ground. "My God, if only you knew! I've never wanted anything else! But I'll not let you swive me in the bracken, like a peasant!"

Rupert released her, so abruptly that she almost collapsed. He turned and went crashing through the scrub, nearly tripping over a pair of lovers lying in the grass. Venetia, catching up with him, met his gaze as if to say, "D'you see what I mean?"

She had no idea of his intention, miserably certain that he was going to escort her back to the inn. Silently, he helped her into the saddle and she could not bear it, wanting to fling her arms around his neck and beg him to take her, then and there, on the ground, like an animal, any way he wanted, but not to leave her. Who was she to dare dictate terms to him—of all people?

The road was unfamiliar and he drew rein at last at an imposing gatehouse, set in a high wall. In the courtyard beyond, Venetia looked up at the colors of the Palatine, flying high above the chimneys, silhouetted against the dark perimeter of the sky.

The back of the house was deserted, although cheerful sounds came from the direction of the kitchen, a clash of pans, and the smell of suppers being cooked.

"Get down, and wait for me there," Rupert said curtly, pointing to an open doorway, before riding across to the stables, leading Orion.

She shrank back into the gloom, obeying his order, nettled because he did not want her to be seen, trying to convince herself that he was considering her honor, while the new cynicism, which she was rapidly deveolping, insisted that it was more likely his desire to retain that reputation for stern self-sufficiency which was part of his mystique. He was respected as an austere, abstemious man. *Il était toujours soldat!* as one of his acquaintances described him.

Then he was at her side, sweeping her up a twisting stairway to his bedchamber, flooded with the scarlet of a dying sun. Only his valet, De Faust, occupied the bare, functional quarter, and, after one startled glance at the Palsgrave's face, he could not get out quickly enough. Venetia was trembling and unable to control her breathing, wanting Rupert so badly that she did not know how to cope with the reality of having him.

63

His arms encircled her waist, dragging her hard against him.

"I am afraid," she said.

"Why?" He was muzzling her ear, the rasping of his jaw sending shocks down her spine.

"Because I love you so much and you are going to hurt me." The last of her pitiful defenses was being stormed; now he could destroy her with mockery or contempt. If only he would say that he returned her love, even if it was untrue. But he did not; Rupert never lied. Instead, his hand came up to stroke over her hair, and he was gentle, so strangely gentle, that she was lost; condemned to belong to him for the rest of eternity.

He lifted her against his chest, running his tongue over her tears, then locking his mouth on hers with a hunger which emptied her of all thought. He pulled her down into the canopied bed, caressing her inexpertly, with the eagerness of a young man who has been used to the offices of harlots. Venetia envied the leaguer drab of some foreign army who had initiated him, early in his teens.

His possession of her was quick, as impetuous as one of his famous cavalry charges, and she wanted it that way. At the moment when cautious Michael carefully withdrew, Rupert was beyond control. Venetia did not care; it would be no disgrace to have His Highness's bastard.

He lay quietly, his mouth on her breast, and she smiled into the dusk, aware that there were hours ahead till dawn, plenty of time to show him just how clever she was at loving; she would give him slow, lingering delight. She had experimented with Michael, developing an unerring knack for finding out and exploiting male sensuality. Rupert should benefit from this. Let him rest awhile, and then she would use her skill to rouse him to an ecstasy which he would never have experienced with his whores. She would be imaginative and tender, because she worshipped him. He was her soul, a part of herself.

Damaris had been right; the Prince was an instinctive rather than an expert lover, and it was easy to believe that he was more at home with his gunners and his horsemen than with women, snubbed by his mother who had so often told him, when he was a shy, awkward boy, that he was too rough to please ladies. He shied away from emotional involvement, afraid to put his masculinity to the test, feeling that it would diminish if he could not win and keep the devotion of a desirable woman.

The accolades heaped on him early in his career had given him an exaggerated sense of his own importance. He had been thoroughly spoilt by the indulgent Prince of Orange in whose army he had first served. The admiration he had won, during his captivity, added to his self-esteem. Conscious of his own abilities and claims to distinction, he adopted that arrogant manner which gave such offense to Courtiers and Councilors. Yet Venetia recognized that beneath this apparent conceit, there was still the child, one among so many clever siblings, scrambling for a crumb of attention from that careless Queen who seemed blind to the thwarted love of her hero son.

"You have made me so happy," she whispered.

He stirred and touched her cheek. *"Liebling,* don't cry. *Ach Gott,* can it be that you really do care for me?"

He would need to be told repeatedly and then still doubt it. Her fingers were tracing across his body in the dimness. "You are all I have ever wanted in a man. I've longed for you for years. Ever since I was a child I have been in love with you, though you were just a name."

"All moonshine, surely?" He sounded pleased, though still deprecating. "Girls are always dreaming, my sisters do it all the time."

"Time will show if I speak the truth, Highness." Even at the closest point of contact, she had not dared to use his name, and he had not suggested it. Now she added: "Can I stay with you tonight?"

She felt his wariness; although they were still clasped close it yawned like a chasm between them. Venetia took no notice, continuing to caress him as if it were already agreed that she should remain. She was beginning to know Rupert; he would have perished by protracted torture rather than admit he needed her.

"It will be the talk of the taverns tomorrow," he warned.

"I'll wager 'tis already, they all saw me leave with you." Her new confidence was amazing.

"What of your betrothed? I don't want him to hate

me," his voice trailed into silence as she wriggled against him, warm and voluptuous.

"You did not speak of that a little while ago," she reminded gently. "Did you expect to hand me back to him when you had finished? Don't worry, I will manage Michael."

He no longer mattered; nothing was of any consequence beside her consuming passion. Oh, Rupert would be very difficult. There would be no placid areas of tranquility as there had been with Michael; it would be like living on the rim of a volcano. Three-quarters of his mind would be shuttered against her and with this she would have to be content, checking her feminine desire to probe and peel away layers. She would have to be patient, subjugate her own personality to his, gladly paying the price for this enviable position where so many women wanted to be—in Prince Rupert's bed.

Sometime during the night, the poodle whimpered and scratched persistently at the door and Rupert got up to let him in, making him lie at the foot of the bed, instead of in his usual place, on his master's chest. Annoyed by this banishment, Boye retired resentfully to a chair where the Prince's cloak lay. He bounded onto it, turning around several times to get comfortable, and tried to settle down. His ears twitched, thoroughly disturbed by the vibrations in the atmosphere, eddies of powerful emotions which made him uneasy. His Prince's voice was different, low, vibrant, caressing, and there were the alien noises of the woman, her soft laugh, and gasps of pleasure.

When the sounds stopped, Boye came across, whining, to lick Rupert's hand questioningly. He rested his front paws on the quilt, unhappy to see the woman with her face buried against the moist hollow of Rupert's shoulder, her hair splayed out, mingling with his dark, tangled locks. Boye gave a sharp bark of protest, but though the Prince's hand half raised to quieten him, it dropped back and they were both deeply asleep.

Very early, Rupert woke Venetia and, reluctantly, she dressed and followed him out. Boye was before them, scrabbling down the stairs while Rupert hushed him with forcible Low Country oaths. The yard was graywashed with dawn; they paused in the doorway and Venetia clung to him.

"*Ich liebe dich, Ruprecht,*" she whispered, trying out

the phrase he had taught her during the night. He was still so beautiful to her, though he was dishevelled and in a desperate need of a shave, clad in hastily donned shirt, breeches and boots.

His even white teeth gleamed in a grin. "Good. Your pronunciation is perfect. Tonight, you shall learn to say it in Spanish."

She knew that he spoke six languages fluently; the prospect was delightful, but a chill finger of doubt touched her, "You won't forget?"

"Sweetheart, how could I forget such a night?" He was laughing and relaxed. "If we dwell on it more, I shall be forced to take you upstairs again, and I have work to do. Holmes will bring you to me this evening."

He saddled the horses himself, there were no grooms about yet, and she helped him in the hay-sweet stable. This simple humdrum action and the way in which the animals responded to his sure touch and the sound of his voice, threw them into a rapport deeper than they had known in sexual congress. The world was so still; it was as if they were the only people living.

At the gate, Rupert became a General again, giving a sharp reproof to the sentinel nodding over his musket. They jogged between hedges still wet with dew. When they reached the turning which led to the inn, somewhere among the hawthorns, a blackbird began to sing.

As they parted, he leaned across to kiss her cheek with a look which was like fire and wine to her. Then he wheeled, and dug in his spurs, yelling over his shoulder to Boye, who careered after him, barking joyously as they raced for the Downs.

Venetia started up the gallery steps, wanting to reach her room and think about the past hours, reliving every moment. She was nearly at the door, when it was flung open, and Michael loomed over her.

"Where the devil have you been?" he demanded, grabbing her wrist and snatching her up close to him. His eyes were bloodshot, his face haggard and his clothing rumpled. He had been waiting all night, drinking heavily.

Before she could answer, he jerked her inside and slammed the door. The noise woke Mallory, who, keeping watch with Michael, had fallen asleep in the bed. He raised himself on one elbow, scowling across at her.

The sight of him made her furious, she could feel pity for Michael in his jealous misery, but resented Mallory's interference. She twisted free from Michael's grasp, rubbing her chaffed wrist. "I went for a ride with His Highness," she answered sullenly.

Michael's eyebrows shot up and he regarded her intently. "You must have covered a good many miles!"

Venetia could not decide whether it was sarcasm in his tone, unable to believe if he guessed where she had been—that he would be so controlled.

"We lost count of the time." As she gave this lame excuse, she knew that it no longer mattered what they believed. From now on she would live under Rupert's aegis, and her eyes went over them scornfully, there was nothing they could do about it.

"Don't bother to lie to me. I know where you have been and what you have been doing." Although his voice did not rise, he was murderously angry. "What kind of a fool d'you take me for? Don't you think that I've seen the way you look at him, with drooling admiration?"

"If you know about it, why ask me?" she said tartly.

His face twisted with rage; this was a man she had never known existed beneath the quiet, gentle Michael whom she had taken so casually for granted. For one terrified instant she thought that he was going to strike her.

Mallory intervened, though wanting to thrash her himself, no man must lay a hand on his sister. "Give her a chance! You have said often enough that Rupert is no lecher!"

But Michael was beyond reason, exhausted by jealousy and sleeplessness, his eyes boring into Venetia as if he would unravel all her secrets.

"The Prince is human, and you are desirable." He spoke between clenched teeth. "It is useless to deny it. I know by your face that you have been lying with him. 'Tis true, isn't it?"

He ended on an imploring note, begging her to release him from his torture, willing to accept a lie, if it would blanket his mind from the obscene images which had filled it through those hellish hours.

Venetia stood fronting them with lifted head and steady gaze. It was as if some of Rupert's courage had poured into her along with his passion.

"Of course I bedded with him!" There was a ring of triumph in her voice. "And I shall do it again!"

Michael's face was suddenly gray and old; his fists clenched till the knuckles showed white. "I'll kill him," he ground out. "Mallory, will you act as my second?"

"Don't be a damned fool! You know he's an expert swordsman and a crack shot!" Mallory treated Venetia to a raging glare. "You slut! See what you have done! He was one of Rupert's most devoted officers!"

"Still the war, and the prospering of the war!" Venetia thought savagely. "They are as bad as the Prince! A pox confound all men!"

"You should never have come with us!" Mallory continued to nag. "The leaguer is no place for you."

She rounded on him, blazing. "Oh, no! Not good enough for Mallory Denby's sister, but what about your whores? You are mighty prudish over my morals, but never slow to take your own pleasures where you will!"

"That is different," Mallory stated emphatically, but he frowned in perplexity.

She was repeating views being voiced loudly by many of the younger women now. If they were to be forced to endure the miseries and heartbreak of a war which was not of their seeking, then they too wanted a share in the freedom. Mallory's mouth tightened; letters from Oxford had not been reassuring. Catherine wrote that they were having trouble with Ella, their house swarming with junior officers and students. Sisters were the very devil!

Anger, affection and shame warred in him. "Good, Venetia, be sensible! D'you really believe that you mean anything to him? He is forever on the move. Women come and go—many offer themselves. Sometimes he takes them—more often he turns them over to Maurice. He probably won't even remember your name."

"That's a damnable lie! He was putting into words her own sickening doubts. "I am to go to him again tonight."

Michael groaned, burying his face in his hands. "I swore to serve him to the death. There is no man on earth I love so well. In truth, could never bring myself to harm him, but do I have to sit back while he rides you like a rutting stallion?"

Silence stretched across the room. Outside, the inn was waking. In the yard, someone was applying energy to the pump handle which wheezed in protest, buckets bumping beneath it while servants chattered, maids whisked into bedchambers with pitchers of water, or trays of newly-baked bread and sizzling bacon.

The confident tones of Damaris rang along the gallery, and a tall form passed the window to go clumping down the stairs. Mallory drilled Prince Maurice's uncaring back with wrathful eyes. He had problems of his own.

"Those damned Palatines!" And he was gone in the direction of Damaris' room, where the sounds of a quarrel immediately ensued, with the clang of pewter as she hurled the breakfast dishes at him.

Michael did not stay, recalling his duty; his sense of honor compelling him to endure the agony of close daily contact with his rival—and chief.

As the door closed behind him, Venetia swirled around and ran to the mirror. Surely a woman who had been loved by Rupert must look different from common mortals? She almost expected to see a luminous aura, and was disappointed that her appearance was not changed, except that her hair was snarled and there were faint blue smudges beneath her eyes.

In a churning state of nerves Venetia could hardly believe it when Robert Holmes was announced early in the evening. She had been ready for hours, but now she had Damaris and Nancy searching frantically for last minute essentials, her scent-bottle, a fan, a clean kerchief. Then she swept out in a froth of petticoats, her velvet hooded cloak flowing behind her, while young Holmes smiled and held the door wide.

Rupert was worried. While they supped, she listened to his grievances. The crux of the matter this time appeared to be over the Governorship of Bristol.

" 'Sblood, that they dare to question my right to be Governor!" the Prince exploded imperiously. "I *took* the bitch of a city!"

Venetia, watching him cracking a nutshell in the palm of one hand as if he wished it were Lord Hertford's head, had to admit that she had never seen such self-will and arrogance stamped across one face before. "Someone should have whacked your backside early in life, Rupert le Diable!" she thought.

Maurice's inferior position under the Marquis had rankled the prickly German brothers for some time. His appointment as Lieutenant-General to Hertford had brought no satisfaction to either.

"He fancies himself slighted because I didn't go into a lengthy consultation with him over the surrender terms." Rupert was in a very irritable mood. "I wanted to get the matter settled quickly without giving Fiennes the opportunity to hum and haw. Hertford would have wasted time thumbing through half a dozen text books on correct procedure. Now he's damned well gone behind my back and given Sir Ralph Hopton the post, without a word to me about it! He knows that I will not set up another officer against Hopton. I esteem him highly, he's a gallant soldier and one of my mother's best friends."

"What will you do?" Venetia was refilling their wine-glasses. The Prince had dismissed his staff, and they were supping alone at a table drawn up by the windows which faced out over the garden.

"Do?" Rupert gave a sudden, frank laugh. "I fore-stalled Hertford days ago. When I first wrote to the King, telling him the good news of the city's fall, I requested to be made Governor and he readily assented. The trouble arises because Hertford has publicly de-clared Hopton's appointment." His eyes glinted wickedly. "Theres one hell of a row going on in Oxford about it now!"

Naturally, there would be; once more Rupert was in-volved in trouble. Venetia felt sorry for King Charles, called upon to settle the disputes of his quarrelsome Generals, a kind of minor civil war in itself.

"He arrives tomorrow," Rupert announced. "And he'll do as I want. He always does when I am nigh. But when I am not with him, the others undermine my advice—the Courtiers, and Digby!"

He was lounging moodily in the large padded chair, one leg slung over the arm, and the other stretched out before him. He seemed so preoccupied that Venetia thought he had forgotten her, but he suddenly beckoned, and she went over, sinking to her knees beside him, her arms going about his waist, head pressed against his ribs, hearing the steady pounding of his heart, feeling the heat of his body, the firmness of his muscles beneath the thin linen shirt.

"You won't be able to stay all night," he was saying,

his fingers against her lips as she started to argue. "I must be up betimes to greet His Majesty."

De Faust woke her a little after midnight, and she sat up, dragging the sheet around her, catching sight of his dour Flemish features above the glow of the candle, registering disapproval at his relaxing of the Palsgrave's high-souled austerity.

"Holmes is waiting to take you home, madame," he told her stiffly.

Venetia propped herself up on one arm, able to take her fill of looking at Rupert now that he was soundly asleep. In repose, his face was poignantly boyish, with the frowning lines smoothed away, the lips pouting slightly, not compressed, and the eyelashes lying in dark semicircles against his high cheekbones. A haughty, lonely young patrician, who had taken so much responsibility onto his shoulders. Tenderly, she pulled the blankets up more closely across his chest, bending to press her lips against his damp forehead, brushing back a heavy lock of hair which straggled across it.

She gathered her scattered clothing, dressed and went out, closing the door softly behind her, anxious not to disturb him. She knew how hard he drove himself, often in the saddle for fourteen hours at a stretch, up before anyone else in the mornings, and last to bed.

In the antechamber, she found Major Will Legge chatting to Holmes. He was thickset, of medium height, with nothing particular to distinguish him, except a pair of kindly, observant eyes. Universally known as "Honest Will," he seemed to be able to get on with everyone, and had taken the Palatine Princes under his wing as soon as they set foot in England. He was especially devoted to Rupert, recognized in him a plain-spoken fighting man, like himself.

Venetia had the distinct feeling that his care for the Prince explained his presence there at that moment. Women were a hazard, they might be rebel spies, or even hired assassins. No doubt, he had taken the trouble to vet her background before encouraging her access to the Palsgrave.

"Well, my lass," he said, heaving his heavy shoulders from the mantel where he had been leaning. "I see by the stars in your eyes that you have been enjoying yourself in there."

Will insisted on escorting her back to the tavern himself. In the stable yard the horses were waiting and, from Orion's back, she looked down into his face as he warned her, with rough compassion:

"It is not wise for a young lady like yourself to fall too deeply in love with His Highness. He is dedicated heart, soul and mind to the happy outcome of the war. He spares neither himself, nor those about him in this resolve."

"I cannot help myself, Major Legge," she replied simply.

Will shook his head, sorrowing for this lovely, spirited creature, so fit a mate for Rupert, but doomed to unhappiness if she tried to shackle him.

"I've been with him from the first—I know something of his devils and his deeds, so take my advice, girl, make no demands on him, he must be as free as air."

He heaved himself onto his horse, giving it a prod with his heels. "Come on there, you old dung-bag!" And, before they left the circle of light flung by the lanterns hanging from brackets, he turned to Venetia with a final word; "I think you will be good for him. . . . I've never met a youngster so full of tension . . . he needs to unwind. Stay with him, if you can, for he is a very great gentleman, but be prepared to bleed!"

She recalled those words many times during the following days. Useless to fume, weep, sit at the window waiting for Holmes, or De Faust or even Will, to come with a message. The Prince was busy.

King Charles detached Hertford from the West by the flattering request for his company at Oxford, then he made his nephew Governor of Bristol as he promised. Rupert, having got his own way, readily appointed the faithful Hopton as his deputy, intimating that this meant virtually the Governorship in practice as he would not be there much. Spirited arguments began as to the next move to block Essex and make a successful advance toward London.

Not even the bonfires and revelry with which Bristol welcomed the King could rouse Venetia from her despondency. She hardly showed any interest on hearing that he had taken up residence in the mansion of the Colston family in Small Street, and that the city fathers were finding entertaining the Court an expensive honor. They were already contributing to a gift of ten thousand pounds wrung out of them by Rupert as a testimony of the "love and affection" which the town felt for the Sovereign!

"He could have written to me," Venetia lay on Damaris' bed in a welter of misery. At first, she had not wanted to wash, sure that as long as a trace of his sweat lingered on her skin, some magic would bind them together. But now even the visible tokens of passion, the purple bruises left by his love-bites, were beginning to fade.

"Did it really happen?" she burst out, thumping the pillow with her fists.

Damaris was sitting in the middle of the counterpane, occupied with an intricate bit of embroidery. In and out flashed her needle, an exotic pineapple springing into being in a blaze of yellow silks. "Yes, my dear, it happened right enough! And don't I know it, having to listen to you babbling on about it ever since. I vow and declare that I know exactly what he said at any point during the proceedings, also what he did, and how he did it, with as much clarity as if I'd lain with him myself."

Seeing that the tears were about to start afresh, she changed the subject. "How is Michael?"

Venetia rolled over on her stomach, turning a woeful face to her. "I haven't seen him or Mallory."

"Your brother is not pleased with me." Damaris bit the thread and selected another color from her basket. "He is being very miserly about Maurice. But that dear child moves out tomorrow, taking a train of artillery to besiege Dorchester. He is ridiculously pleased with himself, now that they have made him a General and given him command of the Western Army. Aren't men vain?"

At dusk, Venetia started up when she saw a shadow at the door, uncannily like the Prince, but her cry of delight was arrested on her lips when he entered. It was Maurice, come to take farewell of Damaris. And Venetia could not corner him, as she wanted to do, and demand if his brother had spoken of her; her awareness of his rank made her shy. Damaris had no such inhibitions, pushing him into a chair, setting food and brandy on the table and perching herself on his knee while he tried to eat, then, catching the urgent appeal in Venetia's eyes, asking after Rupert.

"Ah, well . . . my brother is rather angry at present," Maurice replied, munching cheesecake and apple pie, one arm around the distracting Damaris. "Those fools around the King . . . there have been high words!"

Damaris sat bolt upright and raised her eyes to the ceiling. "La! There always are! The trouble with him is . . . now listen to me, Maurice! . . . You always present cloth ears and a blank expression when anyone faults him! Even you, and this imbecile, besotted wench here, must admit that His High High and Mightiness is not at his best in the Council-Chamber! He goes to every meeting as if it were a skirmish with the enemy, and well you know it!"

Before she carted Maurice off to the bedroom to bid him goodbye in earnest, Damaris said to Venetia: "Send Rupert a letter. Maurice will act as post-boy," and she dropped the key of her writing-case into Venetia's lap.

Damaris was a great scribbler, and never traveled without materials. Venetia spread out a sheet of paper, dipped the quill into the ink-horn, hesitated for a moment, and then started to write:

My beloved Prince,

Since your brother has graciously consented to bring this to your notice, I will tell you of my deep unhappiness when denied the joy of living in your presence. I could bestow one side of this paper in making love to you; and since I may with modesty express it, I will say that if it be love to think of you, sleeping and waking, to discourse of nothing with pleasure but what concerns you, to wish myself every hour with you, and to pray for you with as much devotion as for my own soul, then certainly it may be said I am in love. I implore Your Highness, that you will send me word that you have not forgotten me, for, if this were so, it would be the greatest kindness to draw your sword and deal a deathblow to, Sir,
Your Highness' most faithful, passionate and devoted servant,

Venetia Denby.

Bristol. August 3rd, 1643.

Tears fell across the paper, blotching it; Venetia left them, hoping to touch his heart. She had no seal, so secured the letter with a strand of amethyst silk, twined with tinsel threads, borrowed from Damaris' work-box.

75

Maurice stood, regarding her very solemnly, just before he left, and he gave his word he would place it, personally, in Rupert's hands.

No reply came from the Prince. In desperation Venetia took to hanging about on College Green which had been worn bare of grass as the tertias were drilled. Rupert was strenuously training the recruits with exemplary care, refusing to waste his time attending banquets given by aldermen who hoped to placate the King. Venetia watched him from a distance; he was completely absorbed in his work, rarely losing patience, cheerful and encouraging. Once, he noticed her, his eyes sharpening in recognition, and he was about to come across, when an officer galloped up and engaged him in earnest conversation. He made a gesture of regret to her and rode in the opposite direction.

Rupert was so offended because his propositions for the new siege of Gloucester had been overridden that he refused the command; none the less, he was going to accompany the King. Damaris predicted that it would not be long before he turned up in Oxford.

Venetia agreed to travel back with her, immediately regretting her decision when she stood waving to the army as they marched out through Frome Gate, with the Prince and King Charles at their head, the whole town resounding to the tread of soldiers, the challenge and answer of trumpets, the rolling of drums. Too soon they were gone, leaving only the garrison behind, and an air of anticlimax, a hush, and a waiting.

Dragging unhappily back to the inn to commence packing, Venetia found a messenger there with a letter. It was sealed with an immense blob of blue wax, deeply imprinted with the Palatine arms. In a rush she tore at the seal and it was a second before the words took shape and meaning.

My dear Venetia,
Certes, you have no reason to think that I have forgotten you. My time has been engaged with the levies who know so little of war that they are like to ask for "mercy," instead of "quarter," though now grown so big with pride at their attainments, that they will deem it a dishonor to request either. The King would not heed the soldier and the advice of Rupert to take Gloucester by storm, fearing to re-

peat our losses here, and deciding to sit down before it in a formal siege, which may be a protracted affair which I like not, for it will give my Lord Essex time to come to their aid. I desire that you repair to Oxford, and there remain under the charge of Madame d'Auvergne, where, as soon as this business be settled, you will assuredly be joined by by your loving friend,

                                        Rupert.
Bristol, August 8th, 1643.

Hardly a romantic love letter; the sort of communiqué which he could have penned to a member of his staff, but its military brevity was softened by a funny little sketch of Boye, prancing on his hindlegs. It was an instant reminder of their last evening together when the Prince had put him through his paces, showing the tricks which he had patiently taught his clever pet.

Venetia laughed and cried over it, running to flourish it under Damaris' nose, kissing his name repeatedly, as if it were a holy relic.

SEVEN

The coach lurched over the ruts in the dry road and Venetia, wedged in a corner beside Meriel, was having difficulty in keeping awake. They were on their way to Oxford, a small convoy consisting of the d'Auvergne vehicles and those of the players. They did not anticipate any encounters with the enemy in this vicinity but Damaris had, early on in the war, obtained a pass as a French citizen, permitting her to go quietly about the country, even to London, without hindrance, members of the Parliamentarian forces being commanded to treat her with civility if she happened to cross their territory. As a Royalist adherent this amused her. She could not wait to seduce some repressed Roundhead officer, and then tell him afterwards that he had shared her body with the hated Prince Maurice, and that despised debauchee, General Wilmot, to name but two odious Malignants!

"What shall you do now?" Venetia asked Meriel.

"Pa will find a tavern where we can stay for the winter. The troops will want entertainment when they are in winter quarters. There is a lull in activities then, though the Prince, without doubt, will be leading raids into the neighboring counties to keep all fed and paid."

Venetia pressed her hand against her bodice where his letter lay, warmed by her naked flesh. "There will be ample occasion to see him."

"The Duchess of Richmond will be there also," Damaris reminded.

Venetia could now almost pity Mary Lennox, very superior. She had known Rupert, and Mary had missed her chance! Damaris had it on the best authority (that of Maurice with whom Rupert had discussed the matter) that he had found the experience both shattering and astonishing! Adding that Venetia had all the tricks and abandon of a harlot, without the coarseness, and he was hot to repeat it.

Thinking of this, she sat and glowed. "I no longer fear her. He is mine now, and what can she do anyway, she is married?"

"That never stopped a good woman!" Damaris replied firmly.

She had her feet braced against the opposite seat, and, as they bumped over a particularly deep rut she began to curse the state of the roads, and the inadequacy of the springing of this English coach. As if to add to her annoyance, the driver suddenly braked with a force which nearly hurled them to the floor. Damaris thrust aside the leather window-curtains, ready to give him the trouncing of his career. She found herself staring down the wrong end of a pistol-barrel.

"What the devil . . . ?" she began, flabbergasted by the sight of the mounted man who had ordered the coach to stand. Two or three others, on foot, presented muskets at them from the hedge.

"Madam, a thousand apologies for our unceremonious behavior." Their assailant's voice was full of a lazy humor, and his eyes glittered through the slits in his black vizard. He bent almost to his saddle-bow in ironic courtesy. "My friends and I are but poor fellows, torn from hearth and home by this plaguey war, striving to seek the wherewithal to keep body and soul together."

"Why are you not with the army?" Damaris' eyes were running over him as if he were at stud, for he was showily dressed, his body broad-shouldered and powerful, and he sat his horse well.

"I'faith, we were, still my troop is but thin since Lansdown fight. What were left of them lost heart, and went home to look to the harvest. Wih humble duty I request a contribution, my lady, and be pleased to make haste about it. Your gold, your jewels, anything of value will suffice!" He cocked his pistol.

Damaris was intrigued, and in no mind to lose her possessions to this Reformado officer turned highwayman. "How now, sir, would you rob honest supporters of King Charles? Go, seek a rich Parliament man!"

As she spoke, a couple of his henchmen eased forward and pushed their carbines into her coachman's back. He was shaking with fear, his face turned imploringly to his mistress.

"Hold!" Damaris shouted. "God damn you, sir, d'you think yourself a gentleman? Call off your jackals. We are close friends of His Highness, Prince Rupert."

The highwayman paused. "The Prince Robber?" he said in a slow considering way, and then he laughed and reached up, and removed his mask. "Well, in truth, wolves do not prey one on t'other. I have a fellow feeling for the Plunder-Master-General. His whores, if that be what you are, can go unmolested."

He was laughing again . . . laughter seemed to be as natural to him as breathing—a handsome man with plenty of natural audacity, his thick curling yellow hair making his brown face seem darker. But his hellions did not think it amusing, starting to growl and complain, their small mutiny quickly silenced when he knocked up the pistol of one, and rapped another smartly over the head with the butt of his own weapon. Then, wheeling his bay, he ranged in beside the coach.

Damaris' lips were glistening with such invitation that Venetia guessed she would no longer be pining for either Mallory or Maurice. "Get your disorderly soldiers together, Captain, and come to Oxford with me. You may join my husband's troop, when he returns from

Gloucester. You'll be paid, never fear. We need men of experience."

They clattered through the West Port and along High Street in style, with a fine escort, led by Captain Barney Gilbert, mounted on Damaris' spare horses, which she had loaned with the brisk warning that, should they be tempted to abscond, she would report them as deserters and see that they hanged at Carfax gibbet.

It had been arranged that Venetia would live with Damaris, but a visit to her aunt's house could not be avoided if only because she had money there, the remains of a small legacy left to her by a godmother. There was a painful scene with Aunt Hortense who did not mince words, a tearful scolding from Catherine, still weak from childbed fever, and a galling encounter with Ella, grown yet more precocious in the hectic atmosphere of wartime Oxford. Venetia left, vowing it would be a long time before she visited again.

She turned to the Chevalier's house very depressed, sure that she had made herself an outcast, lost the man who really loved her, and for what? Two nights in the arms of a Prince who must look upon her only as some passing light-o'-love. Damaris was in the hall, or her way to a party, squired by Barney. He had slipped very easily into her life, this burly, boisterous blade, typical of the rapidly growing Cavalier legend; brave, devoted to the cause while it profited him, reckless and raffish. A member of the younger element who strove hard to be the complete antithesis of the Puritans, overdressing, drinking to excess, roaring about the countryside, wenching and leaving behind a trail of bastards, choosing to forget that no one led a more chaste life than the King who they supported so noisily. His estates, much as they were, had been sequestrated by the Parliamentarians. He had no alternative but to live by his wits.

He gave Venetia a lopsided grin and made a bow, sweeping off his beaver. Their companionship made her feel even more lonely; though Damaris was smiling at her.

"*Ma petite,* I'm so glad that you have come home early. You have a visitor. He is in the drawing room."

And she was gone, with a laugh, a wave, and a flick of purple silk, the door closing with a bang behind her and Barney, leaving a strong trail of perfume in their wake.

The black and white tiles of the hall shone like water. Beyond the high, narrow windows at the end, a great solemn sunset was tipping the spires with scarlet. Venetia hesitated at the drawing room door, firmly quelling the wild hope which had flooded up at Damaris' words. Of course it would not be him! There was a little chance of his appearing in Oxford yet. It could not even be Michael; he would be protecting him in the Lifeguard. . . .

For a moment she was blinded by the evening rays pouring across the large, elegant room, then, stepping aside so that the damask drapes shielded her eyes, she saw someone leaning against the fireplace. It was Rupert.

Venetia stood perfectly still, one arm braced against the wall, then she was running across the room while he came half way to meet her, swinging her up in his arms with a great whoop of laughter at her surprise.

She managed to gasp out breathlessly: "Highness, what are you doing here?"

His expression changed, his fierce eyes gazing down at her under their heavy lids. He gave an impatient snort. "Forth is in charge. I'm not welcome at Gloucester. I'll be better occupied reorganizing and increasing my horse."

He was dirty, his high boots caked with dried mud, and it was obvious that he had come directly to her after hacking back to headquarters. Still shaken and hardly daring to believe her good fortune, Venetia questioned him and, finding that he had not eaten for hours, she had a hand on the bell-rope for the servants.

"Have them bring a meal up to your bedchamber," ordered the Prince.

Venetia hauled off Rupert's boots for him herself, without waiting for a manservant; he threw aside his sword, cloak and doublet, and the bed creaked as he flung himself across it with a deep sigh, stretching his great arms until it seemed that he would go through tester and panelling alike. They supped off cold chicken from a tray placed between them on the quilt, washing it down with wine, and she produced a long-stemmed pipe and tobacco, getting a flame going with flint and steel while he puffed. He unwound and poured out the indignation of his soul into her eager ear, and although Venetia was impatient for him to make love to her, this rapport was so sweet that she kept asking him leading questions to prolong it.

81

"Holy God, if I could but have a free hand with the King," he burst out. "But there is always some Courtier or elderly commander who will oppose me. Forth is deaf, past his prime and too fond of the bottle, stepping into the place of Lord Lindsey with whom I fell foul at Edgehill. He swore that it would be the last time he'd go to war with boys! Prophetic words! It was there that he received his death-wound!" A grim smile played about his mouth.

It was getting dark and his pipe had gone out. He laid it aside, turning to take her in his arms, running a finger around the lowcut edge of her bodice.

"I like your dress," he said in dusky undertones which made her want to tear it off. "Let us make the most of tonight for I must be away again in the morning."

Venetia was awake long after his breathing had become deep and steady, watching the patterns of moonlight shift across the shadowed room. This would be her life from now on; his sudden flying visits, a few snatched hours, then the waiting when he had galloped back to the knife-edge of danger. Every time he left, she would have to come to terms with the knowledge that she might never see him alive again.

The siege dragged on as Rupert had predicted. Sweaty messengers on foam-flecked horses thundered into Oxford with news, none of which meant much to Venetia except the horror of hearing that a grenade had been thrown into the Royalist trenches, missing the Prince by inches, while a few days later, his pot-helmet was knocked sideways by a stone hurled from the walls. She deplored his rash insistence on lingering about with the sappers, and spoke her mind on it when next she saw him, ten days later. But he only laughed and teased her and hauled her into bed without preamble, sparing her but an hour of his time.

Rupert was in an angry, sardonic mood; trouble was brewing between himself and Henrietta Maria. She was viciously jealous of the way in which Charles leaned on his nephew, blaming him for the move on Gloucester when she had wanted an attack on London, managing to persuade herself and those closest to her that he had agreed on the siege, not from military motives, but from personal spite directed against herself. At this juncture, three Puritan peers had quitted Parliament, and sought to be reconciled with the King.

"The damned woman received them with contempt!" Rupert flung aside the bed-clothes and stood up. " 'Sblood, couldn't she see that there was nothing to be lost, and, in probability, much to be gained by encouraging them? Now her silly action will discourage similar desertions which might be of service to us!"

Venetia listened to him raging as he dressed, moving about the room with restless, animal grace, muscles rippling beneath his smooth skin. How that proud little Frenchwoman must hate this dominating man who had exercised so much influence over her husband during the months that she had been abroad.

"They came wandering down to Gloucester and I took them to kiss the King's hand." Rupert was frowning while he knotted his cravat. "I gather the Queen is somewhat annoyed with me."

The siege proved fruitless and the Royalists had to withdraw. Lord Essex, with a large army, speeding up his usual lingering pace, moved purposefully to relieve the city. Wilmot, with cavalry from Oxford, tried and failed to delay his advance. Finally, there was a battle at Newbury but the King's ammunition failed and he retreated, leaving Essex with the way to London open, and the advantage to the rebels. What could be done to retrieve the Royalist fortunes the Prince did, but nothing could stop the sheer weight of numbers of the Parliamentarian side.

It was a dispirited General of Horse who came seeking his mistress when the army tramped wearily into Oxford. He told Venetia all about it, and she tried hard to understand the military jargon, and to say, "yes," or "no," or "did you" in the right places. One thing was very clear; he had played his part to the full, which was more than could be said for some. Facets of his uncle's character were becoming clear to the Prince; his stubbornness, and the way he vacillated between modes of action, too ready to reflect the opinions of the last councilor to advise him.

When he had talked himself to a standstill, Venetia was able to tell him that she was going to the supper-party which the Queen was giving to welcome them back. Rupert looked uncomfortable, though his hand still continued to pass over her hair, coiling the tawny locks around his fingers.

Stung by the thought that he was ashamed of her, she jerked away from the caressing hand under which she had been almost purring in sensuous enjoyment. She stared up into his strongly-cut intense features, filled with the urge to drag her nails down each side of his face, drawing blood and marring the perfection of his smooth cheeks.

" 'Tis because of her, isn't it? Mary Lennox!" she accused. "You don't want her to know! So, tomorrow night, I must stand by while you ignore me. Oh no, we must not offend the pure Mary by letting her suspect that Prince Rupert sleeps with a leaguer-bitch who threw herself at him!"

"I am but trying to shield you." There was a tightness about his mouth and warning sparks in his eyes. "You have no notion of the cruelty of their tongues. I would not have you hurt, so you had best obey me!"

He dragged her against him roughly, holding her by the hair, excited by the challenge of her anger. "Come, kiss me, *liebling*. I did not come here to argue. God knows, I get enough of that elsewhere!"

Queen Henrietta Maria's drawing room was packed with Courtiers. The ladies were resplendent in silks and taffetas of the pastel shades so popular that year, although black tended to predominate. An almost hysterical gaiety prevailed, a desperate determination to forget that Death waited for their men beyond these cloistered walls. It was the same spirit which had closed their eyes to reality before the war, when, beneath the hunting, the stately masques, the regal grandeur, the slowly speeding poison of rebellion had been spreading, soon to engulf the nation in a torrent of blood.

The room was hot; a thousand points of light from chandeliers sparkled on satins and jewels, sword-hilts and insignias. Their Majesties, seated on chairs upholstered in crimson velvet with their sons on either side, held out their hands to be kissed. When everyone had been presented, formality was relaxed as the buffet supper was served and the musicians at the far end of the room struck up for dancing.

Henrietta Maria, so tiny and volatile, had a passion for company; wherever she happened to be, a miniature Court sprang up, where she surrounded herself with her sycophantic friends, her poets and artists. Every interest was concentrated there, each political or social intrigue gossiped about, places canvassed and schemed for;

behind the suave masks and polite conversations, the gravest mischiefs were concocted. Her winning manner and brittle charm threw a fatal fascination over all who succumbed to it, none more so than King Charles who watched her constantly, like a man in a trance.

Venetia held her head high, but she was nervously aware of so many pairs of eyes coolly appraising, murmurs running around behind spread fans, with feminine giggles and low male chuckles. "How much did they know of her?" she wondered, panicking, or was this just their usual reaction to any new element which might threaten their tightly-knit cliques? Etienne was at her elbow, immensely kind, knowing just how to deal with malicious beau and spiteful lady alike.

Rupert arrived late, bursting in like a blast of fresh air through a hothouse, causing a stir, snapping them out of their lazy indifference into a kind of bored curiosity. Seeing him against the back-cloth of Courtly life, Venetia felt lost, cut off from him. It seemed quite incredible that only a few hours ago they had shared a cozy domesticity. Then, sunk deep in the feather mattress, tinglingly alive from his recent lovemaking, she had watched him as he stood, clad only in his linen drawers, grimacing in the mirror, scraping away at his beard with a cutthroat razor, cursing violently when he nicked his chin.

Now he looked so Royal, dressed in claret velvet and silver lace, wearing the wide blue ribbon of the Order of the Garter across his chest, with its flashing George. The gulf which stretched between them was emphasized when he leaned toward the Duchess of Richmond, who greeted him with the familiarity of an equal.

Venetia felt certain that being broken on the wheel could not have caused her more suffering than seeing Rupert lead the Duchess out in a coranto. For so large a man, he moved lightly, a natural dancer. It was a slow, stately measure, full of formal posturing, requiring skill, elegance and concentration and its very nature prevented any opportunity for flirtation or talk, which afforded Venetia a little comfort. Her face felt stiff with the effort of keeping that fixed smile; she was sure that in a moment it would crack across like porcelain. She wanted to turn a tail and fly, but Etienne was holding her close against his side, understanding and wise:

85

"See, *chérie*, those are the members of the Council of War who vex your Prince."

King Charles was conversing in his slow, hesitant way with Sir Edward Hyde, a bulky, rather pompous-looking individual who had studied law before devoting himself to the King's service. Etienne added that Sir Edward did not much care for the Palatine Princes.

"And those others are Jack Ashburnham and Harry Percy. They are both in Rupert's black books, being in charge of money and ammunition respectively. Powder, bullets, carts and horses provide endless sources of dissention."

"My dear Chevalier, will you not present me to your charming companion?" There stood George Digby, a seraph in shining black satin, with white boots of the softest kid.

Introductions were made, with flourishes and curtsies and small-talk. Venetia noticed that Digby's mouth was not in harmony with the rest of his bland countenance. It quirked up at the corner in the smirk of a spoilt child who intends to do something naughty out of sheer obstinacy. No, on the whole, she did not much like the pretty Lord George Digby.

"I trust, sir, that you are quite recovered from your injuries?" Damaris was fluttering her eyelashes at him over the edge of her fan.

"Dear lady, 'twas but a slight hurt," Digby drawled. "During a brush with the enemy up on the Berkshire Downs, some poxy rebel discharged his carbine in my face. Thanks to my helmet, I was only stunned, a little scorched, and blinded by the powder."

"I hear, my Lord, that you have His Highness, not your helm, to thank for your rescue." The voice was familiar; Venetia glanced around and saw General Wilmot looking at her with his sensual smile.

Digby flicked an imaginary crumb from his immaculate lace collar. "I pray you, dear boy, do not bring the matter up should he join us, or we shall be launched into a tedious reconstruction of the whose campaign. So boring, and 'tis the only subject on which His Highness will discourse at any length."

"At least Prince Maurice is not here to act as his echo, and remind him of fascinating details which he has omitted."

"Thank God for small mercies!" Digby lifted hands

86

and eyes to the painted ceiling, then they both indulged in wicked impersonations of the rather stiff Maurice with his thick German accent, and Rupert's curt speech and brisk soldierly movements.

Attracted by the laughter, Ashburnham and Percy came across to see what it was about, leaning on each others' shoulders, breathing brandy and smelling very high of orange-flower water. Digby loved an audience and responded with his cat-like grin and further panto-miming with his delicate hands, but his eyes kept sliding across to where Rupert was still dancing, adroitly chang-ing the subject when the Prince took Mary back to her husband.

The Queen's shrill laugh and fluting treble swooped and soared above the hum of conversation, her bright eyes resting on her husband's face, and then going to Rupert, when they hardened. Her Courtiers were urging her to tell them again of her ride from Bridlington to York. She had enjoyed every moment of it, heading an army of two thousand Cavaliers, and needed no second bidding.

"I was their She-Majesty and Generalissima! Their rallying cry was, 'For God and Queen Mary!' Ah, such a valiant retinue of soldiers." Her voice rose im-periously to include the young man who was persistently ignoring her. "Rupert! Have I told you how it happened?"

The Prince gazed broodingly at her as he leaned back against the wall, his arms folded across his chest. "You have, Madame, several times!"

The Queen smiled teasingly, but her tone was shrew-ish. "You men try to convince us females of what a terrible time you go through! Why, it was just like a hunting party, but more exciting. Would I had donned the great helmet of my father, Henri de Navarre, and led my troops into battle against this pack of baseborn rebels! I'd not be bringing them to kiss the hands of the Sovereign whom they have betrayed!"

Having loosed this shaft, she glared up at the exas-perating individual who was no longer the gangling, at-tractive teenager whom she had petted in his first visit to England years ago, when Van Dyck had painted his portrait and Oxford bestowed upon him her first honorary degree of Master of Arts. He had been so appreciative, inbibing the tastes of his connoisseur uncle, developing his talent for drawing, and shyly adoring his aunt.

He was looking at her with a strange, aloof expression as if he could not for the life of him see why his uncle placed such great store by her. It was very offensive, and she whirled around irritably, catching sight of Boye making overtones to her lapdog.

"Rupert!" she shrieked in alarm. "Get your great brute away from my spaniel! She's much too small for him. He'll give her huge, hideous puppies which will kill her!"

"A dog? So that is what it is. I thought it was a muff on legs!" remarked the Prince sourly as he prized free the unrepentant Boye, clouting him, and handing him over to Holmes.

"I am surprised that Madame's refined pet aroused him," said Digby *sotto voce,* staring at Venetia in a way which made her want to toss her wine in his face. "He is a foreign cur with a predilection for low company. No doubt, like his master, he would prefer to mount a mongrel bitch?"

Wilmot guffawed; even Ashburnham and Percy permitted themselves a snigger. But Digby's aside had not been quiet enough, and Rupert's hearing was keen.

"You spoke, my Lord?" His eyes flashed balefully as he rounded on him, hand flying to his sword-hilt.

"Your Highness?" Digby turned languidly, an eyebrow raised; all knew it was illegal to draw in the King's presence. "I did but jest with my friend, General Wilmot."

"If it be a good jest, all should share it!" Rupert said, on a note of snarling menace. He had not moved, but the air gathered tension about him, and people began to look around for he had not bothered to lower his voice.

"We English have a peculiar sense of humor, sir," Digby dabbed at his lips with his lace kerchief. "It is not readily understood by foreigners."

Rupert's face was livid, a vein standing out on his forehead, but King Charles was glancing across at them in reproval—they must not brawl in the Queen's drawing room.

"Your Highness, I was but congratulating Lord Digby on your remarkable rescue of him at Aldbourne Chase," Wilmot breathed admiringly, the respect of his words belied by the impertinence in his eyes.

"I did not ask for your opinion, sir!" Anyone but Wilmot would have buckled under the lash of the Prince's scorn. "Save your breath, and use it to give me a satisfactory explanation as to how you let Essex give you the slip and get through to Gloucester. Were you too busy 'jesting' then, mayhap, to attend to your duties?"

That started a rip-roaring argument which rattled back and forth, impossible to carry out with any decorum for, when heated, Wilmot could shout almost as loudly as Rupert. Ashburnham and Percy joined in, trying to hush this unseemly commotion, but they succeeded only in bringing down the wrath of the Prince on themselves. He jabbed a finger at Percy.

"And what happened to my supplies for which we waited in vain?"

Percy bowed so low that his fair curls almost brushed the floor at the Palsgrave's feet, but though he grovelled, his voice had a sarcastic edge. "Your Royal Highness, pray forgive my presumption, but may I remind you that you did not return the carts which had borne the previous load."

"You should know by now, Percy, that His Highness has a weakness for taking wagons unto himself, particularly if they be heavy with plunder." Digby was being deliberately provoking, goading Rupert into losing his temper, so that the scandal-mongers might tattle of this further display of ill-manners on the part of the Prince.

Venetia watched their faces, Digby's so round and feminine, and Rupert's as darkly handsome as the Devil, each determined to have his way. England was not big enough to hold them both.

Rupert swore between his teeth, "My Lord, you lie like Satan, and do it as if you were quoting the Bible!"

Unruffled, Digby threw him a taunting smile. "Your Highness is, perchance, more fortunate than I in knowing this, being on intimate terms with that personage." Never before had he shown his dislike of the Prince so blatantly, but tonight there was an effervescence about him, an air of conspiratorial self-satisfaction, and he added: "Possibly, such an ability may be of assistance in my new post."

"And what, in Gods name, can that be?" inquired Rupert nastily. "The Queen's lickspittle?"

Digby was buoyant, relishing every word as he answered: "I have given my services readily on the field, suffering wounds, bleeding for my King, but now I am content to exchange my regiment of horses for the political scene."

"Sweet Jesus, I cannot imagine how the army will survive such a blow!" sneered Rupert.

"Alas, such sacrifices have to be made for the good of the country," Digby said piously. Before the Prince had time to give vent to his feelings, he continued: "The tragic death of Lord Falkland at Newbury leaves the office of Secretary of State vacant, and His Majesty has graciously asked me to fill it."

There was a long, tense, funereal silence; then a rush of effusive compliments from the Courtiers.

Rupert's voice slashed across the flowery speeches. "Well, my Lord Digby, I fear that the Roundhead marksman who killed Falkland, dealt a more fatal blow to our cause than we have yet realized."

Then he turned on his heel and swung out of the room. Digby stared after him with narrowed eyes before excusing himself and going to lean over the back of the Queen's chair, all flattering attentiveness, while she smiled up at him in welcome.

Venetia wandered down lengthy corridors lit by smoking torches and patrolled by uniformed men-at-arms. Pages and attendants played cards in ante-rooms, forever on call; lackeys skittered up from the depths of the building bearing salvers and decanters. She was searching for the closet. Though the apartments were so fine this office was, as usual, tucked away in a remote corner. The floor was wet, and she held her skirts high fastidiously, the latrines which Rupert insisted that his sappers dug whenever the army pitched camp were far better.

On the way back, she paused in an alcove which gave onto a small balcony. She was looking out across the dark, tree-rustling garden, when someone spoke behind her and arms went around her waist.

"Beautiful Savage, you starve me of hope, and for all others extinguish desire!"

It was Harry Wilmot, drunk and waxing lyrical. His hands were cupping her breasts and his moist mouth was kissing her neck and bare shoulders. Venetia struggled, but he found her lips, his breath retchy with wine and tobacco. She wrenched her face away, twisting in his arms, putting up her two hands and giving him a hard shove. He was unsteady on his feet and tottered back with a grunt of laughter.

"Why so reluctant? Damn and sink me to hell, 'tis common knowledge that you are Rupert's whore!"

Haltingly, she tried to tell him of her love for the Prince, not wishing to hurt his feelings by rejection, hoping that he would understand and leave her alone.

"Love? You love him?" Wilmot screwed up his eyes, trying hard to focus. "Bah! There is no such thing between man and woman. One can love one's fellow-soldiers, one's King, one's country—even one's horse! But woman—never!" He made another grab at her. "Come, confess that you are no better than the *hurweibles* who blooded us when we were boys in the good old Netherlands armies. The *Pfalzgraf* too! Damme, his sword was not all that he fleshed in the campaign at Breda!"

"Wilmot, you drunken sot!" The gigantic shadow of the Prince blotted out the light as Venetia's tormentor was picked up bodily and hurled into the passage. He dragged slowly to his feet, all the breath knocked out of him, while Rupert roared as if he were dressing down a corporal. "When I have finished crushing this rebellion, I shall give myself the pleasure of killing you, after I have dealt with Digby! You may choose your own weapons—rapier, pistol or what you will!"

Venetia clung to that big, protective shape and his arm came about her. "Get your wrap," he commanded.

She hung back, although he had hold of her hand and had started off toward the door. "I thought you did not want them to see us together?"

He paused and, sensitive to every nuance, she could tell that now he had erupted into violent action he was feeling better; he had been wanting to punch someone all evening. "I have told you, I care naught for their good opinion of me. You have seen for yourself how they are. Overnight they can destroy a woman's reputation with their tongues but, if this does not trouble you, then we will stand together."

"Are you quite sure?" Venetia was thinking of Mary Lennox, and how he had gazed into those laughing eyes.

"God damn them to hell!" said the Prince savagely.

EIGHT

When Rupert and Maurice had first entered Oxford in the autumn of the previous year, they had taken over the house of the Town Clerk as their headquarters. Now, it was once again the season of dead leaves drifting across the gardens and mellowed colleges, muffling the noise of wheels and horses' feet, while the smoke rose from bonfires, a sad nostalgic fragrance which touched Venetia's heart.

She could not understand this melancholy; she had everything she could possibly desire. Rupert had relented and allowed her to move in with him, with a smile, a shrug and a warning that it was on her own head. He had a large staff of loyal retainers, known as his "family," many of whom had been with him since early days in Bohemia. Venetia was sharply aware of their suspicion; his chaplains made no secret of their disapproval; De Faust was very starchy and correct, trying hard to ignore the feminine garments which now bestrewed the Palsgrave's bedchamber. Rupert advised her to give them time, which was all very well for him as he was away a good deal.

Meanwhile, she hobnobbed with young Holmes, and struck up a curious friendship with that despot of the kitchen, the master-cook, Pierre Belfort, whom she had met when meandering down into his domain to find a bone for Boye, or collect a tray of food for Rupert when he blew in unexpectedly at some ungodly hour when all the servants were in bed. Pierre never seemed to sleep, snatching catnaps, nodding in his chair in the chimmey-corner, hands clasped over his prodigious stomach.

Another ally was a voluble, energetic Welshman, Arthur Trevor, the Prince's new Secretary.

"What happened to the old one?" Venetia wanted to know.

Rupert was leaning over the table, frowning down at a map which he was trying to study. "Blake? Oh, I got rid of him after Edgehill. We took the enemies' wagons and among their correspondence, I found reports of my own proceedings, sent to Essex by Blake, and a letter from him demanding an increase in pay. He was already getting fifty pounds a week for selling information!" The parchment would not lie flat under his hands; with an oath, he stuck his dagger in one end and unrolled it. "He was brought to Oxford, tried, sentenced as a traitor, and hanged."

Trevor and Venetia exchanged a glance; the post was certainly no sinecure. There had been no regular secretary since Blake, though Will Legge had helped when he could, and now Trevor faced the enormous task of answering the mountain of letters. Rupert suggested that Venetia might like to assist him, and, all afire with his trust in her, she set to work with zeal, and was often present at important meetings, learning quickly how many difficult issues surrounded each project, and how little ease and pleasure it was to be a King's General.

Rupert did what he could to maintain order, to answer the innumerable demands, sort out the confusion concerning the allotment of quarters between different regiments, the clashes over lodgings and forage which regularly occurred. Everyone lacked arms and ammunition, and their wants were poured out to the Prince, whose own supplies were wretchedly insufficient.

Trevor shook his head in despair, sheafing together a batch of replies which required Rupert's signature. "Was there ever such a difficult army as this? Made up of gentlemen who, while scorning to take orders from one another, show themselves equally averse to obeying a foreign Prince, while displaying a remarkable willingness to do anything rather than that which they are required to do! It is far too small, undisciplined, continually on the verge of mutiny for want of pay, scant of all save bellies and grievances!"

Rupert was never idle; with his cavalry he harried the Roundhead garrisons and towns within easy striking distance, making a series of swoops around the countryside. This guerilla warefare suited his horsemen, providing adventures which gave a lift to ordinary army routine.

"*Mon Dieu!* I thought we should be settling down here, warm and snug for the winter!" Etienne came stamping into his wife's parlor, slapping his arms against his sides to get the circulation back into his hands, wearing his high leather boots and long cavalry cloak, his brown hair wet and the feathers in his hat dripping with rain. "But not he! The worse the weather, the more he seems determined that we shall be out in it!"

"Never mind, dearest heart," Damaris wrapped a cloth around her hand and seized the handle of the posset-pot standing on a trivet over the ashes of the fire, pouring scalding ale onto the sugar and cinnamon in a tankard and passing it to him. "I've nearly finished another set of hose for you."

The house resounded to the click of needles these days; Damaris had all the female servants knitting woollen stockings. There was a pair ready to despatch to Maurice who had been ill with paratyphoid which was raging through the armies of both sides.

"Lord, I hope they are big enough," she stretched them energetically. "He has huge feet."

The disappointing end to the victorious summer had brought a harvest of recriminations amongst the Cavaliers. Venetia watched the pressures from all sides taking their toll of his temper. He had been speaking the truth when he had told her, early on, that he had no time for love; sleep was at a premium, sex a luxury. A few hours leave were enough to put him in a towering rage. These were brief interludes in his exacting duties, giving him no opportunity to consolidate his position with the King.

"Why does Lord Digby hate Rupert so?" Venetia asked Etienne, as he thawed out by the fire.

"Trouble started as soon as they met. He had a high command in the army and the Prince was placed over him. Rupert understands war and he does not. His schemes are wild and fantastic, whereas Ruperts are practical and based on experience in the field."

"His is an unquiet, mischief-making spirit," Damaris added; "He is very busy feeding the Queen's overactive imagination, and she needs but little encouragement."

Venetia fretted when Rupert was away, wanting to ride with him, but he would not hear of it, saying, with maddening superiority, that she must stay at home and be about women's work; she could embroider a baldrick for him, if she liked, or knit him a crimson silk scarf to wear across his breastplate. She suspected that she was the victim of his dry humor for his tone was teasing and he knew only too well how such talk would provoke a high-spirited girl, having had experience with his willful sisters.

Fuming, she made him his scarf, giving it to him for his twenty-fourth birthday on December 7th, and he went off on a foray flaunting it. Venetia, nose pressed to the window, watching him ride out of the yard with his Lifeguard through a light flurry of snow, prayed that it would never be used as a sling to help carry him, if he was wounded.

"Now stop moping. If you went with him it would add to his hazards," Damaris said soothingly. "You are lucky, he thinks a great deal of you."

"Not enough to marry me." Venetia was in a discontented mood, forgetting that, not long ago, she had sworn that just to breathe the same air as he, would have been sufficient. "I haven't even his portrait to look at. I've begged him to have a miniature painted but he just snapped my head off and said that he hadn't the time to sit."

"And you know that this is true." Damaris strolled across to the fire, spreading her hands to the flames. She had a fur-lined cloak flung over her shoulders, for this winter it was so cold that it was necessary to wear one all the time indoors, not only when passing through the drafty passages. "As for him marrying you—I thought you had accepted that fact that this is impossible. He could not, even if he wanted to. I don't think he will ever wed, sweetheart. I suppose you have heard that he finally refused that heiress who has waited so long?"

Venetia drew the curtain back into place with a sigh. Yes, he had told her, and she had been vastly relieved.

"Did you also know that King Charles, loath to let such a prize escape, wrote to Maurice offering her to him? Maurice showed me the letter. He suggested that Maurice should 'take his brother handsomely off.' Needless to say, he turned her down as well. Even eighty thousand pounds a year could not induce either of our Palantines to sacrifice their liberty!"

Oxford was preparing for Christmas, and gay—very determinedly so. There were balls, masques, parties and entertainments, with Thomas Carter's players in great demand. Young men galloped over the ice-hardened roads on snatched leaves, citizens braved the frost to go to Christchurch and see the King and Queen dine in public, and, in spite of shortages and sickness, the old traditional merry-making was in full swing.

In the small hours of Christmas Eve, Rupert had come dropping into bed without bothering to take off his clothes, a habit of his which had started the rumor among the Roundheads that he had sworn a solemn vow not to undress until he had brought King Charles to Whitehall. Actually, it was a matter of expediency, but it did not make him the most fragrant of sleeping companions; it was rather like going to bed with a horse, as Venetia had complained to Damaris. Either that, or he would strip and, chilled to the marrow from the night ride, coil about her, rubbing icy feet down her legs, pushing her nightgown up around her shoulders, intent only on extracting every vestige of comfort from the warmth of her naked flesh, using her just like a fire-brick!

Venetia surfaced as it was getting light. Rupert was already wide awake, lying on his back with his hands clasped beneath his head. Outside their snug curtained cocoon, a servant was raking at the ashes, humping logs, busy with the tinder-box, so that when they decided to rise, the room would be warm. Venetia turned drowsily and snuggled against his side, feeling velvet under her cheek, reaching up to run a hand over his face, tracing the firm jawline, the high-bred Norman nose, the deep eye sockets.

"Damaris is giving a party tonight," she reminded gently. "You did say that we could go."

He encircled her with one arm. "Sorry, *liebchen*, I'm taking my brigade out to relieve Grafton House."

"But it is Christmas Eve!"

"That won't stop the war!" he grunted. "You know that the Puritans treat it as an ordinary day . . . that is how it must be for me also."

All those festivities which she had been looking forward to sharing with him; now she would as soon spend the time shut up in their room, awaiting his return. "When will you be back?"

She could feel him growing impatient, the way men do at things which worry women. "How can I say? I hope that it won't be long."

Sadly, she conjectured that this earnest hope was engendered not by a desire to speed to her side, but merely to press on to the next stage of operations. Why could he not catch some disease, like Maurice? Nothing serious, just bad enough to lay him up for a few weeks, so that she might have him all to herself. But he was so superbly healthy; one of those insufferable people who never ail and have little sympathy for those who do.

She sighed and delved under her pillow. "I have a present for you."

It was fashionable for the Cavaliers to wear bracelets plaited from strands of their mistress's hair, and she had ordered Nancy to take the scissors to her own locks. Now she fastened the result on Rupert's left wrist, unbuttoning his cuff, feeling the broad bones, the urgent pulse, under her fingers. She leaned over to kiss him.

"Wear it for me, my Prince, and God keep you safe."

He pulled back one of the bed-curtains to examine her gift more closely, turning his wrist this way and that, the gold clasps glinting against the dark hair on his arm. He shook his head wonderingly, puzzled, strangely pleased, and his eyes, impenetrable in ordinary light, showed reddish depths, like a stag's, in the weak sunshine which slanted across the pillow.

"You loving little fool," he said softly. "Are you aware that your infatuation is the joke of the regiment?"

Venetia stiffened. Damn him! Why was it that he could never accept anything graciously? He still doubted her sincerity, even now. "I am glad," she tried to sound coolly sarcastic, "to be able to provide amusement for your soldiers."

Rupert roared with laughter, pulling her down on to him with both hands, tormenting and tickling and contrite, while she swore at him, vowed that she hated him, and beat at the muscles which scarcely felt her blows, then he was suddenly serious and passionate.

"Love me quickly," he said harshly. "The trumpets will be blaring to horse at any moment."

When he had gone, and the room had fallen back into that dead pool of silence and desolate emptiness, Venetia stood by the rumpled bed, stretching out her hand to smooth away the impression where his body had rested, so that no evil spirit should lie in it and gain ascendancy over him. On her pillow against a cushion of white satin, lay a locket, circled by seed pearls and rubies, with a slither of gold chain. Rupert's dark eyes gazed humorously up at her from the exquisitely painted miniature.

Lonely? Well, not exactly. How could she be lonely in that hive of activity, the quarters of His Highness, where there were always people coming and going. Hollow, was perhaps a more suitable description of how she felt—barren within and without, when Rupert was absent. Oh, she kept up a brave face, bright and cheerful, but down in the warm dark womb of the kitchen where she was wont to seek comfort, Pierre Belfort cast a wise eye at her and said:

"You've had no letter, madame?"

Venetia shrugged and shook her head, building castles on the table with his pots of spices; exotic odors excited the nostrils.

Pierre was stirring a sauce which he had invented to serve with pork for supper, adding sage, a stream of melted butter and verjuice, gravy and the brains of the deceased pig. He ruminated, as the big wooden spoon scraped against the sides of the skillet. "The *Pfalzgraf* is an indifferent correspondent, madame. Queen Henrietta herself has chided him about this."

Venetia shifted impatiently, reflecting Rupert's irritation with his aunt. "I know, and she chose to do so at Bristol, of all places, right in the middle of the siege, adding a postscript to one of Percy's letters containing her hope that his success at arms would not make him forget his civility to ladies! Treating him like a naughty schoolboy!"

Pierre dived a hand into a wide-necked stone crock, coming up with a fistful of currants which he scattered into his sauce. "He is unlike his mamma. She is a great one for dashing off letters to everyone all over Europe."

"Except to Rupert," Venetia could not forgive the Winter Queen this omission.

"I think, madame, that the Roundheads may have intercepted the mail from her. She would have written—I am sure of it—although they had a furious quarrel just before he left for England." Pierre lowered his bulk carefully on to a stool, ordering a minion to keep the sauce stirred and not to let it burn, on pain of being skewered on the jack and roasted over a slow fire! A bottle was produced from its hiding-place, a rare old brandy which Pierre shared only with his favorites; two glasses were filled and one pushed across the table to her.

"You see, madame, she envies her swashbuckling warrior sons. A very marvellous lady, tall and robust—she would be riding at the head of troops herself, all sun-tanned and rosy—inspiring them! This she would enjoy but, as she cannot do it, she is jealous of their freedom, finding fault, bringing out the worst in our Prince, turning him always into a defiant, bad-tempered young oaf! There is an eternal springtime gaiety about her—not that youth-seeking madness of Queen Henrietta—one forgets that she should be a staid matron of nearly fifty, and is only aware of her vitality."

This dazzling mother of Prince Rupert, her radiance blinding her sons to the qualities of any ordinary woman, what an impossible rival she made!

Pierre had served the Palatines for years and Venetia spent hours in his company, listening to anecdotes of this remarkable family. There was the tale of Frederick Henry, who would have been the heir, but, victim of their attempts at economy, he had been drowned when an over-crowded boat on which he and his father were travelling collided with another in freezing fog.

"So sad, madame," Pierre would say, with a deep sigh, "only fifteen, the pride and joy of his father. They found his body next day, tangled in the floating wreckage, his cheek frozen to the mast. The Elector took it badly, dying himself not long after, still hearing his son calling to him over the black, icy waters, 'Help! Father! Father!' "

Pierre could be very dramatic and this story never failed to raise the down all along Venetia's limbs. It was more comfortable to hear about Elizabeth, the studious eldest daughter, or the madcap Louise. "So like our Prince in appearance and temperament, madame!"

And while Elizabeth and Louise, clever and witty, wrote pages to Rene Descartes, the French philosopher, and filled innumerable canvases under the able tuition of the resident family portrait painter, Gerald van Honthorst, the gentle Henrietta made sweets in the Royal kitchen.

Two sons were still at university, dark handsome Edward, and fair shy Philip, and the Queen had had her share of heartbreak; two babies had died in infancy, and her last-born, Gustavus, had not lived longer than nine years, silver-fair, angelic and fragile, he had been an epi-leptic.

"One of the sharpest members of the family is Sophia," concluded Pierre, "such a shrewed little lady, doesn't miss a trick!"

Oh, Rupert, Rupert, how many days must she endure

before he came home? Venetia counted them in her head, and then again on her fingers to make doubly sure, and, to pass the time, went off to bathe Boye, rendering that indignant animal into a soft white bundle of fleece, spending ages working at the tangles in his fur.

"We'll clip him again when the weather is warmer," said Holmes, clearing away the mess.

"And don't you dare go out into the stable yard and roll in the mud!" Venetia held Boye firmly by the ears, looking into his black eyes. He licked her nose.

At night they shared Rupert's bed, consoling one another. Boye pined as much as she did, when parted from his god, but it was not always possible to take him.

The excitements of Christmas being over, Oxford became more aware of its discomforts. There was an acute shortage of domestic staff, not enough laundresses, the influx of population had put a great strain on the scanty water supplies and sanitation, drains and conduits became choked and army fever flourished.

There was the usual crop of plots and counterplots boiling between different factors, culminating in a plan supposed to have been devised by the Peace Party in London. They had sent one Ogle to Digby with an understanding that the Roundhead Governor of Aylesbury had been bribed and was prepared to admit the Prince into the town.

He had been home for three whirlwind delirious days, and now prepared to depart again, striding round the bedchamber, gathering up essentials, huge and alien in a massive goatskin coat, embroidered with bizarre designs, lined with shaggy fur and smelling strongly.

"Given to him by one of his Transylvanian godfathers," Pierre informed Venetia, adding, with a touch of pride, *"Dieu,* he looks just like his ancestor, Attila the Hun!"

Rupert had a hat to complete this extraordinary outfit; a scarlet velvet montero, edged with sable, and with flaps, usually buttoned on the crown, which could be pulled down over the ears.

"Warm" he grunted by way of explanation, tugging on his boots while she dithered, getting in his way. "Very sensible headgear. Hats blow away in these gales, helmets are deuced uncomfortable."

Holmes and Boye were allowed to go along, but not Venetia; no amount of pleading would alter Rupert's decision. Some hours after they had left for Thame on the first stage of the trip to Aylesbury, a galloper arrived with the news that it was a trap, and Essex was boasting that he would have Rupert, dead or alive.

Trevor sent for Barney and gave him his instructions, while Venetia fled upstairs and changed, catching him in the hall on his way out.

"I want to come!"

"Don't be silly, sweetheart," Barney tried the fatherly approach, wrapping his cloak around him, ramming his hat down, knowing he was in for a cold, tough ride through the darkness to catch up with the Prince.

She gave him her most melting, madonna-like looks which never failed to move every man—except Prince Rupert.

"Oh, very well, but you'll get me shot!" Barney capitulated with as much grace as he could muster.

In the stable a lantern glimmered, their own and the horses' breath hanging like fog on the cold air. Orion nuzzled against her gently, nosing in her pocket for an apple, then crunching noisily while she swung onto his back. Barney primed his pistols and produced a leathern bottle from his saddle-bag, taking a swig and passing it up to her. It burned her throat, and made her choke, but sent warmth tingling to the tips of her toes. She felt ready for anything.

The moon had come up, and the hoarfrost glistened. The hunting and hard riding of Venetia's childhood stood her in good stead. Barney was a rock, always optimistic, shouting encouragement, ready with his flask, pleased and surprised at her determination to keep up with him. On and on, through the weird gloom of corpses, between hedges, over wide moors where the wind sawed at the tortured lungs like knives, then, at last, a pale coppery sheen creeping across the east, and watch-fires and the pickets of Thame.

Rupert had already gone. They were told that he was halting at Lord Carnarvon's manor, planning to reach Aylesbury that night. No respite yet for cramped muscles and frozen extremities, and they clattered across the cobbles of Carnarvon's courtyard as the grey daylight grew stronger.

Barney went to find an officer and Venetia watched the scene from her saddle, the steaming horses, the activity of the soldiery taking on a dream quality. Even the cobwebs were spangled, rimmed with a million frozen droplets, the most commonplace objects transformed into crystal by the frosty touch of Faerie. Then Barney was at her stirrup, grinning waggishly, calling her "comrade," making the other men laugh. She slid awkwardly into his arms, he tucked a hand firmly under her elbow and guided her into the house.

The Prince was in bed but he shot up, instantly awake, while Boye's yelping protests changed to delight as he rushed across to leap at her, nearly knocking her over.

"Venetia! What in hell's name are you doing here?" Rupert roared, his black brows almost meeting in fury.

In jerking, disjointed words, she tried to tell him of the peril. Barney broke in, giving relevant details, and Rupert's expression was none too pleasant.

"That traitor Ogle! I knew that he was not to be trusted, but my Lord Digby was so confident. The fool! Ogle shall hang when we get back to Oxford. We'll continue to Aylesbury, and he'll march in the van to share whatever hot welcome they plan for us!"

Now he was safe, she could allow the backwash of terror to swamp her; for hours she had been dead to all save the horror of Lord Essex's net closing over her Prince. Life was coming back, agonizingly, into fingers and toes, so that she sobbed with pain. Holmes had appeared, astounded at the sight of her, kneeling to pull off her boots, then Rupert had her under the covers beside him, thrusting her numbed hands beneath his doublet, warming them against his body. He asked Barney one or two more questions, commended him for his action, promised reward and dispatched him with an adjutant to find some breakfast.

He was angry and troubled because she had been exposed to risk, proud of her too, although she smarted under his tirade. She began to feel rather pleased with herself, now that it was all over.

Succulent chops were rushed up from the kitchen, clapped between two silver platters set over a chafing-dish to keep hot, and served with thickly buttered rye bread, and plenty of sack. Sitting up in bed, pillows stuffed at their backs, they ate, throwing tidbits to Boye, and Venetia said:

"I'm never going to be separated from you again."

"You might have been killed—supposing your horse had slipped on a patch of ice, or you'd run into a Roundhead ambush?" Because he was worried, he sounded cross, and Venetia rested her hand gently against the side of his face. He seized her wrist, turned his head slightly and kissed tht palm, and she put her arm around him and held on tightly, tipping up her face so that he could kiss her mouth instead.

"Can you understand now, how I feel every time you ride away?" she asked softly. "I die a thousand deaths for you."

Rupert was unfastening all the small buttons down the front of her jacket and the shirt underneath. "You make a handsome lad. But do you not know that the army has issued a proclamation forbidding our soldiers to hide women in their quarters disguised in men's apparel?"

Venetia was luxuriating at his touch, her fingers in the dark curls which swung forward as he leaned over her. "You are his General, surely you are a law unto yourself?"

His mock severity became serious. "On the contrary, I should set a good example."

There in the privacy of his hair, just below his ear, she breathed in the heart-breaking fragrance which was always Rupert to her; his unique skin, the outdoor freshness, with a hint of tobacco, wine and pomade.

"Rupert——" even now, the name seemed a shocking familiarity, "they say dreadful things about you, that you drink the blood of innocent babes, and eat their flesh."

"I know it," he answered, and she could tell that the absurd, vicious attacks rankled. Then he laughed: "Shall I devour you too?" His mouth came down to nibble across her throat. Later, he said: *"Sacrément!* I must get some rest if I'm to make any showing at Aylesbury tonight."

Venetia woke up enough to demand: "You'll let me come with you?"

"If I say 'no,' I suppose that you will only disobey me," he was smiling, though his eyes were shut. "Really darling, you are the most mutinous of my soldiers. But, seriously, you must do as I say on the instant, if you ride with us."

She promised and then surrendered to the urgency of slumber. Outside were the sounds of a military encampment, but in the room there was peace, broken only by the tick of the Prince's pocket-watch on the table, the crackle of logs, sending up an occasional shower of sparks, and the noises made by Boye, scratching on the rug.

As soon as it was dark, the Prince assembled his officers, giving instructions and ordering Ogle to be brought to him. The wretched turncoat stood, shuffling his feet, between grim-faced guards, while Rupert, eyes hard as granite, loomed over him and told him exactly what he thought of him.

"I shall see that you accompany us to Aylesbury!" the Palsgrave's voice was as cold as the blizzard outside. "You'll ride right at the head of the column—with me!"

They dressed Venetia in a breastplate and pot-helmet, and there was a new kind of admiration in the eyes of Rupert's Lifeguard, something other than the praise of virile men for a pretty woman.

A blinding snowstorm gave way to sleet as a thaw set in. Moving prudently, the army approached the silent town. Then a couple of videttes sought out Rupert, bringing with them a lone scout who carried the unconvincing message that they were to push on at once to Aylesbury as everything was ready for their reception.

"And we know, don't we, Ogle, just what sort of welcome that would be, made up of steel and shot!" Rupert said grimly.

The scout lost his nerve when confronted by the terrifying apparition of the Prince in his outlandish raiment, more than half sure that all the tales told him were true and that he was an emissary from the Devil.

"Tie him up!" thundered that awesome figure. "Send me Colonel Gerard! We'll assault the opposite side of the town, where we are not expected!"

They rode fast as darkness and treacherous ground would permit, through rain which had increased to a downpour. By the time they reached the far side of Aylesbury, the river was so swelled with melting snow, as to be impassable. Nothing remained but a speedy retreat.

Venetia decided that hell must be very cold and wet, not fiery, as she struggled through the lashing wind, blackness, rushing water and driving rain. Above the uncontrolled roar of the elements came the jingle of harness, the clank of arms, men cursing, and the Prince's voice cutting across the confusion, encouraging his troops, rounding them up, going back for stragglers, thudding up and down the ranks.

At daybreak they reached Thame, with Rupert in a black rage at the waste of time, waste of men, for some had drowned in the river. It was as well for Ogle that his life did not depend on the Prince's mercy that day.

NINE

The newly-created Earl of Holderness and Duke of Cumberland (some punster had already travestied it into "Plunderland" was standing like a colossus at the head of the staircase, bellowing for De Faust. King Charles had made him a "free denizen" and peer of the realm, in order that he might sit in the Royalist Parliament, now summoned to Oxford. He was late, and could not find his insignia—a rich stream of oaths rolled out, mostly concerning his valet's parentage and the morals of his mother in particular. It was the day after the fiasco at Aylesbury. Rupert's mood was still foul, and someone had to bear the brunt. He had already reduced Venetia to tears, upset Holmes, and ranted into the kitchen, bawling at Pierre over some imagined fault with his breakfast which would have gone unnoticed at any other time.

Pierre ducked, and kept his best crockery out of reach, saying happily to Venetia: "Just like when he was a little boy, red with rage and roaring, and his mamma, equally furious and determined to thwart him. You could almost see the sparks fly! He will enjoy an argument with my Lord Digby today."

Much later, Venetia went to find him in the indoor court, working off his temper in a hard game of tennis with Prince Charles. The boy adored his cousin and, whenever he could, Rupert spent time with him, trying to mitigate the influence of his tutors, the domination of his mother, and the fussy, vague attentions of his father. Charles, just fourteen, was a tall, quick-witted lad, with glossy black curls and humorous dark eyes. His features were heavy, and his skin so swarthy that it bore evidence of the Moorish ancestry of his mother.

He thrived in Rupert's company, impressed by his talents his ear for languages, his knowledge of books and art, science and mathematics. His audacious exploits were bound to endear him to a lively youngster, and, beneath that shell of haughtiness, Rupert was very understanding of the sensitivity of children.

"We'll make a player of you yet," the elder Prince mopped over his face with a cloth handed to him by Holmes.

Boye got up, his feathery tail waving, hoping that this might be the signal for a speedy departure out of doors, glad that his master had finished pursuing that silly little ball, one, moreover, which he had been sternly forbidden to chase.

Charles was buttoning his green satin doublet, his bold eyes going to Venetia. "You may present the lady to me, cousin."

With a lift of an eyebrow, and a perfectly serious face, Rupert made the introductions. She found it odd to be dropping a curtsey to this ugly-handsome boy who was looking her over with such precocity; hard to believe that he was the heir to the throne. Women would find him irresistible soon, and men fall under his spell, for he oozed that dazzling charm which the Stuarts possessed in an almost unfair measure.

"You are fortunate, Rupert, to have such a beautiful friend," he remarked, his knowing glance assuring them he was perfectly aware of the nature of their relationship.

A chill, muttering wind swept past them as they left the tennis court. Venetia had her arm through Rupert's, while Charles loped on her other side, giving her sidelong glances of admiration, and Boye rushed ahead, barking.

They took a short cut through the churchyard, with the poodle bounding in and out among the headstones, lifting an irreverent leg against the weathered inscriptions.

"Where will you be journeying now, cousin?" Charles wanted to know; then, without waiting for an answer, adding rebelliously: "Why can't I ride with you? 'Tis wicked folly to be forced to work at one's books when there are father's enemies to beat!"

He was suddenly a child again, moodily scuffing the gravel of the path with his toe, hands thrust deep into his pockets.

Rupert smiled, sympathizing with the boy's indignant feelings. "I am leaving soon to start recruiting in the

Welsh Marches. My headquarters will be Shrewsbury."

"Are you going with him, madame?" Charles was amused by the languishing look in her eyes whenever they rested on his cousin.

They had paused by a stile bridging the dry-stone wall; the fields beyond glittered frostily beneath the misted copper ball of the low sun. The bells of Oxford sounded thin and dismal, their sound muffled by the fog which was drifting over the flooded meadows. Rupert's hands were resting each side of Venetia's waist, ready to lift her, and he was looking down in that compelling way of his, straight and unblinking, which always made her breath shorten, and scattered her wits so that she forgot what she was about to say.

But this question had been hanging between them for days. Now she voiced it: "Will you take me?"

Her worship in turn irked and flattered him; naturally he enjoyed it, but did not want the responsibility, really far too busy to stop and ponder where it was leading. She adored him, offering herself whole-heartedly and without reserve, a balm to his wounded self-esteem when there were so many people against him. Now he laughed and embraced her; there were compensations for the problem she brought, and he said:

"How could I endure the wilds of that barbaric country without you, *liebchen?*"

The horsemen breasted a rise. It was a keen February afternoon and the northerly wind, blowing up the slope, set the feathers in their hats fluttering, and tossed the fringes on their sashes.

Below them lay a manor house, nestling in the valley, mellow stone walls, lichen-shaded slates melting into a background of soft greens. Rupert the artist saw it as an etching, while the General in him listed the dry moat, thick walls set with arrow-slits which could become musket-loops, and the easily-fortified gatehouse, now standing innocently open. He turned to his quartermaster.

"We'll stay here tonight."

They moved down the gentle incline and Venetia was at Rupert's side. This never ceased to amaze her; every time Orion swung into an easy rhythm matching that of his own horse she could still not quite believe that it was true. They were on their way to Shrewsbury, and, when

107

the scouts reported a clear road ahead, with no Round-head pickets, he allowed her to jog up to the van.

In the paved courtyard, enclosed by the house on three sides and with the protective walk and battlements on the fourth, the owner waited apprehensively. He had harbored the earnest hope that he might be able to keep out of the war in such a sheltered backwater, nonplussed at finding himself suddenly confronted by this stern, unusually tall young man with the foreign accent who introduced himself without dismounting.

"I am Rupert. No doubt, sir, you are loyal to the King. I seek quarters for the night, food for my men, and fodder for their horses."

The Prince's tone indicated that he had not even considered the possibility of a refusal and his enforced host recalled every wild story which was told about him. His only aim was to get out of a tricky situation with the least damage to his property.

He pressed his lips to the back of the sinewy brown hand extended towards him. "Your Royal Highness—such a great honor. We had heard that you were in the district—but never dreamed that we should have the pleasure—most unexpected. By all means, use our stables. You want to take over the meadow for your tents? Make it your own. There are officers needing rooms? My wife will be only too happy to air beds for them, won't you my dear?"

In a nervous spate of words, he introduced himself as Miles Farnaby. His wife, in a plain wool gown, a small cap covering her hair, seemed far less flustered than he. In fact, Venetia had the impression that she was rather enjoying this change from routine, it would give her something to talk about for months to come, and certainly Rupert was at his most courteous, bowing gravely over her hand, making his requests with a hint of regret at upsetting her household arrangements.

They dined by candlelight in the hall, where logs roared up the wide chimney, and Farnaby's hounds, stiff-legged bristled at Boye who issued throaty challenge from between Rupert's feet, under the table. There was an awkward moment when Mistress Farnaby first realized that the leather-jacketed, booted and spurred stripling at the Prince's elbow was a woman, and, although playing her part as a good hostess, Venetia kept finding her looking across with scandalized eyes.

Farnaby began to feel easier with his alarming guest, even formulating, in his mind, the phrases in which he would describe to his neighbors how the most famous young Prince of the age had spent a night under his roof. His son, seventeen and impressionable, was listening, open-mouthed, to the soldiers' talk which rattled round the table. "You'll be needing levies, Your Highness?" he burst out, interrupting his father who had embarked on a rambling account of the local hunting facilities.

Rupert saw the anxiety which sprang into Mistress Farnaby's eyes, and his mouth tightened. Fighting he could control and enjoy; military operations were a challenge, but dealing with personnel, their problems, their complaints and unhappiness, irritated him.

"Indeed, we need all the men we can get. Doubtless Major Legge will advise you." Uneasy under the silent reproach of the mother, he turned to Farnaby, suddenly very correct and businesslike. Venetia knew this change of mood; here was a situation which troubled him, therefore he would concentrate on more straightforward matters. "Sir, this is a fine house which could be useful to the enemy were they to capture it."

Pride, puzzlement and apprehension chased across Farnaby's features in rapid succession. "The Roundheads! Is it likely that we may expect a visit from them soon?"

"They will not bother you, 'till they know Rupert is well departed," stated the Prince drily. "In the circumstances I can offer you three alternatives—to man and defend your house yourself—to have it occupied by a garrison of my choosing—or to blow it up!"

Venetia's heart ached for these civilians dragged into a conflict which was none of their seeking. The Farnabys, in common with the majority of the people, wanted nothing but to continue their lives in peace. Now they faced disruption; their son would go to fight and perhaps to die, their house would resound with the tramp of booted feet, and they would be left the poorer. Rupert's vigorous decisions were often hard in individual cases. Love him to idolatry though she did, Venetia could not blind herself to this fact—he had war in his bones!

Her depression refused to be shaken off, hanging like a pall over her when she went to him that night, in Mistress Farnaby's best bedchamber. "What will you do when the war is over?" she asked him.

He looked at her blankly for a moment, as if he never

thought beyond the one objective of placing King Charles back in his palace at Whitehall.

"Years ago my uncle wanted to make me Governor of Madagascar." He was prone across the bed, fingers laced under his head. "I planned to lead an English naval expedition to the Indian Ocean and conquer the island. We spent a deal of time studying ship-building—I was to have twelve warships—we even went into the details of arming and victualling them. My mother was furious when she heard, writing angry letters to poor old Sir Thomas Roe, who was doing his best to bearlead me. 'No sons of hers,' she wrote emphatically, 'should go for knights-errant.' "

"And that is exactly what has happened." Venetia filled his brandy-glass, bringing it over to him.

"It seems like another life. I remember the wrench of leaving, when they recalled me. I think I was more upset than I had been at anything since my father died. On that last morning, we went hunting, and I told the King that I wished I might break my neck, so that I could leave my bones in England."

As he was feeling reminiscent, she asked him if he remembered staring at her on that hot summer afternoon when they had met. She half hoped that he might say that he had fallen in love with her at first sight, though she knew perfectly well that he never would.

"Of course I was looking at you," he answered tersely. "I was making a drawing of you, in my head, 'tis a habit of mine. The play of the light, the curve of your neck, made me want to sketch you;" he paused and grinned, "—in the nude."

She should have known better than to angle for compliments, so set up the chessboard instead. He liked to win and usually succeeded. Now he was studying the pieces closely, scratching his head, tugging at his curls with his free hand. He cornered her queen and she spent some time deliberating her next move, but they had had a gruelling ride and her eyes were heavy. Bemused she stared at the tiny monarch, his pawns, his bishops, and his knights.

"Would you have liked to be ruler of that island, Highness?" she asked. What an Emperor he would make!

Rupert was asleep. Venetia had got used to his habit of suddenly dropping off, a trick he had learned in boyhood campaigns, snatching rest when he could. His doublet was slung over the back of a chair and there was a rip in the sleeve where he had caught it and freed himself with an impatient tug. Venetia found needle and thread and sat closer to the candle to repair it. It was very shabby and when she had mentioned getting a new one, he had given his habitual reply—"No money."

"What are we to do with him, Boye?" she sighed, and he looked up, head cocked at the sound of his name.

Miles Farnaby and his wife watched the brigade march out at dawn. Rupert, on his black steed, bowed from the waist in salute as he passed. Although he could ill spare them, he had left muskets, powder and shot to supplement their meagre arsenal, and instructions on how to make further bullets, in an emergency, by melting down the lead guttering. Farnaby had elected to defend his home himself, promising to assemble a garrison from the village. His son rode confidently in the reserve, head high, clad in an antique cuirass and morion which had adorned the parlor wall for years. His mother's face was like a death-mask as she waved to him.

The Prince occupied the same house which he had used seventeen months before, when Shrewsbury had harbored the King and his forces for a while. It stood opposite the turnstile of St. Mary's Church, large and comfortable and belonging to Mr. Jones who moved in with relatives while Rupert was in residence.

The needs of the north were pressing, but there was much work to be done before Rupert could go to their aid; hostile interests to reconcile, powerful families to be placated, harbors fortified, contributions fairly assessed, commissions distributed, recruits made, trained, clothed, armed and, if possible paid.

He arranged for his own commissariat fought, by letter, with Lord Percy for every cannon-shot, and with Jack Ashburnham for each instalment doled out to his men, and argued with the whole country around him for every soldier's ration unwillingly bestowed.

Arthur Trevor had remained behind as Rupert's agent so now two of the chaplains struggled with the letters which arrived daily, all urgent, all demanding the Prince's personal attention. Venetia helped to sort through this correspondence. Any written on scented notepaper in a suspiciously feminine hand which proved to be yet another female offering her money, her states and mostly, her body to Rupert, she removed. The promise of cash

111

were investigated, the others went in the fire and it gave her a primitive satisfaction to see those words of admiration, sent in by women who had fallen in love with his reputation, consumed in the blaze, leaving her sole possessor of the real man; in so far as anyone could be said to own that self-willed individual.

Rupert was in an exasperating mood, this kind of employment did not suit him, and he drove Trevor to despair by forgetting to answer letters, by signing bills of exchange without letting anyone know and by making wildly extravagant demands, on the principle that if he asked for more than he needed, to be delivered at once, an adequate supply might be expected to arrive somewhere near the actual time that it was really required.

They had been joined at Shrewsbury by a contingent of Irish soldiers, under their commanders, Colonels Broughton and Tillier. Stout fighters, with experience behind them, Rupert much preferred them to the Welsh. They needed all the men they could get if the pressing demands for help from Newark, and Lord Derby's pleas that Rupert should go to the relief of his Countess besieged at Lathom House, were to be met.

Venetia saw even less of him than she had done in Oxford as he darted about the associated counties proving himself a most uncomfortable neighbor. Nowhere could the enemy feel free from the threat of his lightenng raids. Amusing letters were captured, in which captains, holed up in some remote fastness, sent frenzied appeals to their commanders for aid——; "I hear that Rupert is coming!" and then, in a terrified postscript——: "Rupert has *come!*"

And not only rebels were shaken by his unannounced appearance at any time of the day or night. He called on all the different detachments which were to accompany him on his march north, and little bands that had settled down comfortably, up to any number of profit-making wangles, were thrown into outraged consternation when he swooped upon them with his eagle scrutiny which missed nothing and would not countenance laxity. He was particularly dreaded by shifty aldermen, doing very well out of the shortages; their dreams of military neutrality were shattered when the Prince strode across the scene.

Damaris arrived from Oxford, causing a stir in the old market town, bowling through in her coach, finding her way to the house of Mr. Jones. Venetia was overjoyed to see her, running out as she descended in a flurry of stiff silk skirts, her personality as glittering, as elemental, as barbaric as her beauty; sleepy Shrewsbury had never seen her like before.

"And where are the men?" Damaris was carefully working her fingers out of her fringed, perfumed gloves, evaluating the furnishings of the parlor where nothing was later than the reign of Elizabeth.

"They've gone chasing Roundheads at a place called Drayton. The scouts reported its being occupied by important enemy Generals whom they intend to capture or drive out." Venetia ordered refreshments from Powell who had materialized even before she rang for him.

"Ah, a modest little exercise which, I doubt not, your beloved will complete before dinner." Damaris could rarely mention Rupert without irony. "And how is our magnificent *Pfalzgraf?*"

Venetia sighed deeply. "Oh, he is always so busy and preoccupied. I sometimes feel that the only time I meet him is when we are abed."

Damaris laughed, arching her slim throat. "Dearest, don't tell me that this displeases you! 'Tis the one place where I can tolerate men! The vexing creatures! And I suppose Le Diable is being as difficult as ever, riding roughshod over everyone?"

"If he were less domineering, nothing would get done!" Venetia sprang to his defense, her eyes flashing. "You have no idea how hard he works! Each time a Roundhead outpost is conquered an enlistment takes place, more or less freely."

"They are all mad," Damaris yawned, and removed her Cavalier hat, patting her ringlets into place. "Particularly these Welsh, so I hear. Still, I suppose it is better to enlist than to hang!"

"He doesn't hang them!" Venetia's denial held a vehemence which made Damaris lift questioning eyebrows. It was true that, since knowing Rupert intimately, ripples of disquiet ruffled the serenity of her faith in his chivalrous nobility. Sometimes a chill ran down her spine when she looked into his face and read there his obsession with instilling into his soldiers the discipline of that strange, harsh communal life of the mercenary.

"Have you seen this?" Damaris was rummaging in her valise. "Digby is losing no chance to flourish it while pretending to be wild with indignation at its imputations. For-

113

tunately, King Charles has treated it with the contempt it merits."

No, his latest insult to the Prince had not yet come with the post. Venetia read it through once quickly and then, as the full import hit her, sat down to study it more closely. It was titled, "A Looking Glass" wherein His Majesty may see His Nephew's Love, who secretly under pretence of Assisting Him to gain an absolute Prerogative or Arbitrary Power, will disthrone him to set up himself.

It was an unsavory piece of poison pen literature, written by an anonymous "Wellwisher." Phrases stood out among the black lettering, as if written in blood——— "Thus, Prince Rupert is so near the Crown, if law and Parliament be destroyed, he may bid for the Crown, having possessed himself of so much power already———"

"This is monstrous!" Venetia's hands were trembling.

Damaris retrieved the tract, eager to keep it for her collection, afraid that her friend might be tempted to cast it into the fire.

"A man such as he will inspire devotion in his troops, deepest loyalty in his friends, but he will also make enemies," she said soberly. "Rupert has offended a great many important people. It might be better if he had learned to be more suave and patient, like Digby, better attuned to the vagaries of the Courtiers."

"Never!" Venetia was pacing up and down, her skirts rustling, driving her fist into the palm of her hand. "He is too honest! Quite incapable of intrigue, deceit and wanton backbiting. Digby appears to be a master of it! I would like to see him face Rupert, sword in hand, then it would be a different story."

Damaris was cautiously sampling the home-brewed metheglin which had been given to some of the Welsh gentry. It slid over the plate very deceptively smooth, taking several moments for the full devastating effect to be experienced.

"You've heard what Etienne has to say about Digby and Rupert, I suppose?" she asked. "He believes that Digby may have rather fancied the Prince when they first met. There are rumors of his Lordship's exotic inclinations; Etienne swears that his taste runs to boys, and he should know. Even if this is not strictly true, I expect he wanted to be the close companion of such a renowned Prince, and visualized them leading triumphal processions together. Digby must have been disappointed that his charms did not impress Rupert. I think he rather snubbed him, and unwittingly, made a dangerous enemy instead of a doting friend."

She stood up, and then sat down again abruptly; "My God! What did you say this stuff is? Mead? Brewed from honey? What do they feed the bees on in these parts, for Heaven's sake!"

Venetia ignored her, head lifted. With that extra sense which she had developed, she felt, rather than heard, the pounding of hooves.

She turned to the door. "He's here!"

"God has arrived!" announced Damaris.

The cavalry were blown but victorious, and Rupert elated by the brisk and the hard ride home. The room seemed to explode as he came in. And there was Jonathan, waving aloft the captured colors of Sir Thomas Fairfax with its bold lettering, "For Reformation."

Everyone was talking at once, filling bumpers with mead, sending down to the cellar for more, and, between the disconnected sentences, the boasts, the forgiveable exaggerations, it became clear that the Roundheads had fled, leaving the Cavaliers the richer for goods and prisoners; an important part of the booty, representing so much ransom-money in proportion to their rank.

Rupert's eyes were seeking Venetia, over the heads, through the confusion, and his lavish physical presence took her breath away. She waited her cue. Sometimes he took little notice of her in company; his Calvinistic upbringing, which demanded almost Puritanic standards, was constantly at war with his pride and his need for rich, varied experiences of the senses. Now she sat beside him, watching him raptly, while the afternoon faded into evening, the golden light deepening, making little pools of blood beneath their goblets.

His officers were full of drink and brag, and he smiled indulgently, pleased because they had taken Drayton without any loss of life on their part, clapping Richard Crane on the shoulder affectionately, the leader of his beloved Lifeguard of whom he had said:

"I can afford to try things which they are not expecting, and they will go along with it." Indeed, at times, they seemed to have an uncanny knack of moving, even thinking, as one.

"Where next, sir?" Crane was as eager as an old warhorse.

A shadow darkened Rupert's face; the war was dangerously extended and he was in demand everywhere, but there was one person whom he wanted very much to see. Maurice had been dispatched to raise the siege when Chester was in danger in the middle of February. It was so valuable as a reception centre for the Irish forces, that the Prince intended to go himself and inspect it.

More travelling—always in the saddle—and no, this time she could not go with him—it would not be worth it—he would be back almost before she had time to notice that he was gone!

TEN

Barney went down on one knee at the feet of Damaris, seized her hand, planted a smacking kiss on the back of it and proceeded to declaim:

> "Tell me not, sweet, I am unkind
> That from the nunnery
> Of thy chasted breast and quiet mind,
> To war and arms I fly."

She tried to disengage herself. "Lord, sir, rise do! To begin with I could hardly be called 'chaste' and secondly, you are not leaving me—I'm coming with you."

He leaped up with his broad ingratiating smile, making a grab for her. "All this I know, Duchess! But you must admit, Richard Lovelace is no mean poet!"

The cavalry had ridden back yesterday with Rupert from Chester where orders had been received for a force to go at once to the relief of Newark. It had been holding out valiantly since early March. Now they were almost starving, and, while the men were willing to try one last desperate sally, it would have meant leaving the women and children to the mercy of the enemy. Stubbornly they sent back answer to the Puritan summons—they would starve, and they would die, but one thing they would not do—and that was to open their gates to rebels!

The Newarkers sent an appeal to King Charles. There was only one person who would attempt the impossible, and this was easier said than done for as yet Rupert had no army to speak of. Will Legge had been dispatched, hot-foot, back to Shrewsbury, for as many musketeers as could be spared. The Prince followed himself, after a couple of hectic days in Chester, spent inspecting the earth-works, giving orders for a new prison to be built, and sequestrating Parliamentarian estates within a five mile radius to pay for the fortifications.

"And that is not all he did," Barney's pale blue eyes grew unusually serious, and he paused as if he could not decide whether to add more, then said: "News came that Brereton had already put into practice the Parliament law denouncing all the English troops that come from Ireland —good Protestants, most of 'em—condemning them as Irish rebel papists! They are to be denied quarter, and those taken prisoner must hang. Brereton had captured thirteen of the Prince's own men, and strung 'em high at Nantwich!"

"And then?" Venetia said on a whisper into the room which had grown suddenly quiet. But there was no need to ask, that waiting stillness held the answer, and the memory of Rupert's face last evening, so stern and ter-rible, with that black spot of anger on his brow, and the rough way he had taken her as if seeking to smash all thought and feeling in an orgy of sensual indulgence, frighteningly unlike him.

Barney was poking his fingers in and out of the ribbon loops at his waist. "Why then, sweetheart, there was no rest for any of us till the nearest billets of the enemy were stormed and his murdered soldiers avenged in blood."

"And that was the end of it?"

Barney shook his head. "I've never seen him so furi-ous, or so determined. He selected the same number of prisoners as Brereton and hanged 'em from the nearest tree, sending one fellow to Lord Essex with the message that he would hang two Roundheads for every Cavalier who was put to death otherwise than in fair fight."

Barney's arm came about her bowed shoulders. "Be-lieve me, he did not want to do it, but he is much in love with his Irish soldiers and will not tolerate their being slaughtered like animals. And an eye for an eye is sol-dier's law, you know—and no bad law at that!"

The army had changed the character of Shrewsbury,

where once nothing more exciting happened than market-days, when the singsong idiom of the Welsh sheep-farmers mingled with the musical dialect of Shropshire. Venetia found it an enchanting place, roaming through the winding streets where the old, timbered houses beetled over the passers-by, and the skyline was jaggd with topsyturvy roofs, thatching, crazy pepper-pot turrets and twirling chimneys. The Castle, lowering over all from its prominence, was the finishing touch to this fairy tale setting. It should have been peopled by witches and goblins, dragons, knights and fair ladies, not a motley conglomeration of soldiery and their drabs, the washerwomen, kitchen sluts, and doxies, the usual feminine tribe which pervaded every camp.

Now its antique walls reverberated to the thunder of drums, while trumpets shrilled, men-at-arms cursed, captains barked orders, and Prince Rupert's army moved out, taking the road to Newark. Venetia travelled with Damaris, and Boye jumped into the coach after her at the last moment, insisting on settling himself across their laps. Although the morning had been brilliant with sunshine at the start, cloud quickly settled over the blue Welsh hills and it began to drizzle.

"Oh dear, Rupert will get very wet," Venetia sighed. "A state not calculated to improve his humor."

It continued to rain and, as the days passed, even the irrepressible Damaris grew weary, for how could even the most skilled woman look her best in the damp?"

" 'Slife, this is the wettest spring I can ever recall. What a climate! One good thing about France is its weather. Tho', damme, with it all, I'd rather be here. If it had not been for the war, and dear Etienne's interest in it, I should have spent my days incarcerated in that vast chateau of his, among his dreary vassals, bringing up my children in complete boredom, while he had all the fun in Paris!"

Without any doubt, Damaris was in her element, despite the rain. She had all the traditional qualities of a beauty, with her wide-eyed innocence, her superb figure, and her manner which was faintly decadent, mutinous, full of devilry. There was never any lack of escorts riding at the coach window and, as the march progressed, her admirers increased, Rupert drawing off men from every garrison he visited. By the time they arrived at Ashby-de-la-Zouch, the numbers had risen dramatically to three thousand five hundred horse, and more than three thousand foot, all musketeers. It was a patchwork army, but most of the men were experienced, attracted to serve the Palsgrave by the magic of his military repute.

Damaris' coach was roomy and serviceable; Rupert borrowed it, and it became dining-hall, council-chamber, headquarters and bedroom as the need arose. Venetia found it fun to ride in, like a small house on wheels, or a dim, padded cave. It had been smart once, but was now travel-stained and battered, the Chevalier's escutcheon on the door scratched by the brushing of bushes. But it was comfortable, with little cabinets in the panelling to store flasks and documents, and seats that could serve as beds, the whole slung on giant leather springs.

Rupert and Venetia spent one night in it. Damaris, high-bosomed and keen-hipped in a suit belonging to one of her pages, had gone off on some mad prank with Barney, so the Prince and his mistress sheltered in its dark intimacy.

Light filtered between the closed leather curtains, green-washed because they were parked beneath trees. Venetia lay back against the cushions, watching his silhouetted profile. He turned to her, reaching out and drawing her into the circle of his arm, his free hand sliding up under her skirts, finding the soft flesh of her thigh. They talked and laughed in quiet murmurs while the rain pattered steadily down, penetrating the thick leaves of the woods so that his guards swore and pulled their cloaks more tightly about them.

A kind of bourgeois panic seized Venetia, she struggled to sit up. "The coach will creak and rock like a boat, Highness!"

"Let it." She heard the sound of his chuckle as his fingers closed on her wrist and pushed her hand down further through his unfastened clothing, pressing it hard against his skin.

"They will know exactly what we are doing!"

"Who cares!"

She could never have believed such passion possible in such an impossible situation.

Rupert's speed of movement and the complacency of the Roundheads proved their undoing; the besiegers took the news of his approach with light-hearted disbelief, quite unable to imagine that he would have the nerve to attack them. An intercepted letter amused the Cavaliers; in it was mention of "an incredible rumor" of his advance. But a force of cavalry was now dispatched by Essex to tail and, if possible, hinder them.

Ashburnham sent Rupert warning of this in a pithy note, brought by a sweating, blood-daubed galloper: "The strength that followeth your Highness is nine hundred dragoons, and one regiment of horse; which I hope will all be damned!"

"Damned or not, they've been unsuccessful in stopping me," said the Prince, tweaking Boye's ears, sitting cross-legged on the ground, eating his supper by the camp-fire. They were bivouacking undisturbed not many miles from Meldrum's cohorts, and Rupert had sent out spies to observe them. He rolled himself in his cavalry cloak and lay down to snatch a couple of hours sleep before the action, with the dog curled up against him and the fire-light flickering on his face.

Venetia kept watch, unable to rest, nerves taut as bow-strings. She sat with her arms clasped round her knees, her hooded mantle wrapped closely about her, for the night was cold and clear and the moon was rising. God, if she were only a man! Her fingers itched to grasp a sword-hilt and she longed to change her soft, woman's muscles for those of steel, like his. "No need to worry," said a voice within her. "Crane will guard him, and his luck will hold."

What was it that his admirer, Cleveland, had written about him in that long poem, "Rupertismus?" The words came floating into her head:

Sir, you're enchanted! Sir, you're doubly free
From the great guns, and squibbling poetry.

When Holmes woke him, Rupert, fast asleep at one moment, was on his feet the next, grabbing up his sword, taking his helm from the page, and:

"You'll stay with the wagons, Venetia," he ordered. "Tonight is man's work. Keep out of it, and no tricks!"

"Have you managed to get in touch with the town?" Venetia knew that he had dispatched two messengers already who had not returned.

"I've sent in another man with a simple message which I hope that the Governor has the wit to understand." The Prince was standing with elbows raised while Holmes adjusted the straps of his breast- and back-plate. " 'Tis this, 'Let the old drums be beaten on the morrow morning.' He is to sally out against Meldrum at daybreak!"

That cold trembling was beginning within her, she clenched her hands into white-jointed fists to keep them still; familiarity with death had only increased her fears for him. When he was keyed-up for action, he did not like to be touched, nothing must divert him from absolute concentration, but she reached out toward him blindly, her words spilling over. "Be careful, Highness."

He hesitated for a split second, his thoughts running ahead to Newark, anxious to maul Meldrum as well as relieve the town, but then he moved, as black and huge as the trees at his back, yanking her up against him, his armor crushing her breasts, gauntleted hand in her hair, his lips finding her face and then sinking on to her mouth.

The trumpets sounded cheerily to horse, and he swung off across the glade, a long shaft of moonlight striking his helmet so that it shone like a white flame. His men were happy, shouting and singing as they got into the saddle and Venetia caught sight of Michael, his foot already in the stirrup, and she ran over to him, forgetting that it was weeks since they had spoken.

"Michael," she blurted out; "Keep near the Prince. Have care for him."

He looked into her face, tip-tilted toward him, silver-blue, her voice tight with terror for her lover. The touch of her hand on his arm seemed to burn through his sleeve, jangling along the nerves, stabbing his loins with raw hopeless desire, reminding him of all that he had lost to the Palesgrave.

"I shall do my duty, Venetia." Unable to bear her closeness, he mounted his gray gelding, making a totally unnecessary adjustment to his wheellock.

Speed was an essential part of the Prince's plan, and with his cavalry on the spur, he outstripped the infantry, leaving the wagons and artillery to struggle along as best they could. They did not reach Beacon Hill till later in the morning when the battle was more than half over, and disjointed accounts were already beginning to come in from scouts, spies and wounded.

At first light the Prince had gained the hill and looked down on the fine old town with its magnificent castle by the river, and the whole beleaguering host in dense array where Meldrum had withdrawn them into the burnt-out ruin of a mansion, just north of Newalk, called the Spittal. There were four great bodies of horse awaiting him on the lower slopes of the rise. Rupert decided to attack, knowing the demoralizing effect which this sudden announcement of his presence would have on the Parliamentarians.

He gave the order to charge, leading his men down like an avalanche upon the nearest Roundhead troopers, yelling out the war-cry, "King and Queen!," which was answered by the infuriated rebel roar of, "Religion!"

Astonished, wildly confused, struggling to control their plunging horses and beat off the vicious blows, the besiegers broke their ranks and, at the same moment, the Governor sallied out with his garrison who entrenched themselves doggedly on Meldrum's flank.

Rupert had pierced deeply into the *mêlée*, borne forward by the impetus of that first charge, and, in the desperate hand to hand fighting, he was set upon by three burly assailants. He laid about him furiously with his sword, running one through, while another fell back with a bullet in the head, fired by one of his Guards. The third had grabbed the Prince by the collar and was trying to drag him from his horse, when a whistling cut from Sir William Neale, who had galloped up behind, sliced off the man's hand at the wrist. Then Crane, and the rest of the Lifeguard, came up like a tidal wave, sweeping the routed cavalry right back to the Spittal.

The Newarkers, Colonel Tillier and Rupert had them hemmed in on all sides. The Royalists seized the bridge across the river which gave access to the only road by which they could retreat, and the guns and infantry of Rupert's army were beginning to arrive. Meldrum had no prospect but to starve on the Spittal, and presently, Charles Gerard, who had been wounded and taken prisoner, came limping across the open ground toward the Prince's standard, with proposals of peace. He was grinning, although the blood was seeping through his breeches, squelching in his boot as he walked, beads of sweat dewing his face.

"We've got the bastards on the hip, Your Highness!" he shouted jubilantly.

Rupert nodded, relaxing against the back of his saddle. "Good. We'll discuss the terms when you've been to the surgeon, my lad, to get that wound dressed."

Fatigue parties were getting up tents, unloading wagons,

filling water containers, digging latrines. As dusk deepened, fires glowed against the darkness on either side of
that waste land between the two armies where the prowl-
ers were stripping the dead, leaving them naked beneath
the callous moon which had hung over similar scenes
down through the centuries and would blankly survey
many more, long after these present antagonists were but
dust and memories.

When Holmes put away Rupert's armor, he found a
spent shot which had embedded itself in his steel gauntlet.
Luck of the Devil!—Venetia kept it as a souvenir.

When the enemy had retired, Rupert made his entry
into Newark, not as a triumphant General, but as a
blessed deliverer. The populace went mad with delight,
packing the streets, cheering wildly. The women fought
to get close and touch any part of him that they could
reach, kissing his hands, his booted legs, his stirrups, even
his horse, strewing his path with flowers. He received this
adulation with calm dignity, as became a direct descend-
ant from the Emperor Charlemagne.

By speed, surprise and sheer nerve, he had achieved a
brilliant, unequalled victory, and Venetia, jogging behind
him among the Lifeguard, throat aching with pride and
love, knew that this was his finest hour.

" 'Swounds! What the devil do they take me for—a
Goddam midwife?" the Prince exploded, and flung the
King's latest letter across the table in disgust, before adding the afterthought: "But thank God, she's abandoned
the idea of coming here to have it!"

The Queen was expecting another baby and, in the first
flush of the overall enthusiasm about Newark, had considered joining her victorious nephew, but now decided
that Exeter would be safer for this event. They wanted
Rupert to break off his work in Wales in order to escort
her there.

He had hardly paused to refresh his men at Newark,
and around New Year's Day had hurried them back the
way they came; it was unsafe to linger, for the various
contingents had to be returned to their garrisons, rendered dangerously vulnerable by their removal.

Oxford's reaction to his success was one of unrestrained
jubilation. Congratulations flooded into Shrewsbury; King
Charles described it as, "no less than the saving of all the
North," while Digby, not to be outdone, wrote at great

length, praising Rupert's "courage and excellent conduct," which, he was sure, "has made fortune your servant to a degree beyond imagination."

"Which is, no doubt, very fine," Rupert grumbled, unimpressed. "But all that was really achieved was the relief of a loyal town, some arms and ammunition, and the surrender of a few scattered outposts which we have not the troops to man properly."

Will Legge usually managed to coax the Prince out of his pessimistic moods, and Venetia wished that he could have stayed, but he had gone to Oxford which, in spite of its raptures, was not really being very helpful. There were plenty of promises on paper, but few materialized. Will hoped to remedy this.

They had been hard at work recruiting again in Shropshire for less than a fortnight when this new order came from the King. Rupert spent a day, fuming, expending time and energy trying to work out how he could accompany the Queen, and carry on with the enormous task of preparing for the march north. He need not have worried—the next rider brought yet another order countermanding the previous one. Venetia was aroused from sleep by his infuriated shout:

"God! I've wasted a whole day thinking about it! This is Digby's doing! Christ save me from meddling civilians! How am I to effect anything of importance if my plans are to be interrupted by his every whim?"

The usual disputes and jealousies whirled and eddied in the Court, and Will was doing his best to alleviate some of the troubles.

"He is the kindest man in the world," Venetia said to Damaris as they strolled down the gravel walks of Mr. Jones' pleasant garden, enjoying the April sunshine; everything smelled of fresh leaves, blossoms and moist clods. "Rupert has asked the King to give Will a place as Gentleman of the Bedchamber. He really deserves it, for he never thinks of his own advancement."

Damaris produced a hunk of bread, breaking it up and throwing the crumbs to the birds who took time off from their frenzied fervor of nest-building to accept her charity. "Etienne tells me that there is talk of the Mastership of the Horse being offered to your Prince, now that Hamilton has been dismissed for his disloyalty."

There were tall yellow daffodils, and heavy-handed purple tulips aready in bloom and Venetia began to cut the stems. "Rupert would accept, but he is anxious that nothing shall be done to make it appear that he had a hand in Hamilton's ruin. He says, let each man carry his own burden."

"In spite of all their protestations of admiration toward Newark's savior, the Courtiers still sink their own personal squabbles to band together against him," Damaris was smiling under the shady brim of her bongrace, seating herself on a stone garden bench, spreading out her skirts to prevent creases. "His attitude doesn't help. Jermyn protests that Digby has written several times to our *Pfalzgraf*, and that he has not troubled to reply. He says that Rupert exaggerates the Secretary's dislike of him!"

"Which is arrant nonsense, as well you know!" Venetia's scissors flashed; she wanted to plunge them into the smooth-tongued Digby's throat. What chance did Rupert have against the subtle hints, the sly innuendos, while up to his eyes in the real work of the King's war?

The flowers were still wet with dew, droplets darkening the taffeta of Venetia's green gown. She gave them a shake, before laying them across her flat basket. "Digby likes nothing better than giving Rupert orders, provided there are a good many miles betwixt them! He's just sent another, concerning the plight of Lady Derby at Lathom House, and Rupert has taken great exception to his tone."

He was certainly in an angry frame of mind, scribbling a letter to Will, full of ironical and rather unintelligible complaints against his uncle, and dark threats of his own resignation.

Venetia's spirits sank as she read it before he pressed his seal into the wax, for if he were to leave the country, what would become of her?

The relief of York was now Rupert's principal objective. He rode to Oxford to consult with the King about the impending campaign.

Ella called to see Venetia, not, she was convinced, fired by sisterly concern; a much more likely reason was her avid curiosity to set foot in the Prince's headquarters.

"We shan't have to leave Oxford, shall we?" Her voice was jarringly shrill, Venetia had forgotten just how irritating she could be.

"Would you rather stay here, if the Roundheads take over?" Venetia felt far older than the three years' gap between them; living with Rupert was proving a most maturing experience. Ella had been thoroughly ruined by too much attention from cadets, students, the younger sons of peers who were amusing themselves with the glamorous side of war, while making sure that they kept as far away as possible from disciplinarians like His Highness.

"Oh, 'tis all very fine for you," Ella tossed her blond ringlets, madly jealous of the sister who seemed to have won this prize. "Everyone knows all about you and the Prince! I can't think why Mallory permits it!"

"Be quiet, you silly little bitch!" snapped Damaris, having no patience at all with the vapid beauties who hung about the camps, amateur harlots risking disease and pregnancy without the means of the professionals. Oxford, in common with all garrison towns, was short of nubile population, and overflowing with full-blooded males hell-bent on draining the last dregs of pleasure while life lasted.

There was a change in the atmosphere of the Royalist headquarters; Rupert sensed it and Venetia picked up the general tenor. Some of the best and worthiest of the King's officers had died and the character of his present adherents was gradually lowering.

Rupert found his uncle overwhelmed with grief, now deprived of his adored Queen. He had ridden with her as far as Abingdon and there, amidst tears, they had parted. Charles confided his fears to his nephew, but managed to appear confident when he attended the Council of War.

"I wonder how it is going." Venetia was sitting on a bank beside a stream which leaped happily over boulders, twisting itself into all manner of colors as if it gloried in the afternoon sunlight.

"Oh, they'll spend hours arguing, making decisions and then revoking them. A tiresome waste of a lovely day." Damaris kept an eye on Barney, who was fishing further downstream, chewing on an empty pipe, perfectly content to watch the water lazily, refusing to be drawn into idle chatter.

Venetia had met most of the gentlemen who made up the Council, and sympathized with Rupert's distrust of this unreliable body. He usually managed to dominate the gathering, speaking his mind freely and shouting down anyone who disagreed with him. Wilmot and Digby did so on principle; old Lord Forth used his deafness as an excuse for not siding with anyone, while Sir Jacob Astley had the advantage of being able to get along with Rupert. Lord Hopton, honest and brave, was easy game for the vain, dissolute Wilmot, and the ambitious Digby. The King wavered between them all, usually acting on the advice of whoever was highest in his favor at the moment—or last to speak!

"The level-headed Edward Hyde will try to bring order to the meeting," Damaris reminded, giving Barney a gay wave. He responded by kissing his fingers and holding up a big fish on the end of his line; he was keeping his hand in for any possible privations on the intended march. Tender light filtered through the young leaves above their heads, midges danced across the surface of the water. "La, 'tis really quite warm. Soon we shall be able to indulge in the delights of midnight bathing. Stop worrying about the War Council, and dwell on the joys of a communal plunge into some sparkling moonlit stream, everyone playing at being bacchantes and satyrs. Wouldn't Rupert look wonderful, mother-naked, with vine leaves in his hair?"

Sometimes, Damaris' unorthodox notions brought out a prim streak in Venetia. In any case, if that vision became reality, she had no intention of sharing her beautiful Greek God with anyone else! "Rupert does not believe in heavy drinking. He told me himself, that when in Germany on his way home after being released from Lintz, he upset his hosts by leaving the table early. So they made a hunting party for him instead."

"Oh, don't be so stuffy," chided Damaris. "If Rupert would unbend a little, instead of being so sedately abstemious, maybe even joining Wilmot in his carousals, he might get on better with him."

"I'm very glad he doesn't!"

"Give him time," Damaris said thoughtfully. "There may come a point where he breaks. After all, we none of us thought that he would keep a mistress, but you have proved to us that he is but human after all!"

Rupert came striding down the wooded path, while Boye dived along rabbit-tracks into the brambles, coming back with burrs knotted in his coat. Rupert hooked a finger impatiently under his cravat, tearing open his shirtband, disposing his long limbs on the grass at her side, shifting across to lay his head in her lap. Venetia leaned above him with brooding tenderness, running her fingers soothingly over his forehead and hair, ignoring Damaris' expression of comic despair at this display of unashamed adoration. Let them laugh, she did not care—ready to admit to all that she genuflected in her heart whenever she thought of him.

"They agreed to everything I suggest," he volunteered. "They always do—in the end. My plan is simple—all the King has to do is to keep the surrounding towns well garrisoned, to maneuver round Oxford with a body of horse, leave Maurice to finish the affair in the west, and myself free to march north."

He sat up suddenly, "Hell! I'm hot! Let's go for a swim in the river. Come along!" And he hauled her up by the hands, then stopped and scowled as they started to laugh, not understanding why. Women! With their maddening feminine allusions to the devil knew what! He turned on his heel, whistling to the more dependable Boye, leaving Venetia to snatch up her skirts and run after him.

ELEVEN

"God go with you, madame." Pierre filled Venetia's arms with last-minute parcels. "Take care, and make sure that those misbegotten sumpter-masters keep His Highness's food-boxes out of the sun. And thanks be to the Lord, that you are taking that animal with you—I have had quite enough of him skittering through my kitchen—rioting among my sausages!"

Boye was in disgrace. The household cat normally viewed his hysterical antics with disdain, from her perch high on the dresser, contempt for this shaggy clown, exhausting himself in uncontrolled leaps which fell far short of her refuge, expressed in every line of her svelte body. Unruffled, she would pay meticulous attention to grooming her whiskers, but lately her spring had lost a little of its agility, her sleek sides bulging and lumpy. That morning early, while she was absent for a moment only, Boye had come bouncing in through the backdoor, poking an inquisitive nose into her nest of blind, mewling, new-born kittens squirming in their basket under the table.

The lowly tabby was transformed into a fiend of unbridled ferocity. A ball of spitting, clawing venom, she hurled herself upon the astonished poodle, sinking her talons in his back as he leaped away with a shrill yelp of pain and surprise. In his frantic efforts to dislodge this yowling menace, he knocked over a pannikin, and scattered a trug of vegetables. Pierre in pursuit, waving the broom handle, skidded on a squashed onion awash in a sea of cream, landing with a crash which shook the kitchen.

His wrath was forceful but brief, and, as Venetia went out into the yard, he pressed yet another cloth-wrapped package into her hands—bones for Boye.

Having given his advice, visited garrisons who woke up at his appearance, proved to the King that he did not require any more troops but Rupert *did*, and commandeered three hundred barrels of gunpowder, the Prince returned to Shrewsbury. By the 16th of May, his army was ready to march, and not before time. The Earl of Manchester was already on his way northward to join Fairfax and Leven, taking with him the Eastern Association cavalry under his Lieutenant-General, Oliver Cromwell.

There was an electric thrill in the air; everyone sensing that this was the start of a momentous campaign. They forgot the misery of days spent treking through the rain —"pickled with the wet," as Barney put it—now they traversed roads which hardened under the warm breeze, winding into the open countryside with rich rural landscapes of green pastures and fertile fields, unfolding across the valleys.

The soldiers sang as they marched, the women stopped complaining, striding along with a child straddling a beamy hip, or close-wrapped in the fold of a shawl. Some cadged lifts on wagons or gun-carriages, giving the men plenty of backchat. The hedges were heavy with May, a hundred white crowns to garland the brows of the victims to be offered in sacrifice on the altar of political dissention, religious intolerance, and ambition.

Damaris eased her back against the bole of a gnarled oak, while her servants spread a white cloth on the sward and unpacked hampers. A halt had been called for the night, and in the leaguer there was the usual bustle of settling in; the thumping of mallets as tent-poles were driven into the ground, the whining of tired children, the weary sarcasm of sergeants organizing pickets.

" 'Tis na fine life, if it don't rain," agreed Barney, expertly sharpening a green stick with his knife, spearing an egg upon it, and holding it in the flames to cook. "There's nothing like a bit of real service. You may read military manuals till you're blue in the face, but a couple of weeks campaigning will make you a better soldier than a year in quarters—providing you survive!"

He squatted on his hunkers, deftly removing the shell, holding out the snowy contents to Damaris. "Here you are, Duchess. Try that!" They munched in silence for a moment and then he predicted, cheerily: "This war, well managed, will last twenty years!"

"Hark to the voice of the true mercenary, who fights only for pillage, giving his allegiance to the side which pays most!" Mallory's lip lifted in a sneer.

There was a feud raging between them over Damaris, who lost no opportunity to stir the embers of their smoldering rivalry. Barney shot him a belligerent glare, even his good nature stung by the slur, and Venetia quickly enlarged on the subject of the expected duration, in order to postpone the duel made inevitable by Damaris' coquetry. They discussed the war in Germany which had already been raging for twenty-five years.

"That is where we get these wild tales of cannibalism," stated Etienne, who had been watching his wife's games with her lovers with quiet amusement. "I have seen well-authenticated reports of how Wallenstein and his brother-villains have reduced Europe to such a state that it is necessary to post guards, in some areas where famine is rife, to prevent newly-buried corpses from being dug up, and many cases of children being snatched, slaughtered and eaten!"

Venetia and Damaris shuddered, but Etienne was not trying to frighten them; though generally his brand of teasing humor was not to be trusted, this time his face was perfectly straight. "I swear 'tis the truth, and the source of the nasty rumors regarding the *Pfalzgraf!*"

Etienne ordered a lackey to carry up another bottle of wine which had been immersed to chill in the emerald gloom where the brook ran deep. He held out a goblet to Barney. "Try this, my friend. 'Tis a recipe handed down for generations."

130

Barney choked on the first mouthful. "God's blood! What a bite! Does it shift rust? It tastes as if it were brewed from pikemen's feet!"

Damaris' eyes were sparkling at him. "Lord, you'd be a huge success at dinner with my mother-in-law with such talk! 'Tis one of her best wines, I'd have you know. There is nothing so potent to fuddle the wits and bring instant stupefaction. You should take some to Rupert, Venetia."

"If you want my opinion," declared Etienne whose views had not been solicited, "You'll encourage him to relax, *chérie*. He is much too anxious—like to crack."

Venetia knew that he spoke the truth, and the sad part about it was that because of his size and talents, Rupert should have been a genial giant, with flesh on his bones, instead of this savage creature flinging himself into every new enterprise.

"'And whose chaplains swear faster than they can pray!'" he added, and they fell on each other's necks, laughing.

Certainly, the wine supplied by the Chevalier's mamma was every bit as intoxicating as promised. Against a green and pink sky the dense woods massed and Venetia watched, dizzily, as the birds swirled high before dipping down to nest for the night.

Michael had slipped into the party, taking a cushion beside her, and, somehow he had got hold of her hand and was smoothing her fingers, his fair lashes screening the longing in his glance. Sentimental tears pricked her eyes as she remembered the peace of their relationship, the innocent dreams they had shared of a home and children, before everything had been eclipsed by the meteoric blaze of her passion for the Palsgrave. Almost, she wished that she had never met him, though knowing very well that she would have always been unsatisfied, expecting to find something wonderful around each bend. To be exultantly happy with him, even for an hour, was worth a lifetime of contentment with an ordinary man.

As gently as she could, she detached her hand from Michael's, getting unsteadily to her feet and leaving the glade, Rupert's tent drawing her like a magnet. Above it, his standard was flying, nearly five yards long, blazoned with the arms of his House, the black and gold of the Palatine, the blue and silver of Bavaria. Boye trotted out to greet her, and it was like coming home.

She found Rupert talking with two of his adjutants, and

stood aside for some time, waiting till he was done with them. At last he snapped his fingers at Boye who barked sharply in answer, and the three of them started up the wooded slope.

The sinking sun made purple shadows over the velvet green of the vale, throwing the hillocks into sharp relief. From the camp, nestled in the hollow, came a continual hum, and the smell of roasting meat.

Rupert stood looking out over the scene. "England is the most beautiful country in the world," he said slowly. "When first I came here, it seemed like Paradise after flat Holland, and my uncle's Court the very height of luxury and refinement."

At sixteen, a rootless, landless boy of mixed nationality and cosmopolitan upbringing, he had found at last the country that he loved, birthplace of his mother, this island that, ever after, spelled "home" for him.

"Although they call me a bloody foreigner, I'll warrant I care more for it than many of those born here. Between them, your fellow-countrymen are going to ruin it."

"What has happened?"

"Only what I half expected," he said, in that bitter drawling voice which he used sometimes, the words snaking out from his scornful lips. "A dispatch from the King, sent the day after I left Oxford, revoking the decisions which we had made."

Filled with distress for him and a woeful sense of inadequacy, Venetia longed for the clear-sightedness of Hyde, the calm counsel of Will, even the solid reassurance of Maurice. All that she could offer was sympathy, which was met with a surly: "You know nothing of these matters!"

Indeed the convolutions of Court politics would stun a mind even more alert than hers, and Rupert, with his plain language of the barracks, found it baffling, edging his question with an exceedingly forcible oath: "At times I wonder—do they really want to win this war?"

"At least the Queen is well out the way for a while."

"Aye, that is one blessing," Rupert was seated on the ground, his forearms resting on his knees, a long blade of grass between his teeth. "Although the stupid woman has run herself into trouble, going to Exeter. I advised her against it and I'm sure this only made her more determined!"

Boye was badger-hunting, rooting about in the undergrowth. Rupert glanced over with the same fond indulgence which he reserved for small children, and Maurice. "Silly old fool, he's making too much noise. With any luck he might chase out an elderly pigeon."

Venetia, watching Boye clowning, was amazed that anyone could really believe him to be that "devil dog" of the Roundhead pamphlets. He wormed his way into the affections of those who knew him, a valiant, large-hearted companion, as familiar to friend and foe alike as Rupert's famous red cloak. He had a fondness for Venetia, who could well understand why the King allowed him to sit in his own chair, and romp with the Royal children. Rupert had taught him to leap into the air when he shouted "Charles" and cock his leg at the mention of Pym.

The Prince's mood softened. Boye could usually make him laugh and she sensed that they might enjoy what was left of the evening. She perked up at him, but her smile was arrested by his frown.

"Have you been supping with my officers?" he demanded.

"Yes, Highness—and with my brothers also." She wondered if he had guessed that she had been drinking.

He flung aside the grass-stem, his eyes smoking as they slid to where his locket lay on its trail of chain against the deep cleft between her breasts. "That bodice is cut too low. D'you want to be thought a camp harlot?"

Venetia could feel the blood running into her cheeks. He had turned his back to her, staring off into space.

"Highness——" she reached out tentatively to touch him, then, emboldened by the last remaining whiffs of Madame d'Auvergne senior's brew, slid both arms about him tightly, burying her face against his shoulder-blade. "Rupert—I only wanted to look well—to please you."

He turned swiftly, pressing her back on the earth, lithe and furious as a tormented panther. "I am surrounded by knaves and traitors. You'll not betray me too?"

It was more in the nature of a command than a question, and he kissed her very thoroughly, fingers clenched in her hair.

"Damn the King!" Venetia thought, "and all those who can hurt him so much more than he could ever hurt them, for all his magnificent strength."

Charlotte de la Tremouille, Countess of Derby, had

been formally summoned to surrender "her Lord's house and its honor," by Fairfax, on the 28th of February. She gained time, by parleys, to plant gabions, raise breastworks, train her domestics, and send her men out to press others to join her little garrison. On March 12th the first shot was fired against her house-fortress. Vainly the Roundhead's artillery hammered the stout walls, and the siege had dragged on for eighteen weeks. Lord Derby, miles away from her, again entreated the Prince's aid, reminding him of her courage, and the fact that he was her kinswoman.

From almost every quarter came requests for Rupert's help, constant appeals for his presence, the unshaken belief, put forth in many letters "that the Prince alone can do it" and "his very name is half a conquest." Rupert set his course for Lathom House.

Stockport was the first objective. Rupert and his men battered their way in, assisted by Derby thirsting to avenge the insults heaped upon his Lady. The Roundheads drew off their siege and fled to Bolton, which was Puritan to a man, the greatest stronghold for this austere sect in the north.

In the ruined farmhouse which was acting as a base, the women were working with the surgeons, the rain dripping persistently through the gaps in the roof.

"Mother of God! How many more men is he going to send in? They've been hard at it for over two hours now!" Damaris held up a rushlight so that Venetia could see more clearly as she eased Barney's injured arm out of his ripped doublet, trying to staunch the blood running from a jagged gash in his shoulder.

"The first attack had been repulsed, I think he may decide to hold off." Barney gritted his teeth in pain.

"Not any more he won't!" Etienne was shaken out of his usual equanimity, bloody and bruised. "Those damned fools got overbold and have hanged one of Rupert's Irish boys over the wall in bravado. *Dieu!* He's gone berserk! Flung himself from his horse, called up more foot and, storming at their head, he's forced his way back among them, pistolling anyone who resists. They don't stand a chance—and he has sworn to give no quarter!"

"I don't believe it!" Venetia looked up quickly from fixing Barney's bandage. Rupert, in a fury, had said this before, but always when he cooled down, the enemy were given the honors of war.

She worked on, trying to dismiss this sense of foreboding. Rupert's spirits had been low that morning, sick with worry about what might be happening at Oxford now that his back was turned.

His regiments rallied to his reckless example, rushing the Roundheads, dealing out bloody vengeance. Lord Derby was amongst the first, in finding himself facing one of his own former servants, now Captain in the royal army. Derby killed him joyously.

Venetia never forgot the sack of Bolton. In time the impact faded but she was haunted by the booming sheets of flame, the black smoke rolling away before the wind, the screams which reached her, even in the camp. She dreamed of it—everything drenched in scarlet, the color of fire, the color of blood, reflected in the blank insane rage in Rupert's eyes when he came to her. He reeked of the Germanic wars in which he had been raised and she trembled, her loyalty jolted. Did she really know him at all, this cruel General deliberately allowing his men to loot, rape and destroy?

She wanted to shriek that these were her people he was letting his men kill. Badly advised though they might be —they were still English! The phrases used by those who hated him rang in her head. He was half foreign! How could he understand the feelings of Englishmen? At that moment he lived up to his reputation as a brutal soldier of fortune.

Reading the disgust in her eyes, he drew his lips back over his teeth in a snarl: "I'll teach these rebel bastards a lesson they'll not forget in a hurry!"

His accent had become more marked, his face suffused with passion under the tan. His hair was matted with sweat, a red line scored across his brow from the pressure of the helmet he had been wearing for hours. He reached a handful of hay from the floor, wiping his rapier clean before sliding it back into his scabbard.

He looked mad and she was afraid, sensing the undercurrents surging through him, unleashed by bloodlust; the urge to hurt and subjugate, to wreak his will on a woman as a final demonstration of his overpowering masculinity. But his rank stopped him; he could not rampage through the stricken town like a common trooper, destroying and ravishing. Even at this moment of loosened control he would not jeopardize his authority; but the demon whom he had allowed to take over, deliberately blunting all pity

135

and sensibility, was receptive to the wave of revulsion sweeping Venetia and this enflamed him.

"Don't tell me that you are developing scruples, of a sudden?" he said unpleasantly, legs apart to balance his weight, arms hanging at his side. "How do you think we eat every day, if 'tis not through pillage? What is the matter, *liebchen?* Don't you like me as rough, bloody mercenary? Have I smashed your pretty dreams of a knight in shining armor?"

Venetia was more sharply aware of his body across the space between them, than if she had been in his arms. He wanted her disgust, desired that she refuse him, to give him the excuse to force her. Very well. She would play the game of rape. She glanced at the door, as if measuring the distance, skirts gathered in one hand, ready for instant flight. His mouth curved in a chill smile of enjoyment. He let her wait for a moment and then lunged for her, grabbing a fistful of her hair.

The pain in her scalp was agonizing; she was suddenly angry, wanting this harsh charade to stop. But all thought, all feeling, was being knocked out of her in her impotent struggle against those hard muscles.

The smell of gunpowder and smoke was in her nostrils, the heavy odor of sweat and horse from his clothes. He tasted of blood, his skin wet with the heat of battle. He threw her down, pulling her skirts back over her thighs, his hands taking their toll of her. Normally he was very gentle, knowing his own strength which could so easily snap her brittle bones, wanting to give, as well as take, pleasure. But now he used her brutally, as if he would annihilate all his enemies, smash every woman who had ever teased him, and dominate the one who, all his life, had frustrated and hurt him—the Winter Queen.

Venetia lay limp, every inch of her throbbing with pain, but in deep triumphant exultation as well as discomfort. She would share his bestiality, and burn with his shame, become one with the evil genius which dogged his career, his sins would become hers also. Whatever blame was poured on him for this day's work, let it engulf her too. Without him, she was nothing. And she rejoiced when her body became smeared with the blood of Bolton, transferred from his ruthless hands.

When she thought that he slept, she slid out from under him, and she was crying; angry, despairing tears of pity and indignation at the way in which lesser men were dragging down her noble paladin. Whatever happened she would cleave to him, and words learned long ago at her mother's knee, came ringing back into her tired mind:

"For whither thou goest, I will go; and where thou lodgest, I will lodge; thy people shall be my people, and thy God my God."

A drab twilight darkened the room. Rupert got up, coming over to her where she knelt with her face in her hands, jerking back her head so that she had to look at him, her eyes slanting oddly, dragged up at the corners by the pull of her hair.

"What!" he muttered fiercely. "Praying for Roundhead Bolton?"

He released her abruptly and she clung to his legs, her face against the leather boots which reached half way up his thighs.

"No, Rupert!" she cried in anguish. "I pray for you!"

Lady Derby was standing in the hall of Lathom House with her daughters on either side of her, her servants and her garrison drawn proudly to attention to greet their deliverer. But formality could not be maintained by the exuberant Charlotte and, as her husband and Rupert stepped across the threshold, she broke free, running to meet them, kissing Lord Derby warmly full on the mouth, and sweeping Rupert into her motherly arms, laughing, crying and talking all at once.

"Monseigneur! Rupert! My dear, dear cousin—welcome—welcome!"

And they were kissing and he was grinning, suddenly a boy again, as she hung on to him while they jabbered in French, filled with mutual admiration in each other's courage and family pride in their achievements. Venetia, standing forgotten in the background, felt humble and sad, but Charlotte's quick eyes missed nothing, and, when she was calmer, she dropped her voice and asked him:

"Who is this who stares at you with such adoring eyes? Your *inamorata*, eh, Rupert? That is good. A great warrior should have a beautiful lady to love him." She stretched out a hand to Venetia, a plump, fair, lively woman in her early forties, much kinder than her daunting repute led one to believe. "Don't blush, *mignonne*, although such modesty is to your credit. I can see that our Prince has shown his usual good taste in choosing you. Come, we will be friends, yes?"

Rupert was watching their faces, smiling faintly, now hardly recognizable from the barbarian of yesterday. He had kept De Faust busy since early morning, and was once more his usual elegant self, his doublet brushed, linen sparkling, boots as soft and unwrinkled as a calf's belly, sword-hilt and spurs glittering. Every evidence of stubble had been scrupulously scraped from his jaw, his hair, freshly washed, shone healthily, the ends coiling into soft curls falling below his shoulders.

"And what am I to do with those twenty Roundhead standards which you have so charmingly presented to me?" Charlotte beamed on Rupert, delighted with his chivalrous gesture.

"Accept them as homage to my fair relative and companion-in-arms," he said with a deep bow. "Let them adorn your battlements, madame, and rejoice in thinking of how chagrined Colonel Rigby will be at their loss."

Then nothing would please her but that they must go on a tour of inspection of her defenses, Boye pattering behind them, his nails rattling on the stone flags. Rupert was politely attentive as she told him how a cannon-ball had crashed through one of the casements, during dinner, and how her children had not stirred, and, at a nod from her, had gone on with their meal.

"Take good care of them, madame," he advised. "The children of such a father and such a mother will one day do their King such services as their parents have done theirs."

Venetia marvelled; he was perfectly capable of making pretty speeches as the next man—when he put his mind to it!

Derby and his Lady were very willing for Rupert to use their home as his base from which to continue the subjugation of Lancashire. She welcomed fresh company, happy to accommodate Damaris, Venetia and some of the officers' wives, while the dependents of the soldiers lived under canvas, or billeted themselves in the village. Chaplain Rutter organized a school for the children in one of the barns, keeping them out of mischief, busy with hornbooks and slates.

Venetia took to spending a lot of time on the battlements, her eyes on the north road awaiting the first faint cloud of dust, the distant throb of hooves denoting a galloper carrying news. She breathed in the warm air, redolent of summer, apple-blossom and strawberries, mixed

138

with the rich aroma of the cow-stalls which stretched in a straggly line beyond the fortress walls, and the acrid stench of smoke belching from a near-by chimney-pot.

A choke of loneliness strangled her throat now that he was gone and, to combat it, she dwelt on the stupendous fact that she had known him for almost a year and he showed no signs of tiring. Sometimes, she thought about her home and wondered if anyone was tending her mother's grave in that corner of the country churchyard, or was the moss slowly obliterating the wording on the tombstone so that the world would soon forget that there had once existed Cecilia Denby, who had laughed, danced, cried and loved with all the intensity which Venetia now felt. Had she been as passionately in love with Samuel as she was with Rupert? Somehow, Venetia doubted it. A marriage of convenience—as they would have had her make with Michael, had it not been for the war. Blessed war—which had brought Rupert to her.

She pondered on those who had once been her neighbors, wondering how they fared. Mallory had heard that Giles Fletcher, their erstwhile playmate, had gone into the Eastern Counties, that fastness of Puritanism, where Oliver Cromwell was training his brigades of fiery fanatics who were reputed to spend in prayer the time they did not give in fighting.

Life became an endless vacuum, an eternity of waiting; Venetia dreamed, and, at night, was lost in the enormous four-poster, which itself was dwarfed by the gargantuan stone-walled chamber which Charlotte had prepared for her cousin. She was scared, and ducked under the covers, hugging one of Rupert's shirts which she took to bed for comfort, while the moonlight made eerie shadows over the big bulbous furniture which crouched like beasts waiting to spring.

They kept very busy and cheerful, taking time off for hair-washing and baths, having the maids clean the mud from the hems of gowns, and launder those yards of white, frilly petticoats and voluminous smocks, the collars and lace cuffs. The full-sleeved shirts of their men billowed out, pegged on the clothes-lines, and from the kitchen, the smell of slightly scorched linen mingled pleasantly with that of baking bread, as the maids ironed and goffered.

Lathom House settled back into the life in which it had existed for centuries, the siege no more than the wink of an eye to its aged grey walls, one in a series of many which had been waged times before so that it had been well castellated to withstand the attacks of foemen. Charlotte was always so active, seemingly unconcerned that her Lord had once more departed into danger, superintending every household detail with the same detached efficiency with which, not long before, she had carried on during the siege.

But it was dead—to Venetia they were as ghosts—wandering in her desert of loneliness. Even Boye had gone perched on the top of the Prince's sumpter-cart; Holmes, De Faust and Trevor had marched out with those brave spirits which left Lathom bereft.

The reports of Rupert's successes seemed almost phenomenal; in ten days almost all Lancashire had been overrun. He should have been pleased with his progress, but his despatches to Charles crossed with a stream of letters in which his uncle announced misfortunes.

The King had had second thoughts as soon as his masterful nephew left Oxford. Contrary to all plans, he had withdrawn his troops from the circle of garrisons. Essex and Waller had closed in, almost trapping him. When in a tight spot, Charles usually did very well, particularly if acting on his own judgment. Now he used ingenuity and daring, leaving most of the cavalry and making a feint towards Abingdon. Waller fell back, leaving open the road to the west. The King and his men marched through the gap, making for Worcester. It was hoped that Oxford could hold out against siege till Rupert returned.

Everyone shifted the blame for this disastrous state of affairs at headquarters on to one another. Rupert was furious with them all. In a black, sardonic mood he saw knavery everywhere in the King's service.

The way was clear to York, it was mid-June, the weather was good, and Newcastle writing that he could not hold out more than a week. If York were relieved speedily, it would complete the Prince's triumph in the north. He rode back to Lathom House to make his plans.

TWELVE

The hot afternoon was melting into the shadows of evening when the sleepy atmosphere of Lathom was rent by the snorting and trampling of destriers.

Venetia had to force herself not to go flying out to Rupert. Lady Derby must be given precedence and, as always when they had been parted, there was that twinge of fear in case he would not want her again.

He walked into the hall, brushing aside the speeches, the praise of his success, and Charlotte saw at once that he was tired and strained.

"Your Highness, I will have a meal sent to your room. Tomorrow we will talk and you shall tell me all about your magnificent exploits." She mimed with expressive hands to Venetia, indicating that her job was to go with him and be soothing.

Upstairs, in that vast bedchamber with its wall-tapestries of Grecian scenes depicting buxom goddess and ardent swain, De Faust was directing the disposal of the single valise which contained Rupert's clothes. Still he did not speak, pouring out a goblet of wine and tossing it down in one gulp, staring out across the gardens through' the mullioned window. But at last the meal was set, candles lit and De Faust bowed himself out. When the door closed, Rupert was at Venetia's side in a couple of strides, his arms coming about her, burying his face in her hair as if he would blot out the world.

She could feel him shaking. This was no triumphant conqueror. "What has happened?"

He raised his head and his eyes were those of a damned soul. He cursed and broke from her, striding up and down the room—up and down, as though by walking he could leave his fate behind him.

"They are saying that I want to be King."

"Who are saying it? You read that tract published in London earlier, and tossed it aside as of no import——"

"This is more deadly." He no longer looked romantically lean, now positively gaunt, and she had a flash of how he would be in later years, a stern, uncompromising man, when the vicissitudes of life had tamed his youthful fire. "That was put out by the Roundheads, but now letters come from Court. They say the King grows daily more jealous of me, and of my army. My successes have not pleased those treacherous rats who surround him. Digby, Percy, Culpepper and Wilmot—they say it boldly now, what they have been afraid to voice above a hint before—that it is indifferent whether the Parliament or Prince Rupert prevail—the old King will be deposed."

"And he believes them?" She shook her head in denial even as she asked the question, unable to credit that he would not recognize the unfailing loyalty of his most faithful commander.

Rupert stopped prowling and dropped into a chair with so despairing a gesture that Venetia went on her knees at his side.

"If I were there he would not," he was struggling to be just, to remember his uncle as he had once known him. His fingers flexed as if burning to seize his sword and skewer the whole Council of War on it. "Damn them all! I'll send the King my Commission and get to France. 'Tis plain I am not wanted here!"

Tears of rage and pain which he was too proud to shed were making his dark eyes brilliant. Venetia put her arms about him, drawing his head against her breasts, her fingers passing gently over his hair.

"Come to bed, my Prince," she murmured, her lips against his forehead. "Lie with me, who loves you so deeply, and forget for a while. Let them talk. Truth will out in the end."

But this wound had gone deep, coming as it did on top of other troubles, paralyzing all thought, decision and action in Rupert. By next morning the wild rage had gone, leaving him in a cold, unresponsive trance. He no longer spoke of resigning, of leaving the country—but then, he hardly spoke at all—and the days stretched out in a torpor of inactivity. Lord Newcastle was waiting for him at York. Let him wait. The lethargy which had lain across him for three years in Lintz, dulling his mind, imprisoning his great body, seemed again to hold him in an enforced suspension of energy.

"He is worn out, poor boy." Charlotte, in a solar,

looked up from her accounts when Venetia trailed in miserably, searching for Rupert who had disappeared without a word. "He has been running the whole war for two years. He takes so much upon himself, convinced that it is his task to ensure that everything and everyone is in the right place at the right time, and if he doesn't have a breakdown doing it, it won't be for want of trying! And now this nonsense about him wanting the Crown!"

Arthur Trevor glanced across from the dispatch which he was drafting. "There are too many whom it will not at all suit if he returns to Oxford in a blaze of glory."

"I cannot understand the King." Charlotte raised shoulders and hands in a wide gesture of puzzlement. "They were so close, those two!"

They reflected momentarily on the Royal uncle and his impetuous nephew who had had so much in common. Both were transparently honest—Charles did not know how to lie and Rupert had never bothered to learn. They were both mad about hunting, entering into it with hereditary zest, and they shared similar attitudes, decidedly autocratic, sensitive, stubbornly proud.

Venetia could not forgive the King for doubting and hurting Rupert who would never whine, but she could voice it for him, wildly indignant:

"After all that he has done for them! From the very onset breathing life into the King's lukewarm followers! He has given of himself unstintingly, yet he is forever attacked and his authority undermined, by petty, selfish men motivated by spite, envy and dangerous hatred. They are not fit to clean his boots!"

Forced to stop for want of breath, Venetia caught Lady Derby and Trevor staring at her in surprise. Then Charlotte gave a little laugh.

"*Mon Dieu,* what is it about that family which inspires such fanatical devotion? Rupert's great grandmother, the unhappy Mary of Scotland, had the same fatal magnetism. And his mother—look at the noble gentlemen who have devoted their lives and their fortunes, in trying to restore the Palatinate! Rupert has the same magic, people love or hate him! *Sacrément!* These Stuarts!"

Rupert's listlessness was infectious. Discipline became slack, his men loafed with their women in the leaguer while the officers lounged and amused themselves. Lathom House, its parklands and appointments were at their disposal. They could hunt or hawk, and there was

143

plentiful fishing, pursuits which reminded them poignantly of their homes. Given pause to ponder, some wanted to go back to their own countries; it would soon be hay-making time, and the yeomen thought longingly of their untended crops. How good it would be to return to familiar things instead of this continual slog of marching, fighting, falling into bed and starting all over again next day.

And now this old fortified house held them entranced as in some fairy tale. The very air seemed bewitched, languid with the scents of high summer, every movement became an effort, the mind drugged by the heat-shimmer on the turrets, the Roundhead standards hanging limp, as if expiring with exhaustion, along the ramparts. The flat marshy ground enfolded Lathom like the palm of some huge hand.

Inside, it was more than ever like the Palace of Sleeping Beauty. Narrow feudal corridors, tiny rooms shut away, up one stair and down several others, flights of wooden steps which screwed steeply up to the top of any one of the seven towers, impressive halls which stunned both eye and mind, and grand staircases with newels like bedposts supporting handrails fit for giants.

Charlotte opened up remote corners of this imposing structure to accommodate her guests, mazes which led down into darkness and upper storeys which looked as if they needed scaling ladders. Going to bed could be a harrowing experience with smoking candles flickering on the carved balustrading, the thick pillars rearing up to support overhead landings, sprouting tall elaborate finials in the shape of heraldic beasts. This setting gave plenty of scope for such practical jokers as Etienne and Adrian, who exercised much ingenuity with sheets, lengths of clanking chain, and hollow theatrical groans.

Everyone got lost, and, when they met again, it was with something of the sense of an expedition of exploration, and they were merry—most emphatically so—no one wanted to dwell on York where food was strictly rationed, and all the more unpleasant aspects of a closely beleaguered city were being keenly felt.

"The falconry is better lit than the apartment which I have been given," complained Damaris, annoyed because the servants' quarters were at an inconvenient distance from their masters, most difficult for the performance of their duties, especially after dark. But this disorder had its compensations, permitting, by its very confusion, a relaxing of the etiquette which Lady Derby might otherwise have expected. Most of them retired after dinner, during the full blaze of afternoon, either alone or with some congenial companion. Rupert was one of the stalwarts who did not indulge in a siesta. He could usually be found by the beck where a mill-wheel churned, his long limbs in unwonted laxity on the grass, contemplating the water without seeing it; an inert, chained giant, sulky and uncommunicative. Boye would lie with him, whining now and again, thoroughly uneasy with his gloomy master.

Venetia learned painfully that he was best left alone, and would drift away to find Damaris, chatting with her in her bedchamber while she took off her dress, brushed out her hair and anointed her breasts with perfume, in anticipation of delights to come.

"Oh, do be more cheerful, Venetia," she glanced at her in the mirror, irritated by the sight of her drooping shoulders. " 'Slife, I should have thought you would have been overjoyed to have the Palsgrave with you constantly, and so idle too. It must give him plenty of energy for the boudoir."

"He is so unhappy."

"Out of temper, more like," Damaris studied her image critically. "One good thing comes out of this rushing about after the armies—it gives one little opportunity to put on weight."

"I wish I could help him," Venetia was following her own train of thought.

"I'm quite sure you *do*, my dear. He walks all over you—though I have yet to be convinced that it is a good thing to swell his head even more."

Venetia had, long ago, accepted the fact that Rupert was not in love with her, trying to be content with the casual affection and physical need which he expressed, yet, sometimes, she became angry. "You should hear the change in his voice when he speaks of Suzanne Kuffstein or Mary Lennox," she burst out irrelevantly.

"Men always have this sentimental hankering after the wenches they did not quite succeed in laying." Damaris was always so down to earth, her worldly wisdom dashing aside self-pity.

"I cannot imagine Rupert ever being a rejected lover," Venetia gnawed her thumb despondently.

"Well, in these instances he was." Damaris deliberated between two equally ravishing lounging robes.

Venetia was determined to labor the point, almost enjoying the hurt; "It was his fine sense of honor which stopped him."

"Fine sense of fiddlesticks!" Damaris' head appeared through the neck of a rose-pink diaphanous creation cunningly designed to reveal more than it concealed. "You find him devastatingly attractive, I know, but his unpolished roughness may not appeal to all."

Venetia envied Damaris' capacity for amors in which she remained emotionally excited, mentally stimulated, but heart-whole. She never fell in love, though constantly with some affair either being carefully nurtured, or already in full bloom. When Venetia left her after these conversations, she invariably greeted in the winding stone passageway either Barney, already unfastening the ribbon lacing of his breeches or Mallory, more restrained, knowing that he might bump into her. Occasionally it was neither of these, but an unfamiliar officer, or even a ranker; Damaris was not a snob.

Ten days of suspended animation, and, in the oppression of a thundery evening, the men were playing billiards. Venetia paused in the rounded arch of the Norman doorway seeing, in the lurid sunset glow, Adrian's narrow backside, and his heels lifted from the floor as he reached across the table for a difficult shot, while Etienne made encouraging noises. On the opposite side of the room Michael stood, balancing his cue like a rapier. He saw her and fixed her with a long look which she could not meet. Rupert was not there.

"Of course, his Majesty's action outside Oxford is keeping Waller busy, and Essex is trying to break up Maurice's siege of Lyme," Trevor was saying from deep in a cloud of tobacco smoke, nodding, pleased, as Adrian sent the ball bowling smoothly across.

"Prince Maurice has not the craft of war at his fingertips, like his brother." Michael took aim, and Venetia knew that he had to be always bringing Rupert into the conversation when she was present to test her reactions and add to his torture.

Once she had done the same, making seemingly casual reference to the Duchess of Richmond, every sense alert to catch any nuance in Rupert's replies, or even in his very silence! But lately it had not been necessary; Mary wrote seldom, and then purely formal communications; sometimes a rider might be added to a letter from Oxford to the effect that she had found the cash to pay the messenger.

"Even the Roundheads admire His Highness's Generalship." Trevor never attempted to conceal his pride in working for Rupert. "They've no one to touch him—though reports are coming in about this fellow Cromwell. If these are to be believed, he thinks of the welfare of his men in a similar way to our Prince—concerned about clothing and equipment."

"*Sacré nom!* Any competent quartermaster can do that!" Etienne was aristocratically scornful. "I have often considered that His Highness demeans himself with these cares, bothering about such things as boots and horse-fodder—like a tradesman, *mon ami!* He is the great Generalissimo! He has no need to worry about such trifles."

"Pay and provisions are the common soldier's reward for the danger and hardship," Mallory regarded the frivolous Chevalier as if he were some peculiar species and not too wholesome at that!

"The war is dragging on too long." Michael had been saying this often of late. "It should have finished after Edgehill—I shall never forget that battle—no one, I am sure, was more grieved than King Charles, forced to wage war on the people whom God had placed in his care."

Venetia noticed how thin Michael was getting, now his temples seemed almost transparent under the thin sheen of sweat, eyelids half lowered over his strained eyes, fine pale hair lank on his forehead. He reminded her of a young girl she had once known who had been jilted by the man she loved; as the months passed, so she had sickened, with this same pallor, till she became consumptive and died. A pang of guilt shot through her, but no, surely it was the conflict which was upsetting him so much —not herself?

"The King had no choice! It was rebellion—what we did was right!" Mallory had no patience with such talk.

"Was it?" Michael's gaze was turned within, seeing horrors. "When the drums beat to arms in the dark of that first, frosty morning, how many must have wondered what the devil had induced them to fall thus upon their own countrymen?"

"But the exhilaration of that charge!" Mallory's eyes were shining. "They'd never seen anything like it. None of the old-fashioned sedate trotting, stopping to fire—no, we set spur to our horses and swept down, gathering speed with every stride—slashing, pounding onslaught—straight through their ranks."

"When the slaughter was over we settled down to endure that bitter night." Michaels' voice was low. "We built watch-fires and huddled around them and thought about our dead. We could hear the groans of the wounded, and English voices screaming out for help. It was so cold that the wounds froze—congealing the blood——!"

Was this part of that lethal spell which had held them over the past awful days—this brooding on scenes best forgotten? The atmosphere was thick and heavy—soon it would thunder.

Then, abruptly, Rupert came in through the door, a sheaf of papers in his hand. The yawning stopped.

As if he had never spent an idle moment in his life or this had been no more than a pause in which to fix their arms, he gave his orders:

"Get your men mustered. We march at daybreak."

"George Goring, by all that's Satanic!" Barney was leaning far out of the upper casement window, attracted by the uproar in the yard.

The Prince had rushed his army over the Peninnes and now he and his staff were supping at Skipton Castle.

"I was expecting him." Rupert looked up sharply.

"The King wants you to send him to his aid, doesn't he, sir?" Trevor reminded gently.

The black brows winged together. "I have the greater need of him," said the Prince.

He did not add that he much preferred to keep Goring under his eye, knowing that intrigues were boiling in the wandering Court, unprincipled enough to cause untold damage without the addition of an officer such as Goring who had no morals, knew no qualms and was not troubled with a conscience.

Venetia had not yet met this General, her curiosity aroused, looking expectantly towards the door when noisy shouts and laughter heralded his arrival.

Almost before Rupert had called to enter at his knock, Goring was in their midst, flourishing his hat in an elaborate bow, a tall, attractive swashbuckler, disarming those who had been prepared to dislike him, with his gay, affable camaraderie. A ripple went around the table.

"Goring! You old ruffian!"

"Couldn't the Roundheads stand your presence any longer? Glad to kick you out of their prisons, were they? Tired of your debauching their women, eh?"

"Kept you snugly out of the war for a bit though, didn't it?"

He stood there grinning at them mockingly, almost imperceptibly insolent as he bent over Rupert's hand. "Greetings, my Prince!"

Venetia wondered how Rupert managed to refrain from striking that impertinent face. Boye was barking hostilities from behind Rupert's chair, baring his teeth as if longing to fasten them in the seat of those fashionable breeches.

His wayward glance roved to Venetia, reading volumes in the Prince's icy manner, guessing the cause and finding the situation highly entertaining.

"You are to be congratulated, Your Highness, on having this lovely creature grace your camp," he was murmuring, undressing her with his eyes. "Rare solace for us poor soldiers, in our bleak, lonely wanderings, to have life made sweeter by such a delightful votary of Venus."

"What have you to report, General?" Rupert said, as curtly as if he was speaking to an orderly.

Goring bowed again, hand on his heart. "My horse have wrought wonders in the way of forage. We've been playing the cowherds to any number of 'borrowed' cattle, which will be mighty useful when converted into slabs of beef! Since receiving your latest summons, I have neither rested, supped, nor even drank, till I could be instantly in the glory of your esteemed presence, to fling myself at those illustrious feet!"

"My dear fellow, you must be exhausted." Etienne murmured. "I am sure that His Highness will wish you to share our meal."

"I am hardly fit company," said Goring modestly. In fact he was very beautifully turned out and knew it; a little dust, a hint of dishevellment seemed to enhance his velvets and gold lace. In his spurred boots with the red heels and welts, he stood in a spread-legged stance with all the audacity of an Alsatian bravado. He was a King's man—a Cavalier, and proud of it. He flaunted it defiantly, to damn and mock and fly in the face of the Puritans. If the Roundheads wanted copy for their newssheets, he was only too happy to supply it in its most exaggerated form. They would have no need to invent lies about his doings.

Rupert wiped his slender brown fingers on a napkin, pushed back his chair and stood up. "Have your men on parade at five of the clock tomorrow morning. I will review them before we march. Now, I leave you, Your Lordship. I have work to do."

Everyone rose while the Prince made his exit and Goring was loudly and insincerely devastated at Rupert's dedication to toil. "Ah, my dear Palsgrave, always so conscientious. And you, madam"—he was reluctant that Venetia should depart—"are you too equally dutiful? Or may I dare hope that you will sample a bottle of Rhenish with me?"

Rupert did not express his fury, but the room fell silent as he outfaced him, forcing him to look away at last, unable to meet the scornful stare from under the Prince's heavy eyelids.

"Have you really work to do, Highness?" Venetia watched while Rupert lay back in an armchair in their chamber, bracing himself as De Faust straddled his boot in a tugging position. One came off and then the other, and the valet bore them away for cleaning. And Venetia forgot her question, lost in admiration and that glow of happiness because he resented Goring for even daring to look at her.

Rupert threw off his doublet and shirt. "I left because I should have challenged that goddamned rakehell if I'd stayed a moment longer. And there would have been a ripe piece of news—two of the King's Generals fighting, and over a woman too. That should please you, you vain little minx."

He padded across to grip her under each elbow, drawing up to him, re-establishing possession. Her hands were against the smooth brown flesh of his chest, fingers tracing the line of dark hair which ran plumb down to his navel. She caressed his throat and neck where the skin was soft to the touch, like a girl's.

"Why do you look at me so intently?" he asked, smiling.

"I was thinking—it is the way you carry your head which makes you regal—proud and haughty. You are so beautiful, Rupert."

He laughed, embarrassed by her compliments. "I should not carry it for long if the Roundheads caught me.

It would be the block and a traitor's end. Maurice and I top their list."

She shuddered, her too lively imagination filling in the details. "Don't talk about it! It will never happen! You are invincible—everyone says so!"

"I can never imagine myself dead," he shook his head. "I see so much slaughter, yet cannot believe it could happen to me. It is so strange to think that though I now stand here, holding you, by this time tomorrow a bullet, or a blade more skilled than my own, could put an end to it all."

He had changed—tendrils of that spell which had held him in thrall at Lathom still clung to his mind. This was dangerous talk; part of the charm against defeat was that he should have an unshakable faith in himself. . . .

There was an odd expression in his eyes, as if he saw into the future and did not like what it held. "And beyond death, *liebchen*, is there anything more?"

"Of course! There must be!" Venetia felt as if she were tottering on the brink of an abyss, one fact only standing out with blinding clarity—a personality as strong as Rupert's must continue—and she had again that conviction that she had known him before in some other life, and would ever wander, searching for him, until united with him in existences yet to come. These ideas frightened them—she understood. "Do you believe in God, Highness? You have prayers said for your men."

He gave his short, ironical laugh. "And doesn't this infuriate the rebels! Red-hot off their presses come complaints that, 'The Devil Prince pretends piety to his troops! Rupert, that Bloody Plunderer, would forsooth to seem religious!' " His amusement gave way to irritation; " 'Swounds don't they understand that I as well as their own Generals, know the worth of a hymn or two for the men to sing to keep up heart when they are tired of waiting for action."

"You don't really believe in an after-life, do you, darling?" Venetia was sad, needing his strong conviction to strengthen hers, an entrenchment against separation—an eternity of blackness without Rupert would be the worst kind of purgatory.

"Goddam, I was reared to be a good Calvinist! As children we had a most strict training—taught to know the Heidelberg Catechism by heart—without understanding a word of it!"

"Pierre told me that Bethlem Gabor, one of the sponsors at your christening, is reputed to be half a Turk, and more Moslem than anything."

He was laughing again, with that wild mirthless gaiety which she distrusted deeply. "You seem to spend a great deal of time gossiping with my cook! Aye, it is true and my family never let me forget it. They said that my temper proved me to be a heathen."

He rarely mentioned those at the Hague, though she knew that he had been made happy at the rumor that a cache of mail from his mother had been intercepted by the enemy and, because of its contents, words of praise for her soldier son, Parliament had stopped her pension.

But other letters did not please him so well. He was still pursued by contradictory, worrying messages from the King, half-apologetic for having jettisoned his nephew's orders, full of such phrases as: "I confess, the best had been to have followed your advice."

Even the usually calm Richmond had written gloomily: "We want money, men, conduct, diligence, provisions, time and good counsel."

Now Venetia found herself reading yet another dispatch which Rupert had received at Liverpool and brooded over at Lathom.

It was written in Charles' usual complicated style, full of congratulations on Rupert's successes, regrets at not being able to supply him with powder and then arriving at the real point of the communiqué: "Wherefore I *command and conjure you,* by the duty and affection which I know you bear me, that all new enterprises laid aside, you immediately march, according to your first intention, with all your force to the relief of York."

The Prince had bowed to the direct orders of his King; gathering everyone up and plunging them across the border. All he could do was hope that he might be able to complete the operation without having to suddenly fly to the rescue of Charles.

Venetia continued to look at the King's letter long after she had ceased to read it. A draught from the open window made the candle flame waver. Darkness crouched thick outside the circle of light. Rupert stood leaning against the bedpost, lost in thought. Boye was curled up on the quilt, and he stirred and whimpered in his sleep, in the toils of a nightmare.

152

THIRTEEN

"Why do we have to spend the night in this damned wood when we could have ridden triumphantly into the city and found a comfortable bed?" Damaris vented her complaints on Barney, who, instead of consoling, teased her, but then Barney never took anything seriously. He was seated on a tree-stump by the camp-fire, whistling to himself, polishing his weapons.

"You should have stayed in your coach!" Venetia was short-tempered; it had been raining again and the ground was soggy. Rupert had pushed them hard, still gathering recruits as he advanced.

Three armies beleaguered York—the Scots under Leven, the Northern army under Fairfax, and the Eastern Association commanded by Manchester. They had cause to be confident, for they far outnumbered the Royalists, but, as usual, the very fact that the Prince was in the vicinity was enough to cause elaborate marching and countermarching. When he reached Knaresborough, just twelve miles away, it was to find the Puritans reporting: "Their Goliath himself is advancing, with men not to be numbered."

"Holy God!" said the Prince, casting an eye over his very mixed regiments. "I would that they were right!"

Morning showed to the apprehensive rebel commanders, that a formidable body of Royalist cavalry was moving out of Knaresborough in their direction. For days the air had been alive with alarmist rumors and now it was a natural reaction to draw off from their siege-works and marshal the armies into battle array. Hours passed, while Rupert's horsemen curvetted on the skyline, making a spectacular show, but no infantry came to join them and night closed in on all.

The Roundheads were puzzled. Where was Rupert? What devil's scheme was afoot?

They had underestimated his speed and skill in maneuver. While the horse kept the Allies amused by their pretty display, he had struck rapidly northward with the infantry and the rest of the cavalry, crossing the river, then marching briskly down the left bank making for the North Gate of York. As dawn bronzed the sky, the Parliamentarians watched in impotent rage as Rupert's victorious brigades bore down on the city from the side least expected. His men had marched twenty-two miles in a day, but York had been relieved. Now they quartered in the Forest of Galtres, which did not suit Damaris at all.

"We have to sit here in this miserable place, while, I wager, they are having a fine time in there." She pulled the hood of her cloak up around her ears. "I wish I'd gone with Goring—he wanted me to!"

Barney took no notice, sauntering off to join a picket posted to keep the main road clear. There was little rest for anyone as Rupert's regiments passed the bridge. The Prince had already been over, eager for battle, anxious to do his own scouting and select the terrain on which he would engage the enemy.

"It might have been more diplomatic if he had presented himself to the Marquis," Etienne was keeping out the cold with a bottle of cognac. "I hear that he is a very proud grandee, much inclined to send in his resignation every time he fancies himself slighted!"

"Why, surely he will be so pleased that his city has been freed that no petty considerations will enter his head?" Venetia rejoined, busy looking after her pony, giving him an extra feed of oats. He carried her well that day, and another hard one was anticipated on the morrow.

"Maybe, *chérie*, but don't forget that he is something of a poet, and only an amateur soldier. I have heard him described as one of Apollo's whirligigs, who, when he should be fighting, is toying with the Muses—or the Dean of York's daughters; a silken General made out of perfume and compliments."

"He sounds quite delicious!" Adrian was combing the tangles out of the windswept curls. "Just think, my dear, we shall meet William Davenant, the playwright, now Newcastle's Lieutenant-General!" He was atwitter with excitement for, although he had left the players and joined Etienne's troop, rigged out by the fond Chevalier in a fine leather coat, with handsome arms and accoutrements, his first love was the theater.

154

"Venetia, my sweet, did you not hear that poem which he wrote to celebrate your Prince's glorious saving of Newark?" Without waiting for her reply, he began to recite:

"As he entered the old gates, one cry of triumph rose,
To bless and welcome him who had saved them from their foes;
The women kiss his charger, and the little children sing:
'Prince Rupert's brought us bread to eat, from God and from the King.'"

While applauding the sentiments, Venetia thought Davenant's verse excruciating. Lord! Was Rupert to be bedevilled by yet another crowd of dillettantes? This would not be calculated to improve a temper already raw through almost two days and nights without sleep.

She found him by the bivouac-fire, drinking a mug of hot soup and talking with a group of musketeers. He laughed when she repeated Etienne's remarks.

"He'll not give trouble." Rupert sounded confident. He was not really concentrating on the Marquis, his mind already leaping ahead to the impending confrontation. "I've sent Goring to tell him to be ready to march with us against the enemy at four o'clock tomorrow morning."

"Wouldn't it have been more tactful to have gone yourself, Highness?" she suggested—really, he had a blind spot sometimes where relationships were concerned. "After all, he is a commander twice your age who has exercised unquestioned authority here for a long time. And what about his men? Don't you think they will be looking forward to a rest after such an exacting siege? They may not take kindly to peremptory orders from a stranger who has not even bothered to show himself in the town, or offer his praise and encouragement!"

At times her temerity astounded her. She would not have dared to speak thus to him a few short weeks ago. He stared angrily at her down his aquiline nose, and she knew him well enough by now to hazard a guess that she had put a finger on his own misgivings.

"I'm a fighting man!" he said in a sort of snarl. "Not a pampered Court witling! D'you think I have time to waste bandying compliments with the Marquis?"

She plucked at his sleeve. "Won't you rest for a while, Highness? You were up all last night."

"Rest? No time for that—too much to be done."

A quick bear-hug, his cheek resting briefly against her head and then blackness swallowed him up. Venetia dozed in a corner of Damaris' coach, Boye a restless companion; every so often she was disturbed by his rough tongue licking her face and his dreams appeared to be as hagridden as her own. At last she surfaced into the reality of an overcast summer morning not yet light.

The stream was icy, the shock waking her fully as she splashed her face and scrubbed around her mouth with her bone-handled tooth-brush. She would have given anything for a hot bath and clean linen. The leaves of the trees hung heavily, occasionally dripping; there was a good deal of mist about. Then the early bird-calls were drowned by the noise of trumpets, and Damaris was reeling out, yawning and complaining.

Rupert's army was already in position and the sun climbing high when some of the coaches lumbered across the moor to join them. By that time he had stopped fuming and impatiently riding down the ranks, dispatching messengers back to York to hurry Newcastle who had not yet turned up. He forced himself to check his every instinct that was urging him to launch one of his charges on the rear-guard of the enemy infantry. They were straggling along the lanes to Tadcaster, sent to secure the bridges to prevent the Cavaliers moving south, should that be their intention.

So the Prince chafed, chewing his nails till the blood ran, and his caution surprised those closest to him—this new, controlled Rupert, waiting for belated allies, letting the chance of a lightning attack slip away. His men eyed him anxiously, voicing their own disapproval at this delay, making unflattering comments about that languid, lackadaiscal fellow, Newcastle. They eased their horses, watered and fed them and kept up their own spirits by singing rude ditties about the urges of the Puritan women and the inability of the Roundheads to satisfy them.

Rupert was drawing up a battle plan, using the top of a drum as a table. He grunted without looking up as Venetia put down the blackjack of ale, the coarse wheaten bread and cold beef, and there were dark crescents beneath his eyes, tight lines around his mouth, and a kind of sag to his shoulders which was frighteningly unlike him. When he did meet her gaze, she saw, with a kind of sick horror, that the dead dream-state of Lathom still haunted him.

There was constant coming and going, the hurrying feet and churning hooves sending up a stagnant smell from the trampled grass. Around nine o'clock an ostentatious coach and six, with a glittering troop of outriders, drew up near the Palatine standard which marked Rupert's command post. Newcastle had arrived.

He made his entrance with all the pomp of an actor pretending to be a great General in a play. His gentlemen posed in their beautiful armor, elaborately courteous, full of effusive flattery. They were taken aback to be greeted by this powerfully-built, suntanned foreigner with his clipped speech and abrupt manner, silencing their carefully rehearsed words with a brusque:

"My Lord, I wish you had come sooner with your forces but I hope we shall yet have a glorious day."

Newcastle raised a supercilious eyebrow, and there was a split-second pause; "You intend to fight, Your Highness?"

Rupert's face hardened, instantly guarded. "Of course, my Lord. And pray explain why you have been so tardy in arriving?"

A flush spread across the Marquis' thin cheeks, and he replied stiffly "Two reasons, sir. Firstly, our men have been plundering the deserted camp of the enemy——"

"What did you get?" The Prince cut across Newcastle's smoothly modulated voice.

It took a moment for the Marquis to adjust to this rude interruption, then: "A large amount of ammunition and four thousand pairs of boots," he said.

"Splendid!" For the first time Rupert smiled at him. "You'll give us half!"

Newcastle chose to ignore this mercenary demand. "The second reason, Your Highness, is because a great many of our soldiers have refused to march until they have received their arrears in pay. I have left General King to bring them back to their obedience."

"God's blood! And how long will that take him?" Rupert shouted. "The enemy are weak at present. I think we should attack at once before they get wind of our intention and draw their foot back from Tadcaster."

Newcastle risked his spotless boots across the stretch of muddy ground between them. "Would it not be more pru-

157

dent to wait patiently? My spies report much dissention among their Generals. I would swear they will break up their camps and depart, ere long."

"Nothing venture, nothing have!" Rupert replied; some of the Marquis' theatricality seemed to have rubbed off on him. "I have a positive and absolute command to fight the enemy, which in obedience, and according to my duty, I am bound to perform!"

Newcastle had already spent a wretched night soul-searching, tempted to resign, bitterly offended by the Palsgrave's offhand message, delivered by Goring in a way calculated to cause problems. He felt that he was justified in his indignation; after all, he had raised and maintained the whole Northern army at enormous cost, had sacrificed his love of peaceful, artistic pursuits to become a very passable soldier. And now, how was he received? By this haughty upstart, Royal though he might be, tousled, unwashed, wearing a dirty shirt, as lean and gaunt as a marauding wolf, telling him what to do! Just as if the Marquis were no more than some member of staff come to get his orders for the day!

"You have had a direct command from His Majesty?" Newcastle managed to mold his lips around the words.

Rupert did not look at him, slinging his baldrick across his wide shoulders. "I have, my Lord."

"May I see it?"

"No, sir, you may not. You'll take my word for it."

The air was crisp with animosity. Rupert's officers had come up to attention at his back; there was some surreptitious easing of swords in scabbards, and Newcastle's Yorkist gentry eyed these bearded, flint-faced henchmen apprehensively.

The Marquis managed to cling to the rather splendid image of himself which filled his imagination and his genuine feeling for the Sovereign whom he had sworn to serve. What would happen to King Charles if all true noblemen of superlative breeding left him to the mercies of such uncultured ruffians as his nephew?

"Very well, Your Highness, I am ready and willing, for my part, to obey you in all things, no otherwise than if His Majesty was here in person himself—I will never shun a fight, for I have no other ambition but to live and die a loyal subject."

Rupert calmed down, ready to be more reasonable at Newcastle's compliance with his wishes, and he had already abandoned the idea of falling upon the Allies rear without waiting for the York foot to arrive. The morning was wearing on anyhow and not only would he be blamed for rashness if such an attack failed, but really the opportunity had slipped away.

As the day advanced, the atmosphere became increasingly humid, the leaden sky lowering over the activity on both sides. There was some skirmishing and sporadic firing. A prisoner was brought to Rupert who asked him:

"Is Cromwell there? And will he fight?"

The man nodded, and, to his astonishment, was sent back to his own lines with the message that they should have "fighting enough!"

To which Cromwell retorted: "If it please God, so shall he!"

Damaris' carriage was parked near Lord Newcastle's, close against Wilstop Wood. "Heavens, how I wish they would get on with it, if they are going to fight at all today." She fanned herself with her hand, little beads of sweat breaking through her rouge.

"It will start—all too soon." Meriel had insisted on coming with them, though most of the other camp-followers had gone into York.

Mallory pulled in beside them and Damaris handed him a wineskin. He took a long swig, wiping his mouth on the back of his glove.

"I think the Prince was right when he wanted to go after them earlier," he was shading his eyes with one hand, peering across at the enemy ranks. "Then we should have had naught but horse and dragoons to fight."

Rupert's horsemen fidgeted, watching uneasily as more and more men swelled the Allies regiments, and both armies engaged in the elaborate process of drawing into battaglia, with the cavalry on either flank, the hedgehogs of pikemen between rows of musketeers in the center.

The Royalist infantry sat themselves down in their ranks, opened their knapsacks, ate their rations, talked, smoked and cleaned their arms.

"Man, are they never going to begin?" muttered a young Welsh boy, one of the new levies who had not yet taken part in a pitched battle, though pleased enough with the action at Bolton, Stockport and Liverpool which had put money into their pockets.

A more experienced musketeer scratched about under the broad-brimmed grey hat which covered his greasy locks, hoisted his bandolier, heavy with the made-up cartridges, the leather bag containing spare bullets, and a powder flask, and squinted at the lines of men who formed the opposition among the trampled rye.

"If I know anything about it, that ain't all their lads, not by a long shot. I think there's going to be a tough bout ahead." A ripple passed down their ranks. "Ah— there's General King come at last. See, he's brought the Marquis' foot with 'im. That's them, in those undyed wool jackets. They call 'em, 'Newcastle's Whitecoats.' "

It was midafternoon, and all day the Prince had been forced to wait and see his chances of victory ticking away. The enemy infantry back from their vain trek, were taking up their positions; across the humid heat of the July day came the sound of metrical psalms. Rupert and James King faced each other for the first time in six years and the Palsgrave's eyes were frosty as he looked down on the Scottish commander, now elevated to the peerage and entitled Lord Eythin. They had fought together at Vlotho, that battle which had led to Rupert's being captured. King had been blamed for letting him down badly, there had been hints of treachery, he did not forgive the imputation and had borne a grudge ever since. The Prince could place little faith in him, though he was a professional and knew his trade. He was too sharp a reminder of the past, that first defeat, those dreary years at Lintz. His appearance on the field brought with it an odor of calamity.

King stumped up to him, having spent an irritating day calling his surly troopers every name in the book, now finding himself quite incapable of the courtesy with which Newcastle cloaked his frustrating objections. After a curt exchange of greetings, he immediately started to criticize the way in which the Prince had placed his forces, saying that they were too close to the enemy.

Rupert kept his temper. "Very well, my Lord. I can withdraw them a little."

"No, sir," said King truculently, seeming deliberately to forget that he was not still addressing the very young colonel whom he had known at Vlotho. "It's too late."

The Prince refrained from making the obvious remark that if it was "too late" it was due to King's dilatory appearance. He showed him the sketch map he had made, explaining how he meant to conduct the operation. King studied it, pulling at his grizzled moustache while Newcastle hovered at his shoulder. He had made him his right-hand man, glad to let him take over the disagreeable aspects of the York defense which left him free to lose himself in his luxurious library. Now he had a pang of unwonted doubt in his own judgment in giving him so much power, especially when King unceremoniously tossed back the chart with a snort.

"By God, sir, it is very fine on paper, but there is no such thing in the field." The small, sharp eyes ran over the imposing figure of the youngster who was now his superior in every way and he added, tauntingly: "Sir, your forwardness lost us the day in Germany, where yourself was taken prisoner!"

There was stunned silence save for the colonies of rooks rising in noisy complaint, alarmed by the gun-fire which burst forth occasionally from either side to keep everyone on their toes. Venetia could feel the effort which Rupert was making to check his temper and give King no chance to speak of him again as a hot-headed young fool! But his adjutants were bristling on his behalf. Was it to meet such carping inaction, coupled with Newcastle's tepidity, that they had marched and fought from Shrewsbury to York? And yesterday's twenty mile slog when they had bullied their grumbling soldiers to keep up speed so that the whole maneuver had been carried out with unlooked for rapidity, was this done to see the fire drain out of their beloved chief?

Newcastle was most embarrassed by his Commander's lack of manners. He might not like Rupert much, but was shocked to the core at the way the fellow dared to address a grandson of King James!

The muscles tightened about Rupert's mouth. "I think we should take the initiative and attack."

Newcastle and King, banding together, began to argue. The Prince looked from one to the other, asked one or two questions, made a few points, but for the most part listened in silence. At last he glanced up at the coppery, thunder-heavy sky, shrugged wearily and gave in.

A hush fell on the two armies, staring across the ditch at each other, nearly fifty thousand men, mostly of the same nationality. For hours they had endured the gruelling test of being without cover and at a range close enough to see every detail, with intermittent showers adding to the discomfort.

The evening set in with ominous gloom, and distant thunder made the horses toss their manes and sidle nervously. The unearthly light when a struggling sun admits defeat and dies behind a blanket of dense cloud, played over the array of men poised rank on rank, arms sparking sullenly, flags limp on the staves, the pikes as dense as stalks of wheat before it falls to the sickle. That gleaming display of destruction with its color, its magnificence and its foolhardy gallantry, moved the heart in breathless excitement, stirred the spirit like a fanfaronade of war trumpets, and touched the soul with dread.

"Nothing will happen tonight," Rupert swung out of his saddle, put up his hands and removed his helmet. He turned to Newcastle and spoke in a tone void of all expression. "We will charge them tomorrow morning."

His chaplain, William Lacy, was still mounted, and Rupert added: "Have prayers said for the men before they are dismissed."

"I have been thinking about the text, Your Highness," Lacey replied. "These words came to me—'The Lord God of gods, the Lord God of gods, he knoweth, and Israel shall know; if it be rebellion, or if in transgression against the Lord, save us not this day!'"

"'Sdeath! Let us hope we win," muttered Goring in Venetia's ear. "For if not, those damned rebels rinse-pitchers over yonder are going to say we brought a curse upon ourselves which was accordingly answered by the Lord—*their* Lord, of course!"

When the sound of praying rose from each regiment along the Royalist lines, a loud, anwering hymn of denunciation swelled from the throats of the Roundheads; the gloomy psalms rolling, dirge-like, above that dark mass of iron-clad troopers who watched for Cromwell's battle-word.

Boye loped over to greet the Prince, tail swishing joyously, sharing the meat which servants had unpacked from straw-lined boxes. Newcastle had retired to his coach and was already enjoying a pipe of tobacco, and Venetia shared his relief that matters had been postponed—for one more night at least Rupert would not be at risk.

"God, my head aches!" he ran a hand through his hair, scanning the banked-up clouds. "I hope the men are able to sup before it starts to pour."

On the edge of the moorland which rose black to meet the sepia sky, the Royalist army was dismounting, grounding their pikes, resting their muskets, while, in the rear, the smoke from camp-fires spiralled toward the storm rushing in.

Suddenly the sky was rent by a blinding fork of lightning followed by a crash of thunder which broke overhead. Boye started to bark and the rain fell in great heavy drops. Venetia was snatching up the provisions, ready to dash for shelter when she stopped, head lifted. Above the clamor of the heavens, there was another much more alarming noise—cannon-fire and the steady pounding of hooves. The Allies had attacked.

With an oath Rupert was up and had seized the bridle of the nearest horse, vaulting into the saddle, standing in the stirrups to see what was happening. From several points at once, officers pelted, sent by their generals to the command post. The Prince's crisp orders penetrated the din and, within minutes, he was at the head of his reserves, leading the cavalry to the aid of Lord Byron on his right wing, shouting: "For God and for the King!"

Above the pealing tumult of the skies, the smarting sting of hailstones, the salvos, the yells and clash of steel, Rupert's voice rang in anger and incitement as he met his own regiment already in disorder and turning their backs on the enemy.

" 'Swounds, do you run?" he roared. "Follow me!"

Byron's front line was being crushed back against his second by that indomitable wall of armored horsemen who had splashed heavily across the intervening ditch. There was a great heave, then a counter-effort which restored the position, then another heave and sword to sword struggle with the best of the Prince's horse. Rupert fought like a madman, his blade an entrenchment which none passed, something more than human about him, while the long rapiers of his Lifeguard did terrible execution.

After the first immobilizing shock, Venetia pelted for cover, her shirt and breeches already soaked before she reached the coach. She slammed the door shut and looked from the window, but was too far away to make any sense of the maelstrom of fighting glimpsed through the sulphurous glow of storm, smoke and fast enveloping night. She managed to get hold of Holmes, making him pause as he rushed past, the rain coursing like tears across his upturned face.

"Where is Boye?" she demanded.

"I don't know, madam. I thought he was with you."

Usually the poodle was tied to one of the wagons when Rupert went into action, but this had all happened so quickly. She leaned further out, careless of the wet which poured onto her head and trickled down the back of her collar, calling his name repeatedly, hoping to hear an answering bark above the clamor.

Time became disjointed; tiny, fragmented vignettes imprinted themselves on Venetia's mind. A musketeer cursing because the lit end of his match-cord had gone out, a Catholic crossing himself, a pikeman spitting on his hands, amid the hellish racket of throbbing drums, trumpets blaring to the standard, and nature's cannonade dwarfing the human cacophony.

The Royalist musketeers still reeled from the shock of looking up from their suppers to see the enemy brigades rolling down the slope on top of them. The rain ruined their matches and powder and they stood no chance, armed with nothing but a musket-end, against a formed push of pikes. Goring had recovered quickly and was acquitting himself rather well against the Scots, so said the rumors, along with tales of Cromwell and Fairfax wounded. Some said that Byron had made a premature charge, but no one really knew anything, concerned only in straining every sinew to rally to their colors, to keep on their feet, to stay alive.

It was getting ever darker. Usually night called a halt to battles, but not to this one. From the direction of the greatest noise, the most fierce confusion, came a melancholy procession; two pikes and three swords with a cloak flung over all to make an improvised stretcher, and on it a limp form, dyed darkly with blood and rain. A shot had smashed Jonathan's leg, severing an artery, and life was pumping out of him with every beat of his heart.

Kneeling in the mud, they tried to apply a scarf as a tourniquet, but nothing they could do stopped that relentless flow.

Meriel kept repeating in a hopeless monotone: "Help him—help him."

"Get him into the carriage," Damaris recovered her wits. "We'll drive to York and find a surgeon. You'll come, Venetia?"

"No——" Even now, with her brother dying, there was that overwhelming other. "Where is the Prince?"

"In the thick of it—where else?" one of Jonathan's

comrades replied. "He has just led a counter-attack. Cromwell has retired to have his injury dressed."

Cromwell—that name had reached Rupert's ears. He had wanted to fight Cromwell. Her brother was bleeding to death and all that she could think of was her lover. She was like a being split in two; one half holding Jonathan's head, her tears falling onto his waxen face, the other, in that press of hacking, sweating men, with Rupert.

If only it would stop raining. The thunder has rumbled away, but still water sluiced from on high as if the gods wept for the massacre below. It washed over Jonathan till the puddles on either side of the stretcher were red.

They settled him across one of the seats in the vehicle, and he no longer knew them, his breath rasping, eyes rolled up with only the whites showing between half-closed lids. Venetia stood outside in the deluge while the driver whipped up the horses and Damaris lurched at the window, yelling:

"Find Etienne! Tell him where I am. We'll see you in York!"

Strange and terrible were the things Venetia saw as she wandered on the battle's fringe, ever and again returning to the guards around Rupert's standard, dying a little each time a horse was led to the rear with its rider slumped on its neck, or dangling cross-ways over the saddle. But it was not the body of a tall, dark man of unearthly beauty. The legend held good; his life was charmed indeed.

The fighting was still hot, every pike thrust home, every musket levelled low, and the noise was deafening, the thundering hooves, the ringing armor, the maddened shouts, and the roar of artillery. Venetia traversed the broken ground, among the dismounted guns and shattered carriages, where the dead lay heaped. The distinctions which had separated them in life, these sons of a common country, seemed trifling now. Plumed helmet, plain steel cap, rolled in the mire together; the flowing lovelocks of the Cavalier drenched in the dark blood of the enthusiastic republican.

At one point, she found Arthur Trevor. He had ridden from Skipton with dispatches for the Prince and reined in his sweating bay when he saw her.

"Where is he?"

"I don't know." She wanted to cling to that familiar figure, but could only stand at his stirrup and read her own dread mirrored in his eyes.

"I've coasted the country around," he said. "But not a man has been able to give me the least hope of where he is to be found. And the runaways from either sides which I have fallen into, so breathless, so speechless, so full of fears. Yet, some say that we have won, that Goring has carried the day. But you, madam? You should not be here. Let me bear you to a place of safety. Get up behind me."

She shook her head. "I cannot leave till I find the Prince. While the fighting continues, he is bound to remain—and where he is, there I must be."

Trevor looked at her for an instant as if he thought she was mad, then dug the bloody rowels into his horse's scarred ribs and was gone into the gloom. Perhaps, in that sad hour of despair, she was indeed unhinged. Who could survive such carnage and remain totally sane? Oh, they might be ringing a premature carillon for victory in York Cathedral, but she had seen the irrecoverable disorder and Rupert's jaded cavalry fleeing along past Wilstrop Wood.

The rain had stopped and the moon came up, illuminating the field where those stubborn Yorkshire men, Newcastle's Whitecoats, refused to break. They were penned in White Sike Close, attacked in flank and rear by Cromwell's and Leslie's cavalry, but remaining unmoved as a rock amid the surges of the horse and foot hurled against them. So solid did their pikemen stand that dragoons were called in to force a gap for the troopers to enter. And when their square was broken, they still fought on, those who fell goring the bellies of the horses with sword or broken pike, before dying beneath the thrashing hooves. They refused to cry for quarter, cut down in their ranks until Fairfax crashed in among his troops, his face streaming with blood from a sword cut, beating up their weapons and shouting:

"Spare your countrymen!"

It was late—very late—no longer came any rallying cries. The Cavalier commanders who were able had withdrawn their shattered forces. Every soldier who could move had crept away to shelter, the weary to rest, the wounded to die. The constant rattle of fire had sputtered out to an occasional isolated shot. A hush shrouded the

166

moor, broken only by the sound of men crying out in their agony.

Venetia roamed the stricken field, seeking one face only among the heaped up dead, sprawled as grotesquely as puppets whose strings had been abruptly severed. She came upon something which at first sight appeared to be a dead sheep. Why, her fogged mind argued, was the poor beast there? Had it strayed from its pasture? Certainly, under that cold, searching finger of moonlight, it was white and woolly like fleece, except where the blood was clotting blackly. Withdrawn, wondering, she contemplated this phenomenon, refusing to accept that it was Boye, already stiffening, lips retracted over his fangs in a silent, frozen snarl, blank eyes wide as if still searching for his master.

She looked down at her hands, seeing them wringing in woe in the blunt blades of moonshine, hearing a woman sobbing like a lost thing, and turning to trail after the sound—it was herself.

Michael found her at last, sitting on the tail-board of the Prince's sumpter-wagon, from which every guard had disappeared. He fell from his trembling horse, his voice cracking with relief:

"Venetia! Thank God I've found you! Come away—all is lost!"

"The Prince—where is the Prince?" was all that she would say, and he could not get her to move.

Thus they were captured by victorious Roundhead troopers galloping up to plunder the Prince's baggage, when the last of the Cavaliers had fled, leaving the bloodily contested moor to the Puritan fanatics and Cromwell.

FOURTEEN

As the Parliamentary cavalry jogged back to the field, they were raising hymns of praise to the Lord, after ruthlessly slaughtering fugitive Royalists. Predominant among them were those well-armored troopers whom Oliver

Cromwell had made his special unit. They gave thanks to God for his preferential treatment of their side, never doubting that it was Divine intervention which had won the day, rather than superiority of numbers, regular pay, strict discipline and the astuteness of their commander who had turned to his own advantage the lessons learned from his adversary—Prince Rupert.

Venetia and Michael watched mutely as their captors hauled down Rupert's standard, the most important among the hundred or so taken. Anger burned through the numbness which blanketed feeling as she heard them calling him, "The greatest of Malignants, the Prince of Blood and Lies!" and saw them scrabbling in and out of his wagons. The money which had been intended to pay his troops now went to swell Roundhead coffers, and she and Michael were taken for interrogation to a farmhouse situated close to the wrecked rye fields.

Wet cloaks were steaming before the fire in the kitchen where some of the Allied commanders sat at the table, candles glowing on tankards and used platters, a muddle of papers, ink-horns and quills, all very similar to the paraphernalia which surrounded the Royalist officers. In fact, Venetia decided, it could very well have been a meeting of members of her own side. Most of them wore their hair long, but their doublets were unadorned, their collars plain, and when they talked the difference became more marked, for they seemed obsessed with the war-like phrases and names of the Israelite tribes of the Bible, firmly convinced that they were God's elect and that He was their General.

The sergeant escorting them saluted smartly, addressing the elderly man who appeared to be in command. "Sir, we have captured Prince Rupert's sumpter-carts. These prisoners were close at hand."

Lord Manchester turned kindly eyes to them, but the gaze of everyone else was hard and unfriendly. Venetia wished that she made a more brave figure to do Rupert credit, but she was soaked to the skin, her teeth chattering with cold. Before anyone could speak, a figure stepped from the darkness beyond the candlelight. Venetia's flash of hope at recognizing him as Giles Fletcher, was dashed by his first words.

"I know them, sir. The man is Michael Haywood, one of the Prince's Lifeguard, and the woman is Venetia Denby, His Highness's concubine."

168

Fletcher's revelation sparked off an immediate reaction. She felt the full blast of their outraged Puritan disgust and shrank closer to Michael, while Giles watched her like a cat who had had the unbelievable good fortune to come across an injured bird.

"I see God's hand in everything this day. The wicked are being delivered up unto us," said the ugly, moon-faced man in his middle forties, seated by Manchester, staring at her from deep-set eyes under beetling brows. His forehead bore marks of severity, his mouth a touch of pride, and instinct told her that this was the owner of that new name, cropping up with ever increasing frequency among those of Waller, Fairfax and Essex—Oliver Cromwell.

Fear was making a bad taste in her mouth—deep in his trust, Rupert had given her the key to the cyphers for the Royalist's correspondence. If they tortured her, she might tell all that she knew. But Giles had other ideas.

"Think what this means, sir. He will want her back, his Babylonian whore, that they may continue their iniquities together. We can use her as bait with which to trap him."

"Fletcher, verily thou hast the cunning of Machiavelli." The harsh flat voice of Cromwell held a grudging admiration.

"He won't do it!" Venetia flared up. "You'll never catch Rupert like that!"

Cromwell ignored her. "What have you in mind, Fletcher? Speak, man. If we could but take the Prince, the war would be as good as won."

Giles' face was working with excitement. "We'll send a trumpet into York. I hear that he has already reached there with the remains of his army. We can tell him that we hold her and suggest that he come to treat, then we can ambush him!"

Was this the same person who had enjoyed her father's hospitality for years? Once there had been a humane streak, though the rigidity had been apparent, but, nonetheless, they had all grown up together back home. A picture flashed through Venetia's memory, an embarrassing incident when Giles had shown that his interest in her had been more than neighborly. It had been a night of harvest celebrations—she saw again the laden tables in her father's barn, the laughing faces of his farm-workers, the cider and ale flowing in abundance, and herself going out into the garden to cool down after the hectic dancing. Giles had followed her, begging her to be kind, pouring out the story of his unhappy, childless marriage—and she had been sorry for him, but had warned herself against any show of pity. She had been frightened by his insistence, running back to the merry-makers and Michael.

Now she experienced the same fear mingled with contempt as she spat out: "D'you think Rupert is a fool? He'll guess your intent. For a start, you'll have to give him proof!"

Giles came close to her, pleased to see her humiliated, her Prince beaten and her cause threatened. He was the type who would never forget an injury, prepared to use any means, religion, party or country, to gain power. Cromwell was a man after his own heart; Manchester was too gentle, well-mannered and aristocratic. Giles had offered his allegiance to the blunt, verbose Lieutenant-General, that efficient mixture of Welsh and English ancestry, who was already merging his spiritual scruples with his political asperations.

His hand shot out and snatched at the thin chain around her throat. It snapped and he held aloft her locket, side-stepping as she grabbed for it.

"Look, sir. 'Tis his picture. My spies were right when they reported that she wore it always as a keepsake of her demon lover. She should be burned as a witch who has lain with the Devil!"

He flung her into the arms of a grinning soldier who held her fast while Giles chopped off a lock of her hair. "We'll send Prince Robber these momentoes of his mistress, and she shall put her signature to the letter. That will be proof enough!"

"My Lord Manchester! This is monstrous!" Michael protested, struggling with the guards. Mistress Denby is a gentlewoman, not a camp whore!"

Manchester ordered the man to release her. "There is no call for such hard usage, Fletcher. But your idea is sound. I shall leave the details in your capable hands."

"I'll not sign it!" Hysteria was threatening to swamp her reason, the sights, sounds and horrors of the day crowding in on her like a nightmare from which she had no hope of waking. Cromwell's face, marred with tight lines of repression, seemed to swim in space above her.

"It will do little good to be unhelpful, madam."

His voice shed neither animosity nor threat; his only desire to act in the most speedy, profitable manner. A big man, with heavy features, filled with the conviction that he was God's mouth-piece, for whom the Civil War had become something of a Holy Crusade.

Venetia wanted to smash her fist into that dedicated face. She remembered the slaughter of the Whitecoats; they had died out of sheer Yorkshire stubborness, not particularly driven by any sense of love or loyalty. She was blessed with both, therefore she could surely yield up her life as bravely.

"Kill me," she demanded.

Cromwell's eyes were cold. "Madam, mock heroics will avail you naught." He turned to Manchester, barely able to conceal his irritation with his superior; already they disagreed on many issues and Cromwell was fast gathering a party for himself which was likely to split the Roundheads into hostile factions, not unlike the troubles in the Royalist camp. "I suggest, my Lord, that if the lady persists in this obstinate attitude, Mr. Haywood pays the price. At dawn, we will draw up a firing party. He will be shot with his back against the farm-house wall."

"No!" Her lips framed the denial.

"I think it may cause difficulties for our own prisoners in the hands of the Delinquents," Manchester demurred.

Giles shared Cromwell's impatience with these niceties. "My Lord, we all know that the Prince is the most evil of the King's counsellors. Can we but take him, their forces will collapse."

"I am prepared to die," Michael said quietly.

"Don't listen to him. I will sign." Venetia heard her own voice speaking as if it were someone else.

Satisfied, Cromwell stood, begging Manchester's permission to withdraw. "I must go away alone to perform a painful duty, my Lord."

"Ah, yes, my dear fellow—I had heard that your nephew died today. A brave young man, and now you must send word to his mother." Manchester sighed for all of equal courage, on both sides, who had stained the turf with their blood. He was glad that this slender girl standing defiantly before him had relieved him of the necessity of ordering yet another death. They would have him believe that she was a whore and a witch, denying the sincerity and a kind of purity which transformed her white, tear-streaked face.

171

There was a corporal at the door, carrying something. He came across and dumped his burden on the table.

"Sir, 'tis that accursed cur, the Prince's dog, who was valued by him more than honest creature of more worth!"

Giles leaped forward eagerly to peer at the carcass. "Give Glory, all Glory to God! The Prince's wicked familiar is slain!"

The soldier was appealing to Manchester. "Why, look'ee, sir, the lads want to know if they can use it for target practice, seeing as how 'twas no mortal beast. They have already cut off his ears to make him crop-headed, like us, instead of a shag-polled Cavalier." With a grin, he raised the bloody, mutilated head, displaying their handiwork.

Cromwell gave a shout of laughter, but Manchester rose to his feet in disgust. "For the love of Christ, man! 'Twas only a poor dumb brute, following his master into battle! You'll give it decent burial at once, d'you hear?"

The fellow backed away awkwardly, his jest fallen flat, and Venetia could not tear her eyes from the bundle in his arms. Boye, bereft of those soft silken ears which had pricked at the sound of Rupert's voice, so often caressed by his strong, sensitive fingers.

The farmer's wife, Mistress Hazeldean, lit a rush and conducted Venetia to an upper room. A thin sad woman, not really a bad one, owing fealty to none, her only concern to keep her children fed in the holocaust which had hit the land, first Royalist, now Roundhead troops unceremoniously billeted upon her. It was small wonder that there was a dash of vinegar about her speech.

In the dormer bedroom which smelt faintly of herbs, she fixed the rush holder, glancing at the sentry who had taken up his post, leaning against the door. Venetia was shivering violently, and looked ill enough to drop.

"I'll get you some clothes," offered the woman, and ransacked the linen-press. A woollen skirt, laced bodice and plain blouse came out of one drawer. Thick knitted hose, a shift and black shoes from another. "There now, get into those, and I'll dry your things." The guard was watching in sly anticipation but she soon had him out of the room. "And you, sirrah, can wait in the passage while the young lady changes."

"Lady!" He spat to show his contempt. "Captain Fletcher says we shall burn her after we've caught the Devil Prince!"

Mistress Hazeldean made no comment, holding wide the door, jerking her head in the direction of the corridor and closing it firmly after him, then:

"Daned soldiers!" she said. "Coming into folks's houses, as if they owned them!"

Venetia wondered if the woman might be bribed, then remembered that she had nothing to offer. She prayed that Rupert would ignore the letter, stifling the small voice which whispered that if he loved her, he would at least attempt a rescue. There was no time to sound her out, for Giles was hammering at the door, demanding admittance, ordering away both the sentry and the reluctant goodwife.

Helplessly Venetia sought an avenue of escape, but the only window was almost at floor level, letting in a thin strip of moonlight which flashed across Giles' boots as he came toward her. He was well armed, with pistols slung on a belt across his shoulder, and a sword which knocked against his left leg as he walked.

It was difficult to believe that he really meant to harm her. They shared a common birthplace and she wanted to suggest that they stop this masquerade, find Michael and ride home to the Cotswolds together.

For a moment it seemed as if he had the same thought. "Well, Venetia, how fortunate that we should meet again."

She watched his lean face with its high forehead and fleshy nose, his piercing eyes used to probing in his role as a Roundhead agent.

"Fortunate for you, perhaps."

Under the faintly shadowed moustache, his smile deepened, that cold lift of the lips which never reached his eyes. "I need your signature, my dear."

"You know that it is useless."

"D'you mean that your famous Prince will not bother to aid his harlot?" His mockery cut her. "That he may consider the risk too great for such as you, and that there will be other trollops who will take your place within a week?"

She could not begin to explain the Prince's probable reasons; his instinct for treachery and his duty which would dictate that he retreat, not for his own safety, but for that of the King's army. Only when this was done might he make a bid to save her.

The insidious voice was going on: "We have told him

that you will be tried on the charge of witchcraft. I expect he has a strong imagination—he will know exactly what the punishment will be."

He moved swiftly, locking a hold on her impossible to break. Her arm was bare from wrist to elbow and he forced it close to the rush flame, his pupils retracting, twin points of light, boring into hers as pain made her gasp. He let her go and she stumbled back, pressing her palm to her blistered skin.

He was smiling still. "Fire is agonizing, is it not? Have you ever seen a witch burn, Venetia?"

She would call his bluff; this cruel law was no longer put into operation. "Witches are hanged, these days."

"Not always," he said with unconcealed relish. "In the Eastern Counties the authorities are bringing back the stake. And you will be a very special case."

Giles was enjoying himself; still the spiteful boy who had allowed his ferret to savage her rabbits and fed her song-bird to the cat, always the first to come up with ingenious ideas for destructive games.

"How is your wife?" Venetia asked suddenly.

His eyes narrowed in anger. That sickly girl with her wealth, her repugnance of his embraces, her inability to produce a live heir. Prudence—his wife—always bearing, always burying. In Venetia's face he read her awareness of this, the scornful curl of her lip showing that she was comparing the sad situation with her own passion for Rupert. Months before he had received reports about the Prince's mistress, crushing back his envy when he realized who it was, forcing himself to be patient, certain that, with careful manipulation of circumstances, his time would come.

Lately, visions had arisen to torment him whenever he thought of her with the Prince. He could almost believe the accusations of sorcery which he would level against her, so disturbed was he by his own inflamed imagination which dwelt on her while he embraced Prudence. Prudence—this skinny, shrinking jade who always lay like a block of wood in his arms, her silent protest letting him know that it was only her sense of wifely duty which allowed him the use of her body. Dreams of Venetia pursued him still, when he slept at last, sated but unsatisfied.

Now she was here, helpless under his hands, and he asked, huskily: "Do you love the Prince, Venetia? Tell me what you do when you lie with him—talk to me about it."

Venetia could feel her psyche shrivelling away in horror from the unclean rims of his mind, just as her flesh had cringed from the flame. "You are disgusting." Her voice rang with loathing. "No wonder Prudence hates you."

Confident that this time she could not escape him, he pressed closer to her, still talking, in a kind of chant: "He is very tall, isn't he, this demon lover of yours? Very strong. I have heard it said of him, that he has the face of an angle, and the temper of a devil—such a powerful, handsome man. Does he please you, Venetia? Does he rouse your body to ecstasy when he fondles your naked skin?"

"Stop it!" Venetia wanted to gag, feeling as if she had swallowed a mouthful of dirt. "Let me sign the paper and take yourself off!"

He relaxed his hold, watching her keenly. "I could help you to get back to him."

"What do you mean?"

"An escape could be arranged."

"How can you do that?" Her intellect warned her to beward, yet hope flared up.

"I am in charge here for the rest of the night. It would not be too difficult to engineer." His self-satisfaction was nauseating, there was no doubt that he had wangled himself into a position of some importance.

"How much?" she snapped.

"How much?" he repeated, puzzled.

"Your price, Captain Fletcher. I cannot believe that you would aid me for nothing."

His harsh laughter rang under the low beams. "Oh, you are right, my dear Venetia." He was so sure of himself. "I am no gentleman of noble lineage fired by chivalrous motives, as your father once told me in no uncertain terms. Naturally, a low fellow, such as I, will always be on the watch for his own interests. My price is this—your body in exchange for a dismissed sentry and a pass through the pickets."

"How will you explain my disappearance to your commanding officers?" She knew that this conversation had been fated to take place between them always, in the same way in which she had been certain of one day meeting Rupert. It did not seem strange to be here, playing for time, on the edge of Marston Moor where the un-buried dead lay in their thousands, under the pitiless moon. How would Rupert feel when he read the letter? What desolation would strike into him, already crucified by defeat and humiliation? Rupert, her soul's star.

She was bargaining sordidly with this man who wanted her body—and she shuddered with abhorrence, com-mitted to the Prince to whom she surrendered with sub-lime happiness, his embrace a blissful seal of love, and yet with Giles the very same act would be a loathsome test of endurance.

"I can't do it," she said.

"A witch——" he reminded softly. "They will try you as a witch. I have known you for many years and will not hesitate to testify against you. When you have been proven guilty, they will conduct you back to your cell and shave off your hair, then take pincers and tear out your finger and toe nails and drag you to the stake, pile faggots around you and burn you alive. In your agony you will pray for death, and, by that time, your Prince's head will be adorning a pike on Tower Bridge."

He took her hands, pulling them down from her face. "Don't cry, Venetia. Lie with me, and you shall return to Rupert. Save yourself, and him. Come, let me look for witch-marks on the secret places of your body."

She twisted away from his grasp. "How do I know that you will not cheat me?"

"I'll give you back your locket and your hair—you can take the letter too. I am well trusted here."

"And Michael will be free too?" She was trying des-perately to think of every eventuality. He nodded, and she added: "I have no guarantee that you will not go back on your word."

"That is very true." This cat-and-mouse game appealed to him. "But you have no alternative, have you?"

"You had this planned from the moment I stepped into the kitchen, didn't you?" she accused.

He shrugged, wanting to boast to this woman who so openly despised him. "The war has been good to me. I hope to do much better out of it as time passes. There will be parcels of land and titles to be shared out among the friends of Oliver Cromwell."

"Your side have not won yet!"

"This is the begininng of the end. Can you doubt it, after today?"

Doom thundered like a roll of drums—the sense of defeat as strong as her conviction that Giles intended to betray her. He would take her, and then revoke his promise. She would protest to both Manchester and Cromwell, telling them what he had done; and he would stoutly deny her charges, while they pretended to believe him.

She was so tired that she could not think clearly, her very bones seemed to be crumbling with fatigue and her eyes smarted sa if there was grit under the lids.

"Lie down on the bed, sweeting," Giles was purring. "I will write a safe-conduct pass."

He scribbled away busily, using the shelf of the press as a table. Because he was a methodical person, he carefully laid his pistol, sword and dagger beside the bed, before stretching out at her side.

"Venetia—you are so warm, so beautiful——" His hand was passing over her hair. "Why can you not love me as you do the Bloody Prince? You deceived Haywood for his sake, did you not? What madness is it which runs in your veins?"

He muttered in a crazy fashion as he struggled with her clothing, his mouth coming down painfully on hers, jarring her lips with his teeth. She shoved against him as hard as she could, her resolve melting into disgust.

"That's right, leaguer-bitch! Fight me!" he jeered and fetched her a blow across the face which half stunned her. "When the Prince is a prisoner, I shall enjoy telling him that you put up some resistance before I took you!"

His laughter roared in her ears, the cruel mockery of the taunting bully, and he was still laughing when she reached over, seized his knife and plunged it into his back. He gave a grunt and slumped heavily on her.

Escape. There was no room for other thought. So much horror had washed over her since that fateful morning that her emotions were in a state of suspension. She rolled Giles over and searched through his pockets, unmoved by the blood which was spreading out in an ever widening circle on his shirt. Systematically, she took the things which belonged to her, as well as money and weapons. Michael must be found and then they would get away.

Giles had planned his night of pleasure with characteristic thoroughness. A keg of ale, secretly appropriated, had ensured that the guard would absent himself. Venetia could hear him singing happily and drunkenly somewhere downstairs, as she opened the bedroom door.

It was all so effortless, like a dream. She moved lightly, feeling disembodied, almost sure that she was invisible and could float right past the soldiers without being noticed. But to Michael she was solid enough, and he sprang up with a start when she turned the key in the lock.

She thrust the pistol into his hand, giving him no time to argue, her only concern to put as much distance as was humanly possible between themselves and the farm before daylight.

They stood at the head of the stairs, looking down into the black well. Deep in the bowels of the house, a clock boomed the hour—it was two in the morning and quiet as the grave. Even the sentry was asleep, his head in a puddle of ale on the kitchen table.

A door behind them opened abruptly and Mistress Hazeldean was framed against the candlelight. Michael jabbed the pistol into her ribs.

"Lord save us, sir, don't shoot!" She understood the situation at a glance. "I'll not raise the alarm!"

In her bedchamber, Michael kept her covered while Venetia negotiated, using Giles' money as a further incentive.

"You'll not get through tonight," the goodwife shook her head. "There is still much activity out there. I'll hide you, and later you can mingle with the country folk."

There was a cupboard built at the back of the room and she led them there, pushing her way among the musty clothing.

Michael held the candle, shielding it from the garments so that they did not catch alight. Mistress Hazeldean fumbled with the panelling, seeking a vital knot-hole. A narrow door opened, a draught of cold damp air rushed from the black aperture beyond.

"You'll not be the first runaways to hide here. This secret has been handed down through the Hazeldean women—the men were never told it—they blab too freely. I'll bring you food and drink when I can—you'll find a bucket for the relief of nature."

While she talked, she gathered up blankets, thrusting them into Venetia's arms, and they stepped into the pristhole. The panel slid into place behind them and both had the sobering thought that perhaps she had gone to betray them.

"We'll fight," said Michael grimly. "I'll take a couple

178

of the bastards with me before I die!" He settled down to keep guard, both pistols cocked.

"Michael, d'you think she means to leave us here to die of starvation?" The full terror of the day's happenings were swamping reason in this claustrophobic situation, making her tremble violently. Michael held her firmly, drawing her head onto his shoulder, as he sat with his back pressed against the wall. His voice was soothing as in the old days when they had played hide-and-seek, secreting themselves away from the others, waiting in the same dry-mouthed suspense. He reassured her, making his tone confident, rocking her gently like a frightened infant, so that she slept at last, drugged with exhaustion.

With the dawn, Fletcher's murder was discovered. Michael and Venetia clung to one another, listening to the shouts, the bumps and crashes as the house was searched. She had the wild urge to jump up, hammer on the panelling and scream out their presence, ending the nerve-racking tension. But she did not do so, burying her face against Michael's chest and praying instead.

Tiny dots of light from air-vents high above their heads made it possible to judge the passage of time. The day passed and it grew dark again. True to her word the goodwife pushed in food. They dozed, woke to speak in whispers, and slept again. Venetia found herself being glad that it was Michael with her and not Rupert. With his height and size such a cramped compartment would have been torture, and she could not bear to think of him uncomfortable or cold, hungry or unhappy.

Michael told her something of the battle, of how Rupert, separated from his Lifeguard, had striven to rally a few deserted followers, but in vain. Wherever a group was gathered, the Roundhead hores were upon them in force, and eventually the Prince was left alone. Michael's last sight of him was when he broke from his assailants and roused his destrier to one final effort, clearing a high fence into a bean-field.

Early next morning Mistress Hazeldean came again, saying that it was safe to leave. They stumbled from their nook, blinking like owls in daylight, and she fed them and found Michael rough clothing as a disguise. "I can't let you have horses." She was apologetic. "They've taken all but a couple of spavined nags which I must keep for the ploughing if we are not to starve. I'll put you on the right road and you'll have to make your own way."

It was a sobering experience, to walk calmly away from shelter and into the open ground bordering the moor. No one heeded them, taking them to be either spectators drawn by ghoulish curiosity, or else some of the villagers who had helped dig the shallow pits into which the dead had been tumbled, soon to become no more than a melancholy legend of the bleak, windswept heath.

Venetia was eager to push on to York, strength pouring into her at the thought of reaching Rupert. It was afternoon when they entered by Micklebar Gate, to find the streets filled with wounded, most of them in a sorry state, helped as much as possible by the citizens who were panicking, some already packing up and leaving. The Prince had departed at dawn, and the Roundheads would be back to besiege them again.

Venetia wanted to sit down and cry, but Michael would not allow this, insisting that they search until they found someone who could give them news. And, after a deal of enquiry and false trails, they came upon Thomas Carter. He was able to tell them what had happened, details which he omitted filled in by the players who were still dazed by the shock under which all were reeling.

"Ah, my dear, our Prince did not give in readily. When he had hidden for a while, he rounded up such fellows as he could find unparalyzed with panic and led them to where narrow lanes afforded the only approach to York. He lined the hedges, and fired so fiercely upon the pursuers, that even Cromwell stopped and called them off. He was one of the last to get back here, dropping in with his weary officers about eleven at night."

Venetia was hunched up, rocking in misery. "Oh, if we'd only left sooner, I should not have missed him."

"Sometime during the turmoil of that night, Rupert, King and Newcastle came face to face and warm words were exchanged," Carter continued, and Venetia could well picture the scene. Warm words! Surely this must be the understatement of the year!

"General King asked him what he intended to do, and the Prince made answer: 'I will rally my men.' "

The tired faces lit up, they nodded their approval of this stout reply, and Carter's voice strengthened as he went on:

"Then the General says, 'Know you what Lord Newcastle will do?', and the Marquis himself replies, 'I will go to Holland,' looking upon all as lost. The Prince would have him endeavor to recruit his forces, but, 'No,' says he, 'I will not endure the laughter of the Court.' King was determined to go with him, though Rupert tried vainly to detain them and, in the end, he let them depart, wasting no more time, but he was very angry."

"As he had every right to be!" blazed Venetia. How unfair of the Marquis to run away, leaving all the onus of failure on Rupert, as well as the heavy work of re-organizing his shattered forces for their dangerous march south.

She jumped to her feet. "I must go to him."

Carter reached out a hand to clasp one of hers. "My dear, wait for us. We but delayed to arrange your brother's funeral. As soon as Meriel is fit to travel, we shall follow the army."

Jonathan had died in the coach before they reached York, and now Venetia mounted the wooden staircase to find his mistress and try to bring consolation. But it was Meriel who comforted her when grief surged up in an uncontrollable torrent and she cried until it seemed that there could be no more tears left within her.

At last utterly spent, the two women huddled together for a long time and then Meriel stirred. "I must go and help father. He gets into such a wax if I'm not there to sort things out. We'll be away from here by nightfall. Will you come with me and see Jonathan's grave before we leave?"

They managed to find a few flowers and took them to that new mound of earth in a secluded corner of the churchyard.

"We buried his sword with him," said Meriel softly. "Laying it on top of his coffin."

"We won't forget you, Jonathan," whispered Venetia, kneeling on the turf, the soil fine and warm under her hand. "When the war is over, we'll come back and fix a headstone, I promise."

Meriel's touch was gentle on her bowed shoulder. "He is not there, Venetia. 'Tis but a husk which lies rotting beneath the earth. It was selfish of me to grieve for him, this only made him sad and held him fast to those poor remains, but now he is free to come and go at will, like that bird there."

She pointed to where a skylark was soaring, high in the

blue vault above, its joyous notes barely descernable to their ears. But Michael's eyes were still on his friend's last resting-place and he said quietly:

> "Oh, blessed Peace!
> to thy soft arms through death
> itself we flee;
> Battles and camps and fields
> and victory
> are but the rugged steps
> that lead to thee!"

And they turned their backs on York and its unhappy memories, setting out in search of the Prince.

Cavalier

ONE

There had been talk of Rupert making for Richmond so the players took that road on the off-chance, and days of frustration followed; whenever they arrived at a place where he was said to be, it was to find that they had just missed him. Venetia was eating her heart out, growing thin and wan, unable to sleep, impatient with any activity not directly concerned with bridging the weary miles. They met up with stragglers on the way, and she realized that she had been lucky to fall in with Carter in the confusion; Etienne, Damaris and Mallory had departed with the Prince, leaving the actor detailed to search for her.

At Chester, Venetia sought out Will Legge, temporary Governor. His mournful face did nothing to allay her fears.

"His Highness is taking all the blame for the rout on himself. The disaster has cut him to the heart, but you know how proud he is, he'll speak no word of self-justification."

He told her that Rupert was already recruiting again and building up a new train of artillery. He had marched back to Shrewsbury and his own headquarters.

At last, the weary little procession plodded into Shrewsbury and reached the house of Mr. Jones with the Palatine colors floating over the chimney-pots.

In the hall she ran into Barney whose eyes widened in delighted astonishment and relief. "Venetia! Thank God! We thought you dead!"

"Where is he?"

"The Prince?" A shadow crossed his face. "Inside a bottle!"

"Drinking? Rupert?" Aghast, she made for the stairs while Michael watched her wistfully, her dear companion on the journey whom she had already forgotten.

Holmes was outside the door of the bedchamber, and,

when he had greeted her warmly, he hesitated: "He's given orders not to be disturbed."

"God dammit, man, stop tiptoeing around!" She was furious at any further obstruction. "That is more than half the trouble—every one is so afraid to cross him!"

She flung open the door and was over the threshold before he could stop her. A girl was standing in the middle of the floor, skirts hitched up, fastening her garters. She shot Venetia a defiant stare, giving a toss of her tangled locks. Venetia recognized her; she was one of the camp harlots.

One quick glance round the room showed Rupert sprawled across the bed, asleep or dead drunk. Murderous rage swelled to a crescendo in Venetia's head. "Get out!" she yelled.

"I want my money." The whore flung out an arm with dirt-seamed palm extended.

"Money!" The scorn in Venetia's eyes should have blasted her to dust. "You demand money for letting the Prince swive you? My God, if he was in his right mind, d'you think he'd have a creature like you in the same room?"

The woman paced slowly towards her, and her mouth was twisted in a cynical smile. "And what is so special about him, I'd like to know? He sent for me, and then acted as if I didn't exist! I've been better served by a crookbacked beggar than your famous Prince! Swive me, quoth you! He was so bloody drunk, he couldn't do anything!"

Relief made Venetia weak in the knees, her only thought to get rid of the wench. She fumbled in her purse, throwing over a coin. The whore caught it expertly, bit down on it, and then tucked it between her breasts. She sauntered to the door.

"I wish you better luck with him, deary. Prince Rupert indeed—" she jibed, making her exit. "Fine stallion he turned out to be!"

No time now to be hurt because he had wanted a woman, any woman, in his hopelessness. The room smelled foul and Venetia went to the window, opening the casement. Holmes was behind her, very apologetic.

" 'Tis the first time one of those trulls has been here, madam. I swear it. He thought you were lost, you see. I'll vow that what she said was true and that he did not touch her. He is in no fit state."

"Thank you, Holmes." Venetia was grateful for his kindness, his concern, and his excuses.

The Prince was flat on his back, arms wide. Venetia leaned over him in anxiety and despair. His face was sallow, eyes glittering through narrow slits, mouth open as he breathed deeply, a trickle of saliva on his unshaven chin, a pool of dried vomit under his head.

Angrily, she seized him by the shoulder. He blasphemed in some unknown tongue and shook off her hand.

"Rupert! Wake up!" she shouted, continuing to punch him, beginning to sob.

His eyes opened, red-rimmed, bloodshot, sunk in muddy circles. "Go to hell, slut!" he snarled, taking her for the harlot. His speech was slurred, heavily accented; in drink, as in passion, he lost his hold on the English language.

"There is naught to be done with him, madam." Holmes was standing nervously at her side, nearly as distressed as she. "Leave him to sleep."

"Well, help me move him over. We can at least spread on fresh sheets and get him into a clean shirt."

This they accomplished with some difficulty, and then Venetia washed Rupert's hands and his unconscious face, tried to untangle the spew from his hair while he tossed and complained. She understood only too well why he was acting in a manner so strangely unlike himself. It was the shock of Marston Moor. That massive failure had hurled him from the heights of success into the abyss of humiliation.

Venetia dozed, her head on her outspread arms. She had only to lift her hand to be able to touch him and peace, such as she had not experienced since they had parted in that grim hour of battle, lapped over her. De Faust came in to light candles, moving with exaggerated quietness, as if someone had just died. Venetia lay on the bed beside the Prince, her arm across his chest, uneasily aware that there was something missing—it was the weight of Boye at their feet.

She was awakened by Rupert struggling to sit up and the sound of his retching. She ran for the chamber-pot and was in time to thrust it under his chin. He was violently sick, and then lay back groaning. Venetia reached across to wipe the sweat from his face and he looked directly at her. His glazed eyes open in wonder.

"Venetia! *Liebling,* is it really you? I had to leave— could not wait to search for you——"

"That is all right, darling, I understand," she assured him gently. He had been blamed enough for everything that had gone wrong. She would not add to his cares.

He was mumbling something incomprehensible under his breath, almost asleep again, then he suddenly said clearly: "Boye is dead."

In that awful accumulation of anger, disaster and shame, one thought had been reeling over and over in his agony of mind—"Boye is dead." That good friend, companion of six years, unquestioning, ever loyal. Rupert had forgotten to tie him up so that he could not follow him into the heat of battle.

He was shivering now, clinging to her and she began to stroke his forehead, his shoulders and back, murmuring pet names and endearments.

He needed tactile contact so desperately, this being who hid his innate reserve and sensitivity behind a mask of dismissive hauteur, the lesson learned in infancy when he had been thrust away from his mother, not cruelly, just carelessly and too early. He had been suckled by wet-nurses, not at the breast of the Winter Queen who could not spare time from more interesting pursuits among her hounds and thoroughbreds to bestow this benediction on her children. That strict upbringing in the care of tutors, entering university at ten, already familiar with the pikemen's eighteen postures and the musketeer's thirty-four, followed by the tough army discipline, war, prison and more war. No chance to let up, to be weak— to cry sometimes, when he was hurt.

Now he poured out all the bitterness of the past months which had culminated at Marston Moor. He did not need the jeers of his enemies to convince him of his defeat. His projects crossed, his work unavailing, and, in his heart, he was sure that his uncle's cause was doomed.

How different from the indomitable Commander, this heart-broken boy who, stripped of his pride, still young enough to be wounded by the venom of his enemies and the injustice of his friends, wept wildly until, exhausted, he slept at last, his head pillowed on Venetia's breasts, the tears tanging his lashes.

Now that his nephew had taken a beating, Charles was more kindly disposed towards him, and the Courtiers feared him less and stopped tainting the King's mind against him. They had troubles of their own. The intrigues in the army continued; General Goring's new prominence and importance was one among the many unfortunate results of Marston Moor. He had played a gallant part in the battle, fighting drunk, recklessly brave, and was going around bragging of his share in it. Digby was only too happy to join with him in ignoring the Prince's gallantry, dwelling only on his defeat. Another person whom they were determined to ruin was Harry Wilmot.

The crisis came when Wilmot married a wealthy widow with relatives who were Parliamentarians and laid himself open to a charge of treason. King Charles had been quietly contemplating his removal from command for some time.

"Goring keeps me informed of what is happening," Rupert was going through his mail and bringing Venetia up to date with news at the same time. "He amuses himself by writing to me in terms of passionate devotion, while conniving with Digby to strip me of everything. Now, it seems, they are united in their efforts to get rid of Wilmot. No doubt they will implicate me, so that I can be blamed."

Venetia remembered Harry Wilmot very well, a less fascinating, more unprinciples person than Goring. Like him, he was a hard drinker, but not to the detriment of his military duties, and with the dissolute wits of the army he was exceedingly popular. Rupert, usually so temperate himself, had no sympathy for the failings of either of them. The seeds of his dislike stretched back to the Netherland campaigns, blossoming into detestation at Edgehill where Wilmot had refused to make a second charge, with the frivolous comment that, having won the day, they might as well live to enjoy the fruits of victory.

As the Prince had anticipated, Wilmot told everyone that it was Rupert's doing, although he was miles away when the blow fell. Goring was given the treacherous General's command. And Rupert when he heard of it, just laughed. He laughed at everything these days, when he was sober enough to take it in.

In a mood of black depression, he roamed the Welsh Marches with his cavalry, looking for men to swell the ranks, dispatching them to Shrewsbury. Venetia went with him always, clad in man's clothing, sharing his lot. Most onlookers thought her a junior member of staff, or, if they suspected differently, they were prudent enough to keep their opinions to themselves.

In London, there were uneasy speculations as to his possible next move. Would he break out toward the North, or strike across the Midlands? He did neither—with a small force, he rode down the Welsh border, forded the Severn, and made for Bristol.

This was his own city, he was still Governor, though several had served as his deputy, and he was greeted enthusiastically. But if this was calculated to lift his spirits, the news which awaited him at headquarters did nothing but pull him up short.

Venetia, giving orders to the servants for the disposal of their baggage, took one look at his face when he stormed into the room, and waited for the blast.

Rogue! Turd-colored dog!" His voice set the goblets rattling.

Without speaking, she speculated on who, out of a dozen possible persons, this might be.

"Charles Louis is in England again. Rooms have been made ready for him in our uncle's own palace at Whitehall. It would seem that Parliament favor the idea of joining with the Scots to put him forward as a candidate for the throne! God, I'd like to get my hands on him!"

This could not have happened at a worse time; there were plans afoot to make Rupert supreme Commander-in-Chief, as soon as Lord Forth could be honorably retired. The Elector's arrival would call a halt to this and, sure enough, a letter came from Charles conveying discreetly that he could hardly appoint Rupert to such a high position when, at any time, his brother might be set up for King in London.

The Prince cursed Charles Louis to hell, then ordered a couple of horses to be saddled and took Venetia down to the quay where often, nowadays, he idled in the dingy taverns.

He got on well with seamen, conversing with them in a multitude of tongues. Venetia could almost imagine that they were seated in the great-cabin of some pirate galleon; Rupert, so swart and tanned, his hair tossed in disarray, his smoldering eyes, curved nose, all the fine arrogance of him, suggesting an untamed corsair captain giving orders to his ruffianly crew.

The sailors, recognizing a brother-adventurer, wove a verbal tapestry, telling of heavenly islands, remarkable beasts, and fabulous wealth to be found overseas. He nodded and smiled lazily, inhaling deeply of their tobacco, liberally spiked with potent herbs from Arabia which burned with a sweet smell, like autumn couch-fires, having the power to bring about a merciful state of release. Rupert's eyes glittered while he talked, and Venetia was dazzled by the revelation of his words.

He was highly intelligent, immensely talented and well educated—she listened, spellbound, while his thoughts expanded as the hashish instilled itself into his blood. Here was no mere *sabreur*—no thick-witted trooper—but a bright intellect which now displayed its inventive skill and limitless curiosity. He was fascinated by the challenge of opening up new continents—of building a ship which could move beneath the water (someone had already shown him the plans for such a one)—and the proposition of that far-sighted artist, Leonardo da Vinci, for the construction of a heavily-armored vehicle, which would roll on many wheels over the roughest terrain.

When speech proved inadequate, he pulled out his pocketbook, sketching diagrams to illustrate his own ideas for a repeater pistol, doing away with the laborious business of reloading every time. Venetia hoped fervently that this would not be developed, knowing how often Rupert's life had been saved through the misfiring of the existing clumsy weapons.

The night deepened around them, the noisy, crowded tavern with its thick foggy atmosphere, proved no barrier to his imagination which streaked ahead to the outer reaches of the Universe. The mariners scoffed, but he was very serious as he discussed the incredible notion of a machine capable of carrying men through the air—even to the planets! It was easy enough for Venetia to visualize him leading an expedition to the moon!

Hours later in their bedchamber, she alternated between blissful drowsiness and a sharp, unnatural awareness. She could do as she willed with Rupert's body—it was hers, a beautiful plaything—his mind God, and his own devils, only knew where, freed to roam boundless regions in pursuit of visions.

Venetia lay at his side in the light of the guttering candles, marvelling at the perfection of this creature, made up of muscle, flesh and bone, welded by some strange alchemy into a being of magnetism and high-powered personality, who had the right to command her for ever. She wanted to fall on her knees and worship him, every facet of his diverse nature worthy of adoration.

She told him so, over and over, unsure if he even heard, lost in his own fantasy world, while she ran her kisses over his ears, his face, his hands and his body. Her tongue circled his navel—this was where the umbilical cord had bonded him to that celebrated dam. He had been in her womb when she was crowned in Prague—for his sake the ceremony had been curtailed—typically, he had made his presence felt even before birth.

Venetia sobbed, tears dripping on to the black hair of his belly, wanting to be his mother, to suffer pangs to bring him forth, to nourish him at her breast—or to become the well-loved Maurice—or that soul-mate artist, sister Louise—above all she yearned to be Rupert himself. Had she been born male, she would wish for nothing but to resemble him exactly, in every way.

While she was still trying to piece together this jigsaw paradox of need, an unbidden surge of joy swooped over her because she was his mistress, able to know an intimacy which the envied others could never share.

Filled with an overwhelming sense of power, she lipped his skin, her mouth closing over him, dragging his spirit back from the shimmering spaces of widening experience to the physical ecstasy of the body, bringing him to the edge again and again, then carefully holding off, just before the tension became too great, hearing the heavy thud of his heart, the slow gasps of his breathing, feeling his frame shudder and buck, till that final moment when, for an instant, flesh, soul and mind were fused in a blaze of pure sensation. At that point in time, Rupert belonged to her, utterly dependent, wanting to think of nothing, to know nothing—denying all save drugged dreams and sexual gratification.

The strain under which he had worked for over two years suddenly relaxed. He who had looked upon an hour of lolling as a time-wasting, if not downright mind-destroying indulgence, now took his full share, sunk in apathy, his usual vigilance grown careless, the rigid self-restraint given over to sensuality.

They went to bed early and got up late; there were days they did not bother to leave their room. He continued to drink hard and Venetia made certain that he never drank alone; it was her avowed intention to share in his every experience, no matter how degrading.

Sometimes they were joined by Damaris with one of her current paramours, and then, lying in the Prince's arms while he fondled her sleepily, she knew the vicarious pleasure of watching another couple making love. But, above all, she preferred to be completely alone with him, isolated in their ivory tower.

And Arthur Trevor, that loyal, impartial secretary who forgave much and would never speak ill of his master, voiced the dismay of all the more sober-minded Cavaliers, lamenting in his letters to Ormonde in Ireland: "Prince Rupert is so much given to his ease and pleasure that everyone is disheartened that sees it. The city of Bristol is but one great house of bawdry, and will ruin the King; and by all that I see, Prince Rupert is resolved to lie by it."

Will Legge was on his way. Very early on the morning of the day in which he was due in Bristol, Rupert got up, went out into the yard, and stuck his head under the pump.

Venetia, peering from the window, saw the water cascading over his hair, heard him shouting and swearing at the icy shock, while Holmes, grinning with delight and relief, vigorously applied himself to the handle. She knew that the awful, wonderful period was at an end.

The Prince's spirit burned with too bright a flame to be quenched, and the deep unshaken faith of such friends as Will and Richmond managed to convince him that the King still needed him. A new Rupert emerged from the crisis, more controlled, guarded, cynical and cool.

He had met his match in Cromwell. "Old Ironsides," as he had nicknamed him at Marston Moor, finding an opponent worthy of him and watching his movements closely. It was vital to understand this man who had risen rapidly through the ranks, grasping military principles with astonishing speed for a civilian, developing a charisma almost equal to Rupert's own, that mysterious power to turn raw recruits into first-rate, enthusiastic soldiers.

Because she had spoken with him, Rupert questioned Venetia keenly and his countenance was murderous when she haltingly described her treatment by the Roundheads.

King Charles had spent the summer traversing the West Country, chasing and beating Lord Essex and now, heartened by that endearing optimism of Digby, he was advancing from Devonshire into Dorset, once again confident in his ability to deal with the rest of the rebels. And that gay, good-for-nothing Secretary of State, blithely ignoring news which would have oppressed a less buoyant individual, continued to send chirpy missives to all and sundry, full of sugared thoughts and hopeful suppositions —"God hath blessed his Majesty's affairs even to a miracle. . . . We are now marching eastward, victorious and strong. . . ."

Rupert roused himself and rode to meet his uncle at Sherbourne. Venetia stayed in Bristol; they had a tacit agreement that she must never flaunt her relationship with the Prince in the King's vicinity, also she was sensitive to his need to stand on his own feet once more, to lead out his troops, with the chance of fighting ahead.

His consultation with the King was brief, within a week he was back in Bristol and Venetia's welcome was arrested on her lips by the extraordinary spectacle of Lord Digby riding on his right hand as if he were a lifelong companion. When Rupert pulled her into his arms for the greeting kiss, he muttered his instructions that she was to be civil to him.

Strange days followed, with Rupert actively engaged in preparing his men and planning to meet up with Sir Marmaduke Langdale and General Gerard, and Digby dancing attendance, so suave that butter would not have melted in his mouth!

When they met, which was usually at supper, Rupert would slump in his chair, far down on his spine, legs stretched out under the table, a brandy goblet between his hands, watching Digby unblinkingly, making little comment on the Secretary's fanciful absurdities.

Digby had a fine flow of eloquence and a finished grace of delivery. He laid prime stress on witty conversational ease, delivering his thrusts with skill and rapier-like precision.

Seeing them together, it was easy to understand their enmity—the Prince had no time for Digby's foppish pose, which veiled a deadly drive, ambition and ego; a most dangerous man, very willing to undertake everything, but unable to carry out the smallest part of that which he took on so airily.

He smiled demurely when asked how matters stood with the Western Army, exaggerating their success, minimizing their difficulties, and there was much to relate— the King's flight from Oxford and subsequent wanderings, his defeat of Waller at Cropredy Bridge and Essex at Lostwithiel. Digby's gushing phrases gave way to genuine admiration as he described the assured manner in which Charles had conducted the campaign. Their Sovereign had become their Generalissimo in the full sense of the word, controlling the whole wide-flung front, his studious, cautious disposition, his dignity and energy, ensuring an unusual harmony, no easy feat with this factious, over-officered army.

Venetia pondered on Digby's bland affability and just why Rupert was being so tolerant. It was an obvious strain, the claws sheathed, the fangs covered by tight-lipped smiles. On the surface the Prince was making a mighty effort not to fall out with the Secretary for the sake of his uncle, but she suspected that, as it was becoming apparent that no one was going to offer the Elector the Crown, he was playing the Courtier, and cultivating Digby for the purpose of removing Lord Forth.

There was nothing he wanted so passionately as to be appointed Commander-in-Chief; only then would he have any hope of mobilizing the scattered Royalist forces into a cohesive body strong enough to face the ever increasing might of the Roundheads.

"And I wish them joy of Charles Louis," Rupert had spoken contemptuously when it was confirmed that his thick-skinned, opportunist brother had settled down in London to live comfortably at the Parliament's expense. "Let them keep him! He'll cost them a pretty penny!"

Digby re-joined the King while Rupert was still not ready. Although Charles had promised to wait for the Prince, he decided to hasten on without him, persuaded by Goring, who had no desire to share his present glory, thoroughly enjoying himself skirmishing with Waller.

Digby, effusive and sparkling, bore the glad news of victory which came from all sides, to his Royal master, and the King, hourly expecting the arrival of Rupert, occupied Newbury. Within days, Manchester, Waller and Essex converged on them, and the King's men were once more engaged in battle.

The Prince got his army on the march, arriving at Marshfield the day after the battle. He was met by a galloper bearing tidings that the King had been defeated, and had retired to Bath. This blow was capped by the rumor that Maurice was dead or a prisoner.

"No!" Rupert's voice cracked out, startling his adjutants

who were standing in an unhappy group about him, deflated by the news. "He is perfectly well."

Rupert possessed an uncanny awareness of anything concerning his brother, and had been proved right before; Venetia accepted this—it was how she felt about *him*—it was as if the sun would go out, or her own heart cease to beat, if he died.

Of course, he was right—it was a little galling how he so often was—when they rode down into Bath, tucked into its misty bowl between surrounding hills, it was to find Maurice with the King, sharing the apartment kept for visiting members of the Royal family above the West Gate, overlooking the meadows toward Bristol.

Although she wanted his happiness more than anything on earth, it was with mixed feelings that she saw the brothers together again. That Prince, born in the chilly castle of Cüstrin to a refugee Queen, was a shadow of the remarkable child who had made appropriately dashing entry into the world in Prague, a year earlier, six weeks after Elizabeth's coronation.

Unobserved, because they were so absorbed in each other, Venetia looked from one handsome face to the other—she could have fallen in love with Maurice if Rupert had not been there to eclipse him. There was a charming diffidence about him; he was a much less complex person, happy to share the limelight without being the center of it, shy, awkward, often underestimating his own abilities, limiting his performance, blinded by the brilliance of his brother.

At first, they were lost for words, and then Maurice's eyes grew anxious as they searched Rupert's face, noting the new lines of strain, while the Palsgrave was equally concerned because Maurice was still pale from the recurrent attacks of fever which dogged him.

The King enjoyed a brief respite in the company of his heir, and the sons of his only sister, whom he had not seen since 1613, when, as a bride of sixteen, she had embarked for her new home in Heidelberg. He reflected that it would have been as well if she had been contented to remain the Princess Palatine, instead of ambitiously driving her adoring husband into risking all in a throw for the crown of Bohemia.

In many ways she resembled his beloved Henrietta Maria, who had been forced to run from Exeter in July, leaving behind her fortnight-old daughter. Disguised as a peasant woman, relentlessly hounded by Essex, she had made her way to the coast and escaped to France.

For a moment Charles could pretend that the war did not exist, lingering over the meal, so different from the snatched, indigestible fare which had been his diet too often lately. His hesitant, precise voice was extolling the virtues of the medicinal springs of Bath.

"And now other visitors take the waters," he remarked slowly, "to cure wounds, instead of aching limbs."

Maurice and Rupert exchanged a glance, but managed to keep their patience with this exasperating little man (their mother had often referred to him as "Baby Charles") who could blather on about non-essentials when there were so many vital issues at stake. Yet his worn, tired face wrung their hearts, making them want to leap up and clout someone over the head, much as he might infuriate them with his endless prevarications.

He was always so correct, with his quiet attention, his polite denials—"By your favor, I think otherwise," never descending to arguing, merely giving a mild rebuke—"Sir, I am not of your opinion." Weighted by his stammer, such reproofs reduced everyone to an uneasy silence, squashing any opposition—with the exception of Rupert's.

But at last: "Sir, we should go back to Oxford." The Prince broke across the ripple of polite conversation.

The King looked along the table at him. "This was indeed our plan. But we had hoped to bring relief to our brave garrisons first." He touched his lips with a lawn kerchief.

"We should have made a better showing at Newbury had Your Highness but followed the King's summons to make haste," reminded Digby unnecessarily. In the company of Charles, he found it almost impossible to keep up pretences, resenting anyone whose opinion to the Soverign might value above his own.

There was a fraught silence. Rupert's face darkened. "I made all possible speed, my Lord. There was much work to do."

The damask cloth stretched like a snowy plain between them, the cutlery, the silver plate, slender-stemmed wine-glasses and squat decanters, parading down its length like a well-drilled regiment.

"It was rumored that Your Highness was not aways engaged in arduous duties." Digby's eyes were wide and guileless. "And I gave answer to such defamatory talk, saying, why should you not take your ease? Was there any other who had given of himself so unstintingly? 'Twas only just that you should seek enjoyment, though your manner of so doing might alarm some."

Goring, leaning on a lazy elbow, watched them with amusement from under his slack lids. Maurice, as usual, going that bit too far, was very haughty, staring down his nose at the Secretary with open animosity.

"My Lord, you should not have concerned yourself in my defence." Rupert's sarcasm coiled round the softly-lit chamber, smooth and menacing. "It would have been more to His Majesty's service, had you spent your time dealing with that double traitor, Urry, who gave the Roundheads intelligence of your movements."

King Charles passed a hand wearily across his eyes. Loud, angry voices distressed him. "Nephew, let us talk of your promotion," he said placatingly. "This must be done as soon as we enter Oxford."

"All the more reason for going at once, sir." Prince Charles beamed across at his hero, unswervingly in his loyalty in spite of the varying influences which boiled about him. He had been with the King for most of the summer, at Newbury fight, and in this latest fifty-mile trek to Bath.

Goring winked at him broadly, raising his glass. To the boy, he was a dashing attractive figure, fun to be with, and he flattered and amused him, treating him in a delightful man to man fashion, making light of heroics when they became boring, exciting him with his talk of women.

The King turned to his son, a smile lighting up his features. "You are right, Charles," he patted him on the shoulder. "We shall repair to our loyal city without delay."

"And may I propose a toast, sire, to cheer us on our journey!" Goring leapt to his feet, drink held high. "To the damnation of Essex, head and horns!"

The Princes came to bed late, bearing bottles and tankards and settling themselves by the fire, while the logs burned low, the level in the decanters sank, and they talked as if they would never stop.

Venetia sat at Rupert's feet, wrestling with that hot, heavy lump of jealousy which weighed her heart. They were having a post-mortem on every battle (Marston Moor in great detail), each skirmish was re-enacted, each siege examined in depth. But at least they were speaking English, and, astoundingly, Rupert included her once or twice, actually asking her opinion! She was pleased to find that Maurice remembered her, but even this was soured by his expression of surprise that she still interested his brother.

From the war, they progressed to their family. Charles Louis' character was dissected, found to be faulty, and cast aside. Maurice leaned forward to light a spill and then touch it to their pipes. Venetia leaned her head back against Rupert's knee. He absent-mindedly stroked over her hair, in the same way as he used to play with Boye's ears! Then Maurice gave a cracking yawn and Rupert, all concern, remembering that he had so recently been ill, hustled him off to bed. Venetia was relieved, wanting to re-establish her own part in Rupert's affections, but it was not to be; Damaris would wait in vain for Maurice that night.

The Prince rolled out the truckle from under the four-poster, hauled off half their blankets and would not be satisfied until Maurice was comfortably settled.

She drew the curtain with a sharp indignant swish, jerking the rings along the poles, tossing off her clothes behind them. Still the deep voices boomed on, but now, maddeningly, they were discoursing in French. Some of it she could comprehend; living with Rupert it was almost impossible not to pick up a smattering of different tongues, though most of what she had learned had been curse-words, or love-phrases.

She was more than half asleep, cross and unhappy, when the Prince came to bed, but even then he did no more than twine his fingers with hers, freeing himself suddenly to rear up on one elbow, poke his head out through the hangings and make yet another point.

Venetia retaliated by tugging at the inadequate bed-clothes, miserably sure that she was in for a cold, restless night. Rupert stretched on his back with a deep contented sigh; she listened to the twin breathing becoming more regular, and knew that the brothers had succeeded in leaving her isolated in the darkness—they were both sound asleep.

TWO

"Ale, madame?" Pierre put down two mugs on the scarred table-top and filled them from a pitcher; golden-brown, it frothed out like a rain-swollen stream, sharp and strong to the tongue, making Venetia shudder, much richer than that brewed at home. Pierre popped a glistening pearl onion into his mouth, crunching happily. Venetia declined the offer, not wishing to taint her breath.

That morning, on Bullingdon Green, the King had reviewed his reassembled army, and proclaimed the appointment of Prince Rupert as Generalissimo and, at the same time, he had been elevated to one of the most important places about the Royal household, that of Master of the Horse. Venetia had been glad to be under cover in Damaris' coach, for it was a gray November day, with lowering clouds which threatened rain, and a biting wind which scudded through the Oxford streets. She had come home early, eager to go to the kitchen where Pierre was preparing a celebration dinner, a surprise party for the Prince.

Pierre would not let her have a hand in it, and she had to content herself with watching him work. He resembled a sack of turnips himself, a shapeless man, his apron covered with food stains, grease, blood and powdery icing sugar, his hairy forearms dusted with flower. He had the spatulate hands of a butcher, yet no one could refute that he made the most delicate pastries, fairy-like spires of frosting, masterpieces of confectionery.

Venetia was no mean cook herself and they exchanged recipes, both deploring Rupert's seeming indifference to the refinements of elegant cuisine. They decided that his palate had been ruined by years of army fare, coupled with the poverty of his mother's palaces, where the staff were rarely paid, and they existed on the goodwill and patience of the Dutch merchants.

All through that trying autumn, Pierre's attitude toward her had not altered; if anything, it had grown warmer. With his unspoken sympathy for Jonathan, and a sorrowful shake of the head over Boye, he had let her know, diplomatically, that the "family" appreciated her support of the Palsgrave. She had become accepted as one of them. To prove this, he let her into his closely guarded secret of creating creamy omelettes, frothy and rich, just crisping at the edges and garnished with a whisper of Parmesan cheese.

"Thank God we are back in civilization, madame," he commented. "Those addle-pated dolts in the West, and the diabolical Welsh!"

It was difficult to keep the domestic side of Rupert's household running with any degree of predictability, constantly disorganized by his erratic wanderings. The locals, called in to help, could not grasp the finer points and, consequently, all his regular staff were promoted to posts of extra responsibility. This went to their heads and they tyrannized over the common rabble.

"Barbarians——" Pierre continued, champing away on a handful of raisins. "They failed to understand why I would not have the farm animals and chickens in my kitchen. And their little children!—they always seemed to bring a horde with 'em, all without drawers and untrained! The mothers were most offended because I grumbled and made them clean up when these brats soiled my clean floors!"

His hands became delicate birds, hovering over a thick slab of pastry. He rolled, patted, shaped and then asked: "How did he look?"

"Magnificent!" Venetia's breath came out on a sigh.

Pierre snorted down his nose, satisfied, taking up a sharp knife and cutting the flat white carpet of paste into petals. "Ah, madame what it is to be in love!"

"You should have seen him, Pierre!" and she could say no more for the tightness in her throat, remembering him this day and how he had been—back in Bristol.

The quick-thinking Rupert had seen the sense of Digby's hint that it might be prudent to make Prince Charles Commander-in-Chief, with himself as Lieutenant-General, less it should appear that he was aggregating too much power.

"A shrewd move, madame." Pierre nodded approvingly. "Though no doubt suggested by my Lord Digby to keep a curb on the *Pfalzgraf's* supremacy."

Head on one side, he was considering the blue glazed platter, nearly hidden beneath rosettes of transparently thin ham, rings of sliced, hard-boiled eggs, verdant parsley sprigs and papery slivers of onion. He turned his attention to the side of beef which an admirer of Rupert had donated.

"It is high time there was a change. How the King tolerated Lord Forth for so long remains a mystery. Oh, don't mistake me, madame, he is a man of unquestionable courage and integrity, but getting too old—and failing after years of immoderate drinking—a habit, madame, which I can never understand. More ale?"

He rapped out a sharp command, a boy got busy with the bellows, and there was the rattle of jack-chains. Pierre drove skewers through the massive joint with the ease of a hot knife slicing butter. Then he took up a cloth and drew out a tray of crusty rolls from the bakeoven at the side of the hearth, deftly splitting one open, a mouth-watering smell twirling up with the steam from its moist interior. When he handed it to Venetia, yellow rivulets melted and dripped on to her fingers.

She chewed and mused and put her thoughts into words. "Oh course, the soldiers are delighted about it, but I'll wager it will be exceedingly unpopular with the Courtiers."

"Pah! Courtiers!" Pierre slung the beef on a massive hook suspended on the spit, placing a copper pan to catch the juices as they ran out. "I've seen them come and go. Lord Wilmot now, taken boat to France——"

"Where, doubtless, he will be telling tales to Queen Henrietta about the Prince, adding his spite to that of Newcastle and King." Venetia knew that Wilmot had directed his animus against Rupert, and he would be supported by his friend Percy, who, implicated in his disgrace, had resigned. Lord Hopton had been given his job in charge of the Ordnance which might mean that Rupert would get his supplies with less arguing and loss of temper all round.

"And you, madame," Pierre fixed her with a steady look. "When are you going to present His Highness with a little princeling, eh?"

She shook her head regretfully, wondering this herself for some time now, longing for it to happen.

Pierre screwed up his round face, eyes almost disappearing into the folds of his cheeks. "So? No signs of motherhood yet? I shall have to concoct one of my special dishes for you. In the past, they have proved mighty beneficial in these cases. In fact, my posset, especially brewed as a bridal-night cup, has been ordered by some of the best families in Europe. It never fails. A bowlful of this, containing all the ingredients to ensure that you have a boy, and a bedtime drink for the *Pfazgraf*, and very soon you will be running down to tell me that his physicians have pronounced you *enceinte*. This will be good for His Highness, every man should have a son, and, as yet, he has fathered no child."

This was exactly what she wanted to hear but, "How can you be sure of that?" she insisted.

He tapped the side of his nose sagely. "Word would have reached me!"

This she could believe, his efficient grapevine among the servants would have done credit to the rather muddled intelligence system of the army.

From somewhere in the depths of her being Venetia was now forced to draw on reserves of patience which amazed her; she had no idea that she possessed such fortitude. Nothing to be gained and much lost if she yielded to the temptation to stamp and yell and storm in tearful rage when Rupert left her behind, accompanied always by Maurice, on the exploits which occupied them in the weeks before Christmas. She was able to tell him goodbye calmly, lovingly—even to wish Maurice well, instead of six feet underground!

It was only after they had taken their exuberant departure with their Lifeguard, that maddeningly exclusive masculine coterie, that she could let go, flinging herself across Damaris' lap, scattering that amiable courtesan's bobbins, silks and bits of embroidery, and into her arms where she could cry freely and rant about the injustice of life, with the clash of hooves, the triumphant war-cries, echoing on the breeze to mock her.

Winter closed in; snow blanketed most of war-ravaged England, and both sides welcomed the respite. Loyal households began their preparation for Christmas. Venetia was more than ever thankful that she did not live in dismal Puritan London where jollifications had been banned; even with all the tribulations of wartime, in the Royalist great houses and at the Court, the Lord of Misrule still reigned triumphant at this season.

She longed to see her little brothers and sisters again,

and spent a lot of time wrapping gifts in colorful, crackly paper—whips and tops, rag-dolls, wooden horses, hoops, a coral and ivory teething-ring for the baby. Pierre allowed her to spend one blissfully sticky day making toffee, gingerbread and marchpane, unable to resist the challenge and himself producing the most exotic sweetmeats which were duly boxed, ready for delivery to the young Denbys.

Nowhere was Christmas celebrated in such fine style as at the house of the Chevalier. He held a party on the Feast of Lights Day, when every window shone like a beacon with a multitude of candles. The Murmurs came stamping in from the frosty night in their masks and strange costumes, to caper and dance and act out their ancient ritual play of death and resurrection. The Yule-log was dragged across the hall and ceremonially lit, amidst cheers and singing.

The evening grew late, and an air of *bonhomie* prevailed. Venetia leaned against the back of the settle, Rupert's arm about her shoulders, laughing and listening to the others capping verses, or making up anagrams out of each other's names, none of them flattering.

This new confidence in her hold over the Prince was like a heady wine; she was recognized as someone of importance, respected, courted even, by those who desired some favor from him. And though the women were fascinated by him, he was rather an alarming person, likely to lash out with his withering sarcasm. Maurice got on much better with ladies of all ages, they were captivated by his school-boyish charm, his quick flush and shy smile, his habit of clapping himself on the brow when at a loss for the right English phrase, which always made them rush to his aid, enchanted by his accent.

Damaris was being possessive, keeping him at her side as she announced; "Draw closer to the fire everyone. Meriel has promised to tell fortunes, this being the season for such mysteries."

A sudden shiver gave Venetia goose-pimples, though she smiled and exclaimed as brightly as any among that interested circle. Pictures of the dying Jonathan flashed through her mind and, more horrible, the face of the murdered Giles, as in the darkness of night when she clutched Rupert in a paroxysm of fear, sure that he was haunting her for having sent him into eternity without preparation.

"Come, let her read your future first, Rupert," urged Maurice.

Meriel had altered since Marston Moor, becoming fine-drawn and serene. She had immersed herself in the life of the theater, spending her time studying plays. Listening to her when she sometimes read aloud from the poets, Marlow, Ben Johnson or Shakespeare, Venetia would feel the prickle of tears at the back of her eyes.

Rupert was openly sceptical, as those who are psychic themselves but refuse to admit it, so often are. " 'Tis nonsense. Games for children and old women! There must be a scientific reason for the stars in their courses. Take the theory of Copernicus, for instance——"

"You take it" Maurice interrupted in a rude way which would have provoked an argument had it been anyone else. "Give her your hand, brother——"

The Prince shrugged and consented. Meriel took his right hand and looked at it; first the lean brown back, showing veins and sinews and long strong fingers, and then turning it over, studying the network of lines in which she could see the pattern of his life.

When he told her his date of birth, she said: "You were born under the sign of Sagittarius the Archer, he who shall trample his enemies beneath his hooves and transfix them with his shaft!"

Etienne was bending over Venetia's shoulder, murmuring close to her ear. "Le Diable, indeed! And his shaft? Has he not speared you with it many times, *mignonne?*"

Venetia hushed him crossly, eager to hear every word Meriel spoke.

She was still poring over the broad palm, telling him things about his personality and incidents in his past, which made Maurice, who knew him best, exclaim in wonder.

"When you were very young, you had a serious illness—I feel a constriction in my chest—it is difficult to draw breath. Your mother nursed you devotedly."

A puzzled frown knit Rupert's brows. He suspected trickery. "That is true. How could you know it?"

"She had been bribing your servants, *Monseigneur,*" Etienne broke in lightly, trying to laugh it off, attuned to the drop in atmosphere.

Meriel seemed unaware of the interruption. "Later in life, I see that you must have a care for old injuries which will be troublesome."

"His Highness is never wounded!" The spectators chorused joyously, glad to discredit her, to prove this just a game, not to be taken seriously.

"There is a head wound indicated." Her calm insistence was dampening. "And one to the leg."

"I'gad! 'Tis sorcery! I vow it sets my head atwirl and chills my blood!" Adrian gripped Etienne's arm in feigned terror, rolling his eyes theatrically, then flippantly tossing out a question, "And the hurts to our Prince's heart, my girl, what of those?"

"You will never marry—but there will be children."

This raised a laugh, but Rupert was unconvinced, still trying to catch her out. Her voice went on, in a low monotone.

"I do not see you ever being a rich man——"

"There she speaks truly—he doesn't pay our arrears now!" someone shouted, amidst a gust of merriment.

"There are other skills besides those of the sword. The crucible—and metal treated with lines to make pictures—do you understand?" Meriel's eyes were clouded.

"When will he win the war and hang all the Goddamned rebels!" Barney wanted to know.

Meriel shook her head. "Nothing is clear—but wait—there are ships, and fighting—decks slippery with blood."

"But he is always seasick, aren't you, Rupert?" Maurice was getting impatient, wanting his turn. "What a future! On the sea—always throwing up!"

Rupert went to draw away, tired of what he still considered fairground chicanery, but Meriel gripped his wrist, saying, on a note of urgency: "Wait, Your Highness——" and there was something in her tone which stilled the relieved chatter which had risen on a wave of sound. "Oh, sir—a great prize will be dangled before you very soon—the temptation will be strong. I hear a multitude of voices lifted in one cry, 'Rupertus, Dei Gratia——' "

"What mean you?" He snatched his hand away as if scorched.

Maurice elbowed in, with drunken obstinacy ignoring his brother's warning stare and Meriel's pallor. "Here—read my future. Tell me what you see."

Meriel flinched. "Not now, Your Highness—some other time—I am tired."

"I insist!" Maurice could be very stubborn if he felt himself slighted.

"Leave it, Maurice," Rupert muttered uneasily.

But Maurice, still laughing in an angry, determined manner, pushed his palm almost into Meriel's face, forcing her to look at it. Sweat beaded her forehead, while she faltered, "I see water—towering waves—and the noise!" She bent double, clapping her hands over her ears. "My God! Such a wind—howling—raging—please, Your Highness—no more!"

"*Mon Dieu!* There has been too much talk of water; if't was sack now, I would welcome it!" Etienne broke the spell.

Experienced host that he was, he signalled urgently to the musicians who had been supping during the lull, getting them going again. Damaris, taking her lead from him, hauled Maurice on to the floor.

"Come, dearest. They are striking up a jig. Let us try once again, and pray don't stamp all over my chilblains this time!"

Rupert was drawing Venetia. In the short winter days when the weather put a stop to outside interests, he returned to this earlier hobby. She was glad to pose for him.

He threw himself into sketching with the same furious intensity with which he undertook everything. To his half closed eyes, Venetia was reduced from a woman to an object, made up of plains, broad hunks of light and shade, simple forms to be skillfully reproduced on to paper through the medium of the charcoal-stick in his fingers. He was unapproachable, locked in fierce concentration, swearing when the point snapped under the pressure, snatching up another, and, if she moved a muscle, cursing her crisply.

"Be still, damn you!"

She had pins and needles and her neck ached, and he looked as if he was in full spate and likely to go on for a long while. To keep her mind from the discomfort, she watched him, trying to figure just what it was about his face which was so attractive. As his critics said, his nose was certainly formidable, and his expression could be harsh, yet just to think of touching him made her feel limp.

But it was his eyes which were so compelling, deep, sensitive, darkly brooding; the eyes of a hurt child or a wounded stag, bewildered, reproachful. She wondered if it had been that incident when his parents had fled from Prague, which had stamped them with this wistfulness. Pierre thoroughly enjoyed recounting it to her very dramatically, while Venetia's heart went out to the baby Rupert, not yet a twelve-month-old, who had been forgotten by his mother in that agonized panic of flight.

No doubt Elizabeth had been overwhelmed with terror for her husband, wild with rage at the affront, and anxious for the unborn child which she was almost due to deliver. Quite probably, she had believed Rupert to be safe with his nurses, but the fact remained, damning and indisputable, that her care for her third son had not been uppermost in her mind. It had been almost as an afterthought, as the jumbled train of carriages and wagons hurtled from the beleaguered town, that she had drawn breath and asked where he was.

Consternation followed; riders were sent galloping down the line. There, in the boot of the last cart, almost suffocated by the luggage thrown in on top of him, the Prince had been found, scarlet in the face and roaring his indignation. He had been abandoned on the palace floor by his hysterical nurse, and only snatched up at the very last moment by some fleeing menial who had tossed him in among the bundles.

Venetia's leg had gone quite numb—she had to move. Rupert threw aside the charcoal, stood away from his drawing, squinting at it critically. She sat up, waiting for the life to tingle back into her limbs, then shrugged her shoulders into her dressing-robe and pattered over to look, standing beside him, very tiny in her bare feet against his height.

Was she really as lovely as he had depicted? It was the drawing of a lissom woman, lying on a couch, arms stretched above her head, limbs languorously relaxed; a woman who enjoyed revealing the splendor of her body.

Rupert grinned, looking down at her quizzically. "You have a beautiful body, *liebling*. Rubens would enjoy working from you."

"But his women are so fat!" she wailed. "They have hips like bolsters! You don't think I resemble them, surely?"

It was a nine day wonder and the talk of Oxford, this more mature Prince, taking his new responsibilities with a gravity which impressed even the older counsellors. He erupted once, disappointed because, in addition to the promotion already conferred, he had expected the colonelcy of the Kings' Lifeguard, and, when this was bestowed on Lord Bernard Stuart, felt himself so injured that he had proclaimed his intention of laying down his command. Venetia was quite ashamed of this childish display of temper.

Will Legge was able to talk him into a more reasonable

mood, and, more sullen than truculent, he had apologized for his outburst. He was sincerely doing his best to avoid an open breach with Digby and as for Goring—he spent a few halcyon weeks *persona grata* with His Highness who seemed prepared to forget past misdemeanors of that unpredictable individual, until the time that Goring left Oxford for Hampshire.

From then on the good feeling cooled. That accomplished dissembler began to write letters in the most flowery terms, addressing Rupert familiarly as, "My Prince," and signing his screeds as coming from: "Your Highness's all-vowed, all-humble, all-obedient Goring," while having made up his mind never to serve under the Palsgrave again. He had requested the King to grant him an independent command. This was but one among a string of troubles coming from every quarter, and Rupert was beset by the usual problems; demands for oakum for "match," timber for gun-carriages, cloth for uniforms, horses, arms, forage, bread, cheese, beer and, above all—money!

"I hear that my dear little Maurice is to be sent into Wales. Alack! We were becoming such close friends too." Damaris was sitting with her feet propped on a stool. Outside a snowstorm was pasting white blobs to the window.

No one except Damaris would have dreamed of calling Maurice "little," but Venetia understood. "Can you not accompany him?"

Damaris snuggled deeper into the fur collar of her robe. "I think that I shall do so, though Etienne is determined to remain near Rupert. But I consider it my duty to go with Maurice and offer comfort in those remote regions! Besides, he is so very kind that he finds it nigh impossible to tell a woman no! 'Sdeath! Who knows what wicked Jezebel may get her hands upon him if I'm not there! I trust that he won't be dispatched hither until Dobson had finished his portrait. Have you seen it yet? He wishes to paint your Prince, does he not?"

"I believe so." Venetia found it hard to imagine Rupert having the patience to sit.

"I do wish that he would paint Etienne, but there is such a waiting list. My dear, everyone who is anyone poses for him these days. And he is so shockingly expensive too! Who will pay the bill for the Prince, I wonder?"

"Lord Craven, I expect." Venetia was feeling lazy after a fencing bout. She and Adrian were having lessons together, both wanting to improve their chances of survival

208

when next called upon to stare down a length of cold steel in earnest! She liked wearing breeches, finding them so much more practical than voluminous skirts which restricted movement, picked up leaves and twigs about the hem, and were so quickly reduced to bedraggled rags in anything but the most clement weather. It was impossible not to feel gay, enjoying the freedom, aping the strutting lads in high boots, swinging cape, and rakishly tilted hat.

"Ah, yes, Lord Craven," continued Damaris, beckoning Nancy to light the candles. "The champion of our two heroes' mamma! And I know of another among her knights who will not be sorry to see the back of my Prince. That is Lord Hopton. Have they told you that it was he who aided the Queen, years ago, when he was plain Captain Ralph?"

Venetia shook her head. "Rupert rarely speaks of her."

"It was when she was fleeing Prague. Her cortége came upon a snowdrift, blocking the mountain road on the Silesian frontier. A young English volunteer came to her rescue. He had a horse strong enough to carry two—nay, in truth 'twas three, for the Queen was big with Maurice—and thus she travelled for forty miles up behind Lord Hopton. I'll wager, there has been many a time of late when he has wished that he had abandoned her to give birth in the snow!"

"Their lives are full of such strange coincidence." Venetia had ceased to be amazed at anything appertaining to the brothers.

Their affinity was uncanny. She had heard Rupert laughing and saying, half serious, half mocking: " 'Tis my belief that you were got on my christening day. In such haste were you to follow me into the world, forsooth!"

Venetia missed Damaris when her blue coach had jolted off in the rear of Maurice's army, heading for Wales. He had resigned his command in the West and had been made Major-General of the counties of Salop, Hereford, Monmouth and Worcester at Rupert's behest.

Maurice's letters confirmed his fears, warning him of disaffection. Down with the dispatches came letters from Damaris full of complaints and humor and worry about Maurice. She was of the opinion that it needed the iron-will of Rupert to quell the troubles, and that the younger Prince had taken on a much higher part than he had the experience to discharge. But, with it all, she wrote that she adored him and did not regret her departure.

Venetia laughed over the latest missive, sitting up in bed

one evening in February. "Oh, you Palatines! Why is it that even the most sensible of females are prepared to go through fire and water for your sakes?"

Rupert was hunched in the wooden bathtub, rubbing soap on his chest and arms while De Faust spread towels over the back of a chair before the fire. "You should see my brother Edward," he grunted. " 'Tis said that he is the best-looking of the lot, and has, furthermore, the most elegant French manners."

"He must be quite devastating!"

His broad back glistened, the muscles rippling smoothly as he moved. He stood up, the water cascading from him, puddling the carpet, and De Faust held out a towel. Rupert knotted it around his hips. "The Parisian ladies seem to find him so. Our mother, no doubt, fears that they may make a Papist of him. That is ever her dread for us—even Charles Louis!"

There were meetings in progress at Uxbridge to discuss peace, and the outlook was not very hopeful. The obstacles to agreements seemed almost insurmountable, religion, the King's autocratic attitude, and the long list of persons to whom the Parliamentarians would give no pardon. It was headed by the names of his nephews.

The Palatines, both present when this was read out, had laughed aloud rudely, but the King had taken it very seriously and ordered them to be quiet. In spite of this incident Rupert was forwarding the treaty by all the means in his power. He had been one of the first to meet the Commissioners on their arrival, and had attended all the discussions, occasionally speaking to remind the King of some forgotten point, but otherwise keeping silent. She could not help wondering how his saturnine presence affected the Parliamentarian representatives—it must seem that Mars himself presided at the Council-table.

He rose, went to the hearth, knocked out his pipe, then came back to her. In his long white robe with the great belled sleeves caught in at the wrist, silhouetted against the flickering fire in the darkened room, he seemed more than ever like a fallen angel.

He smelled of soap and clean linen and she coiled closer against him, but he was in an abstracted mood. She waited, schooled to bide her time. The Prince would communicate, when he was ready.

"I fear that the peace talks will be of no avail," he said

at last. Uncle will not yield in his determination to maintain the Church, and keep his power over the army."

"Would you have him bend to them?"

Rupert did not reply at once, then: "I have suffered exile and deprivation—he has no notion of it. Perchance, this is his last opportunity to make a treaty that is not a surrender."

His words hung heavily on the thickening darkness with something in his tone which she had never before heard.

"But we shall win, Rupert!" She almost shouted it, suddenly afraid. "We must! If the King will not treat—and we were to lose! My God! Rupert—what would they do to him?"

THREE

There was little shelter on Phene Heath; the blustering March wind tore through the assembled army, ruffling feathers, tangling manes, so that cursing troopers hung on to their hats and grappled with their flapping cloaks. Many of them grumbled at having been marched out of Oxford with almost indecent haste after the news had been received that Shrewsbury had fallen.

Rupert, on the rampage at the loss of his training center, would not rest until he was on the hot spur to avenge the outrage.

Shrewsbury had been betrayed from within whilst Maurice was away at Chester. The Governor was killed as he tried to rally his men, and, after only a little ill-managed street fighting, the Cavaliers were trapped in the castle. They had surrendered on disgraceful terms, withdrawing to Ludlow with their arms, leaving behind the whole magazine, the stores, fifteen cannon, and soldiers who had come out of Ireland. Colonel Mytton promptly hanged thirteen.

The peace treaty had failed dismally, the armistice was over; Sir Jacob Astley and his foot were sent for from Gloucestershire, and Langdale had received his marching orders.

Now, with grim satisfaction, the Prince sat his horse and looked over the dense array; everyone had arrived at this rendezvous on time. The gaunt, laconic Marmaduke Langdale had brought his lawless Northern Horse, sweeping down like a desolating whirlwind through the West Riding with pillage and rape marking their path.

Maurice, who had been unhappily roaming between Chester and Maelor, trying to salvage something from the wreck of his brother's hopes, had also obeyed his summons. But Rupert did not reproach him. What was there to say? The damage had been done long before Maurice reached the area.

The country all around was impoverished, the conduct of the war had brought trade almost to a standstill, garrison commanders kept their soldiers and horses fed by indiscriminate raiding, and Rupert had recently authorized cavalry patrols to exact contributions from those who were tardy in payment. Added to this was a whole complexity of regional feuds, quarrelling between rival leaders, misunderstandings between the Welsh and the English. Division, strife and poverty threatened to cleave asunder that land once known as the "nursery of the King's infantry."

It was Rupert's plan to ensure the safety of Ludlow and Hereford, to support Maurice's operations, and to prepare the way for an advance northwards, which was to be the summer campaign. Now his amalgamated forces moved away from the heath toward Whitchurch where they intended to quarter.

The roads were terrible, consisting of narrow forest tracks, or antiquated hollow ways deeper than head of horse or rider, where the mire of January was hardly dry by June. In the rear of Rupert's train the going was slow, the heavy wagons having difficulty in getting along, and troopers galloped up and down the line, alert for trouble with Colonel Mytton's men who were tailing them.

Venetia was travelling in the van, concentrating on controlling this still unfamiliar chestnut cob which Mallory had selected to replace Orion. Meek as an angel when the Prince was about, no doubt recalling that he had whacked him smartly across the nose when he tried to bite, he gave Venetia trouble, and she was unconvinced that her brother had made a wise choice. She sighed for her own gentle pony, bleakly wondering what Roundhead horseman now rode him.

She had grown soft in winter quarters, forced to learn

all over again the best way to endure freezing winds and sheeting rain. At the end of the first miserable day, she had had to fight back tears at Rupert's hoots of derision when she climbed stiffly from her horse, sure that she would never make her knees meet again.

It was still raining by the time Whitchurch was reached. The unprepared garrison bestirred themselves to welcome their honored guest. The commander, once he had recovered from the shock, expressed unfeigned delight, overjoyed to be greeted in his own language by the Prince who had spent many hours cloistered with Arthur Trevor, picking up the difficult Welsh tongue.

Captain Huw Morgan was large and black bearded, living in decaying splendor and wielding an almost feudal despotism over the surrounding countryside and his gang of brazen fighters. They stood, drawn into uneven lines, grinning all over their faces at the novelty of being reviewed by the great General.

This manor-fort was typical of other outposts scattered at strategic points up and down England, and Rupert encouraged these adjuncts to open warfare. They formed contacts between towns, sheltered troops which could be drawn upon when needed, and overawed as well as protected the area.

Morgan was eager for news of the outside world, but Rupert was subdued, eating little, drinking too much. Maurice picked up his mood, uneasily certain that it was in some way connected with Shrewsbury and feeling guilty.

"Is not this a miserable life?" inquired Morgan rhetorically, before embarking on a long catalogue of little dissensions. "And, to add to all, Your Highness, the damned locals here about are beginning to riot. 'Sdeath, I am in accord with Colonel Scudmore at Hereford who had become so provoked by their thwarting and taunts that he threatens to hang the dogs and drown the whelps!"

As a servant heaved another log onto the sooted hearth, a gust of wind blew smoke back into the hall. The cushion beneath Venetia felt damp, and moisture gleamed on the stone-hewn walls. The state of the bed which she and Rupert would later occupy did not bear thinking about.

"These people make such an accursed whimpering if a man take bread for himself or fodder for his horse," Morgan raised his tankard to Rupert. "God prosper your Princely enterprises with happy success, Noble Sir!"

The badly cooked meal had been brought in by a blowzy

213

slattern with whom Morgan seemed to be on intimate terms. Aided by a couple of equally unprepossessing serving-maids, she had not even bothered to tidy the strands of hair coiling down from her cap, nor change her bodice which was marked with rusty sweat-stains under the arms.

"She's a good wench," declared Morgan under cover of the general hum. "Can't speak much English, but then, it's not talk a man wants. The Prince now, he'll not be seeking the use of her tonight. Brought his own, I see!"

He gave a monstrous, ribald wink in the direction of the wild-looking girl who had been such a pleasant surprise, swinging down from her pony in his muddy courtyard, and was now seated close to Rupert, resting her cheek against his sleeve while he took no more heed than if one of the hounds had fawned on him. Morgan combed his fingers through his beard—her mouth was of such an enticing shape, a little parted as she gazed at the Prince—but then —when did she not keep those almond-shaped eyes riveted on him? The lucky devil!

As had been expected, Colonel Mytton had set his men to worrying the Royalist rear that day. Prisoners had been taken in the scuffle. The Prince ordered Morgan to have their leader brought to him.

He sat at the head of the board, clad in black velvet, his cloak, a splash of sullen scarlet, flung over the back of his chair.

The Roundhead Lieutenant stood stiffly, correct and formal, between guards, and the dark brooding eyes opposite fixed him.

"Sir, Colonel Mytton saw fit to hang my men after taking Shrewsbury." The foreign voice was level, chilling. "When this practice was first begun against the Irish soldiery last year, I promised my Lord Essex requital, man for man. He was wise enough to cease. Now it appears to have started anew. My part is plain, and what must be done shall be performed in the open, for all to witness. You, sir, will select twelve of your men by lot. They shall hang before we depart this place. Yourself shall then take horse and bear word to your leaders that Rupert keeps his oath!"

"Your Highness!" the lieutenant burst out, taking an involuntary step forward. "These men are guiltless—you dare not!"

"Dare not? To me!" Rupert snapped imperiously. "No

214

more, sir! I cannot help your soldiers. Colonel Mytton himself doomed them."

Oh, these ancient creaking houses where sudden blasts of damp air sent the rushlight wavering madly and every move, after nightfall, was fraught with hidden dangers. At the very least one might trip on a broken step and break one's neck in a headlong plunge down some unrailed stairwell.

Venetia found Rupert sitting in the dark, lost in thought. The sulky fire warmed nothing but its immediate vicinity. The Manor had changed hands several times during hostilities and showed it. The hangings were ripped, tapestries sagged, lopsided, from the walls; no one had bothered to replace them. Water dripped ceaselessly somewhere, and the smell of mildew fought for supremacy over other fetid odors.

De Faust and Holmes had done their best, but the hot brick wrapped in flannel did nothing but draw out the moisture from the lumpy feather mattress, and Venetia curled into a ball, shuddering, under the other pulled on top. Rupert came to bed at last, his body a bulwark against both cold and darkness.

When morning paled the stars, creeping through the smashed windowpane, Venetia hazarded a guess that the condemned men had slept as little as he who had sentenced them.

Before beginning their march to Hereford, the army was drawn up on a stretch of open ground. Venetia would not stay at the manor, nor occupy a position in the rear, though Rupert tersely advised it. She took her place at his side, watching the huddle of prisoners with a kind of sick fascination.

The victims were set on horseback with their hands tied behind them, each with a noose around his neck, while men scrambled up to the branches above, knotting the free ends securely. The remarks, the nervous jests died away and a hush fell on the mass of waiting soldiers.

One of the Roundheads, a very young trooper, was sobbing—his face a queer, greenish hue—while a comrade tried to speak words of comfort—then even they became quiet, listening to the chaplain who had begun to pray aloud.

Rupert barked out the order for their mounts to be whipped from under them.

"What ails the peasants?" Etienne asked, very annoyed. He was being attended by the camp surgeon having been hit on the head by a stone flung by an enraged rustic. "We would know how to deal with them in France. The ring-leaders would be caught and flogged to death!"

Venetia was holding a bowl of blooded water in which a sponge floated in a red halo. "It is a warning sign, Chevalier. The yeomen will take so much—then they turn."

"*Mon Dieu!* I did not volunteer to be attacked by a mob with staves and stones!" In the mirror he was surveying the ruin of his yellow doublet, only somewhat mollified by the eye-catching bandage which they wound about his head.

Plagued beyond endurance by the demands of the sol-diery, the countryfolk, led by a few small gentry and cler-gymen, were banding together against both parties. Calling themselves "The Clubmen," for they had few arms but these improvised weapons, they cared little for the ideals of the warring factions, more concerned in preserving the hard-won produce of their fields. They were sick to death of seeing their cattle and flocks driven off by soldiers, of having troops quartered on them with hungry mouths and empty pockets, and having to scrape together that regular monthly contribution.

Hereford became the new headquarters, but hardly had they settled in when the Prince, his energies at full strain, was determining a *volte-face* for a gallop to Oxford and a rapid consultation on the impending campaign, in the light of his findings in the Marches. He deprecated his uncle's decision to set up Prince Charles with a Council and a Court of his own in Bristol. Such an arrangement played straight into the hands of ambitious officers who would lose no opportunity to intrigue with one Court against the other and against himself into the bargain.

He had written to Will Legge, whom he had promoted to Governor of Oxford before he left: "I expect nothing but ill from the West; let them hear that Rupert says so." This was for the benefit of George Goring!

He and Maurice had mulled over the situation, even mooting a dash for Bristol to take charge of Prince Charles; a high-handed act which would have prevented the danger of a divided command. But watching his fierce, impatient face, and that of the "Twin," who would agree to any mad scheme and follow him to hell if he asked,

Venetia knew that it was but idle speculation. He was too loyal to the King to carry out such a *coup*.

When Rupert had convinced himself that Maurice and his staff could manage for a few days, he made for Oxford at a searing pace. Barney, borrowed from Etienne, proved invaluable. He knew the Severn Valley like the back of his hand, making full use of by-ways, short-cuts and diversions.

Rupert remarked, with a grin: "My friend, I would that every scout be recruited from the ranks of highwaymen!"

It was Easter, and they rode through moist, green country, assailed at every turn by the burgeoning of nature.

The Cavaliers paused in a village where the single street meandered like a sluggish brook between the cottages, ending at the church. The gardens spoke of industry; thick pink blossom decorated the fruit trees, promising a fine apple-crop.

At the far end there was a green thronged with people enjoying the festivities. The younger element, dressed in their best, were rolling colored eggs, and there was a great deal of giggling and pushing as the girls waited in delicious excitement for the youths to "lift" them in a chair decorated with garlands.

Venetia smiled wistfully; it was not so very long ago that she had joined in such simple frolics, yet it seemed a million years. She was glad to see that the maypole was still standing; in some places these had been condemned as pagan by those of ultra-Puritan persuasion.

At the appearance of horsemen, the crowd became quiet, the music of pipe and tambour stopping in mid-chord, the bells of the Morris dancers jingling into uneasy silence. Cavalry spelled trouble, and the faces turned toward them were apprehensive. The leaders pulled up their mounts, bringing them to a prancing nervous halt on the edge of the road near a group of girls whose expressions of alarm quickly changed to admiration. There was still a magic quality about the Cavaliers to bedazzle village belles; they had lost none of their gallant swagger, with their long, curling hair, their suits of rich velvet garnished with silver embroidery, contrasting sharply with the white lace collars and cuffs.

Word went around, like a breeze, gathering momentum: " 'Tis the King's men!"

And then a soldier, wounded and home to recover, recognized Rupert and the cry was taken up:

"The Prince! Prince Rupert is here!"

Venetia caught the wave of curiosity and fear, and something primitive within her stirred in response, exciting her. She always enjoyed Rupert more after some demonstration of his power and authority.

She straightened her shoulders, looking down, faintly patronizing, on these wenches who might dream of him, before being hustled into marriage with some homely, unimaginative clod, but would never know the blissful joy of lying with Prince Rupert. Their expressions were comical, changing to gaping astonishment when they recognized that she was a woman. She made her horse sidle; her knee bumped the Prince; he turned his smile full on her and left no one in doubt that they shared the closest contact.

Barney swept off his hat and spoke to the prettiest of the girls. "Your servant, my dear. We seek an inn. Is that one yonder suitable for His Highness, think you?" He pointed with his ship.

The girl blushed, wriggled and stammered.

"Which of you gentlemen be the Prince?" she gasped at last, peering around fearfully, expecting an apparition with horns and tail.

Rupert leaned forward, crossing his arms on his saddle-bow. "I am he."

The Lifeguard was grimly amused by the consternation which this simple statement never failed to produce.

On Easter Tuesday, April 8th, they reached Oxford. Rupert went to see the King, and Venetia staggered thankfully into their house, greeted by the "family," delighted to have even this fleeting visit from the Palsgrave and his lady.

Never one to mince words, Rupert drove home the hard facts at the meeting which was convened, disrupting the atmosphere of happy optimism which Digby was fostering. The Prince had no illusions about the prospect before them.

Oliver Cromwell, in the House of Commons, had demanded an intensification of the conflict and a clean sweep of such inept political Generals as Essex and Manchester. The upshot had been a decision to raise a regular army which would be properly paid and equipped. He was ordered to form, train and lead a force organized on professional lines, calling themselves the "New Model Army."

Rupert thoroughly distrusted rumors of unrest in the

218

Roundhead camp, and had little faith in the chimera of further troops from Ireland. In his opinion the King was in a strong enough position to win a negotiated peace, but not to win the war. These sensible counsels of caution amazed the older Couriers who had been vainly trying to persuade His Majesty to follow just such a course. Once Rupert had arrogantly brushed aside their timid policies; now he found himself adding his weight to their pleas for a renewal of peace talks at the earliest possible opportunity.

And at the King's side expressing, in the nicest possible way, an almost pained surprise that His Highness could suggest such a thing, sat the smiling Lord Digby. Rupert did not return that smile—his eyes those of a dangerous panther. Their *rapprochement* of the winter had been short-lived.

Very well then, if they insisted on fighting, Rupert would, of course, support them with all his ability and resources. He set out his plan—the King must bring his train of artillery from Oxford to Worcester, prior to a thrust Northwards to relieve Chester. Recruits could be raised in Lancashire and Yorkshire, it might even be possible to join Montrose, whose victories in Scotland were giving Charles such false hope.

In a dirty, evil temper, Rupert prepared to leave for Bristol—snarling at Venetia. What hope had he that his seriously given orders would be carried out? Oh, Will would do his best—delighted to see one another, they had talked far into the night, going over all the possibilities— and respectable old Secretary Nicholas would remain faithful to Rupert's interests and endeavor to transact business in a straightforward manner, in spite of his tortuous colleague, but. . . .

"God damn Digby!" he spat out, smashing his fist into the palm of his hand. "With his idiot diplomacy and dastardly advice!"

At Bristol there was little to lessen his disquiet. Everyone was at loggerheads about respective duties, while complaints about Goring's troopers continued. That obstreperous individual was ordered to take his cavalry toward Salisbury, while dispatching his guns and foot to help Sir Richard Grenville who was besieging Taunton. Determined to do things his way, Goring carried out the second part of Rupert's order, but then refused to stir himself, leaving his horsemen idle and, pleading ill-health, retiring to Bath to take the waters.

And Rupert, pacing up and down till it seemed he would wear a groove in the carpet, vented his irritation and worry in a stream of cursing fury to which Venetia listened patiently, trying to make sense of the troubles.

"If he is ill, which I do not believe for one moment, it will be as a result of his damned debauchery. He has, no doubt, got a dose of the pox!"

"Etienne tells me that he was wounded years ago and has recurrent bouts of pain which may explain his erratic behavior," Venetia suggested mildly.

The Prince stopped dead, glaring at her. "I know all about that! It was in '37, at Breda. *Sacrément,* I was there!" His black brows drew together in an intimidating scowl. "By Christ, Venetia, are you defending him?"

Then she had to swivel around, clasp her arms about his waist and coax him out of his jealousy. Presently he gave a short laugh: "Edward Hyde spoke truly today when he said of us: 'Well, you Generals are a strange kind of people.'"

The little hill-top town of Stow-on-the-World, bursting at the seams with soldiery, sweltered under an early heatwave. The King had arrived at last for this general muster, and not without delay and difficulties.

Gallopers winged to Rupert. The note of Digby's dispatches was that of an alarm bell—Cromwell was beating up the neighborhood—soon Oxford would starve; the draught horses had been driven away, without them the train could not move; Goring had been sent for but had not yet arrived! Would His Royal Highness please come to the rescue?

His Royal Highness cursed Cromwell for a hell-spawned cur, dropped everything, rounded up Maurice, a stout troop, all the horses he could lay hands on, and spurred to Oxford. There he drew off the stranded artillery, King Charles, his splendid Lifeguard (known as the Show Troop) and the Royal army, and escorted the lot to Stow.

While the great ones furrowed their brows at a Council of War, the rank and file, all eleven thousand of them, made the town their own, roistering noisily far into the dusk, trampling carelessly over sprouting barley and springing wheat. Goring's wild cavalry rollicked through the city gate in a cloud of dust, full of themselves because they had skirmished with Cromwell on the way and captured forty of his horses.

The townsfolk looked askance—welcoming the trade, but wondering when they would be paid.

Damaris and Venetia were lodging in the best tavern. They rustled down to the taproom at the sound of horsemen clattering into the yard. Etienne, Barney and Mallory, with some of their troopers, were ducking their heads under the lintel.

An acute pang of disappointment—Rupert was not there.

"He is still engaged with the War Council," volunteered the understanding Chevalier without having to be asked.

Damaris was enjoying herself; Venetia was envious of her ability to flirt with two other men whilst anticipating a passionate night with a third—Maurice was sure to come looking for her.

Trestles were filling, tapsters on the run to supply the urgent demands for refreshment. Soon a putt school was flourishing in a corner. They were shouting for Adrian to fetch his guitar and choruses of marching songs reverberated under the beams.

The wine flowed freely, the talk became bawdy, the men exchanging lurid tales of the brothels of Oxford. Laughter crackled in the smoky air.

"Did you manage a brush with Cromwell?" Damaris wanted to know.

Barney shook his head, his lean face breaking into its usual teasing smile. "I fear not, Duchess. And the Prince will be mighty vexed to hear that Goring had the good fortune to do so. He is hot to meet his in the field."

"Old Ironsides is following the *Pfalzgraf's* methods, but with a pious ruthlessness all his own," put in Etienne thoughtfully.

The hours were leaden and yet they passed. It was nearly a week since Venetia had seen him—they had been deposited at Stow when the Princes marched past from Broadway.

Staring out of her casement into the frustrating emptiness of the May night, willing it to be filled with Rupert's coming, she could see pin-points of light beyond the town. The watchfires of the camps: Langdale's independent Northern Horse, Astley's stalwart foot-sloggers, Goring's Roaring Boys, the cohorts of the Princes, and the King's Oxford army.

It grew late, the sounds died, and she wrapped a shawl over her nightgown. Nancy had left a pitcher of cider, a covered platter of food, should the Prince not have stopped to sup. Venetia sat in the big padded chair and tried to read; these nights she was afraid to be alone—she and Damaris had shared a bed all week. The flame waxed and waned, dimmed and glowed, and fantasy began to smother her mind—she seemed to float back to that farmhouse bedchamber; in an unnatural stillness the blood was seeping across Fletcher's shirt. She jerked herself awake, wondering yet again if others would feel that ghastly moment, frozen in time.

Venetia shuddered, forcing herself to concentrate on the normal, itemizing the Turkey rug, the dull empty grate, the tent-like interior of the bed with its curtains drawn on the door side to cheat draughts, and the pillows stripped of their embroidered daytime covers, primly white, side by side above the sedate edge of the sheet.

She jumped, fully alert, with her neck and shoulder stiff from leaning in a cramped position; voices outside and the skid of hooves on cobbles, then Rupert's boots were loud on the boards of the passage, and he was shouting a hearty goodnight to someone, probably Maurice, and his sword banged the door as he came in, unbuckling his baldrick.

"Wake up," he said, laughing at her, and he scooped her from the chair, her hair tangling his buttons, and carried her over and fell with her onto the bed. They did not talk —this would have been not only superfluous, but downright impossible at such a moment, but later Rupert got up, lit the candle, filled a tankard, clapped a wedge of cheese between two hunks of bread and told her about the meeting.

"A stormy one, *liebchen*," he was talking with his mouth full.

He, Langdale and the Northern Horse, wanted to march toward Chester. The reasons Rupert gave were for the relief of that city, the weakness of the Scots, and the eagerness of Langdale's troopers to campaign near home. He did not add his strongest argument—his burning eagerness to wipe out the stain of Marston Moor.

"Goring, Digby and the rest were for trying conclusions with the New Model Army——" a wide grin, "my lads have already christened it the 'New Noddle.' "

"Highness, you have been out in the sun without your shirt." She ran a lazy hand over his chest and shoulders.

222

He scowled and flicked a glance at her. "You've not heard a word I've been saying!"

She composed her face into an expression of intense interest. "You gained your point?" Somehow she never doubted it.

He nodded, yawned and eased down under the covers. "Naturally. Though not without a deal of murmuring and complaints. The King and I leave for the north in the morning."

"And Goring?" She reached out to snuff the candle, then moved over to lie in the circle of his arm.

"Goring is to return to the siege of Taunton. I have given him a more extensive commission."

This surprised her. "Why?"

"He and Digby are as thick as thieves. Christ's blood, 'twill be enough to bear with Digby's company. If Goring were with us also, God knows what plots they would hatch between them to my cost."

"Can you manage without his soldiers?"

"We'll recruit as we go. Holy God! Give me a month and I'll double our numbers! Langdale is loyal to me, we'll pick up Gerard on the way. I shall have Maurice to hand, and Edward has written begging to come to us. 'Wilful Ned,' we called him at home. The King has given permission and I've sent for him."

"Oh, dear," thought Venetia as sleep fogged her senses. Not another Palatine warrior coming to thunder across England!"

FOUR

"Le Diable may well prefer to lead a charge of horse, yet there is little at which he so grimly excels as the sudden assault on a fortified town." Etienne rested his shoulders against one of the gabions which protected the guns. He was seated next to Venetia in the warm sunshine on the south side of the city, where Rupert had set up his command post and his artillery.

Leicester, wealthy and falsely secure behind its medieval walls, was having a demonstration of his aptitude for siege-craft. The Royalists had taken it by surprise. They had appeared without warning, startling an outpost, who so little expected to meet an enemy that they had their greyhounds with them and were coursing hares instead of attending to their military duties.

The Cavaliers had swung aside from the northern march on hearing that Fairfax threatened Oxford. Rupert had absolute faith in Will Legge's ability to safeguard the Royal Headquarters (he had made him Commander as well as Governor) and Leicester was a rich town which would be a spur to the soldiers and, he hoped, prove a bait to draw the Parliamentarians away from Oxford, and send them speeding to defend the fat Puritan countries of the Eastern Midlands.

Sir Richard Willys, the Governor of Newark, had come over with a thousand troopers, a welcome reinforcement, and the next day the Prince had Leicester invested. With Langdale and his patrol, he rode round the outskirts and inspected the fortifications. It was in poor shape to resist, its bastions had been neglected, its walls were rendered vulnerable by suburban dwellings which no one had bothered to pull down, and the other defenses were drawn too wide. There was an improvised citadel on the south side, known as the "Newark," and, facing this, Rupert put his pioneers to work building a battery. The share he took in this toil was marked by his usual contempt of personal risk, his continual presence and the cheering ring of his voice encouraging his men far into the small hours.

Venetia had her cob saddled early and went seeking him. Grayish light was smearing the horizon as her horse picked his way over the uneven ground toward the fresh brown gashes where newly dug earth had been levelled to make a base for wooden platforms, and the excavated material packed into protective mounds fronting them.

It was essential to have a firm flat surface along which the guns could move without interruption in order that the recoil energy would be harmlessly dissipated in motion which, if prematurely checked, could cause the rapid disintegration of the carriage! Venetia was thankful to see that the Prince was being prudent, wearing his breastplate under a coat of a nondescript gray instead of his usual flamboyant red one, and remembering to keep his tall head well down, for their movements were being closely studied by marksmen on the city walls.

He was absorbed in conversation with Bernard de Gomme, the young Walloon whom he had promoted to Quartermaster General, and they were busy pointing and aligning the cannons with the aid of a quadrant.

The morning wore on and Venetia was joined by the Chevalier, Holmes, Sir Richard Crane and several others, either watching, waiting instructions, or lending a hand, and still Rupert would not rest or eat until all was prepared. The army was drawn up in array before the town; he sent in a herald offering pardon to all if they opened their gates to the King, and fired off two calverins to show that he meant business.

The blast was terrific. *"Il fait plus de peur, que de mal,"* murmured Etienne against her cheek as Venetia clutched him. "It frightens more than it hurts! Cling closer, *ma petite,* some pleasure must be found in adversity, although our armor clangs like anvils!"

The city worthies, made over-confident by the presence of officers of the New Model, retained Rupert's man, sending back an emissary of their own bearing a protest because His Highness was continuing to raise his batteries while a parley was in progress, and asking for further grace to consider their reply.

Rupert examined the man through slitted eyes; he had been up all night, and this tried his temper. "Such insolence is not to be borne! Come no more to me with saucy messages or I'll lay you by the heels! They have but a quarter-hour to make up their minds!"

It was a rule of this dangerous game that the lives of the defenders were forfeit, if they went so far as to compel the beleaguering hosts to deliver a storm.

The Palsgrave stood on the platform, hands on his hips, raking the stubborn city beneath the steel peak of his zischagge, his expression forbidding between the metal ear flaps and the single vertical bar which protected his nose. His mouth was compressed as he contemplated the dust-haze of the messenger's departure toward the gates. He gave an impatient snort, turned away to find Venetia and dropped on his heels at her side, taking a long pull at the wineskin.

"If they don't surrender—and I doubt they will—get you to quarters, and keep that damned helmet on!" he barked, having just taken his off.

With any luck, in the heat of the moment, he might forget ordering her to retire. She had come prepared to stay, fully armed and wearing sensible inconspicuous clothing.

When the time was up, Rupert took the delay for a challenge and gave orders to open fire on the "Newark."

"The attack is like to be as hot as hell!" said Crane, his eagerness reflecting that of the Palsgrave.

And he was right. The defenders answered resolutely, their own ordnance in constant deadly play. Musket-fire from both sides dispensed destruction, lines of flame and smoke tracing about the walls, shattered across by the wider glare of cannon.

Those great beasts, vomiting death, mesmerized Venetia; the noise stunned thought, the reek of sulphur made her eyes smart and choked her throat. Each gun had its own crew, every man well drilled and, barring accidents, the operation was carried out smoothly enough. As soon as the cannon had recoiled, the men fell upon it, hauling it back into place and depressing the breech to elevate the muzzle and reload. A spiked staff was inserted, raking out a glowing shower of debris from the last shot, wet and dry mops were brought into instant use to suppress the hot residue. A ladle was taken to the budge-barrel of powder, standing handy but perilously close, and then thrust compressed the charge, followed by wadding, packed down on the powder.

Meanwhile, the gunner was carefully examining the intended projectile, checking it for the correct diameter.

Then the moment of truth; with almost the flourish of a Master of Ceremonies, he lightly touched off the explosive with a linstock holding a piece of smoldering cotton rope.

Bang! Whizz! Boom! The bombardment continued relentlessly and the walls crumbled, bit by bit. By nightfall a wide breach had been opened.

At midnight, Rupert, having carefully made his dispositions, let loose his assault parties with their ladders and hand-grenades. It was launched from several points at once, but the heaviest pressure was concentrated on the "Newark." For over two hours the Roundhead soldiers, the citizens and their womenfolk, shared a bitter struggle. Attack after attack was repulsed—the scaling ladders set up, only to be toppled from the walls. There was a timeless gulf filled with grappling, explosions, shouts and screams and sword thrusts.

As Rupert's infantry fell back, his cavalry drove them on again, some even went so far as to dismount and support the wavering column ahead, struggling over the fascines in the ditch, pressing fiercely to the gap. The Prince was everywhere, galloping along the graft beneath the storm of shot, Crane and the Lifeguard crashing behind him.

The foot managed to overpower the guards on the city gate and let the cavalry pour in. The fire of the enemy faltered, and the shouts of conflict at the breach grew into a yell of triumph, the attackers bursting through, the skirmishing scattering away among the streets. But even then the work was not ended; every home became a fortress, citizens fighting doggedly from roof and window, women standing at the casements, firing with steady aim, the combatants illumined by the leaping light of blazing buildings.

The horsemen streamed through the narrow alleys, killing all who stood in their path; this continued defiance after the town had been entered exasperated them. In the market-place, by the cross, the last bloody stand was made; the defenders set up ordnance, and the Royalists found themselves in for another, smaller siege which they crushed mercilessly.

At daybreak the town was the King's; Rupert's black banner flying over the broken wall. Venetia discovered him near the breach, restless with victory and already scanning the smashed citadel and planning refortifications.

There was a brilliance radiating from him, he seemed drunk with triumph, catching the frenzy of his troops who were scouring the town on a hot wave of bloodlust and greed.

"What do you here?" he cried, grabbing her wrist in a gloved hand and hauling her up against him. "Did I not say to keep away? My *Walküre!* Battle-maid, eh? I'faith, no Roundhead rogue should be borne to the halls of Valhalla—but my men—ja, they are heroes, fit to feast with the gods!"

He talked so wildly and in such broken English that she did not fully understand him, knowing only that he was happy, and rejoicing with him. Now he was prepared to honor her. Keeping an arm tightly about her, he wheeled to his officers.

"Look to your men, especially the new Welsh boys. See that they do not run off when they have done plundering. Keep close watch on the prisoners, mine in particular—I could use their ransom money!"

The Lifeguard were gathering and the Prince mounted

his charger. "Come, *liebchen*, we will ride in together, yes?"

And she was deaf and blind to all save the light in Rupert's face, the warmth of his voice, and the savage surge of pride in the achievements of her man—pitiless and primordial.

So they passed through the breach and the dead who still guarded it and, crossing beneath the Palatine standard, entered the conquered city.

He had every reason to feel gratified by the action; it had gone well, planned with Teutonic thoroughness. The King had witnessed his success; once more he had proved that he was a man to be reckoned with, not a licked foreign whelp from some impoverished German family. Venetia was the last person to detract in any way from his elation, yet, next day, when the excitement had given place to the aftermath, the brutality of the whole business sickened her.

She needed assurance that their deeds were justified—some one to tell her that—yes, this was a city held by rebels who had denied their lawful Sovereign, and that the Royalist fought on moral grounds to lead back a misguided people corrupted by such leaders as Oliver Cromwell.

She longed to run out into the fields, to fling herself down on the fresh green grass and breathe in the scent of clover instead of carnage, to lie on her back and become lost in the layers of light fluffy cloud where birds were shrilling a glad, mad carol in praise of summer—to feel cleansed of man and his works.

Only in Michael's face did she read an echo of her own misgivings. He hardly ever came near her now; rarely could they stretch across that gulf which had split their too delicate structure of misunderstanding and desire. Waking at night, listening to Rupert's deep even breathing, knowing sadly that sleep had fled, she would stare into the darkness and see Michael's wounded eyes. He was gentle with her, showing an infinite pity—the pale warmth of his kindness making her ashamed.

Prior to Leicester, Rupert and Digby had been in accord, unanimous in agreeing that if Fairfax could be tempted to give battle, somewhere in the Midlands, confronting the united forces of the Prince, Goring and Gerard, his defeat would be almost a certainty.

But concord could not last. A Council was called in Leicester, and Rupert was again in opposition. No news yet suggested that they had been successful in making Fairfax withdraw from Oxford, and the councillors, anxious for their property at headquarters, lent eager support to Digby's suggestion that, instead of continuing their march north, they turn back. Letters had come, clamoring about the danger to the Duke of York, the stores, and all the fair ladies of the Court.

Venetia was smitten with violent jealousy when Maurice told her that they had sent a petition, begging Prince Rupert to save them!

He smiled as if he guessed her thoughts. "The King has bidden the city to be patient and bear the stringencies of a siege, even if it does mean that cousin James has to go on short rations."

Venetia had warmed to Maurice, understanding why Damaris was so charmed with him. Now that she grew ever more confident of her place in Rupert's affection, she no longer resented the devotion of the brothers. Maurice talked freely, telling her all that she wanted to know. Rupert could not always be prevailed upon to discuss the Royalist disagreements which made his life so complicated.

He was overborne by the War Council and all his plans for the campaign set aside. The army which he himself had mainly raised and prepared turned southward. They must now make for Market Harborough, and there await news of Oxford's predicament, and the expected reinforcements which Goring and Gerard had been urged to bring. The army was depleted, its ranks thinned by the garrisons which had to be found for Leicester, its casualties in the storming, and the large number of deserters who had decamped with their booty. Willys took four hundred of his men back to Newark, leaving the rest to serve under Langdale.

In the midst of this delay, came intelligence that Fairfax had abandoned his half-hearted siege and was advancing toward them. The *Wheatsheaf Inn* at Daventry housed King Charles and the Prince for a few days, whilst the cavalry spread out to sweep the country-side for sheep and cattle. The flocks they collected went to supply Oxford, with a convoy of over a thousand horse. Rupert was forced to hang about until they returned and, once more, the arguments broke out.

"His Majesty is overjoyed at the relief of Oxford." Rupert flung around in his chair in the parlor which was still stale with the fumes of last night's ale and tobacco. He did not sound as if he shared that enthusiasm. "He has already written rapturously to the Queen, and Secretary Nicholas, gaily predicting a merry winter."

Maurice had unfolded the inlaid chessboard and set out the men. Rupert made an opening move, then sat back, frowning at the game. Maurice, with customary lack of foresight lost one of his pieces.

"Mort Dieu! Will you never learn?" His brother was in an irascible mood. "You used always to make that very same error at home."

He was sprawling in the carved chair, wearing his shirt sleeves, the billowing linen rolled up above his elbows untidily. He nibbled his nails, scowled and brooded. Maurice, now over-cautious, took a long while to move.

Damaris yawned beyond her hand. "La, men are dreadful unless fully occupied."

Venetia watched Rupert anxiously; she recognized the warning signs. Something was gnawing at him. She sighed, wishing that he could take life more philosophically, like Maurice.

"He is a lovely boy," Damaris had recently confided. "So big and gentle. He makes me feel tiny and frail, most flattering to someone of my build. But for all his size, he is a mere baby in the amatory field. I am having much sport teaching him everything that I know."

Now Damaris, bored with chess, struck a languorous pose and waited; when nothing happened, she crossed the room, sat at Maurice's knee, and ran a hand caressingly through his hair.

"That will put him off the game entirely." Bad-tempered lines spoiled Rupert's face.

"My dear Diable, why else do you suppose I am doing it?" Damaris made an impertinent moue at him. She treated him exactly as she did any other man, impudent and debonair, undeterred by his bullying. Rupert often grumbled to Venetia about her, disapproving of her alley-cat morals and fearing that she would give Maurice the pox.

"But she has the very finest apothecary," she protested, annoyed to find that she was always forced into the position of defending her. He remained unimpressed, but if Damaris could be said to show a preference among her lovers, Maurice was the most favored.

The Prince leaped up to pace the room but forgot the

230

low ceiling and sat down again abruptly, swearing and rubbing his forehead.

"You must be pleased, Rupert, to see Digby put out of countenance, now there is no longer reason for us to return to Oxford?" Venetia was trying to be helpful, but the very name of that instigator of the frustrations in which Rupert was unwillingly embroiled, brought him upright in his chair.

"It was a plot!" He smashed his fist down on the table, making the flagons rattle. "Digby and Ashburnham feared that the soldiers should take from them the influence which now they possess with the King!"

Maurice grinned. "Langdale's fellows soon put a stop to it with their mutiny."

"Pish!" Rupert was not to be consoled by the angry dead-lock in which the Council of War now struggled. "Digby is up to something, going about looking as sober and demure as a whore at a christening! And where is that damned cup-shotten Goring? We are desperately undermanned."

"Ah, well, Your Highness, you know Goring," said Damaris lightly.

"And have you *known* Goring?" Maurice murmured into the bunch of curls over her ear.

Damaris laughed and teased him, refusing to give a direct answer. Their love-play was plainly annoying Rupert. He wanted Maurice's attention, and leaned his elbows on the table, chin in his cupped palm, glaring at him.

"Reports come about the strength of Fairfax's army. It will need the utmost skill and vigilance to draw him to fight at a disadvantage."

"Is it really so serious?" Maurice's eyes sharpened and he grew still, quietened Damaris with one large hand, as if she were a frisky filly. "I thought there were rumors of quarrels in their army. I've heard the King talking of this."

"If our uncle chooses to underestimate their strength and unity, deluding himself and listening to the advice of fools, I certainly do not!" said Rupert, and stalked out of the room before the crushed Maurice could reply.

As the spirits of the King and his sanguinary gentlemen grew lighter, so the Prince's premonition of disaster deepened. Every leading man in the Royalist army, except himself, seemed to have lost all sense of reality. It was certainly with no blessing from him that the King was hunting in Fawsley Park, and the soldiers lolling at ease, when patrols hacked into Daventry reporting that Fairfax was only five miles away, accompanied by a force of eight thousand men.

Venetia was dreaming of Marston Moor, reliving the bloody field stark under the white glaze of moonlight, and Boye, running before her, nosing among the grisly heaps, looking for Rupert. She woke sobbing at the urgent banging at the door and men's voices. Rupert was shouting to enter, out of bed and reaching for his breeches. Venetia sat up, her dreams giving way to a waking nightmare.

They had evacuated Daventry and were spending the night in Harborough, while King Charles had retired to the Old Hall, Lubenham. Rupert had left an outpost at the village of Naseby and had come in late, drenched and cross, after seeing to his men. Now there was this disturbance.

The King was below, calling for an immediate Council of War. His troops had been having supper, well content with their comfortable quarters around the inn at Naseby, drinking and playing quoits, their weapons and armor laid aside, when they were taken unawares by a patrol of Roundhead horse. One of the vedettes had escaped over the hills, wounded and bleeding, galloping to seek the King.

Charles roused his councillors and rode through the wet darkness to the only man who could deal with the situation —his nephew.

Venetia crept to the head of the stairs, peering through the banisters like a child watching the grown-ups arrive for a party. The King's advisers came straggling in, blinking at one another in the sudden glare of candlelight. Rupert was shrugging his shoulders into his doublet, his hair a disorderly mop.

" 'Tis strange," the King was saying in his studied way, sounding calm in the midst of this confusion, although his face was gray with exhaustion. "I was dreaming of poor Tom Stafford when they awakened me. He was warning me not to engage the enemy. This is the second time he has appeared to me in a dream."

No one answered; this reference to the executed friend of Charles, sacrificed for the safety of his Queen, seemed singularly ill-timed.

For once, Rupert counseled retreat, astonishing even Digby into silence by such unwonted prudence. "Why should this make any difference to our plans to go north? We can continue our march but at a quicker pace. There will be additional troops at Leicester, also Gerard and Goring should arrive at any time."

"And Fairfax is already here," Digby said silkily, his cold, pale eyes on the two Princes whom he detested so heartily.

"I am not in favor of accepting a battle with him yet." Rupert was keeping a tight hold on his frayed temper. "Let us retreat in good order and draw him after us until we have more men and a better choice of both time and ground."

"What does Your Royal Highness require? A guarantee of safety?" purred the Secretary of State, enragingly calm.

"No, my Lord—just a guarantee of success. Every failure is a waste of time." Rupert's voice was full of menace.

"Sir, I beg leave to disagree with His Highness." Digby turned to King Charles. "Would not this be a glorious opportunity for that final battle? We could then return triumphant to Oxford."

Charles did not reply, his large tired eyes going from one to the other, floundering helplessly when faced with alternative moves. They were in a tricky situation, either course was a hazard; with Fairfax tailing them, there was a grave danger that the retreat might turn into an ignominious flight.

It was this which Digby stressed with such flowing eloquence, echoed and seconded by the King's favorite Gentleman of the Bedchamber, Jack Ashburnham, both making it a point of honor of scorning to retire. This chivalrous reasoning appealed to Charles, and the rest of the Council, with the exception of the Palatines, allowed themselves to be persuaded.

"Oh, God, why are they so stupid?" Venetia wondered, sitting cramped and chilled on the stairs as the meeting drew to its conclusion with remorseless inevitability. "They should know better—Rupert is against an engagement—and when a fighter such as he can bring himself to refuse a challenge from an enemy so close—then those foolish amateur tacticians ought to heed him."

She lost all patience with the King who was siding with the Courtiers against his Commander-in-Chief. At the same time, it tore at her heart to see how much he had aged lately.

The voices rolled on, and Rupert listened in a kind of

hopeless anger, his eyes hooded as they rested on Digby. Once the Prince would have stood his ground and browbeaten them into doing as he willed, but now, suddenly, a weary indifference swept over him. Even old Astley was nodding his snowy head in agreement and Maurice was yawning fit to crack his jaw, summing up the conference as one prodigious bore. They were determined to fight—very well—so be it!

He rose abruptly, terminating the discussion, brushing aside protocol. There was much to be done in what was left of this short June night, his men were billeted in the surrounding villages—it would take time to muster them.

The town burst into alarmed life, lights springing up, men and horses in movement. Venetia, dressing quickly, beseeched him, as he swirled out of the door: "Can I come?"

Rupert was too worried to argue. "Very well, until we are in battaglia—then you must dispatch to the *lager.*"

Morning was dulling the stars, tree-shapes looming out of the drizzle. The cantle rubbed her backbone, beaded drops fell from her helmet peak and wet her cheek, leather creaked, scabbards thumped on saddles, bridles jingled, hoofbeats thudded dully on sodden turf.

Ruse, the scoutmaster, had returned, assuring Rupert that he had been forward two or three miles and had seen nothing of the foe. The Prince swore at him for an incompetent dolt and went to make his own reconnaissance. In the early summer dawn, he breasted a rise and stared across a boggy hollow to where the New Model were moving against the skyline on rising ground opposite.

" 'Sblood, what is amiss with Ruse's eyesight?" he demanded gruffly of Richard Crane. "If this be a fair example of his industry, I now know why our intelligence is so poor! I had been better advised to employ Barney!"

"Easy enough to miss them, sir." Crane was screwing up his lids against the brightness.

Rupert grunted and nodded. Open as the view was, between the ridges there rolled a series of lesser undulations which were sufficient to hide a troop as soon as it moved from the heights.

A couple of peasants were brought to him, apprehensive, ducking and touching their forelocks, big with news. They had been minding sheep close to Fairfax's camp and had seen a body of horse ride in to join him just before it was light. A great shout had gone up from the Roundhead ranks—"Ironsides is come!"

Maurice cantered up with the cavalry and his brother wheeled to him, speaking with intent quickness: "Cromwell has come!"

"Good. Then we will meet him together."

Maurice relaxed—this was more like Le Diable. He had become alarmed by the profound melancholy which had seized Rupert, and his inability to shake off the remembrance of his losses which weighed heavily on his spirit.

Rupert was pointing out that the Parliamentarians seemed to be intending to occupy the Naseby ridge. At the same time he was taking note of the stretch of ground between, marshy and treacherous, impossible for horsemen. The Cavaliers must either turn their position, or else remain on the defensive higher up, declining battle. But the Prince had already seen what looked like more promising terrain on the right, by which his troopers might ascend and launch an attack.

"It will mean a flanking movement, sir." Crane sniffed the air, feeling the direction of the strong breeze. "And it will bring us to windward of 'em, so we'll not have their powder blowing in our faces."

Following his instinct, Rupert found what he wanted—a gentle slope leading down to an open expanse of moor which rose again on the other side a little higher, but still easy for cavalry, leading up to the westward end of the ridge where the New Model were maneuvering. He sent back an urgent message to the Royal army to come up with all speed.

Behind them straggled the light field-pieces, the carts and coaches, and, as the opposing armies drew into battle array, Venetia reluctantly trotted her pony to the rear.

The wagons were already positioned in a wide circle within a strong guard of musketeers, and the women were busy seeing that their men had full canteens, and a meal inside them before operations began. Damaris' coach was parked beside several others, which included Lord Digby's, on a hillock where they might have a good view of the field.

Etienne was using up a deal of energy making sure that his men were at their station in the Prince's Regiment of Horse. He paused while Damaris leaned from the carriage window and pinned a beanstalk in his hat; this was the fieldsign for the day.

"Did you hear that singular tale of panic which happened when we were in Hereford?" Barney took meat and bread from his saddle-bag, sat on a fallen log and chewed. "It was told of a trooper who, being beaten up at night in his quarters, strenuously attempted to bridle his comrade instead of his horse!"

Barney was a splendid person to be with at such a moment, utterly fearless, full of initiative—his forte was to fight, to tease, to laugh and tell a good yarn, and he was a most useful member of any brigade in that he had a rare talent for getting goods out of the most stubborn locals.

The tension was mounting—there was the smell of battle in the air; the horses sensed it, moving restlessly and giving trouble. Etienne's spritely animal caught the excitement, fretting as he climbed into the saddle; he gentled her in soft French phrases.

"Courage, *ma belle,* you will recover when we are on the hack!"

They had climbed on to the coachman's seat, the panorama of the wide Royalist front spread out before them. A pale sun washed over the spectacle, winking on breastplates and swords, silk sashes and bright doublets.

"What a fine sight!" Venetia said, a lump in her throat —they were so gallant. "It should give pause to that rebel carrion!"

"Oh, look at that!" Damaris was pointing to a cavalry standard of green flowered damask with the bold inscription "cuckolds we come" surmounted by a pair of horns.

Venetia was more concerned to find Rupert's banner, and that of Maurice, at the head of the right wing.

The standard-bearers were selected from among the most stouthearted and athletic gentlemen available—the task of carrying the colors was not altogether enviable. At the beginning of a pitched battle, they made a fair target for the enemy cannon, and in a *mêlée*, both sides strove lustily to seize the standards of the opposite party. A common practice was to chop at the hand stubbornly clasping the staff. Although protected by a bristling wall of pikes they still had to cope with the unwieldy six foot spread of fringed, painted taffeta and, if all else failed, to defend themselves and it.

In spite of the impressive display, Venetia's heart gave a lurch when she saw how few they were compared to the vast force of the Parliamentarians. She thought bitterly of Goring's seasoned troopers, far away in Somerset. His wayward disobedience might well cost them the day, unless, by some miracle, he suddenly arrived. It would not be unlike him to come dashing impetuously along at the last moment, in high-spirited *bravura*.

Venetia shadowed her eyes with her hand, chafing for Rupert's perspective glass, straining to see his minute figure, far away on the right.

It seemed that he was not going to lose the initiative a second time; to catch the enemy before they were quite ready was his best chance of making up for the inferiority of numbers.

His sword flashed, a trumpet howled, the whole line moved forward towards the moor, marching at a smart pace and keeping formation. As the foot began to climb the slope on the other side, the Roundhead infantry streamed over the brow to meet them. There was a jolt and a crash as they came to push of pike. Astley's musketeers fired volley after volley and then fell on them with swords and musket-butts.

Rupert was galloping ahead, his horse forming long uneven columns which bulged and bellied, thundering into the valley towards the opposite hillside. As they began to prick up the rise, the Prince checked, a breathless pause held his cavalry as they stared at the whole dense mass of the Parliamentarian force which now lumbered into view on the crest. But the halt was only momentary—urging his men on, he swung them uphill at the gallop, and his crack front line did not falter, running the gauntlet of the dragoons behind the hedge on their right, whose carbines galled them as they swept past, emptying many a saddle.

Panting and snorting, whinnying with excitement, as fiercely eager as the men who spurred them on, the destriers struggled to the ridge, smashing into Ireton's troopers like a wall of steel. They staggered at the shock, then recovered and drove on again, the superior swordsmanship telling—Rupert and his Lifeguard making fearful havoc, breaking through their ranks, pushing them back to trample their own infantry and throw that too into confusion. The huge force of rebel cavalry was crumbling, scattering and dwindling as men turned to flee headlong, pursued by the yelling, victorious Cavaliers, who chased them off the field.

There was turmoil in the vale below, where fallow fields were being mashed by flaying hooves and stamping feet— time was out of phase—it might have been minutes or an hour since hell had broken out. Voices shredded back on the wind, cries of rage and agony, the rattle of shot, the terrified screams of maddened horses—and still there was no sign of Rupert.

In the leaguer, the surgeons, overworked and short on staff, did what they could for the injured who staggered in, hacked or trampled or bleeding from bullet wounds.

"Where is the Prince?" Venetia demanded of every new face, but all they could tell her was that his cavalry were last seen making for the enemy wagons far behind the line. There was some encouraging news; Ireton had lost control of his wing, he had been wounded twice, a pike had run him through the thigh, a halberd had slashed his face and, for a while, he had been a prisoner.

"And Cromwell? What of him?" She was getting as neurotic as Rupert about that formidable Lieutenant-General. Cromwell was alive and doing very well.

He had stationed his horse up the hill. Langdale's troopers were threading their way through the furze bushes and rabbit-warrens toward him, and as they began to climb, he gave a signal and his cavalry poured down, firing their pistols at almost point-blank range and then attacking with their swords. The fight was short and vicious, Langdale's men gave ground, then turned to run with the leading three of Cromwell's regiments in pursuit. But he had them well controlled; they rode in knee to knee order after the demoralized Northern Horse, uttering no war-cry, grimly silent, steel caps glinting, a solid wave inexorably progressing, perfectly disciplined, ony going just far enough to see that they did not rally and reform. Then, at the command, they turned back to press home their crushing weight on the Royalist foot.

Sick with anxiety, Venetia climbed once again to Damaris' carriage, and there was someone else also eager to view the battleground from the roof of his ornate vehicle. She looked straight into Lord Digby's eyes.

"Why are you not out there fighting, my lord?"

"Rupert's trull!" he spat out with feline vindictiveness, his mouth turned down in petulance like a child who invites you to slap its face. "I might have guessed that you would be nigh, eager for him to swive you, between his bouts of plundering!"

There was no mistaking his emnity, and she recalled Etienne's insinuations, suddenly convinced that he was right. Digby's behavior towards the Prince was very much that of a woman scorned. When they had first met, he must have been attracted by the magnificent young savage. Rupert was no innocent, and he would have quickly realized that more than friendship was offered; his years at university and in camp would have opened his eyes to sexual deviations. Rupert, for all his beauty, was essentially masculine—and overtures from Digby would have been frigidly rejected.

Venetia looked him up and down, slowly and insultingly. "My Lord, I am of the opinion that you are green-sick with jealousy. What would you not give to be in my position?"

Digby went white with temper. "You speak like the whore you are, madam! Where is your lover at this moment? Looting the enemy baggage, forsooth! His unruly hellions have ever thus betrayed the cause!"

There was a stir on the Naseby ridge and a cry went up. Rupert had returned. He was scanning the field from the crown of the hill, deliberating where he and his men might best assist.

The long line of infantry was still swaying together, locked in hand-to-hand struggle all along the slope. Little knots of cavalry circled and fought among the gorse; there were bodies sprawled on the ground; riderless horses bolted; remnants of the Newark troopers galloped for survival to the rear of the King's reserve.

The enemy forces were converging on the Royalist foot who were giving such good account of themselves, but now, beset on three sides, they began to fall back down the valley. Only one thing could save them—intervention by the King's reserve, and Charles moved, urging on his Lifeguard. His voice rang out, firm and true, with no trace of stammer.

"One charge more, gentlemen! One charge more, and the day is ours!"

Rupert plunged down the incline, launching himself into that heaving, struggling mass of men and horses, cleaving his way towards the King.

But just at that moment, when it seemed that their Sovereign's courage might put new heart into his dismayed soldiers, some well-wisher, anxious for his safety, seized his bridle and pulled his horse's head around. This movement was taken for a command. Someone shouted, "He means us to march to the right hand'" and part of the horse wheeled away, carrying the King with them.

Chaos ensued. Everywhere the colors began to fall, men were throwing down their arms and crying for quarter, except for Rupert's own brave Bluecoats, who stoutly kept their ranks, fighting chest to back, their pikes repulsing the pick of the New Model horse, with the same dogged courage of Newcastle's Whitecoats at Marston Moor, and meeting the same bloody end. Its square was only broken at last when Fairfax brought up his infantry to climb their way in, while the cavalry charged on both sides simultaneously. They died in their ranks, heaped one upon the other, fighting with resolute, hopeless valor to the last.

When Rupert succeeded in reaching the King, it was already too late. In vain he tried to rally his cavalry for one last effort, his voice ringing like a trumpet-call on a fine-drawn note of desperation, but the battle-heart of his men was broken; the horse were in disgraceful and tumultuous retreat.

"All is over, save the slaughter!" came the cry, and panic spread. Cromwell's men turned on the stampeding Royalists and this time the pursuit was not checked, and their swords did heavy execution all along the road toward Leicester. The Cavaliers left everything behind; their standards, their baggage, their wealth—and their women.

The victorious Roundhead infantry poured into the leaguer despatching the guards. They were shouting: "Kill the Cavalier drabs!" and clubbing any who tried to stop them.

They ransacked the coaches; clothing, goods and personal effects flung aside and trampled in the frenzied search for money, hauling out the cowering women, ignoring their protests that they were officer's wives, excited by their terror, hunting them among the wagons, holding them down on the crushed grass and raping them before putting them to the sword.

Venetia ducked behind a cart. A woman rushed towards her, mouth agape in fear, sobbing breath labored, burdened by a howling toddler. She tripped and flung the child into Venetia's arms, before being borne down by the gang of ruffians who fell upon her. The swords flashed up and then down, and she shrieked. Venetia pressed the child's face against her so that it should not see its mother murdered.

The wives of the Welsh foot, crying out in their own language, were taken for Irish witches, the men believing the tales of their chaplains who said that the knives they carried were intended to cut the throats of their victims. The women fought savagely to protect their belongings, before being overpowered and butchered.

Then they turned their attention to the whores. Many of the wealthy ones, forced on their knees in the mire, screaming for mercy, were able to buy it from their victors —but the others—the poor doxies who had been the perquisite of the lower ranks, were mutilated in the brutish manner in which these bigoted fanatics marked harlots.

They were seized and held firmly. Venetia, half hidden by a wagon, still holding the sobbing baby, saw them squirming and heard their shrill animal cries as their faces were slashed, blood spraying from between their fingers as they covered the wounds where their noses had been hacked off and their cheeks laid open to the bone. And the preachers walked among them, praying and giving thanks to God for a glorious victory over the heathenish vermin.

Soldiers found Venetia and dragged her from her hiding-place. She fought, bit and swore, till stunned by a swinging backhanded blow across the face. The hysterical child clung to her legs, adding to the furor, before being kicked away.

"Here is another of the wicked queens!" her tormentors were yelling, ripping her shirt open from neck to waist. "Dressed as a man, the shameless slut!"

They pushed her, face down, in the bloodied puddles at the feet of one of their chaplains.

The blood was salting Venetia's tongue from her cut lip, but she choked out: "I am English—let me go!"

The hot eyes of her captors were raking over her, for her torn shirt exposed her breasts, and she could feel the waves of lust sweeping out from them, almost tangible. Even the preacher wore the same expression, appetite roused by the massacre. There was blood everywhere, running from the pathetic corpses, clotting on the hands of the men, while the maimed huddled togegher, moaning.

A hand grabbed her by the hair, holding her rigid, and there was the flash of steel raised to strike; one slash and all her beauty would be reduced to twisted monstrosity, healing into livid, puckered weals, a vile disfigurement from which men, sickened, would avert their eyes.

The sword hung for a frozen instant, then commenced its downward swoop, but Damaris was there, knocking up the Roundhead's arm, demanding, in high indignation, what the devil he considered that he was doing!

The chaplain glared at her. "Who are you, madam?"

"I am a French citizen." Damaris was supremely haughty, her air of authority halting them, more angry than Venetia had ever seen her, a blazing-eyed termagant, well used to dealing with rebellious peasants with the iron-fisted autocracy learned in a country where the feudal system still held sway. "Unhand my friend at once, sirrah!"

The preacher was reluctant to lose a victim, instantly hostile because she was a foreigner, probably a Papist and follower of the hated Queen Henrietta.

A band of Ironside officers clopped into the circle of wagons. "Are you having trouble with the prisoners, chaplain?" enquired their leader.

Whatever he or his troop thought of the actions of the foot, they made no comment, stern-faced, uncompromising, believing that God had given them victory that day, rejoicing in Him and their leaders.

The Captain listened to the preacher, then shifted in his saddle to address Damaris. "Madam I trust that you have papers to prove your claims?"

"In my coach, sir." Her face was imperious, but now unbending slightly as if recognizing a gentleman among a rabble. "If your men have not already plundered it."

He dismounted, shouldering his way through to Venetia. He reached down, put a hand under her elbow and helped her to her feet. Beneath his helmet, his expression was deadpan, but he had recognized her instantly and she remembered him and a day in Oxford, months before, and Rupert bidding her to write a pass as he dictated.

He escorted her to Damaris' carriage, his men falling back to let them through, giving a curt command so that the belligerent soldiers bullying her servants took themselves off. Then he spoke to her, his voice low and urgent.

"Get away from here with all speed. I cannot keep your identity hidden for very long. You are wanted by our people after the affair at Long Marston. But I will give you this one chance. Prince Rupert was very fair in his treatment of me."

They could do no more than mutter their thanks and he stood back, the whip of the coachman snaking across, flicking the leader of the team of six horses. The vehicle jerked into motion, and Venetia leaned out, catching a last glimpse of the Ironside captain standing in the mud, watching the coach take its awkward, uneasy course along the track leading to Leicester.

FIVE

Venetia caught up with Rupert before nightfall. She found him sickened beyond words by the totality of the rout. He was badly bruised, his sword arm hanging useless at his side and they spent a miserable few hours trying to get some sleep. Next day, with the dejected King and the pitiful remnants of cavalry, they pushed on to Hereford.

The news which filtered through was increasingly depressing. King Charles had lost his infantry, his guns, and most of his baggage-train at Naseby. The Stuart standard had been taken, the Queen's beautiful colors embroidered with the lilies of France, those of the Palatine and the Duke of York, together with the flags of every foot regiment on the field.

Digby should have looked after his Royal master's correspondence and possessions; he kept his wits about him enough to make his escape in his own carriage, but the entire collection of private letters belonging to the King fell into the hands of the enemy.

Incredible though it seemed, he managed to talk his way out of his criminal negligence. Rupert fulminated at the injustice of the situation; he had been against giving battle and was now exposed to the odium of defeat, while Digby, so hot for it, was not called upon to answer for the fatal outcome.

Rupert wanted to link up the surviving horse with the still intact army in the West, moving rapidly, before Fairfax and Cromwell swept down on that part of the country and prevented amalgamation. But a subtle change had come over the King; always obstinate, victim of his own incorrigible infirmity of purpose, he now displayed an unlooked-for tenacity, stubbornly insisting that he must raise levies and join Gerard and his Welsh troops. This meant delay. Rupert fumed, unable to sleep, tiresomely restless. It was small wonder that his uncle sought refuge in Digby's sympathetic company.

"I fail to understand how a man of the King's intelligence can be so blind!" Rupert prowled the room. "He speaks as if military defeats are of small moment—unfortunate accidents—regrettable, but not calamitous, and then goes on to speak of 'moral victories.'"

"Is it really so disastrous?" The well-trained Maurice was keeping a weather eye open for sudden spurts of temper. "Gerard has a few thousand men and Goring is still at large."

Rupert glared. "You ask me that! 'Sdeath, man, you were there! You saw it all! For any serious purpose, we have no army to put in the field. Worse than that, we are a command divided against itself, and nothing will heal the breach."

After three stormy days, Rupert took leave of the King, rode to Cardiff, packed Venetia off to Bristol under escort, and went by boat to Barnstaple to seek out Prince Charles and his roaming Court and take measures for the defense of the West.

Bristol—a place of many inhabitants, a center of shipping, a busy city jumbled untidily round its river, dominated by a tumbledown medieval Castle; the King's last remaining major town, and gateway to the sea. There was plague in Bristol, a pesthouse had been opened between Stokes Croft and the River Frome. As Venetia jogged through the gate with her bodyguard, she averted her eyes from the red crosses daubed on doors. There was a brooding heaviness in the atmosphere, it was almost possible to smell the despondency and disaffection which were being played upon by rebel agents scuttling about their treacherous business in the heart of the old port. It was insufficiently supplied and badly garrisoned; the Commissioners had fled and, when Rupert returned, he would find that he had the work of many on his hands.

Matters in the West did little to mitigate Rupert's gloom. He stayed ten days and was in Bristol early in July. One of his first orders was for immediate cessation of the knells tolling out monotonously for the plague-dead, grating on the already raw nerves of the garrison.

Venetia, rapturously happy to be in his arms again, put

all her own problems aside, wanting only to please him. She pressed her body into his, her fingers probing at the small of his back, while his lips moved over her temples, eyelids and mouth with small exploring kisses as if he had forgotten the taste of her.

Every time he came back, it was like discovering him anew; there was always that same intense, irrational excitement which she had known the very first time she saw him. The war—King Charles—all faded into insignificance beside this huge emotion.

She could never have enough of his kisses, hungering for them when he was away. That lovely mouth closed on hers, firmly at first then softening, seeking, as if he would suck out her very soul and absorb it into himself. Eyes closed, ripening, sweetening under his touch, she marvelled at those lips which could bark commands, make acid comment, mould round complicated languages and give her such ravishing delight.

He had come in not long before dinner, and there had followed an oasis of peace and closeness. It was cool shadowy dusk, though not dark enough to light the candles, when they awoke. Venetia got up and crossed to the table to fetch goblets and a decanter.

Rupert stirred, opening his eyes and smiling at her, calm and relaxed, the way men are after loving women.

He shook his head dubiously. "I wish that I need not leave the West in Goring's charge, but there is no other way."

"Why did he not come to Harborough, as you commanded?" She snuggled under the covers beside him.

" 'Swounds! Why indeed!" he rejoined with an angry flash of his eyes. "He has a multitude of plausible excuses —says that he was sieging Taunton and pressed to defeat the enemy there. But I have heard that he spent a deal of time vaporing at Bath."

Venetia rested her cheek against the back of his hand. "And Prince Charles?"

Rupert laughed. "Having the time of his life! Idolized by all, he can ride and sail to his heart's content. Hyde fusses around him, but he is developing a mind of his own and, by God, he needs it when dealing with Goring and Richard Greenville, who are up to all manner of knavery."

They were both busy plotting, quarrelling violently, neither willing to concede that the other had any right to forage or contributions, upsetting local Justices of the Peace by their habit of kidnapping civilians and holding them for ransom, while their badly-behaved ruffianly troops terrorized the district.

Goring was going through a bad patch; showing occasional bursts of his old brilliance, then lapsing into long stretches of debauchery and equally incapacitating courses of physic. Athough such bitter rivals, he seemed to have an extraordinary power over Grenville; they were much alike, a pair of arrogant, corrupt intriguers.

Rupert told her how Goring had bungled an attempt to intercept Fairfax. His men had converged from opposite directions on what they thought was the retreating enemy and fought each other for two hours before realizing their mistakes. "That unrepentant rogue gaily reported that it was the most fantastical accident since the war began!"

Rupert could see the humor of this shocking blunder, and Goring's natural charm and audacity were so great that, no matter how he maddened by his errors, no one could hate him for long.

Not long before, an uneasy truce had existed between them; they had been drinking companions for a day or so, during which time Rupert told Goring, with evident relish, all the evil that the Council of the West had said concerning him, and Goring returned the compliment with notes and additions.

Now there was real distress in Rupert's tone. "If only he and Grenville could be brought to work together for the King! They are good soldiers, and badly needed."

Venetia echoed these sentiments in her mind, applying it to every member of the disrupted Royalist command.

Rupert got up, throwing back his hair, suddenly resolved. "I shall send for Maurice and we will see to it that Bristol remains in His Majesty's hands."

There was no rest for Rupert. He had arrived on Friday, worked hard till Wednesday, then, to cheer his low-spirited men, took them on a successful night raid on enemy quarters at Wells. On Friday he saw leaders of the Clubmen outside Bristol. Like their counterpart in Herefordshire, they were seething with unrest, blowing their swineherd horns, calling nocturnal assemblies so that they might plan an attack on the city, hoping to indemnify their own losses. On Monday evening he parleyed with another group, to try and win them over to the King. But whereas once the Royalist successes carried weight, now the down-hill slide of their fortunes went against enrollment.

There were flares dotting the skyline, illumining the dark shapes of men whose voices rose to a roar as Prince Rupert and his Lifeguard thundered up the slope of Landsdown toward them. They drew rein, steam from their blown animals hanging on the damp air, and the circle of set, determined faces closed in. These wild ones who rampaged through the countryside could not really hope to oppose an organized force. But they were a nuisance with their numbers and their English hardihood.

An argument broke out among them as the Prince's men waited in ominous silence. Then their spokesman, a broad-shouldered young husbandman with angry intelligent eyes shouted down his confederates who wanted to crack open a few heads. The troublemakers were frog-marched ignominiously away.

Much of Rupert's startling publicity had preceded him, and they tended to lump him and his troopers together with Goring's undisciplined rascals, but now his calm impressed them. He addressed their leader.

"What is your name, my man?"

"Tom Chapman, sir." He was respectful but not servile.

"And what is the trouble, Mr. Chapman?"

A discontented rumble came from the yeomen; Rupert's accent did nothing to still their suspicion, rousing their clannish hatred of foreigners, which included anyone born outside the boundaries of their own country.

"We want no more soldiers in our villages!" Chapman declared adamantly, while his comrades shouted in assent. "We can't afford to support 'em, and we've no mind to do so further. They upset our lives and unsettle our women. Terrified of 'em, they be!"

Venetia caught an inference which made her smile. She guessed that they had trouble with their wives, daughters and sweethearts, impressed by the swaggering adventurers who brought color into drab lives.

Rupert was attentive and polite. "I offer my regrets, sir, if any of my men have cheated you or used my name in justification of their actions. In truth, if they so did, they disobeyed my instructions. It has always been our desire to pay for supplies."

An intention not always possible to carry out. Living at free quarters, a troop of horse would soon outstay its welcome, even in the most loyal area.

Some of the heat had gone out of the gathering. Rupert was addressing them, telling them that men of the soil made the best soldiers and the King wanted their support. It was a never-failing wonder to her to see how he always managed to inspire respect, if not liking, in a foe.

Before he left, the Prince coerced them into a half-hearted promise to stop badgering his cavalry, and to sell him the beef which he required.

They supped in Bath, arguing all through the meal because Rupert was insistent that she should return to Bristol while he intended galloping through the darkness and crossing the Severn to meet King Charles near Cardiff.

"I'll be home tomorrow," he promised as he kissed her farewell in the courtyard and then he was off.

He was as good as his word. Next afternoon, Venetia, hanging from an upper window, saw him throw his bridle to a groom and disappear indoors in a couple of strides. He came bounding up the wide, shallow staircase and she met him at the door.

"The King is coming here!" He sounded jubilant. "At last I shall know, first-hand, what is going on."

Venetia pushed him into a chair, setting a bottle at his elbow.

"Did you sleep at all last night?" She was studying his face, seeing the fatigue lines, the dark smudges beneath his eyes. She sent for De Faust.

"Sleep? We didn't arrive till dawn and there was much to discuss."

"And the King was reasonable?" Venetia seated herself on his lap in a rustle of silk skirts and his arm came about her.

He nodded, but she knew him too well not to recognize that there must have been reservations. "He still talks of reinforcements from Ireland. I don't think it matters a damn if he brings in the Turks, so long as we get men!"

"You didn't tell him that?" Venetia rubbed at a streak of dried mud on the side of his jaw.

"I fear that I did. I think he found me a little discouraging. My uncle knows not what belongs to war."

"But he is coming here to you and that is good news, surely?" With her sensitivity to his every mood, she knew that more had happened at the interview than he had divulged.

He leaned his head against the back of the chair. "Jack

Ashburnham made it his business to inform me that Digby intends my ruin."

"I thought he was Digby's friend." De Faust was tardy, so Venetia began to tug at his boots herself, astride his leg, skirts hitched high, while he thrust with the other foot against her backside. Then he stood up, groaning, and stretched widely till his joints cracked, making for the bed. He fell into a deep sleep as soon as his head hit the pillow.

The Prince's visit to Bath had been in vain; his attempt to reorganize and strengthen the garrison had merely provoked mutinous discontent and when Fairfax appeared before the town, it surrendered without a struggle, following the example of Bridgwater. Bristol was no longer regarded as a safe haven for King Charles.

For Venetia, the war had narrowed to one West country port, plague-stricken and in danger of being besieged. No help seemed forthcoming from the Court now at Raglan Castle, where the whispering campaign continued and the only reports were disquieting ones of Digby's machinations.

"Could I but spare one day to ride to them and find out for myself what is going on!" Rupert raged, but there was no time. Bristol was badly stocked and short of men, the desertion rate was high, and the city full of rebellion. He did his best to remedy these problems, ordering the citizens to victual themselves for six months, importing corn and cattle, and starting factories for match and bullets.

One thundery morning, Rupert was in his shirt sleeves laboring over his correspondence with Trevor. He pushed the letter aside, drew a clean sheet toward him and began to write to the Duke of Richmond.

"My Lord, it is now in everybody's mouth, that the King is going for Scotland" . . . he paused, pen poised, trying to control his anger. Once more, those about his uncle least suitable to be trusted with any secret intention were party to them, whereas the one person who should have been consulted was deliberately kept in the dark. Then his pen flowed on, urging the gentle Duke to press for peace: "His Majesty has no way left to preserve his posterity, kingdom, and nobility, but by a treaty. I believe it a more prudent way to retain something, than to lose all."

He expressed grave doubts as to any help coming out of Ireland, and ended "One comfort will be left; we shall all fall together. When this is, remember I have done my duty. Your faithful friend, Rupert."

He stabbed the quill into the squat silver ink-well and added the date "Bristol, July 28th, 1645."

Anxious to keep Will Legge in the picture, he scribbled a note to him, betraying his annoyance and fear of the King taking offense. Honest Will, one of those among Rupert's friends who were proud to call themselves the "Cumberlanders," after his English Dukedom. Digby's spies were trying hard to implicate him in their hints of treachery, using the cowardly means of anonymous letters.

Venetia felt sure that Rupert's latest blunt epistle would upset the King, yet hoped that he would recognize that this desire for peace was sincere and disinterested. Rupert had far less to gain from it than many of the Royalists; being foreign, he had no stake in the country's future, and the very fact that such incorruptible men as Richmond and Will were his staunch allies must persuade Charles of his absolute integrity.

Rupert plunged into action. He gathered a troop, marched all night and beat up an enemy horse-quarter at Dursley, took a Parliamentarian's house at Stinchcombe, slept at Berkeley Castle, travelled like the wind through Wootten-under-Edge and Chipping Sodbury, skirmished with Roundheads outside Bath, and hacked back to Bristol in fine fettle.

He felt much better after a good fight, and he was singing as he changed into a clean shirt before supper. Afterwards, Venetia rose and went to the window, while he sat on, drinking, and watching her.

"It is going to be a fine night, Highness, with a great full moon."

"Splendid for a raid." His lips curved into an indulgent smile.

"Oh, you and your raids!" she said with mock impatience, delighted because he was so jovial; he had been animated all through the meal which they had shared with Crane and de Gomme, discussing plans for the protection of the city.

"There will be few opportunities for more," he said soberly. "Fairfax is tightening his lines."

"Will Maurice be able to get through?" Venetia had hoped that Damaris would accompany him, missing her endearing spontaneity.

"He cannot leave Worcester, it is too vulnerable."

"And Prince Edward? I thought you expected him daily." She was very curious to meet this handsome younger brother.

"Ah, there is mention of him in a letter from Paris sent by Harry Jermyn. It will interest you." He was searching through his pockets; one crumpled paper fell out, but it was the dog-eared, creased dispatch sent to him by the King before Marston Moor which he always carried. He dragged out another, smoothed the pages and read the relevant passage while she listened with enjoyment to the rise and fall of his voice.

" 'Your Highness is to know a romance story that concerns you here, in the person of Prince Edward. He is last week married privately to the Princess Anne, the Duke of Nevers' daughter.' "

Rupert paused to say: "Jermyn adds that the Queen of France was displeased, and that he was commanded to retire into Holland. There he will have met the vexation of our mother, for I believe the bride is a Papist! Poor old Ned! Jermyn goes on: 'She is very rich, and is a very beautiful young lady.' "

"Do you envy him?" Her throat closed inconveniently. Oh, to be wealthy, titled and a beauty! Would Rupert marry her then?

"What!" he sounded astonished that she should even suggest such an extraordinary idea! "Holy God! I would not be wed!"

"Not even to a fortune?"

"Especially not to a fortune! I'd not be some rich woman's lapdog! Here, darling, what ails you?"

He came to stand behind her, his hands going to her breasts, and his head bent so that his mouth touched the nape of her neck. Gently he turned her toward him, troubled by her sadness. And how could she tell him? But in her eyes he read her sorrow, and understood.

He drew her to him, her face against his chest, his lips resting on the sleek top of her head. "You are so good to me," he said wonderingly, with pity and perplexity, "and I treat you more harshly at times than I would a dog. Yet I think that you are the only faithful friend I have, save Maurice and Will, in the whole of this island."

"I love you." There was no other answer to give, and he was quiet for a moment, and then:

"Tomorrow I must work, but now we will do anything you wish. What would you?"

Her arms were around his neck and she tipped back her head to look at him. "D'you recall the woods, across the Downs, where you took me on that first night?"

He smiled with amused male tolerance of her womanish whims. "Nightingale Valley? Oh yes, I remember it well. You would not let me do it there."

"I should not stop you now."

She felt his sharp intake of breath, the instant response of his body. "We will take horse, then go to the quayside to buy herbs from the sailors." He jingled coins in his pockets.

"What of the plague?" Her pleasure was shot through with alarm.

"If you catch it, then doubtless, I shall also!" He was so confident that it was possible to believe that even the Black Death would cringe before him. "We will go to the woods and lie beneath the stars and you must show me just how much you love me." His voice was low, husky, and there was swift demanding impatience in his dark face.

The valley was cool and black and mysterious. Nothing jarred their serenity; even a nightingale obliged and performed for them. He spread out his cloak, laid her down on it, and stretched out at her side. There was a strange intoxication in the air. She had never realized that she had such an abundance of skin or so much hair to be caught on the breeze and fall like a veil over the Prince as he pulled her on to him, his cold buttons indenting her flesh.

"Oh, Rupert," she breathed, "Oh."

"Do you love me? Tell me."

"Oh yes, I love you."

He did not answer except to kiss her very long and deep. She held him closer, shuddering with passion and cold. And then he said, his lips against her ear, "Shall I give you my son?"

She cried with joy and made him, laughing, say it again, in all the languages he knew—and later, she stood in the centre of the glade where a shaft of moonlight notched through a roving cloud and bathed her in blue radiance, dazzling her sight. She raised her arms wide, face rapt and uplifted, like a votary of Diana, goddess of childbirth, praying to her and to all the ancient pagan deities, that they might pity and bless her and plant Rupert's seed in her womb.

252

Within a month of their capture, the Roundheads gleefully published the Royal letters in a volume called *The King's Cabinet Opened*. It placed before a shocked, excited public the indiscreet discussions on policy between Charles and his Queen, covering a period of almost two years. They left no one in doubt as to his intention to bring over an Irish army and in return, to abolish the penal law against Catholics in England, exposed both his efforts to hire foreign mercenaries and his attempts to get money from France, Denmark and the Prince of Orange.

The Royalist party was affected—the Welsh gentry cooled and withdrew offers of aid. Rupert raved at Digby's blundering imbecility in losing such inflammable documents at a moment when it was vital that they hang on to every vestige of trust and goodwill.

There had been no direct reply from the King to Rupert's peace proposals. Richmond had passed on the message, and written telling his cousin how it had been received. Rupert whacked the paper down on the table, the draught lifting the quills and sending loose leaves dancing to the floor.

"He was very calm about it apparently, Richmond says that he read it graciously! As if he need be 'gracious' to me! He found it impossible to swallow his pride and ask for another treaty." His voice fell with disappointment, then rose again in anger: "The King was pleased to say —'dear Rupert was right to use perfect freedom, and that he had expressed himself with the same generosity that appears in all his actions!' God damn him, he'll not do anything about it! I'm beginning to know my uncle."

Rupert had called a Council of War and his officers would be arriving at any moment. Arthur Trevor was already there, sharpening quills. Rupert's mind was still running on the King.

"I envy him his certainty! He was brought up in an atmosphere of unshakable succession to an assured throne, convinced that he was given this right by God. I've always wanted to protect him from the fate of my own family. I know what it means to be reared in the poverty of an exiled Court. Mother is an expert at keeping up appearances against fearful odds! The King doesn't know what he is talking about when he speaks of preferring to face total disaster than to compromise, and the trouble is he never *does* face it. He never loses hope!"

"He is right on one point, Highness," Venetia said tact-

253

fully. "If he intends to fight on to the bitter end, then it is very undesirable for you his greatest General and kinsman, to appear in favor of a treaty."

"The man's either a fool or a saint!" Rupert ran his hands through his hair, despairing of the gulf between himself and his stubborn uncle. They were divided by experience and temperament, yet alike in so many ways, and there still existed that strong bond of affection, not only a matter of blood, but of deep respect. "I wish that my mother were here," he exclaimed explosively. "She might talk some sense into him!"

His Colonels began to come in and take their places at the table. Fairfax and Cromwell now ringed the city, preparing for a formal seige.

"I told His Majesty that I would hold Bristol for four months," began the Prince, glancing at the familiar faces of these commanders, Murray, Tillier, John Russel and many others of tried courage who had fought beside him for such a long while. "However, I see by closer inspection of our manpower and resources that this may well have been a vain boast."

The meeting was lengthy; there was little doubt that they were in dire straits, and there was still no clear news from the King or Goring.

All points were gone over once again; they could only muster fifteen hundred men to hold a wall five miles long; they had plenty of artillery but were short of ammunition; the forts were good, particularly the new one opposite Brandon Hill, but the Castle was practically a ruin. De Gomme had made a thorough survey of the fortifications and was not over-enthusiastic about his findings.

"But we are strong on horse." Rupert was trying to raise their drooping spirits, even against his better judgment. "My troopers and I will harry them, and when they attack, we must repluse the first storm. With any luck they may withdraw and, with the onset of winter, we shall have a respite."

"One of our greatest difficulties lies in the fact that the town is against us." Henry Tillier put into words what the rest knew but had not cared to mention. "It takes the heart out of our soldiers, defending a city for people who want it surrendered. The Bristolians are concerned only about their shipping and their damned commerce—they'll support whoever promises 'em the least disturbance."

The temper of the people everywhere was violent, the

moral and material devastation threatening to leave a permanent scar; it had already dragged on too long. No one anticipated, in the beginning, that it would be more than a skirmish quickly concluded. Plague was spreading fast, some said it had already reached Worcester; famine could so easily follow.

Rupert lay back in his chair, touching the tips of his fingers together, awaiting suggestions. Then he straightened, suddenly decisive. "Gentlemen, there are three things we can do."

"Three? There's not one Goddamn thing, save to die!" muttered Russell, but Rupert ignored him.

"I shall propose them and leave you to come to some resolution on our wisest course of action. I will bow to your decision, then no man can say that I have influenced you unjustly."

No one answered, they watched him and waited, and he continued, "I am prepared to take as many horse as can be spared and make a dash for it through Fairfax' lines to raise a relieving army on the other side, leaving the rest to hold the Fort and Castle. Secondly, I will undertake the defense of those two citadels myself—or, lastly, we can make the best of it, man the wall as well as we are able and share alike in the result."

They did not take long to reach their conclusion; it was deemed neither safe nor honorable if Rupert left with his cavalry, all agreed that it would be an unfair division of forces and chances. The next choice did not meet with approval either. Those for whom there would be no more room within the fortresses would be put to the sword by the revengeful enemy. So the third suggestion was adopted and the Prince disposed all the Colonels to their posts upon the line. His first command was to fire Bedminster, for intelligence had been brought that the Roundheads intended to quarter two thousand men there that night, and he was determined that they should find only ashes.

The thin gray clouds had cleared by noon into a day that shimmered with heat under a blue-white sky. Venetia climbed up to the battlements of the Royal Fort, seeking Rupert, who had left in a hurry after the meeting. But she was disappointed; the only person present, besides the sentries, was Richard Crane. He was lying back against a buttress, shirt undone over a brown, hairy chest, soaking up the sun like a big tomcat and idly watching the black column of smoke rising, away to the south, where the village was burning.

"Can't stomach setting houses ablaze," he commented. "Dirty part of war that, to send women and children and old folk flying from under flaming beam and thatch."

"What has he said to you concerning our chances?" she asked.

Crane looked at her. His humorous eyes, like the corners of his mouth, were crinkled with laughter and vigilance. "The Palsgrave? He says little, but I know what he thinks—that the game is played and lost."

Crane was as loyal as Maurice and as fearless a fighter and he knew her Prince very well. She was always a little less anxious when he rode at his side, with his piercing eyes alert for any danger to his beloved charge. He had served the Palatines for years, and had been detained with Rupert at Warrendorp after the defeat of Vlotho. It was he who had carried a secret note to King Charles in England, written by the Prince on a page torn from his pocketbook.

Venetia looked down from the newly-completed bastion, built on the rise, not far from where, two years ago, Washington's men had made that first breach and beaten Fiennes' troopers. Now the wheel had turned full circle—the hedges, hollow lanes and ditches provided cover for Roundheads. Rupert had not had time to destroy them all.

She remembered Fiennes and his disgrace and said to Richard: "What if we cannot hold the town?"

He shrugged sleepily. "Then we lose it, and maybe get some rest which his energetic Highness grudges us now."

"But Richard—the Prince?"

"He will either hang on till the very last, which he'll do his damndest to perform, or he'll die and the rest of us along with him, or . . ." he paused, as if uncertain whether to go on.

"Well?" she prompted.

"Or he will surrender—but I doubt, for all his valor, that our *Pfalzgraf* has courage enough for that"'

"Courage enough—to surrender!" She was astounded—Rupert's Colonel of the Lifeguard to say this of him! "You must be mad!"

He chuckled, his expression full of genuine affection for her. "And you, my dear, are very young, and very much in love!"

SIX

It was no longer safe for anyone with Royalist sympathies to walk abroad in Bristol. The Parliamentarians had taxed and oppressed the people in equal measure when the town had been in their hands, yet now, as ever, Rupert was held responsible for the sins of all fighting men. The citizens felt that they had been ruthlessly mulcted for the upkeep of his garrison.

Through wet, blustery weather Rupert's cavalry harassed Fairfax's men without respite. They captured the redoubtable Coloney Okey, whose dragoons had stung their horse at Naseby, but had to pay dearly for it. The Prince came back to headquarters with ashen face and stunned eyes; Richard Crane had received his death-wound in the sortie.

One evening, shortly after Crane's death, Rupert had just sat down to supper when his aides interrupted the meal. He listened to the hurried tale of a prisoner taken under suspicious circumstances, then shoved back his plate and prepared to go out again. Venetia ran to keep up with his long stride. They took horses and in a short while were in the guardroom of the Royal Fort. Spluttering flares made the atmosphere smoky, gleaming dully on the racks of guns, the tall pikes, the furled colors. Cards and dice were scattered on the plain boards of the trestle—obviously they had interrupted the pastime of the watch. The prisoner was fetched and stood defiantly between a couple of guards.

"Has he been searched?" Rupert wanted to know.

"He was on the point of destroying these when we caught him, sir." An officer handed over a packet.

Rupert broke the seal and his brow darkened as he read aloud: " 'Instructions to the citizens for the delivery of Bristol to the Parliament——?' Christ's blood! What knavery is this?—Promises of protection if they make no resistance—offered their lives, their liberties and estates, in return for 'delivering up the said city'—and signed by 'Thomas Fairfax and Oliver Cromwell!' "

Like a thundercloud he hung over the prisoner. "What do you know of all this?"

The man held his ground. He was inclined to be insolent, one of those seduced by anti-Royalist propaganda. "You will never succeed in witholding the truth from the people! They'll not see their city ravaged by idolatrous Irish and mercenaries!"

"*You* certainly won't live to see it!" said the prince. "Tomorrow morning you will hang!"

"This is not the only copy, sir," another adjutant announced from the door. "They have been discovered in different parts of the town. It would seem that they planned a surprise for us tonight."

"Did you say that the soldier with whom he was talking was shot down?"

"Aye, Your Highness."

"He may have further papers on him. Where is he?"

Several men piped up at once, all eager to point out the place, a dangerous spot, just within the defenses at an outer angle of the bastion. The Prince ordered no one to follow him and took up a lantern as he passed. Venetia pattered alone beside him. It was cold on the ramparts, the wind blew a soggy spray of drizzle into their faces.

Rupert called out to the sentry: "Don't shoot me by mistake. I go beyond the walls, and have no mind for one of our own bullets!"

"Your Highness, 'tis not safe," the guard ventured uneasily, "the Roundheads are very near on this side."

"Rupert, take some men with you," Venetia pleaded when she realized his intention. "Why must you be so rash? There are a dozen who would go in your place willingly."

"No!" he snapped, one leg already over the ledge. "D'you think I want to prove to them how easily these fences can be scaled?"

He had knotted a rope firmly to a stanchion, and dropped down and crossed the ditch without trouble. The dead soldier lay not far across the line and Venetia strained every sense, probing the dark hollow of the meadow between the two forts, certain that there were forms flitting against the blackness.

"Highness," she called in a whisper. "For God's sake hurry!"

But it seemed an eternity before he reared out of the blackness and landed beside her, a paper in his hand. In the guardroom, he tore it open, his frown deepening. "*Dieu!* 'Tis a list of the city gates with the hour that they shall be opened to admit the enemy. The damned traitors!"

He turned brusquely to the waiting soldiers, giving instructions. Nothing would satisfy him but that he personally visit every postern, each fort and redoubt. They spurred to Brandon Hill and through the rain which gusted across King's Down, rousing the guard at Prior's Hill Fort, putting them on the alert, leaving there to enter the city by the Frome Gate, clattering through the echoing streets to Redcliffe, and up to the ancient hulk of the Castle.

Having stirred all into life at the citadel and despatched men to seize the insurgents, they passed out under the jagged teeth of the portcullis. The sky was beginning to clear, though mist still drifted, phantom-white, over the murky river. Planks drummed beneath their hooves, but the lofty, gabled houses lining the bridge were shuttered and dark.

Silence, mute as the grave, closed about them again as they climbed the steep road which led back to headquarters. Venetia shuddered and tugged on the bit so that her mount swerved closer to Rupert's. The air was thick with hostility. They had saved Bristol from betrayal this time— but for how long?

Fairfax and his men were active, encircling the city on both sides of the river, building a bridge without Royalist interference, while a fleet of Parliamentarian ships landed reinforcements and kept watch to prevent any assistance coming from the sea.

Venetia, tired of being left so much to her own devices with nothing to do but worry, collected her sewing-box one morning and traversed the backstairs to the kitchen.

"Shut the door quickly, madame!" Pierre was frantically flapping with a cloth at a zooming bluebottle which had crossed the threshold with her. "*Sacré nom!* I am beset by flies and their demonic cousins, the wasps! They are more nuisance than the Ironsides!"

Venetia sat on the window-seat with her mending. She was darning Rupert's hose; although there were seamstresses in plenty, she loved doing little tasks for him, jealously guarding the privilege. New garments were a problem; he and Maurice had been fitted out during the winter, giving time grudgingly to their tailor, but they were hard on their clothes.

Despite all difficulties, Pierre's cooking was still superlative, partly due to the wealth of fresh produce. Although it was now hot, the year had been a wet one on the whole, bringing forth a generous crop of fruit and vegetables. Just below the window, a little gaggle of sparrows were luxuriating in a dust-bath. And the cat, basking in the sun at Venetia's side, opened emerald eyes and regarded them scornfully, then got up, stretched languidly and went to rub around Pierre's leg. Her deep purr thrummed across the noon torpor.

"She is a nice plump animal," he observed, looking her over expertly. "Let us hope we are never reduced to popping her into the pot!"

"D'you think it will ever come to that?"

"Who knows what is in store, madame?" Pierre had grown philosophic in the Prince's service.

It was a strange, inopportune time for it to have happened, yet it seemed to follow a predestined pattern. Her wish had been fulfilled. "Pierre," she said, suddenly bashful, "I wanted you to be the first to know. I am with child."

"Madame! That is wonderful news!" Delight spread over his rubicund features. "But are you sure?"

"Yes, I am sure." Putting it into words finally convinced her; she had been anxiously counting days and doing sums in her head.

"Have you told him yet?" His eyes twinkled, inordinately pleased to be party to such a secret. She shook her head, not at all sure how Rupert would take it. "He will be delighted, surely?" Pierre reached for the brandy. "Just a sniff, madame. We will drink to the-little-one-that-is-to-be! The Queen of Heart's first grandchild—unless Charles Louis has been busy among the Puritan wenches in London. But I am confident that Gallois would have kept me informed."

They touched glasses and pledged the baby and she thought of it, curled down in the darkness of her body. Did its heart beat yet? Was it boy or girl? When would it quicken? Trapped in this bristling environ of warriors, she wanted to run to that experienced mother, Damaris, to find answer to these vital questions.

The brandy was having a mellowing effect on Pierre; he waxed reminiscent; "I recall when the Prince was born. I'd not long been in the palace kitchen—felt myself im-

260

portant, I can tell you, to be serving the new King and Queen of Bohemia. Your Prince came into the world—somewhere between nine and ten of the clock at night. The people of Prague were wild with delight—he was their princeling, you see, born in the capital. Wonderful gifts poured in for him—an ebony and ivory cradle studded with gems, and a casket to match, full of infant's clothing of the very finest lace and lawn from Cambrai."

As he talked, Venetia pictured the citizens filing past the presentation crib ostentatiously exhibited in the gloom of Elizabeth's magnificent antechamber, their broad Slavic faces wreathed in smiles.

"And his christening! What a show! The snows had melted and it was a day of sunshine. I managed a place in the church, and, madame, the great personages who attended! The arrival of each was heralded by flourishes on kettledrum and hautboy—such a din! 'Tis no wonder that he grew up to be a soldier, for he was handed by the Chief Burgravine to Count Turzo, who uttered the single name 'Rupert,' in a voice which thundered through that glittering cathedral, and thence, in turn, he was passed to the representatives of Moravia, Silesia and the Lusatias, all of whom were clad in full armor!"

"Was he frightened? Did he cry?"

Pierre wagged his head reprovingly. "Not he, madame! He watched everything with his big solemn black eyes and, when the procession emerged into the square, there was the King of Hungary's gift for his godson."

"The Moslem—Bethlem Gabor!" she said, smiling, knowing how often Maurice baited Rupert about this.

"The very same! And what a gift! It was a wildly neighing Turkish courser, wearing a saddle, bridle and housings ornamented with gold and jewels which flashed fire as it stamped and snorted. And then there was a feast; and dancing in a silken pavilion where the lovely Queen held court by the light of sparkling torches. Oh, yes, Prince Rupert's christening was a great success."

Pierre refilled their glasses, sipping slowly, eyes gray-filmed as he looked back over the years. "Even the Jews, who do nothing without careful thought, sent him a costly present. Out of the quarter where they lived, the Josefska Trilda, came a silver alms-dish fashioned like a ship."

A big tear wandered down his cheek, to be caught and wiped away with a corner of his apron. "Ah, madame, if their good fortune could have but lasted. They were the

261

Winter King and Queen, no more. Less than twelve months did they reign, by the time snow fell again, they were gone—their kingdom snatched from them. They lost everything, and we went into exile with them. My poor lady—what poverty she has endured since then—what hardships those fine children of hers have known."

"I wish I could have seen him then."

"You will have something even better, madame—his child. There will then be two of them to love, eh?"

Venetia sat on the high stool, hugging her knees, while joy grew and blossomed in every corner of her being. She counted months in her mind—it would be born in the spring, the very best time of the year. She felt holy and rare and of incalculable value. What was a mere siege compared with this?

On September 4th, a trumpeter rode into the city and was escorted to the Prince's quarters. Fairfax had formally summoned Rupert to surrender.

Silently the Prince read this epistle from the man against whom he had fought for three years. A soldier, like himself, who had always behaved with honor and courtesy; but for the vagaries of Fate, they could have been comrades, giving their skills to one cause. This summons was more in the nature of a private appeal to the sense and humanity of Rupert himself. Fairfax began with a conventional request for the rendition of the city with all the forts. Then the tone of the letter, changed, becoming much more personal.

It was a very carefully worded message and doubtless Fairfax had spent some time on its compilation; it was couched in masculine, energetic language, straight from the shoulder, in a way sure to appeal to the Prince. He did not hesitate to remind him of the popularity once lavished on him and the help given to his family.

His family—Rupert's mouth turned downward at the corners as he thought of the treacherous Charles Louis feathering his nest in London, and of the disquieting news which had come to him from Worcester. Maurice was ill. There was a rumor that it was the plague. Brotherly hate, brotherly love, warred in him. But he knew where his duty lay. He passed the letter around the War Council, while the messenger stood waiting.

Before dark, he rode back to his own line, bearing a terse couple of lines, asking whether Fairfax would give leave for a galloper to go to His Majesty to know his pleasure.

"That will give them something to argue about," said Rupert to Venetia with a tight smile. "If I can play for time, it is possible that help may arrive."

Now that the heated talk on the precise wording of the reply was stilled and everyone departed, a curious hush hung on the twilight.

Rupert was absorbed in some document or other, the swaying light from the candelabrum planing shadows on his face. Venetia went across to weave her fingers through his hair. "Have you much more to do tonight, darling?"

He frowned at the ridiculousness of such a question. "*Sacrément!* I'm only holding a damned rebellious town against an enemy three times as powerful, that's all!—I've naught to do! Jesus, I can roll into bed and sleep till cockcrow like any fat-arsed burgher!"

"I want to talk to you." With the deepening of danger, she felt it imperative that he should know about the child. Supposing that he were killed without ever realizing that he was to be a father?

"Well, I'm not stopping you. Talk away." He was laughing at her, hauling himself to his feet. "Though I think everyone talks far too much—'tis one of the problems in this Godam world."

Why would he never take her seriously? She could not divulge her precious news if he were in this frame of mind.

He came behind her, pelvis pressing against her buttocks, bending over to murmur into her neck: "You should not stand like that, sweeting. It is much too inviting. Have you ever been taken on the top of a table?"

Venetia wriggled in half-hearted protest. "You would know if I had, there has been no one else. Stop it, Rupert! Fasten up! Trevor may come in at any moment!"

He is a tactful fellow and would go straight out again." He was rubbing his chin over her bare shoulders, making her shudder, goose-flesh stippling her limbs. And what about my predecessor, Michael? Was it with him that you practiced those delightful tricks which rack me with pleasure, eh?"

Don't tease me tonight, Highness, I have something important to tell you." Her serious tone arrested him. He saw that tears shone in the clear eyes which regarded him; English eyes, which went well with her fair hair and flawless complexion. Was it these which attracted him so

263

much? Eyes which reflected whatever color she was wearing, sometimes green, at others tawny, or blue, or dark gray as the sea on a rainy day.

He pretended to be suitably impressed, looking down at her and pulling his face straight, staring at her unblinkingly. "Ah, this matter of weighty significance." He reached out to snuff the candles between thumb and forefinger. Let us to bed and you can tell me there and, if 'tis something which is going to annoy me—keep it till afterward."

So she had screwed up her courage in vain; Rupert wanted to make love and she wanted to talk—they ended up by doing both—in that order.

The room was very still, and then came the soft whisper of rain.

Damn!" said Rupert. This bloody weather makes the ground too slippery for horse."

He turned over so that she lay in the bend of his arm, her head on his shoulder. Now was the moment—with a great effort she said, "Rupert, I am to have a child." There—it was out—the next move was up to him.

His hand paused in its sleepy stroking, then he said: "You should not be here—the plague—the fighting—it is too dangerous."

She wished that she could see his face clearly. "You don't mind?"

"Mind! Holy God, d'you take me for an utter rogue?"

"But you are not pleased." Whatever happened she must keep this shrewish edge of disappointment from her voice.

"I don't know what I feel. I'm not exactly surprised. The possibility had occurred to me!" He answered dryly. "But you must give me time to get accustomed to the idea."

He said nothing more and when she raised herself to look, she could see that his lids were closed. He was asleep and she wanted to weep.

She woke to find him propped on his elbow, studying her face with such a wistful expression in the watery dawn light, that she caught her breath. He leaned over to brush her lips with sweet, unexpected tenderness.

"I'm sorry, *liebchen*." He was humble and contrite; Rupert, the lordly and arrogant, was apologizing to a woman! "I robbed you of your moment of pure joy. That was un-

264

forgivable—a shoddy way to treat you, when you have given me so much."

"Oh, no, Rupert," it hurt her to see him looking like that. "You have blessed me. I have had more than any woman alive. To know you—to touch you! No one has been happier than I! And now—to bear your child——"

Tears welled up, spilling over, sliding across her temples. He reached out to brush them away with gentle finger-tips and looked at her with something akin to awe.

"I've never been loved like this." Part of him was determined to be as soaringly free as a sparrow-hawk. "It overwhelms me—I don't know what to say."

She laid her fingers on his lips. "Say nothing, my Prince. Feel it—accept it as your right. I worship you. You are my life."

For several days a lengthy correspondence passed between the opposing Generals, while every one waited in overwrought suspense, and Rupert hoped against all hope that reinforcements might arrive.

"The prospects are gloomy, madame, and I'll be the first to admit it." Pierre was directing the scullions in the packing of his kitchen goods for yet another move, this time to the Royal Fort. "Not very comfortable quarters, I fear. They tell me that the well is not yet completed— the building is raw and new—we might hold out if food is low, but water we must have."

Venetia was finding it increasingly difficult to keep up heart. Rupert was appallingly strained and anxious, for he had still received no letter from the King nor the Prince of Wales nor Goring.

"Even if the King did raise a large enough force to march towards us, I doubt that it would do much good. The enemy are absolute masters of all the passes, and have so blocked up the way that a small force might stop even a great army."

"What is to be done, Pierre?" Venetia wrung her hands in despair; with him she had no need to keep up the optimistic front which Rupert and his Colonels expected. Pierre was at the hub of ordinary life, away from the purely military preoccupation of the soldiers. "The Prince swore to keep it for King Charles."

"Rash——" He was directing the removing of the flitch of bacon slung up near the ceiling in its muslin shroud. "He could not have taken proper heed of the fortifications.

Unlike him to be careless—but still, I have noted that he does, at times, behave somewhat out of character."

Fairfax, that shrewd veteran, was not in the least fooled by the Royalist procrastinations; he would have done the same himself in a like position, but, as the wind and rain had at last changed to fair weather, he cut across further delay and ordered a concerted attack, early on the morning of September 10th. Rupert's spies got wind of this and he was ready for them when the Roundhead trumpets sounded for a general assault.

No one had slept that night. Venetia and her servants dealt with the people who were pouring into the Fort for safety, the soldiers' women, those townsfolk who supported the King. As the enemy pushed further into the suburbs and Rupert's men fell back through the streets, so these terrified refugees increased. Once more, there was the pathetic stream of women trying to pacify frightened children and cope with the bulging bundles which contained all that they had been able to snatch up, and the elderly, staggering in with precious belongings of value to none but themselves.

Pierre was managing the enormous task of providing for all these people, who were bedding down on the cheerless stone flags. Other rooms were used for the wounded, and Venetia organized a rota among the women so that there was constant help at hand, and set them tearing up sheeting into makeshift bandages.

Fairfax had begun his attack at two o'clock in the morning, firing four of his great siege-pieces at Prior's Hill Fort. Rupert's guns gave answer. They were numerous and cunningly placed and they made the storming of the long, sparsely manned defenses more dangerous and costly than the Roundhead General has anticipated.

It was beginning to get light, a dawn rent by fire and noise and death, when Venetia allowed Pierre to press her into a chair and put a bowl of gruel in her hands. Then she realized just how tired she was. Her back was aching, and her eyes felt raw with lack of sleep. Again she asked that question which seemed to have been with her through all eternity.

"Where is Prince Rupert?"

"Now, now, stop fretting." Pierre scolded, full of protective concern. "He is in his usual place at the head of his men, but he'll come through without a scratch as he always does, mark my words."

266

The Royalists, though fighting heroically, gradually began to give way. By five in the morning Prior's Hill Fort had been taken and all its defenders slaughtered. The Cavaliers withdrew to the shelter of the Fort, and, as Cromwell's troopers rushed in through the town, the citadel was cut off from those who still maintained an isolated resistance in the posts on the outer line.

Rupert gathered his commanders for a final Council of War. It was eight o'clock and they had been fighting all night. A single ray of morning sunlight, played over their features, haggard, hollow-eyed and desperate.

"Well, gentlemen?"

They rustled uneasily—they were in a death-trap and all knew it. If they fought on, they were faced with nothing but destruction; some of their best men were still in the outposts and would be condemned to the brutal killings of Prior's Hill. There was no longer any possibility of relief, further resistance would only expose the citizens to the fury of the enemy.

As he had passed through the hushed Fort just now, Rupert had been painfully aware of the white faces, the frightened eyes fixed on him; those helpless women and children—he remembered the massacre of the camp-followers at Naseby, an atrocity which had turned his stomach. He thought of his valiant cavalry, those gallant lads who had so faithfully served the King, and he thought of Venetia and his unborn child. What would those insane fanatics do to her? And into his mind, unnaturally sharpened by exhaustion, came the memory of words she had spoken to him not long before—that love was not negotiable—if you did not like it, you still could not change it—neither could you avoid its responsibility. It would have been so easy to defy the enemy and go down fighting.

"The Fort has been damaged, sir," Tiller was saying to him. No one wanted to recommend surrender but all recognized that this was the wisest course. "How long is it possible to fight on without water?"

There was a pause. His weary officers shuffled their feet and eased off their helmets, defeat written clearly on every face. Rupert, with his high ideals, would once have forced himself to defend the citadel while life lasted; now he was in no mood to advise anyone else to die in a hopeless struggle.

He had nothing on earth left but his honor; he had given his word to his uncle to keep Bristol. He revoked this

267

promise in order to save lives and prevent further blood-shed, making the sacrifice with his eyes wide open, know-ing only too well that his motives would be misunderstood and used against him by those who hated him.

"I shall send a trumpet to Sir Thomas Fairfax to know whether he will treat."

Fairfax agreed, commissioners were nominated, and while the treaty was in progress, a cessation of arms was ordered. The Prince laid down his own terms, and very haughty they were, full of cool assumption.

"Trust Le Diable," said his troopers proudly, holding their heads a bit higher, still Rupert's *élite*. "Just as if he is the Goddamn victor instead of the vanquished!"

He demanded that he, his men and all others who were attached to the army, should march out, unmolested, with colors, pikes and drums, bag and baggage. The sick and wounded were to be allowed to stay until they were re-covered and then given passes to rejoin the King. He wanted twenty wagons for goods and a convoy to conduct his force safely on its way. He insisted that every citizen, regardless of politics or religion, should be protected from plunder and violence. In return, he agreed to deliver up the city without further damage, with all the ordnance, arms, ammunition and stores, promising that his men would not take any booty with them, and that he would at once set free those prisoners whom he had already cap-tured.

Hostages were selected and dispatched with Rupert's ultimatum to Fairfax. Surprisingly, for he was in a posi-tion to be harsh, Fairfax agreed. Maybe, knowing the Prince's reputation and bearing in mind that Bristol had already been fired in three places, he feared to goad him into ripping up the treaty and sending the lot sky-high be-fore he and his men died in a last suicidal stand.

Now that the decision was made, the surrender terms concluded, Rupert could be persuaded to rest. His face was grey under the tan, his eyes burning pits set in dark hollows.

"I have never before been forced to give up a city, though I've made others do it," he said quietly to Venetia. "It seems that I am fated to experience every bitter aspect of defeat."

"What else could you do?"

"I know what my enemies will say that I should have done." He threw himself on the narrow pallet which was too short for him. She knew whom he meant—and they were not Roundheads.

It was morning and almost time to leave. Somehow, between them, De Faust, Venetia and Holmes helped Rupert to get ready. The valet shaved him expertly. Since an early hour, Holmes had been fussing over his armor, plying his cloth on imagined rust flecks.

De Faust wore the mournful air of an undertaker, holding out the scarlet doublet richly overlaid with silver lace for Rupert to slide on over his shirt. He was already wearing matching breeches, cut straight, and fringed at the knee. Holmes adjusted the corselet, then draped the baldric across his chest slipping the sword into its three-strap carrier at his left hip, kneeling to fasten the silver spurs.

Venetia reached up to smooth his collar, and rested her palm fleetingly against his cheek. He was very pale, and a tremor was running through him; his hand, brushing across hers, was like ice.

De Faust tut-tutted in the background, but she took no notice, elbowing him aside, tying Rupert's sash. He swung his cloak over one shoulder and reached out blindly for her with a gruff, "You'll be close by?" Then walked out to where they waited for him to lead them from the city.

His magnificent black Barbary horse stood patiently as he sat, very tall in the saddle, while his foot regiments filed out of the fort to join the eight hundred cavalry who filled the green just beyond the gate. The baggage-wagons creaked into line, the conglomeration of servants, women and dependents, all sharing the ignominy of having to pass their conquerors who were drawn up to watch them go. And it was a subdued, dejected-enough company, jests and raillery fled, thankful to be escaping with their lives. The Prince rode last, with his body of firelocks and his Lifeguard, bringing up the rear deliberately, lest any of the leaguer should be attacked.

His head was high, his back straight, like a victorious emperor, not the General of a beaten army, and only Venetia, riding just ahead, knew what it was costing him. The cavalcade halted at the great main gate while the keys were handed over, and the Prince's fierce falcon's eyes gazed down on the party of senior officers who jogged up to escort him to Fairfax. They were headed by Lieutenant-General Cromwell, his plain helmet tucked under his arm.

Venetia, swivelling round in her saddle, saw Rupert

sweep off his plumed hat and bow low over his horse's neck, his face inscrutable, and she had never been more proud of him. They would not find him sullen and uncouth, these Ironsides who were now so confident that victory was assured—his breeding would show—he would bear himself towards his conquerors as a soldier and a gentleman.

Her fidgeting annoyed Mallory who wanted as much dignity as possible to be maintained in the troop who were already smarting because, as they passed under the archway and came into the sight of the well-fed, regularly paid soldiers of the New Model, they burst into laughter at the shabby appearance of the King's men. It was quickly suppressed by their officers, but those smirks and mocking eyes were hard to bear for they knew they were a sorry sight on their jaded nags, wounded, ill-equipped and wretched.

Undoubtedly the Prince heard the sniggers, though he did not betray it by as much as a flicker of his supremely haughty eyelids. He was as gaunt as his men, but no one laughed at *him,* there was nothing of the broken-down Cavalier about him!

Sir Thomas Fairfax seemed to be particularly taken with him, and they rode together and he gave the Prince the right hand all the way. He was another tall, personable military man, as dark and lean as Rupert, and he also liked to wear a red cloak.

It was rumored that, although by nature a quiet, controlled man, he became inspired in battle, galloping the field bareheaded. There was instant empathy between him and the Prince—they understood one another; two immaculately behaved contenders, acknowledging similar courage and qualities. They were aristocrats, marked with that indisputable stamp of authority, and though both would have given Cromwell credit as a fine leader, he could not but appear homely and coarse beside them.

Rupert told Fairfax that he wanted to march for Oxford. The General listened gravely, obviously much more at ease with his illustrious counterpart that was Cromwell. Venetia wondered what was going on in the mind of that bulky, awkward man, with his heavy features and tight mouth, speculating as to whether such good terms would have been allowed had he been in command.

"I would appreciate the courtesy if you would lend us muskets to defend ourselves against the Clubmen," Rupert requested. "I shall see to it that they are returned with your convoy."

Venetia was dumb with admiration at his control and ability to carry out his part in this charade. He was keeping an iron grip on that morass of nerves, shame and humiliation which had made him physically sick during the night. And there was no escape for him yet, the torture had to be endured still further.

" 'Sblood! Just look at them!" Mallory muttered savagely as they mounted the steep incline which wound from the Fort to Durham Down. "He seems to have won them over completely! Damme, I believe they intend to ride with us!"

And they did accompany the Prince for more than two miles, almost as if they could not bear to part from him, stunned by the discovery that they had been much mistaken in their idea of him. This was no mad Wizard, no outlandish foreign plunderer—but an intelligent young man, as much concerned for the welfare of the country as they, and they ordered their soldiers to drive back the hordes of country people who had gathered on the outskirts to hurl stones at the Royalists.

Morning mist had melted into a fine golden day—it was pleasantly warm—faintly nostalgic—tinged with autumn. In the valley behind them, the river lay low and turgid between cracking mud-banks, and the old grey city hummed, already on the way to recovery, concentrating on the really vital things—the manufacture of soap, the importing of sugar, sherry, oil, and that increasingly profitable commodity—tobacco.

Colonel Butler was in charge of the convoy, a bright, cheerful person, accepting with alacrity the Prince's invitation to ride with him. At his almost imperceptible signal, Venetia dropped back to her customary place at his right hand.

They supped together, Rupert and his Colonels and the Roundhead officers; a very curious scene with the conversation stilted, though they discussed matters of war and State, but with the reserve of enemies, temporarily at peace. But alcohol builds remarkable bridges and, before long, Butler was expounding the ideals of his party and the Prince was listening, and asking questions, nodding in agreement on many points.

"But what of Cromwell?" asked Rupert, tapping his tankard with his finger-nail, to indicate to Holmes that it

271

was empty. "Is it not true that he quarrelled with Manchester?"

"Certainly, many of the other Members of Parliament do not see eye to eye with him on every issue." Butler, though mellow, was not prepared to divulge too much.

"It seems that Sectarian enthusiasm has spread through your army."

"That is true! The New Model were much heartened by Naseby," Butler blurted out, before checking himself, afraid that this tactless reminder would be painful. "It gave the soldiers faith in their officers, their cause, and the Lord. Never have I heard such a ferment of preaching —far beyond the bounds of our orthodox chaplains——"

"And what of the slaughter of the women there? What has your Lord God of Hosts to say about that?" Venetia could contain herself no longer—she hated the Roundheads and everything that they stood for—she had seen them in action. Normally, she did not join in discussions, content to remain in the background, but this was beyond endurance.

There was a moment of shocked silence. Every male eye turned on her reprovingly. Why could she not hold her tongue and take part in the masquerade as they, officers and gentlemen, were forced to do? There were certain subjects it was best to eschew if they were to get this convoy to Oxford all in one piece!

Damned hypocrites! Venetia stared back at them defiantly.

Butler cleared his throat. "They were mostly Irish, madam."

"They were not, sir!" Venetia's eyes sparked. "I was there and saw it all. Many of them were the wives of the Welsh, and many more English ladies!"

"And Cavalier's whores!" This came from one of Butler's men who looked as if the fire of bigoted intolerance had already been kindled in his breast. His manner plainly suggested that he numbered her among that tribe.

"What if they were?" She was in too deep to draw back. Rupert had not even glanced in her direction, his face shuttered. "Does that make them inhuman monsters, outside the realms of mercy? There was no excuse for the outrage, which your news-sheets reported without a hint of shame. Is this a good example of the New Model Army? Making war against women? Where was their religion when they were brutally raping them? Our men have never done anything as bad!"

"It was the ill-disciplined infantry, not the horse!" He was furious with this brazen strumpet who dared to bring up this blot on their record which they were already trying to justify. "They were still engaged in pursuit."

"Yes, striking men in the backs as they fled, giving no quarter, hacking them down—Cromwell's godly men! Mighty is the arm of the Lord!"

"You blaspheme!" he hissed, and she saw again Fletcher, using his new-found cant as an excuse for his own ambitions.

"Sit down, Venetia," said Rupert quietly, without bothering to look up. She obeyed, and she was shaking. All right! So she was being hysterical and unreasonable and feminine! She didn't care.

She was still trembling when they went to their chamber, afraid that Rupert would be angry; but he was only functioning with the top of his mind, having reached that peak of stress where he moved as an automaton, outside himself, watching it all dispassionately, beyond anger or tears or repining. As a sop he would seek brandy, hashish and Venetia's body and it would be days before he regained any sort of equilibrium.

Camp-fires were glowing beyond the windows and the maimed, angry and depressed army settled down as best it could. But there was no singing, no ribaldry, all felt themselves involved in the Palsgrave's disgrace.

"Was there any other way?" Rupert said, one hand on the casement, the other round a botte.

Now that they were alone at last, he had no need to pretend and his face betrayed his torment.

"You were right, Rupert. Think of the lives you have saved. You will feel more helpful by the time we reach Oxford."

"Oxford! Aye, and how do you suppose the news will be received there? Digby will be beside himself with joy!" He raised the bottle to his lips, tipping back his head and taking a deep swallow. "I would that time might stop so that we never reach Oxford!"

SEVEN

Over Will Legge's dining-table, the whole of the Bristol siege was being re-staged; the salt-cellar became the Royal Fort, the decanter, Prior's Hill. Rupert and Will had been engaged in this earnest table-top war game for some time, dishes and platters laid aside, glasses filled to sustain them in the exertion. And Will listened and commented and watched his Prince with the anxious eyes of a concerned friend.

Venetia was having difficulty in keeping awake, struggling against the desire to sleep which swept over her willy-nilly nowadays. Then she jerked upright to find Rupert saying:

"Venetia, you are snoring! 'Sdeath, the siege may have been a damn nuisance, but it was surely not that tedious!"

She mumbled something, coming awake; this somnolence, along with morning sickness, were scarcely topics for conversation with gentlemen. She could not wait for a heart-to-heart talk with Damaris, but the opportunity had not yet presented itself, though they had been in Oxford two days.

They were dining with the faithful Will who would always tell Rupert if he thought that he was in the wrong— but he had agreed that, faced with such an enemy in overpowering numbers and revengeful mood, he had done well to bring off his army safely. Choosing his words, so as not to depress the unhappy soldier further, Will had been trying to tell him of the rumors being lovingly fostered by Digby and his cabal. He was still with the King at Hereford, but he had a sidekick in Oxford, one Edward Walsingham, on whom Will had been keeping an eye for some time. He was a malicious intriguer, busily occupied in culling poison for Digby to pour into the Monarch's ear about his nephew.

Walsingham was not the soul of discretion and, in his position as Governor, a good deal of what passed between the plotters got back to Will; most of it was an unsubtle rehash of that old story that Rupert wanted the Crown. His earnest proposals for peace had put the finishing touches to Digby's hatred of him, and also afforded excellent means of exciting the King's distrust. Even after Naseby, the Secretary had continued to take the reversal of their prospects breezily, refusing to accept the magnitude of that disaster.

Digby hotly resented any suggestion of compromise, clinging to the bright vision of a resounding Royalist victory, with himself in a blaze of glory, holding lofty sway over a grateful King. The Prince's level-headed sanity blighted this dream. He had become Digby's *bête noire;* his energies were bent in one direction only—that of getting rid of Rupert.

Will had thought himself in the know, but even he had not been anticipating the visitor who was later announced; Sir Edward Nicholas requested an interview on a matter of the utmost importance. As he came in, leaning on his cane, Rupert and Will rose to greet this venerable nobleman who served as State-Secretary jointly with Digby.

He had always liked the Prince, and many and varied had been their dealings together, now he respectfully asked him if he might speak with him privately in the withdrawingroom.

"What is it, Will?" Venetia's mouth had gone dry, watching them go, but he could not enlighten her. In a short while Rupert and Nicholas came out. The old man seemed distraught, there was the glint of tears in his eyes, while the Prince was pale as death.

"You will let His Majesty know at once," he was saying, "tell him that I humbly bow to his will, but that I am very innocent of anything that might deserve so heavy a punishment. I shall write to him myself now."

Venetia was on her feet and at his side, eyes going over his face, tender as a mother's caress; he was so still, so blank, like someone suffering from a severe shock. She ached to take him in her arms and kiss away that terrible look.

"What has happened, Highness?"

Silence yawned for a dead instant, broken by the purring of the sea-coal fire between the iron dogs, and Nicholas fumbling in his hanging sleeves to find a kerchief, blowing his nose resoundingly. Rupert moved abruptly, throwing down the paper which had hung limply in his hand, turning away to reach for the decanter. And while she read this letter from the King, behind her the Secretary was repeating incredible things to Will, depriving him of Governorship of Oxford, placing him under arrest. King Charles, like most stammerers, was an eloquent writer, and never more than now.

The bald facts about the surrender of Bristol sounded so damning—but had Charles been there, would he have acted differently?

My conclusion is, to desire you to seek your subsistence, until it shall please God to determine my condition, somewhere beyond seas; to which end I send you herewith a pass; and I pray God to make you sensible of your present condition, and give you means to recover what you have lost; for I shall have no greater joy in a victory, than a just occasion without blushing to assure you of my being.

Your loving uncle, and most faithful friend, C.R.

The passport was attached to the letter, and was signed by George Digby.

The gravel scrunched softly under Venetia's high-heeled slippers. It was pleasant, luxurious even, to trail a skirt again, moving slowly, body held in rigid dignity by a tightly-laced stomacher, arms a little bowed by virtue of the big, full sleeves which seemed to slip from her shoulders, borne down by their weight, exposing the rounded curve of breasts pushed high by buckram and whaleboning.

Her body had not changed visibly, there was as yet no thickening of her slim waistline, no indication of that mysterious tiny occupant—only her breasts betrayed her—larger, harder, more globular and, Rupert said, more beautiful—the skin creamy and smooth, marked by the submerged tracery of blue veins—the nipples darker than of yore, still rising hard and eager under his knowledgeable fingers.

The night had been a bad, sad one; Rupert, submissive at first, had become very angry later, more for the injustice done to Will than to himself. Seriously to suspect that loyal man of treachery was ludicrous; it had obviously been done because he was Rupert's friend.

Now it was morning and he had gone to see Richmond, though both he and Will were under house-arrest. She supposed that Mary would be there too, cooing sympathetically—this jealousy was unworthy—he would be far too worried to add to his cares by alienating his kind cousin—smarting under the disgrace of having his commission publicly revoked. Every officer in the army had been commanded to take no more orders from him. Nevertheless, Venetia was looking forward to the time when her pregnancy could no longer be concealed—longing to vaunt it in the Duchess's face.

She strolled in Damaris' garden, listening to the rustle of the poplars, the sun warm where the fruit trees were trained along the south wall. There were a few late still-blooming roses, and her skirts whispered across the drift of yellow leaves. Idly rounding a corner, she was in time to see a little collection of riders trotting towards the stables, hawks on their wrists, falconers following behind. Damaris gave her a wave, leading the group, elegant as ever, her wine-red skirt cascading over her saddle.

Dinner was not a success. Damaris was serious and subdued, concerned over Maurice's illness, and the others had caught the prevailing mood of indignation at Rupert's treatment. Whatever subject someone brightly brought up, inevitably the conversation turned to the Prince.

"He has written to the King, asking to be granted an audience," Venetia told them. "He cannot embark without leave from the rebels and, without asking His Majesty's content, he will not demand their permission."

"The whole thing is a scandal, and a conspiracy on the part of Lord Digby!" Damaris knit her wing-shaped brows. "Maurice will be furious! Etienne is seriously thinking of sending Digby a challenge, are you not, dear heart?"

The Chevalier looked up to nod, breaking off from the sporadic hawking talk in which he had been engaged with Barney. Damaris, with an eye to her guests' needs, continued:

"Oh, we have been well aware for a long while that there was something afoot. That slyboots, Digby, must have worked very hard to make the King believe that Will was planning to deliver up Oxford and making private overtures to the Roundheads! Have you ever heard anything so ridiculous?"

Bleakly, Venetia began to see even more clearly, how calamitous for Rupert had been the Bristol affair, coming as it did at this juncture. Digby must be transported with delight at the way fate was playing into his hands.

"He could do naught else but surrender!" The pain and urgency in her voice captured their attention. "Why didn't the King send help? And where was Goring and his army?"

The King, it appeared, had been called upon to relieve the threatened town of Hereford; he had been drawing up several plans, on paper, for coming to Bristol's rescue; there was little news dribbling out of the West about Goring since his crushing defeat by Fairfax at Langport.

Etienne and Barney had returned from Hereford, with the remainder of their men, to see if there was any way in which they could have reached the Prince, but, by then, it was already too late.

All the time she was remembering his distress of yesterday and how he had sat down and written to his uncle—a rather incoherent letter—with sincerity pouring through every line. He had bowed to the King's decree and begged to be allowed to render his account of the siege in person. It was imperative that he justify his actions and clear himself in both the eyes of the King and the world. His honor demanded it.

Barney summed up her feelings. "I would that the king were back in Oxford, Digby clapped in irons and soldier's work left to the soldiers!"

Even cards and dice failed to cheer them, and only Adrian was vivacious. He kept up a gossiping commentary about his friends in the army and at Court, and his anticipation of carousals to come, cornering Venetia with yet another tale of the talk rife in the town.

"I saw that creature, Walsingham, and a friend, hurrying along, heads together, and overheard one say to t'other, that he would show him our new ruler. Naturally, I followed, and we came upon Prince Rupert and Will Legge walking in serious conversation. Those two jackals stood their goggling, no doubt building upon the fact that the nobility and gentry were treating the Prince with respect, standing bareheaded at a distance, and Walsingham said, 'The House of Palatine do think themselves assured of the Crown.' I vow that I was so enraged, I nearly called the saucy varlet out!"

"For the love of Christ! Why did you not?" growled Barney, glaring at the boy. "You should have given him a bellyful of cold steel to digest the lie with!"

"It seems that a man must fight with more than his sword, if he would hold his own in this world!" Etienne smiled whimsically, piling his winnings into neat stacks before him.

" 'Sblood! It was more fun in the old days when we would gallop into a town yelling, 'Fire and sword to all rebels! Pack the mayor in a barrel and roll it into the river!' " Barney was as disgusted as the Prince by these political convolutions. "Give me a plain, simple skirmish any day!"

Things went from bad to worse as the scrappy information, alarms and hearsay merged into a cohesive picture of a chain of regrettable coincidences and ill-luck. By an incredible stroke of misfortune, at the very time during which Rupert was exchanging civilities with Fairfax in Bristol, Charles Louis, lording it in London, had received the sum of eight thousand pounds from Parliament, and, almost at once, Rupert had surrendered!

"They could not have thought there was any connection?" Venetia listened to Etienne with growing horror.

"Whether 'they' did or did not, they have managed to persuade the King that this was really a bribe for Rupert to hand over the city—that the Palatine brothers were all in it together— even that Maurice had given up Shrewsbury as part of the deal!"

"My God! But they've never exchanged a single letter with the Elector since the war!"

All Etienne's flippancy and mannerisms had been laid aside. His face was unusually grave. "Articles of impeachment against the Prince for high treason have been drawn up by Digby, and he swears he shall have his head, or it shall cost him a fall. I have seen this coming for a long, long time, Venetia."

Oxford was in a ferment. The soldiers came out to a man on the side of the Prince, the fact that Will was universally popular and had been shabbily treated, helped his cause, and Richmond never wavered in his trust in him. The favorable impression which Rupert had made in Fairfax and his men now proved a mixed blessing. The London news-sheets did nothing to allay the suspicions of the Digby party, for a number of them sang his praises! —seeming to be yet another proof of his collusion.

To make matters worse, there were not any serious undertakings on hand now, nor any army to execute them.

Boredom was giving people plenty of time to exercise their imaginations, tongues and pens.

The King had written to Maurice absolving him from any connection in Rupert's disgrace but his loyalty was unshaken. Enraged at hearing his brother traduced, he had lost no time in letting him know that he had his full support, and had shakily, for he was still confined to bed, copied out the whole of the King's letter himself, enclosing it.

"I've sent a galloper to him, telling him to meet me at Banbury." Rupert got up, lighting a candle. It was still dark, a chill October morning.

"What?" Venetia woke sharply.

Rupert was suffering from insomnia; he who once could never get enough sleep, dropping off immediately even in the most noisy, uncomfortable conditions, now lay awake, tossing restlessly.

His disgrace made him writhe—his name would be blackened all across Europe—no doubt the tattling scribblers had already sent their dirty little messages speeding over the water to the Queen, who woud be busy spreading it around Paris that her nephew had sold Bristol to the enemy! He did not add the other thing which would stick in his craw above all others—the fact that Elizabeth of Bohemia would get to hear of it and be ashamed of him.

"I thought Maurice was too ill to travel," Venetia demurred, stifling a yawn, watching him as he moved about the room, hauling on his clothes, wrenching open the door to shout for DeFaust and Holmes.

"He'll come," the Prince said with grim confidence, honing his razor purposefully. "And the Lifeguard are ready for action."

"But you had orders not to leave Oxford." A silly remark she knew, for who would dare try to stop him?

"I am for Newark," he said.

"Newark!" That shifted her right out of bed and around to his side, the cold tiles imprinting themselves on her warm bare feet. "But, Rupert, you can't! That is straight through enemy territory!"

He gave a boyish grin, much more balanced now his mind was made up; he had spent a miserable few days, either sunk in brooding apathy, bitterly angry, or roaring around belligerently, blaming everybody. "That is what Digby is counting on. Why else do you suppose he has hurried the King off there?"

De Faust was opening drawers and cupboards, filling bags. Rupert paused, giving her a questioning look. "Have you any money?"

"A little." There was still a small amount of her inheritance left.

"Good. Bring it with you." Rupert, fully dressed, was ducking his tall head in the mirror, combing his hair. Venetia swallowed hard and got busy—before he changed his mind—having already faced the dreary prospect of being left behind.

"I've no money coming from any source." He took his cloak from Holmes, while Venetia flung on her clothes, screened by the bed-curtains. "I'd be hard put to it to lay my hands on fifty pounds and can't pay my servants. Unless something is done, I shan't be able to feed them soon. So much for that bribe of eight thousand golden Jacobuses! Christ's blood, what I'd give to meet Charles Louis!"

They left Oxford without incident, and Venetia still could not believe her incredible luck. Of course, it would not have entered Rupert's head that such a ride might be unwise in her condition. The Winter Queen had never missed a day's hunting when pregnant—he could expect no less from the mother of his son.

Damaris would be very cross with him when she knew —she had already lectured Venetia about getting enough rest, eating the right food—and not going horse riding!

Rupert was straining ahead, hair and cloak streaming behind him and Venetia let her animal go, bending low over his withers, hanging onto her hat, her mouth full of lace collar and strands of hair. She caught up with him and he turned to her, laughing uproariously, with the exaltation of a wild creature suddenly freed, his eyes, reckless and ferocious, flashing over his hallooing followers who had rallied to his call.

Maurice was waiting for them at Banbury. They found him quartered at the most comfortable inn which the tiny own could provide, huddled over the fire, pallid and cadaverous.

"What the devil have you been up to?" Rupert demanded, his voice hard with worry. "Getting ill again as soon as I turned my back."

Emotion rippled the brothers' faces like wind on sullen water—each so concerned about the other.

"Well, thank God it was not the plague, anyhow,"

Rupert said when Maurice had explained that it had been another attack of the army disease. They had good cause to dread the plague—their father had died of it when only thirty-six.

After he had received the King's letter, Maurice, sick as he was, had dragged himself into the saddle and gone to see him at Denbigh, leaving no one in any doubt that he considered his brother's disgrace a travesty of justice and that Digby was at fault.

"And Digby?"

"Oh, he is still going around making loud and confident noises." Maurice was trying to look better than he felt, ashamed of this weakness which set his teeth clacking, while sweat beaded his upper lip. Rupert gave him a brief résumé of his troubles, heartsick to see how the Twin's vitality had been reduced by the fever, his hair lank, his bulky frame fined down.

Venetia gave Maurice a letter from Damaris which he opened eagerly, read with a smile, and tucked away in his pocket.

"As well she did not come in person," he joked sheepishly. "I've not the energy."

"To horse with me at dawn." Rupert tousled his hair with rough affection, looking down into his face which seemed filled with his great dark eyes. "Goddam! How many times have you been ill now, or getting yourself wounded? Will it not put new life into you to see Digby plucking my rapier out of his bowels?"

"He's been playing a damned dangerous game with you, Rupert." Maurice, lifelong shadow of le Diable, knew better than anyone just how dangerous. "And how the hell do you propose getting through the enemy line? I have not been able to bring above a score of men with me."

The flames flickered over their faces, cheek-bones gouged by shadows, both so swarthy, so sinister, with their untamed eyes and beaked noses—fired by family pride and a determination to avenge Rupert's tarnished honor. If Digby had any sense at all, he would get away fast, as soon as the faintest ripple of their approach reached him.

"I'd kill him myself, were it not my brother's privilege," stated Maurice simply to Venetia, when Rupert had gone out for a while. His expression was set in angry brooding lines, and he hunched forward in his chair, spreading his big, gaunt hands to the warmth, the red glow behind rendering them almost transparent. "They had best watch out, lest those aspersions about his wanting the Crown prove true."

She stared at him, startled. He had a queer look, as if, on his bed of sickness, delirium had evoked fantastic images and longings.

"Months ago, the rebels put out a tract averring that Rupert was aiming at the throne. This notion was taken up and cherished by Digby."

"I know it well." Her voice sounded thin in her own ears with the effort to be normal. "Rupert took the libel very hard."

"And what would you say, if it were true?" he challenged suddenly.

"He would never——" she began, while madness ran in her blood. "It is unthinkable—isn't it?"

"Of course." There was a total lack of conviction in Maurice's tone.

In each other's eyes, they saw mirrored the hopes and aspirations which they hardly dared dwell upon even in their most secret thoughts, bewitched by that splendid being to whom they had dedicated their lives.

Venetia drew in a sharp breath, and there was something ruthless in her voice, banishing scruple, as she said: "He could take the Crown, betray England, sell the whole of mankind to the Devil, and I would still love him!"

"And I also!" affirmed his brother fervently.

When he returned, a few minutes later, they both started like sleepers awakened. His eyebrows went up in amusement.

"You look like conspirators! D'you want to lie with her, Maurice? Or is she telling you our news, eh?"

Rupert's face was as flushed and feverish as his brother's, but it was drink, not sickness, which burned him up. He sprawled across the settle, pulling her down to him, pushing open her skirt and kissing her throat, her collarbone and her breasts.

Maurice was laughing, puzzled, and asking: "What news is this?"

Very pleased with himself, Rupert shouted at him: "She is *enciente!* What think you of that?"

Parliament had sent fifteen hundred horses to intercept the Prince. He was undeterred and grinned at the information; this was more like it! The autumn had set in with early frost, cold winds and rain squalls. The weather deteriorated the further north they progressed, mud sucking the horses' fetlocks as they traversed the wagon-ways of the wild uplands.

Passing through Northampton, they came to Burghley, a house now garrisoned by Roundheads. They had been alerted to catch the Prince, strung out untidily across the road, barring the way. Rupert halted and sized up the barricades and the cluster of "forlorn hope" pointing their muskets through the damp morning.

"I know the Governor of this place, a renegade who was once in my own troop. Thinks to stop me, does he!"

He brandished his sword, inclined forward in his saddle to urge his courser on and led his hundred Cavaliers in a furious charge on the unfortunate musketeers. Rupert's horse leapt the barricades first, landing square on a group of them who scattered and fled.

Round the bend of the road came troopers, headed by the Governor himself who galloped straight up to the Prince, raised his pistol and fired in his face. There was the empty clatter of hammer against pan but no report—Rupert was still unharmed. The man's expression changed to horror, he threw down his weapon and yelled for quarter. Rupert's lips curled in contempt at such presumption and he shot him dead.

When their leader toppled from his mount, struck down by the huge, mad Wizard Prince who, once again, had proved himself impervious to natural arms, his followers turned, dug in their spurs, and rushed back to the shelter of Burghley.

Rupert was using his old tactics of night marches and bewildering speed to slip through the enemy posted to catch him. Venetia, used though she was to travelling with him, had never before been subjected to such intensity of danger and constant movement. They slept by day, rolled up in cloaks on the damp ground, it was too dangerous to risk inns which might betray them. Occasionally a cottager would give them shelter for a few hours, alarmed into compliance by finding himself staring down a pistol-barrel.

Venetia was dirty and lousy, always hungry, saddle-sore and tired; the only female among this band of hardened rapscallions, expert at raiding chicken-houses and screwing supplies out of unwilling rebel smallholders. She forgot what it was like to live among women, now warmed by the bluff good-fellowship, the coarse humor, the cursing and the courage of Rupert's men. Whatever modesty she had managed to retain after over two years of following the army, disappeared completely in this enforced close proximity. The men treated her as casually as if she were one of themselves, but gave her the respect she merited as being Rupert's woman.

They were nearing the end of the journey, Belvoir Castle in Leicestershire, where they would be safe, for it was governed by Colonel Gervase Lucas, and only a day's march from Newark. Rupert, eager and impatient, was keeping up a jolting trot through the darkness, with the horses skidding on cart-ruts, slipping in mud, picking their way over fallen logs.

Venetia was half asleep, lulled by the rhythm of her mount, no longer even aware of the dull ache of the bruises on her buttocks. After miles of riding in the dark, her thoughts floated aimlessly, outside human experience. She could see little but the shoulders of Barney ahead of her and Rupert on her left, the tree-trunks each side making blackness denser, lining the way like foemen waiting in silent ambuscade. Close at hand would be Etienne and Adrian, Mallory and Michael; without being asked they had formed themselves into her own private body-guard.

The deep black mystery of the heavens which had hung above her, began to thin, she was made wide awake by the chill dawn breeze on her cheek, the cold dampness in her hair. Her mouth felt furred. She turned her head— daylight carved harsh shadows beneath Rupert's eyes.

He was on familiar ground—he had stayed there once as a boy, and hunted all over the surrounding countryside. They came out of the forest track onto a wider road and his scouts plodded up to announce that they were not the only early risers. The bridge ahead was swarming with enemy troops, a good three hundred by the look of it. Rupert's plan was simple. They rode coolly on as if to charge the Roundheads massed so solidly against them, then he suddenly wheeled his horse, leading his troopers in a feigned retreat, pretending that they had just realized the odds against them. The duped cavalry gave chase and, having lured them into the open, Rupert swung around galloping hell for leather, charging straight at them, in-tending to get between them and the bridge. But they were far outnumbered and twice this ruse failed. The Prince rallied his men for one final attempt; they could see further enemy reinforcements coming up—if this effort did not pay off, they would be surrounded.

"We have beaten them twice, we must beat them once more, and then over the pass and away!" he urged, yanking his blown animal around.

Venetia's cob swerved with the rest, hardly needing her guidance and she gritted her teeth to endure yet again the savage pounding. The saddle jabbed her crotch and skinned her thighs and the reins seared her fingers as they bore down on the rebels, crashed right through them, hacking and cutting, and careered over the bridge, outdistancing pursuit.

They slowed their pace, easing their horses, but Rupert knew that the Roundheads would not give up. The sumpter-beasts, laided with baggage, were a hindrance. He paused long enough to divide his force into two parties, despatching one contingent to escort the goods to Belvoir by the main road, and slipping down a side lane with the rest, following a path remembered from nine years before.

It was winding and overgrown, slippery with wet leaves fallen from the almost bare trees. They heard the sounds of the enemy hurrying after the baggage-train, their excited shouts fading into the distance.

Maurice passed his sleeve over his wet face. *"Mort Dieu!* D'you think we've shaken them off?"

"Maybe. I know this way well. The King and I hunted here once. We used to shoot conies in that valley." Rupert was looking Venetia over to ascertain if she were unharmed.

She managed an unsteady smile, shaken to a pulp, not sure herself if she was still all in one piece. "Lord, the babe must be stuck fast as a limpet," she thought wonderingly, "or surely, I should have miscarried by now."

They let the tired horses idle along. Then Rupert pulled in sharply, head lifted to listen.

"Goddam! They are after us again! And we leave a trail a blind man could follow!"

There was the ominous drumbeat of hooves churning the mud of the lane behind them, and Ironside morions and red coats came into view. Rupert ordered his men to turn, blocking the narrow way. Now within earshot, the Roundhead captain shouted:

"Will you have quarter?"

The Prince laughed in his face and went hurtling down

on them, his men hard behind yelling war-cries. Carried forward by the impetus into that pandemonium of shouts, oaths and shots, Venetia found herself hacking at an enraged antagonist who reared in her path. A numbing blow on her wrist cost her her sword, a hard face, under the iron peak of a helmet, glared into hers. And then Rupert was suddenly there, treading down deep in his stirrups, clubbing the man with his pistol so that he rocked in the saddle and slid sideways into the mire. Rupert caught the battle-axe from his saddle-bow and thrust it at her— disarmed, she was helpless. Michael and Barney closed in, and there was the clash of steel behind her. One terrified glance showed Rupert fighting the rebel Captain, who gave a yell as his sword went spinning off into the bushes and the Prince's rapier pierced his throat. He keeled over, dangling at a crazy angle as his horse bolted.

This finished the Roundheads; they broke, crashed through scrub and undergrowth, scrambling, helter-skelter, back to the road. The Cavaliers gathered themselves together, winded but cocky—it had been a good fight. They teased Venetia good-humoredly while she sat sucking the gash on her wrist and Barney called out to the Prince.

"Your little she-devil has been blooded, sir!"

He rode over then to examine it, and wrap his kerchief round the wound, stroking her fingers, saying little, but very proud of her.

"Your Highness." It was Lord Molineux leading a fine mare. "It belonged to the fellow I've just shot. Take it sir. Your nag looks done for."

When they had taken a breather, they ascended the track through steep woods, flanked by bare rock worn into uneven ledges like stairs, and came at last to Belvoir Castle. Yet another old, obstinate fortress, gripping the spur which dominated the rugged landscape, still holding out for the King. A short parley at the gate, then under the spiked archway into the keep, enclosed by high machi-colated walls.

Colonel Lucas had to tell them that some of the baggage and men had been lost in the Roundhead attack. The Cavaliers dismounted slowly, yawning and hawking, suddenly too weary even to curse.

In the ballroom-like proportions of the chilly bedchamber, Venetia luxuriated in a copper bathtub, up to her shoulders in herb-scented water, her hair skewered on top of her head with bodkins, while a very embarrassed

Holmes had been cast in the role of lady's maid. A whole log blazed in the stone fireplace, with its carved supports, and mantle carrying the armorial bearings of the Earls of Rutland, whose home this had once been. Rupert, shaved clean, and looking remarkably handsome, seated himself astride a chair, arms folded on the back, watching her as she bathed and making funny remarks of an indelicate nature which convulsed her and sent Holmes crimson to the ears.

These small corners of peace, little breathing spells in the turmoil, were happiness to Venetia—compensation enough for all the hardships. Such wild frantic joy, pleasure that was almost torture, love always tinged with tears, threatened by loneliness and longing and that unspoken knowledge that it could not possibly last for ever.

She pushed melancholy from her resolutely. The hot water was blissful, and she played at washing, looking at the Prince from the tail of her eye, with the smile of a pretty woman who knows that she is being admired by the man she loves. Life was good—she would think only of the moment. The smell of roasting venison wafted up from the great hall—soon they would be amidst merry company, to talk and drink and laugh. Rupert would forget for a while the gravity of his mission. And later, in the depths of ensorcelled night, he would be there—a tangible reality—and she would be steadied, not lost in that nightmare labyrinth where she wandered sometimes when sleeping, crying, seeking him—waking with tears of ice on her cheeks, to clasp him close and sob with relief, knowing that, for a while at least, she had been reprieved.

It happened just like that—an evening to treasure and remember, but in the morning, as they sat at an early breakfast, a rider came in from Newark bearing a message from the King, forbidding Rupert to come any nearer.

"He says, among other things, that I am no fit company for him." Rupert tossed the letter across to his brother, threw down his napkin and slammed out of the room.

Maurice and Venetia looked at one another without comment. In the courtyard they could hear him barking orders for the men to get to horse.

EIGHT

The sky was like lead and the air uneasy. As they rode through the woods, the bare branches sawed, and the shrivelled leaves whirled and eddied on the ground. Breaking from cover the cavalcade slowed, wary of the troops making toward them from the direction of Newark.

It was a large body of horse, led by Rupert's friend, Sir Richard Willys, the Governor. They had risked the King's displeasure to make this demonstration, coming two miles from the city walls to escort the Prince.

Maurice's lips widened in a grin of pride and pleasure. "That will show 'em!"

Venetia understood, sharing his satisfaction, before the joy in this reception was marred. Rupert exploded into a passion when Willys told him that Digby had not stayed to face the music. Montrose had sent for help, and Digby, well aware that the Prince was hot on his trail, had convinced the King that he was the very man for the job, taking fifteen hundred soldiers, and flourishing a brand new commission making him Lieutenant-General of all the forces north of the Trent.

"But that was Rupert's command!" Maurice could not prevent the rush of angry blood which colored his face.

"He will not be able to run forever." Rupert's jaw was clenched, his eyes narrowed to venomous slits as he started over their heads, towards Scotland, as if he could descry the fleeing Secretary. "One day I shall catch up with him."

An even greater welcome awaited him at Newark. The soldiers were unanimous in their support, fuming because the man who had broken their Prince and lied away his good name, had been given an even higher honor.

Rupert had now only one objective, and Willys and Gerard accompanied him into the courtyard of the turreted Castle where the King lodged. Silently, the two Palatines swung down from their mounts and, unannounced, without any of the usual ceremony, they strode into demand audience.

Reluctantly, Venetia permitted Willys to lead her to his house, there to begin the agonized wait. He was very kind; a lively person, black-haired, stocky, devoted to Rupert, he quickly made Venetia feel at home, ushering her into his parlor, producing a decanter of claret, understanding very well how she was feeling.

In a while, the slow, dismal clop of hooves gave them their answer.

By the time she went to bed late that night, Venetia's head seemed to be bursting with fatigue, confusion and talk. Rupert had been so upset by that terrible interview with his uncle that it was not until he had been seated for some time by the crackling fire tearing up the chimney, and had got several beakers of mulled sack down him, that the stunned look had faded from his eyes.

"What did he say?" she demanded of Maurice.

Maurice shook his head slowly, disbelievingly, sinking onto the settle. "That was just the trouble—he would not say anything."

"Not to me," said Rupert.

Sir Richard had supper brought in. They ate and thawed out and, gradually, the story could be pieced together Venetia had known, right from the start, that such aggressive action would not work with the King—to go barging in, so rudely, could do nothing but alienate him further.

"The poor man must have felt that you had come to murder him!" she burst out, vexed with them both. "At the very least he probably believed that you intended to force him, at sword's point, to make peace with the rebels."

Rupert's eyes switched to her, black with misery, "Why should he have thought that I intended to harm him?" He still could not credit that the real affection which his uncle had always shown him, could have been so changed. "I told him that I had come to render an account of the loss of Bristol. He made no reply."

"He probably did not know what to say, sir," suggested Willys.

It was more likely that the shock of seeing his rebellious nephew had robbed the King of his speech—he always needed time to compose his sentences and control his impediment.

They had arrived just as he was going in to have his

supper, and he had turned away from them, walking into the dining-room. Now, rather ashamed of such boorishness, Maurice told how they had followed him and stood, one on either side of his chair, while he tried to eat. Exasperating as she found the King to be, Venetia could feel little but pity for him, missing his Queen, distressed for his ravaged country, and finding himself fenced in by these two enormous young barbarians who had deliberately disobeyed him, forcing themselves on his person with singular lack of respect.

"It was terrible." Maurice pushed the food away, sickened by the memory. "He spoke a few words to me, asking after my health, but would say nothing to Rupert. We stuck it out though, until at last he retired to his bedchamber."

"Do you mean to tell me that you did not hound him here also?" The strain was making Venetia fractious, uncomfortably able to see everyone's point of view. Oh, she would always give the Prince her whole-hearted support, yet she found his present behavior atrocious.

His face set in sullen lines, his mouth drooping, eyes hooded. "He'll hear me yet! I insist on a court martial! Even the lowest soldier in the ranks deserves nothing less if he is falsely accused."

Venetia was already in bed and sliding off to sleep when Rupert came in. She sat up crossly, annoyed with herself because she had wanted to be alert, fully conscious, to offer whatever solace he needed. He stripped rapidly to the skin in front of the fire, red as a fiend in the glow, coming over to douse the light, and the bed sagged on one side beneath the coverlet —a stone effigy on a family tomb. She reached for, and found one of his hands.

"Oh, God, Venetia, what have I done?" There was such distress in his low tone that her heart gave a lurch. "If you could have seen him this afternoon—he has aged so much—he looked so tired, so careworn—and there was I, who have ever wanted only to serve him—adding to his burdens."

"You have to be vindicated, darling. He must grant you this."

"When I first came to offer him my sword at the outbreak of the war, there was nothing I would not have done for him." He was tormented by self-reproach, anger and bitterness. "What went wrong? Was it my accursed temper which has ever been my bane?"

She wished that she had known them in those early days, when King Charles had been so delighted in the loyal enthusiasm and achievements of his big, healthy nephew, newly-released from prison and hungry for action. The issues had been clear-cut to Rupert then, while the King's views had been for moderation. Now their roles were almost reversed—Rupert was the peace-maker, having seen too much in his youth of the damage done in terms of life, property and trade, crippling taxes, the break-up of families and the disruption of communities caused by a lengthy conflict.

"I am the butt at which envy shoots its arrows, all my uncle's losses are laid at my charge" the Prince said somberly, then added: "When I looked at him, I had the most curious sensation—I was so angry because he ignored me, and yet, it was as if his face floated, disembodied, in the light of the torches—so pale and drawn, staring at me without expression, as if he were dead!"

He rolled on his side, his arms going round her, pressing his face against her hair as if he would blot out that frightening vision. Venetia held him tightly, unable to find words to help him, running her lips over his face, tasting the salt of his tears.

"Oh, Digby," she thought, cradling him as she would soon rock his child, loving him more than her life. "You must be hugging yourself with glee at your success in overthrowing the bravest of the brave. Can't you see that your Royal master will come crashing down with him?"

Rupert got his court martial. His case was heard before the Council of War on October 18th and it was a body made up, very fairly, of his friends and his enemies. He submitted a declaration in which he had stated his actions at Bristol and his reasons for them. Also, there was a very full description of the conditions in the town and the events which had led up to the surrender, signed by all the well-known officers who had been on his staff. He stood up and made his own defense in a characteristically terse manner, nonetheless impressive for being very much to the point. There were two hearings and the King presided over the second. The result was an unqualified verdict of acquittal.

It was a great triumph for the Prince's party, but brought little contentment to Rupert. His honor had been redeemed, the stigma of treachery and corruption cleared from his name, but the King, though agreeing with the council, had not forgiven him, still unbending in his mien, avoiding his company, cold and distant. There were savage undertones and tensions, a sharp cleavage between the King's faction and the Prince's. It was almost a relief when matters came to a head.

The enemy was approaching Newark and the King was planning to leave for Oxford. He had taken umbrage at the behavior of his officers and their show of fidelity to Rupert, and had no intention of leaving the most powerful of them, Willys, in position as Governor. Following his usual policy of giving with one hand and taking away with the other, he ordered him to change places with Lord Belasyse, who was now commander of his Life-guard.

Willys paced his parlor furiously, putting his grievance to Rupert. "He thinks that by promoting me, he can cozen me to his real motive. Belasyse is a friend of Digby's—if he becomes Governor here, and I am dragged back to Oxford, everyone will know it is a mark of the King's disfavor!"

Rupert was already making for the door with Maurice at his heels. "This is not to be endured! We will see His Majesty!"

Unconsciously, he had been waiting for something like this to happen—simmering at his treatment—growing hourly more contemptuous of his uncle's pettyfogging attitude, and his weakness which allowed him to be dominated by a scroundrel like Digby.

It was Sunday and the King had just come back from church to take his place at the dinner-table, when there was a disturbance in the antechamber, angry voices, the heavy clump of boots, the rattle of swords. Maurice, Gerard, Willys and a crowd of officers marched into the presence. Rupert was at their head, his face dark with rage.

Charles gave him a haughty stare, icily calm. He ordered his attendants to take the meal away, rose from his chair and went over to the arched recess of the window, beckoning the leading malcontents to follow him. He was stiff with injured majesty; a tiny man, dwarfed by the soldiers looming over him, yet every inch of him proclaimed him their ruler.

It was Willys who broke the charged silence, brushing aside all etiquette and shouting: "Sire, the whole town is saying that I have been dismissed from my place as Governor. I have been publicly affronted and demand a public explanation!"

Before the King could reply, Rupert rudely interrupted: "By God! This is done in malice to me, because Sir Richard has always been my faithful friend!"

Gerard, out of control and excited, released the pent-up resentment which had been festering for weeks, since his dismissal in Wales. "Digby is behind all this! Digby is a traitor!"

The King did not flinch under this gust of passionate hostility. He outfaced these stormy agitators, led by his intolerable young kinsman who glowered defiance at him. "Digby is an honest man and they that say otherwise are traitors."

"Then we must all be traitors!" flashed Gerard, and Venetia despaired, standing in the background among the Prince's adjutants. It would have been far better for Rupert had this hothead not been there.

"You have spoken the words." The King fixed him with a freezing glance.

This was too much for the Prince and he roared his support for Gerard. "He is right. The cause of all this is Digby!"

He spat out the name viciously—baulked in his desire for Digby's blood—cheated of revenge—determined to force his uncle to see the Secretary in his true light—a black-hearted villain!

But King Charles was blind to everything except his fear of Rupert's power, and his outraged indignation at this shocking breach of conduct.

"I am but a child!" he retorted with bitter sarcasm, all trace of his stammer gone in his anger. "Digby can do what he will with me!"

The formal correctness had been shattered; two bright spots of color appeared on the King's pale face and Rupert was glaring down on him with furious intensity. They looked very alike at that moment, full of stubborn pride, both quite unable to retract.

"*Sacrément!* But that is true!" the Prince cried. "He *can* do as he wills with you! You believe his every lie. All through the war it has been his desire to see me ousted of all command!"

"He would have been your friend, had you let him." That chill, toneless voice cut like a lash.

"Friend!" Rupert threw up his head, eyes blazing. "His jealousy made him determined to ruin me and, by Christ, he has damn near succeeded! But in so doing, he has lost you the war!"

"Nonsense!" The sharp rebuke cracked through the room.

Rupert was almost insane with fury, grief and hatred. "If you had heeded me, we would have finished this business long since. We should have taken London after Edgehill—but no—you followed the advice of the Courtiers, not the soldiers! You were acting for Digby when you ordered me to fight against odds at Marston Moor! And Naseby! What a disaster that proved—carried out at his urging! Was it he who prevented aid coming to me at Bristol?"

The mention of the city was like lancing a septic wound. Its loss had shaken the King from his customary calm. He could not forgive the man who had delivered it to the enemy—yet this was that same ardent boy whom he had loved like one of his own. It was as if all the horror of this costly war weighed suddenly on him—an unbearable burden, cracking asunder that self-imposed reserve, that mask of serenity.

His shoulders bowed, and his eyes, raised to that tense, bitter face above him, were sunken, empty of anger, bereft of hope.

"Oh, nephew——!" The words came out on a long sigh, and then stopped short. He turned away, gazing blankly from the window. Colors rainbowed from the heraldic devices on some of the panes—blue, crimson, amber—throwing warm patterns on the bare stone floor, then fading as cloud obscured the watery sun.

At that finely-balanced moment, they could have buried their antagonism, both in desperate need of a renewal of trust, and Venetia prayed that Rupert would find it in him to make the first gesture. But he was worked up into a raging temper, consumed with that hot sick wave of fury which would leave him shaken and dazed. He would not keep silent, bursting out, for the third time:

"Digby is the man that has caused all this distraction between us!"

The King's face closed into a mask; he would endure no more of this insolence. "They are all rogues and rascals that say so!" he answered sharply, "and in effect traitors that seek to dishonor my best subjects!"

It was a disgraceful scene, and deeply disturbing to all who witnessed it. The three who were with the King squared their shoulders and exchanged glances—they were not going to be called traitors! Gerard and Willys bowed and went away, embarrassed and already regretting their hasty words. But Rupert stalked out proudly, showing no reverence, his staff trailing, miserable and shamefaced, behind him.

They cantered back to Willy's house in deathly silence. Willy's parlor was crammed with huge, violent men, throwing aside drenched cloaks, slapping bedraggled hats against their thighs, bawling for pots of ale, while servants hovered. The whole town joined in the rumpus—soldiers gathered in loud, gesticulating knots on every street corner, circulating wild yarns, each adding his own bit of color. Soon the incident had grown out of all proportion—the officers had forced their way into the Royal presence, fighting the Lifeguard—the Prince had drawn his sword and threatened the King—the King had called him a traitor!

And the eager partisans who formed the ruck of the Rupert-party, clamored outside the ex-Governor's house, shouting for the Prince, till Willys was forced to go out and order them to go away. The Prince's secretary was sent for and, before the evening was through, they had concocted a petition.

They asked for a court martial or, if this be refused, their passes to go abroad. Rupert, waiting for the return of the petitioners, listened to the excitement in the streets outside. Drums were beating to call the men to arms, and the chief officers thundered about on their leggy steeds, preparing to leave.

He rested a foot on the window-seat and leaned forward with his arm on his knee, gazing out.

"*Mort dieu!* Look at them. Mine to command!" He pondered for a moment and then muttered, almost as if he had forgotten that Venetia were there: "Gustavus Adolphus was right when he said that a King should be his own General or——" he checked himself, but she finished it for him.

"Or a General his own King!"

He looked up sharply, straight into her eyes, with so quick a change of expression that it was impossible to tell if it was anger, agreement or sadness. Before he could answer, they were interrupted by the appearance of Willys's men.

"Well?" the Prince demanded.

Silently they handed him the passports.

Gerard was on his feet, hand flying instinctively to his sword-hilt. "We are with you, sir, to the death! What would you have us do?"

Rupert was not listening, firing questions, wanting to know every detail of what had taken place at the Castle.

"One of the officers very humbly expressed the hope that His Majesty would not call the action mutiny," Willys answered in a low voice. " 'I shall not christen it,' said the King, 'but it looks very like.' "

Cavalry, growing denser as daylight strengthened, jostled in the market-square, till there were three hundred ready to obey Rupert's bidding. In the sobriety of dawn, many recognized that, no matter his injustice, their loyalty should have remained with King Charles, but pride would not let them recant—and the Prince would not apologize.

Maurice pleaded with him to yield a little. He felt strongly that if Rupert made the first move, then their uncle would unbend. But it was hopeless—he had shut himself away in black brooding silence. Maurice looked to Venetia for help; she shook her head, reflecting sadly that she had never been successful in influencing Rupert. Though she pretended otherwise to herself, she was still oddly shy of him—when he was with equals and she felt inferior, or when, by his glance, she guessed that she had said or done something foolish, or at early morning when his sleeping face was a stranger's.

They went to take their leave of the King—Rupert, Maurice and Gerard. He received them privately, in his bedchamber, and the meeting was brief and painful, bringing ease to none. Stilted, formal, the empty words dropped into the atmosphere, with the King stiffly and, it seemed to Rupert, grudgingly acknowledging their fidelity and innocence. Gerard muttered something about regretting the folly of yesterday's scene. Rupert, stony-faced, offered no apology and, following his lead, neither did Maurice, though he was unable to conceal his discomfort.

Down in the courtyard, the three men got to horse. They rejoined the cavalry, still patiently waiting direction in the square. And Venetia had never seen Rupert look so bleak, not even when he rode out of Bristol. Maurice was plucking at his sleeve, a habit which infuriated him at the best of times. He rounded on his brother as if he would strike him.

"For the love of God! What ails you, dolt?"

"Did you notice him?" Maurice was too upset to be silenced by bullying.

"What are you gibbering about?" Rupert was running his eyes over that company of first-rate soldiers who were there only to do his pleasure.

If he gave the word, they would raise such a furor in the country that a second war would start, which might well finish more successfully than this one, with himself on the English throne. And why not? That black demon was whispering in his mind which was clouded by bewilderment and loss.

Maurice's voice was booming on relentlessly, determined to make him listen.

"It was the King. I looked back, up to the window, and saw him standing there watching us go, with the tears running down his face."

Belvoir Castle became the temporary home of the Prince and those who had thrown in their lot with him. No time was lost in sending to Parliament for permission and safe convoy for all those who wished to leave the country. While they waited for a reply, news came through of Digby's doings; it gave Rupert grim satisfaction to learn that he had lost the Northern Horse, having been routed in Yorkshire where he had again left behind important papers, this time the whole of his own private correspondence on the King's affairs. On a false rumor that Montrose had rallied and was in Glasgow, he had pushed up into Scotland and, on learning the truth, had planned to winter in hiding, but the busy enemy found him out, his men deserted, and Digby got away by the skin of his teeth, taking ship to the Isle of Man, where he now enjoyed the hospitality of the Countess of Derby.

The Newark fiasco was the climax of the strife between the military and the civilian parties. It was heart-warming to see how popular Rupert was in this crisis; men arrived to attach themselves to his troop, letters came promising support.

And, of course, Rupert wrote to his "dear Will," telling him all about it. Lieutenant Colonel Osborne, who had taken the Prince's request to Westminster, sent back their reply. Parliament would give passes on condition that the

Princes promised never again to bear arms for the King.

Rupert would not agree to this. But some move must be made before the winter closed in—he got his followers together and they fought their way back to the village of Woodstock, not far from Oxford.

The Royal Manor squatted on its rise in the midst of a valley, reached by a wooded forest path, promising shelter after the exposure of that final gruelling stage of their journey, when rain had sheeted on them remorselessly all day. Venetia was so tired, wet and miserable, that even the meanest hovel would have been welcome. Something told her that she would not be able to keep up this roaming existence much longer. Rupert, sullenly preoccupied with his own troubles, seemed to be unaware of the toll it was taking, not only on her, but also on Maurice, still absurdly delicate after his illnesses.

It was a rambling mansion, built originally as a fortress by Norman barons, still presenting blank walls, pierced by arrow-slits, to the outside world, but inside the courtyard were larger windows where lights now sprang up. Rupert's scouts, riding ahead, had brought warning of their imminent arrival. Venetia had a jumbled picture of crowding gables, dormer windows, steeply angled tiled roofs of varying heights, richly ornamented chimneys and a tower or two.

Conveniently close to Oxford, it was possible to send for the "family," and, within a few days, Pierre appeared with a pack of servants, De Faust and Gallois, essential goods, and messages from old friends. He opened up long-closed kitchens, setting the menials to work scrubbing at soot, grease and cobwebs, while the place resounded with the hammering of carpenters fixing more shelves for his fussy requirements.

"Christ knows where the money is to be had to pay for all this!" Rupert exclaimed in despair.

"Fear not, *Monseigneur*" replied Etienne with a grin and a flourish of his feather-burdened beaver. "My dear wife will be here any day, with further supplies. I am still in good standing with my goldsmith!"

Damaris never just arrived anywhere, she always made a dramatic entrance, and her appearance at Woodstock Manor was no exception. Her enormous crested coach, drawn by powerful horses, swung into view. The Chevalier did not wait for the step to be lowered. As soon as the door opened, he reached up and she jumped into his arms, and he held her close while they murmured greeting and tender endearments in French.

She swept into the solar, unfastening the strings of her fur-lined hooded cloak of emerald green velvet, taking immediate charge of Maurice, lecturing Rupert on the folly of dragging him around the country in his state of health. She whisked down to Pierre's kitchen, insisting on preparing some potion of her own for the invalid, ignoring his cross looks.

"And I had best move in with you, darling. Perchance you may have need of something in the night." She leaned solicitously above Maurice where he lay on the couch and arranged the cushions beneath his head.

His pleasant mouth curved in a smile, delighted to be fussed over, his eyes on her breasts as she bent nearer, enveloped in a warm wave of her musky Frangipani perfume. *"Dieu!* Would that I felt stronger!"

Rupert was lolling in unaccustomed idleness in a deep chair. Venetia, seated on a footstool at his side, watched him adoringly.

He made some sarcastic remark, pooh-poohing this coddling, resentful of the inference that he neglected his brother. Damaris handed Maurice the posset-pot which she had prepared.

" 'Tis high time someone cossetted him," she stated firmly. "Really, Highness, your lack of concern for others is somewhat alarming! Have you no pity for that poor wench of yours? 'Twill be a marvel if she does not drop that babe before it's due!"

Rupert's expression was surly and Venetia wished the floor would open and swallow up her outspoken friend. She was painfully aware that Rupert was by far the more sick of the Princes, his depression affecting his magnificent physique, making his sluggish, over willing to seek insensibility in the bottom of a bottle.

Damaris fetched a blanket and laid it across Maurice's legs. "And while I'm speaking plain, Your Highness, 'tis my opinion, and that of many of your real friends, that you stop lingering about here, sulking like Achilles in his tent, and get back to Oxford. Why not make your peace with His Majesty? He has arrived there and released Will Legge——"

"I know!" Rupert snapped. "I've heard from him!"

"Will thinks that you should apologize. He tells me that the King desires it." Damaris could be very persistent, undeterred by Rupert's scowls. "Can you not see what is happening to the army with no one to lead it?"

"Why should I care? The civilians have taken over from the soldiers. 'Tis what they have ever wanted. Let them get on with it!"

Maurice had managed to seize one of Damaris' hands as she tucked in the blanket, saying softly: "And I thought this was going to be a damn dull winter."

"Never believe that, dear heart," Damaris sparkled at him, her gaze direct, her smile alluring. "We'll hunt, fish and ride—and all in your room!"

Rupert gave a sardonic smile when she told them how Digby, with typical mismanagement, carefully preserved his love-letters in cypher, while all those of political importance were written in plain language. The Roundheads wasted valuable time decoding ardent words of passion of no significance to anyone except his paramours, when they pored over the recently captured cache of mail.

Unable to rest, Rupert wandered the room a couple of times, stared hard from the window, seeing nothing, and then went back to the fire.

Damaris took up the tankard of lamb's-wool from the tall stand at the end of the fire-dog, where she had placed it to keep hot. "Rumor has it, that even the Ironsides feel the King has treated you shabbily, Highness. You seem to be held in high regard by everyone in the Kingdom——"

"Except His Majesty!" Rupert kicked at a log with the toe of his boot, sending it crumbling in a heap of glowing ashes.

Venetia, for her part, would have been quite content to remain in the friendly house for ever.

"Let the men rumble away to their hearts' content," said Damaris, as they slipped off to the bedroom. She had settled her beloved invalid, making him promise to go to sleep, mixing some herbs into his caudle to make sure that he did. "I want to talk about you. How are you, my dear? None of you look very well, I must say. Rupert is so pinched and peaky, seems even worse than Maurice."

"So you have noticed?"

"Of course I have!" Damaris paused to smile and throw an arm around her. "He's in the devil of a scurvy humor!"

Venetia gave her a brief account of their adventures and Damaris was exasperated, expressing the strong opinion that she had been lucky not to miscarry. "All that

301

jogging! Such treatment may have been very well for his mother—from what I hear, she has the constitution of an ox! 'Tis a thousand pities that you cannot remain here, in peace, till the child is born."

Woodstock was a house to love and Venetia had already explored a great deal of it, dragging Rupert along with her, more interested than he cared to admit. They had faced a freezing north-easter, muffled to the noses in cloaks, going to view the ruins of "Rosamund's bower," with its strange winding labyrinth of walls and turnings. The wind had whistled mournfully around the square paved well where she had wanted to linger, sighing over the legend of the fair Rosamund Clifford, mistress of Henry II, for whom he was supposed to have built this dwelling beyond the walls of the Manor, protected by its complicated maze.

But inside, the house was quite sumptuous, with ornamental ceilings and magnificent staircases, a vast hall, a chapel, arched galleries, a tennis-court, apartments for the King and others for the Queen, all with a fine view of the parklands, abounding in game for the Royal sport. It was all a little seedy and run down—a sign of the times where there was no longer a bottomless Treasury to pay for its upkeep.

The Prince's bedchamber was furnished handsomely. There were table-desks and oaken joint stools, and box chairs of uncompromising hardness, but there were also others, with matching footstools, covered in fringed galloon secured by a multitude of brass-headed nails. The oak bed was of truly majestic proportions where even Rupert could stretch out full-length without his feet touching the bottom, and it rejoiced in twisting pillars and an inlaid headboard. It was hung with deep-red drapes, festooned with a great deal of somewhat tarnished gold swagging, but still very impressive.

Damaris seated herself in a "farthingale" chair, without arms, designed to show the decoration of a hoop petticoat to its fullest extent. "Thank God, our fashions are more graceful now, so that we look like women, not walking sideboards. And these high waistlines will help to keep your secret, my dear. What does Michael say about the baby?"

"He is very upset, but he still wants to marry me." Venetia backed up to Damaris so that she might unlace her tight bodice. Her gowns had arrived with the servants, bringing home the reality of her pregnancy—nothing fitted any more.

"What you need is one of those short, loose, fur-edged jackets which are all the rage in Paris and just coming into this country," advised Damaris sagely. "I have one which I will give you, then you can leave your bodice unfastened, the gap won't show at the back." She sent Nancy off to fetch it, and pursued the subject of Michael. "A useful young man," she mused. "You will need a husband."

"I have Rupert," Venetia said, her voice brittle.

"For how long?" Damaris was holding her spread fan to act as a fire-screen between her complexion and the flaring embers. "You know very well that he will not wed you. He cannot, even if he wishes—which I doubt."

Why did Damaris have to come along, pointing out so brutally, all those bald facts which stalked across Venetia's mind in the dead small hours when she could not sleep? She went on, relentlessly:

"You know what his family are like and what will be expected of him with regard to matrimony. A Princess, no less. There are so many considerations when people of their station think of wedded bliss!"

"I know——" Venetia was close to tears, grabbing desperately at the straws of Rupert's affection. "But he is pleased about the child—truly he is!"

"Oh, I expect he is very proud of himself!" Damaris gave a cynical smile; for a woman who spent so much of her time making love to men, she had really a very low opinion of them. "They think it mighty clever to get a woman with child. A proof of their manhood, I suppose. I always tell 'em that it takes far greater skill not to!"

"I cannot wed Michael." Venetia shook her head. "Rupert will look after me."

"My dear child," Damaris said and her voice had softened with pity. "What can the Prince do for you?" He has no money. Michael still has his estate, though, God knows, if things continue to go as badly for Royalists as they do at present, this may not be worth much! But your baby will have a name. Believe me, I am more familiar with the ways of the world than you, my innocent, and this is important!"

All this Venetia knew—going over it in her mind a hundred times—but her chin set stubbornly as she clung to the one plain fact which loomed over all else. She would not put a further barrier between herself and the

Prince. Marriage with another man would but add to the problems, if, and when, Rupert decided to make her his legal wife.

Damaris wanted to enlarge on the subject but Venetia gave her a stricken look which cut her off in the middle of a sentence. "Oh, very well, I'll keep my peace!" She gave a rueful grin. "Alack, what a poor thing is a woman in love!"

"And, Damaris, do not tax him with this, if you care for me," Venetia urged—Rupert needed careful handling and Damaris was more than just a shade tactless with him. "Also, refrain from further talk of his duty to his uncle—he is so unhappy. You do not know him— all is not as it appears on the surface." How to explain, even to this understanding woman, the diversity of his character. "He is a sensitive person, and really very kind," she ended lamely.

"Lord help us all!" Damaris lifted her eyes beseechingly toward the ornate ceiling as if begging guidance for her mad friend. "Of course, 'tis plain to see that beneath his rough exterior there beats a heart of *pure granite!*"

NINE

An iron frost gripped the land; the last days of November brought with them a winter of exceptional cold. The roads, difficult at the best of times, became mostly impassable for heavy vehicles, even the rivers froze and at Woodstock, hunting became a necessity rather than a pastime. The Chevalier was open-handed, presents of money came from Lord Craven and other well-wishers, but there were still a large number of mouths to feed. Rupert's horsemen spread themselves out to forage on their own account, and they were often assailed by flying bands of the enemy. This was typical of what was happening all over England; the last attempts at discipline among the Royalists were breaking down everywhere.

Venetia wished that this isolation might go on forever.

Woodstock was a snug nest; the world could not get at them and Rupert had no cause, or desire, to reach out. Drugged with dismay and anger, he hardly bothered to open his letters—and Venetia was happy, with him every hour of every day and night, using all her energy, all her will, each thought and waking moment for him. Whatever the future held—and common sense told her it could hardly be rosy—she had these few weeks, as at Bristol after Marston Moor, when he belonged to her completely.

Huge, roaring fires, one at each end of the great hall, did much to combat the cold. Candles smoked in circular holders hanging on chains from the painted ceiling. Thick curtains shut out the night; Flemish tapestries were drawn across the doors and, at the two long tables which ran parallel from the shorter one at the head, Rupert's friends feasted.

Woodstock had its own dairy where Pierre supervised the making of cream, butter and cheese, besides a brew-house, very necessary to keep us the large quantities of ale and beer needed for daily consumption. That night the demand was even heavier than usual.

The wenches recruited from the hamlet to help, poured sack and metheglin, brandy and wine, as well as home-brew. There was an air of festivity in the room and, their work done, they lingered, half pleased, half frightened by the mock gallantries of the Cavaliers, till Powell hustled them away, wanting no trouble with his staff. Not that there was any shortage of women—wherever there were soldiers, so females appeared out of the blue!

The gentlemen had eaten well and now they settled down to the serious business of the evening—drinking.

Rupert was seated at the top table and had chosen to dress not only as a soldier, but also as a Prince of the blood. He wore dark blue velvet, the star on his cloak, the flash of his jewelled order, made more brilliant by contrast. He exuded that mysterious and compelling force which made him the center of attention at any gathering —it was the recognition of the ability to take command.

Venetia was intensely proud of her position as his mistress, it gave her the edge on every other woman there, a primordial satisfaction in which she indulged to the full. She let Damaris' loose jacket fall open, wishing that her belly were larger, wanting them all to know that she carried his child.

It was a very good wine. The room swayed and every

face appeared to be swimming in a circle of gold, and in each she saw reflected her own emotion—they all revered Rupert, and she had the greatest difficulty in controlling the urge to make obeisance.

The Prince had been drinking deeply, though only the glitter of his eyes betrayed him.

"What a fine place is this!" Gerard was exclaiming to anyone who would listen. "What a citadel! Why, with these rich pastures and parks, it could be practically self-supporting, like Lathom House. An army could hold out here for months. Would it not be a safe retreat for the King, were Oxford to fall?"

"The King? Charles, d'you mean?" This came from a fair, middle-sized young man with a little golden fuzz on his face, one of those junior officers who made a cult of the Prince. He jumped up to pound the table, knocking over someone's tankard in his eagerness. "We have no need of him! Our leader is here!"

Cheers drowned his voice and he fell back into his seat in tipsy triumph.

"No truer word has been said." Maurice wanted to join in, already levering himself out of his chair, but his brother told him sharply to shut his mouth.

Gerard was leaning across Venetia, eyes keen as the sought Rupert's. "You have but to say the word, sir. You'll have three-quarters of the army behind you. We can raise a force big enough to march on London!"

The youthful revolutionary was on his feet again amidst whistles and yells. He addressed Rupert, throwing aside all caution: "Your Highness, 'tis plain that Charles and his Popish Queen will not be suffered to rule England again! But a Protestant Prince—one who had fought for and been imprisoned for his faith, one, moreover, coming from a House whom the people love—to him all things are possible!"

He should have been warned by the downward swoop of Rupert's brows, but was too carried away by his own eloquence to notice, rushing recklessly on: "Sir, in London—nay, in the whole of the Kingdom, men are longing for your leadership! I pray you, step into the place which the Elector is not strong enough to fill! Accept your destiny! Turn your sword into a scepter!"

Now they were cheering themselves hoarse—it was out at last, what they had all been burning to express. The boy bared his rapier, swinging it high, while they stamped and applauded and followed his example, shouting Rupert's name.

The Prince made no movement or answer, sitting like a man in a trance, all the color draining from his face. Venetia waited breathlessly to see what he would do, while the sudden astounding thought sprang up in her that if he yielded, as she so much wanted him to, this prospective usurper would never be the Rupert whom she served and loved.

He rose slowly, a tall regal figure, and the noise thundered to a crescendo, abruptly silenced as he held up his hand. It burned into Venetia's mind, that hectic moment, lit by glaring torches and leaping flames—an instant which might have altered history, plunging England, even the whole of the civilized world, into the greatest conflict it had ever known.

Without taking his eyes from them, Rupert snapped his fingers at the guards who leaned their shoulders against the panelling at his back. They acted promptly, descending upon the startled boy and marching him up to face his Commander.

"Give me your sword." Rupert spoke quietly, sternly.

With a miserable, hangdog look, the prisoner fumbled with the buckle and handed it over. Rupert took it, drawing the blade from the sheath, glancing down its length once. There was a sharp crack as he broke it across his knee, throwing the pieces on the floor at the officer's feet.

"I would not be served by the sword of a traitor!" said the Prince.

A chapfallen silence followed, with the miscreant escorted away to be locked up in the guard-house, there to kick his heels in suspense, fearing the worst. But gradually spirits revived, with the musicians hurriedly filling the hiatus. Venetia wondered why Rupert had not given the order for the lad to be shot. If he really believed his action was tantamount to treason, then this would be the punishment.

The argument continued in the solar when the Princes retired with their intimates.

"He was right, of course." Gerard cornered Rupert· there was no need for discretion here. "The troops will follow wherever you lead."

"It is madness—madness," repeated the Prince, but there was no clear ring of certainty in his voice.

Venetia had not yet come down from the clouds where

that wild *débâcle* had tossed her. Her imagination had soared, keeping pace with theirs, putting Rupert on the highest pinnacle of acclaim. With Charles Louis controlling Europe, and Rupert as King of England, they could rule half the world between them with the power of their military might. And why not? He was young, full of practical skills and knowledge, and all this, combined with his athletic powers and his remarkable talent for inspiring boundless enthusiasm in those who came under his spell, made him a perfect candidate for the throne.

The magnitude of it flamed through her, kindling aspirations which had lain dormant till Maurice first mentioned it at Banbury. She was almost sure that he loved her, confident that she was becoming an essential part of his life. Were he King, a law unto himself, he would be free to marry her. Their child would be the heir.

"As we stand, all is lost," Maurice commented, stretched out on the bed, hands laced under his head, tongue loosened with drink, "for you, Rupert, and for the King. If, by some miracle, you could triumph over the Roundheads in this, whom would you wrong?"

And later still when they were alone, the two brothers and their mistresses, with the four-poster a comfortable meeting-place for drinking and loving, Maurice continued to grumble. "You must do it, Rupert! It is what everyone has always wanted. You've said yourself that the Puritans refused to share the gaieties when cousin Charles was born, how they openly announced that they had prayed for a barren Queen. King Charles is finished—they want you!"

"Who wants me?—Parliament? They have Charles Louis already—they can give him the throne."

"Parliament too—they are much disposed in your favor now, you know that! The affair at Bristol pleased them—and your genuine desire for peace." Maurice was encouraged to continue as he had not yet had his head bitten off, all his repressed ambition for his brother coming to the surface.

Rupert was staring into the darkness beyond the light, without seeing anything, his ears still filled with the cheering, mind rocking at the riotous exhibition in the hall. Coldly, deliberately, he allowed himself to harbor that dishonorable thrill of power. He had only to raise a finger to set the whole world on fire.

"Give a dog a bad name," he said suddenly, startling

them so that Damaris looked across from twining her limbs about Maurice, eyes big and filled with wonder. "By God, they've given me one—the whole damned pack of them!"

"But not the soldiers. Never the real fighting men. They love you!" Maurice could speak from experience, he was more in touch with the rank and file than the unsociable Rupert.

What was stopping him? Why did he hesitate? Rupert saw King Charles in a sudden cruel light, that light which shines so conveniently on the object which we intend to wrong, blinding us to any good points.

Once Rupert would have been proud to agree strenuously that King Charles was a good father, a model husband, a devout Christian and conscientious ruler, and would have fought any man who denied it! Now he saw him as a bigot who felt safe only when following inexorable routine, unable to reach the common people, obsessed with his high notions of the majesty and rights of princes from which he would never swerve. What use to recall the kindly uncle of pre-war years, the art expert, the superb horseman, and the brave heart who stoutly led his men, though knowing little of military arts.

Rupert groaned and buried his face in his hands. Venetia refilled his glass and drew him down gently beside her. Maurice rambled on, while Damaris added her word. Rupert was silent, his eyes smouldering, goblet lifted to his lips. And Venetia caressed him, her hands going beneath his robe, stroking and fondling his body, her mouth against his throat where a pulse throbbed, wanting to make him forget for a while to put off any decision till the morning.

His fingers had been combing through the heavy mass of her hair, but his grip suddenly tightened, forcing back her head so that she had to look at him. "And you?" he muttered urgently. "What think you of this?"

Question, and answer flashed between them in the white heat of silence, and, without words, he knew. He looked at her with bewilderment and sadness which was worse to bear than his rage. His voice was deep and low and shaken.

"You, too, would have me do it? You, who have lived by my side for so long. How little you know me."

At some point during the night, Damaris was prodding

309

Venetia awake, leaning over the sleeping Princes, saying, with drunken solemnity: "He won't do it!"

"What—Who?" Venetia struggled back up through layers of consciousness, seeing the candles guttering. Some had gone out. "Oh, Damaris,—it's too early."

"Early?—late, you mean! I've not been to sleep yet. But it's no use you know, he just will not agree."

"Why?" Although Venetia coiled closer to Rupert and shut her eyes again, she recognized, resignedly, that slumber had fled. The baby was making its presence felt by little kicks and thumps, and Damaris was determined to talk.

"Because he would drive himself mad with remorse! That is why! If you have any sense at all, Venetia, you will see this. He would end up hating you, his followers and, mostly, himself. He won't do it!"

"Of course he won't do it!" Will echoed Damaris' assertion when they told him all about it, seizing a brief opportunity before Rupert came into the room at a rush, grinning like a schoolboy for the first time in weeks, pumping his friends' arm as if he would never stop.

Will let him talk and gave his quiet, considered opinions, watching this dark, forbidding young man, in whose hands lay the power to plunge the country into another blood-bath.

"He needs you," he said simply, his broad, open countenance inspiring nothing but confidence, his whole heavily built body, clad in a rather shabby doublet, a barrier against the pressures put on his dear Prince from every side.

"Have you heard how things are going? Goring has swept up all he could lay hands on and gone to join the Queen. Sydnam Poyntez, that German-born professional, working for the enemy, is scouring the Midlands. Belvoir still holds out against him, but he ordered the killing of all the prisoners taken in the unsuccessful assault."

"God damn him!" Rupert set his mouth grimly, remembering the garrison who had given him shelter.

"You knew, of course, that Basing House had fallen? Cromwell took it in an attack of unbridled ferocity. Civilian refugees as well as soldiers were slaughtered."

"That seems to be an Ironside habit!"

"This time, they explained it away by calling the place a 'nest of idolatry.'" Will warmed his hands around the

310

hot tankard of mulled ale, his knees close to the fire, the snow melting on his boots. He had had a hard, freezing ride from Oxford, and Rupert had already given orders for a meal to be hurried along, grateful for his care and overjoyed to see him.

"Lathom House has capitulated." Will reached for the long white clay pipe and tobacco jar. "Thank God, Lady Derby is in the Isle of Man."

"Entertaining Lord Digby, and listening to his smooth lies about me, I doubt not!"

Will speculated on Digby's chances of being alive for many moments if he and Rupert ever met again. "She is a sensible woman, my Prince, she'll soon see through his Lordship!"

Will was very careful not to allude at all the hopes of the Prince's supporters. And under his calm, which refused to give credence to the smallest whisper of treachery, the others became ashamed of such unworthy notions. Rupert saw mirrored in his friend, his own ideals which still existed, though shrouded in anger and hurt pride.

They went into the library and there spent the morning composing a letter to the King. When Venetia dared to interrupt, she found Rupert laughing at some ribald tavern joke which Will was relating, and looking about five years younger. They rose to greet her and Will's eyes widened.

He bowed over her hand, then straightened and came out with it: "God's faith! No one told me of this!"

Venetia felt ashamed suddenly, and hung back, but Rupert was at her side, his arm about her. "Now, Will, don't lecture! You must have known that it would happen, sooner or later!"

Will's eyes were twinkling at her. "A child, eh? And what do you suppose the Winter Queen will make of this piece of news, sir?"

Rupert's black brows twisted. " 'Swounds! She's not bothered one whit, till now. No letter have I received, not a message in three years. This gentle creature has shown me more love and kindness than any living woman!"

Will's glance, sweeping over her, was full of compassion, and later, when they were alone for a space, he took one of her hands in his and raised it to his lips.

"My dear, you will not let ambition for your little one guide our Palsgrave into action which would destroy him —particularly were he to succeed!"

"I'm so glad you came, Will." Venetia spoke from the

311

heart, nothing could have been more timely; he had quietly
averted disaster. "There was a kind of delirium seizing
us——"

"I know it," Will sighed, easing forward to touch a spill
to the flames. "A madness seems to be spreading through
our party. The most harebrained schemes are being considered seriously by sensible men who, six months ago,
would have dismissed them as poppycock!"

"Was this one so mad?" She knew that he was right, but
there was a lingering hint of regret that she would never
see Rupert crowned in Westminister Abbey.

"No," Will was saying, having trouble in getting his pipe
to draw, seeming far more preoccupied with this than the
weighty matters under discussion. "There was such a
measure of sanity about it that it would have persuaded
even the most loyal amongst us. And it would have finished
the Prince—he would never have forgiven himself."

It was exasperating, humorous, and very ironical, the
way in which the helpless, almost defeated King quibbled
about his nephew's letters of apology. Several communi-
qués passed between them and still Charles was not satisfied. Finally, he sent Rupert a carefully-phrased epistle,
telling him what he ought to say, and asking him to sign it.

The Prince read it and Will stood waiting for the storm
to break. Matters were balanced on a knife-edge; one
false move and this touchy, inflammable being frowning
down at the sheet of paper in his hands, could rip it up,
refuse to consider further overtures, and topple their
known world into the abyss.

There was a pause, and the rider held out his numb
hands to the flames gratefully. The ice was beginning to
thaw, darkening his cloak and leather doublet, falling to
sizzle on the embers. Venetia moved over to make room
for the cold, wet man who tried to grin his thanks at her
with a stiff face.

With a sudden impatient oath, Rupert pushed the letter
away from him, seized a clean sheet, stabbed the quill in
the ink, wrote his name at the bottom, sanded it and
tossed it across to Will.

"Take that to him! Let him write what the devil he
will! He has my signature!"

This was no gesture of humility. It was an arrogant
statement of his determination to do things his way.

King Charles, of course, did not see it like this. Will
came back a few days later, to report that he had been so

moved by his unhappy, rebellious nephew's complete capitulation, that he had stared at the blank parchment and the large, gracefully formed hand, with tears in his eyes. There was nothing now to detain them longer at Woodstock.

The coaches and wagons struggled through the stark, ice-bound countryside, where the wind cut like swords and on the outskirts of Oxford, they were greeted by the familiar sound of church bells.

Rupert was nervous—he would rather face a battery of musketeers any day than an embarrassing scene. He lingered in the courtyard of his headquarters, mooching around with his hands in his pockets, giving totally irrelevant orders to Powell, putting off the interview. Then he spluttered out a few curses, gave Venetia a grin, and swung into the saddle, riding off to Christchurch to seek his uncle.

He seemed relieved, buoyant even, when he described it to her later. In that mellow room in the Royal apartment, all warm panelling, tapestries and firelight, the tiny upright figure of the King had risen to greet him eagerly, as if he had been waiting. He had reached up to grip him by the shoulders while Rupert bent his head so that Charles could kiss him in each cheek. For a moment, neither of them had been able to speak.

"Which was, perhaps, just as well, under the circumstances," Venetia thought to herself with a smile.

The winter was passing and with it the Cavaliers' hopes. The eight weeks of immobilizing cold ambled by. It was strange, after so much wandering, to stay in one town for long; the days assumed a mantle of routine, and Rupert was slowly dying of boredom in the inbred atmosphere of Oxford. Then the wind turned warmer, trees dripped, streams swelled, the snow became dirty and yielded to the green spears of grass, and the New Model army was on the move again. Like some inexorable juggernaut they rolled across England taking Royalist towns and garrisons piecemeal.

Rupert could do nothing to help, the jealousy and fear of the Courtiers still prevented Charles from giving his best soldier any military command—not even that of the King's Lifeguard. Lathom House, Belvoir and Hereford were rendered. All South Wales, except Raglan, had fallen leaving the King with little to call his own in the Welsh Marches, and making the recruiting efforts of Lord Astley, striving to build up another army, almost impossible. Rupert, at his headquarters, was in a state of profound dejection, mingled with bursts of irritation.

"I wonder how Lord Goring is enjoying himself in France," he brought out sourly, while the charcoal moved across the sheet swiftly. His eyes noted the play of wintry light across his brother's features, and he transferred what he saw to the paper.

"As triumphant as St. George in a Christmas mumming, no doubt." Maurice tried to answer without moving his cheek muscles.

The Prince flung the sketch aside, unfinished, and a hound stirred on the hearth-rug, stretching, yawning wide with lolling pink tongue. He got up, rested his chin on Rupert's knee and gazed up at him with most soulful eyes.

He shot a glance at the lazy Maurice. "Come, stop dozing! Let us to horse. There are some stags to be hunted, if not old Noll Cromwell!"

Venetia moved absentmindedly through the day till afternoon, then she suddenly put on her new cloak, ordered up a gentle mare and, with a servingman at the leading-rein, went to visit her father.

There had been little fighting during the terrible cold, although some Puritan outposts had sometimes felt the wrath of Royalist raiding parties. Round Woodstock, Banbury and neighboring villages, the King's flying horsemen still intimidated the land, and it was in just such a minor skirmish that Samuel Denby had been wounded. After a stormy meeting with him at Christmas, Venetia had sworn never to speak to him again but now Mallory had brought word that he was gravely ill.

As she rode past the noble Oxford buildings she remembered the hurtful quarrel. On perceiving her condition, Denby had gone beserk. He had called her a whore, lashing her brutally with his tongue because she was to have a bastard, albeit of His Highness's begetting. The unfairness of his accusations infuriated her. Ella, hastily married to a Cornet of horse, one of half a dozen lovers, had admitted to Venetia, with a deal of spiteful satisfaction, that she had no idea which one was the father, and now preened herself in her married state, accepted into the bosom of the family. In fact, Denby had been going round boasting that he was soon to be a grandfather!

Aunt Hortense greeted her with tight pursey mouth, and Catherine's eyes filled with tears of pity and sorrow; she was the only one, apart from the children, who had remained her friend.

"I'll take you up to see him," she said, and Venetia wondered how she would manage if he died. She had such a brood to rear and, while still young, her prettiness had faded, though she was pleasant looking in a well-bred way.

Nothing broke the stuffy silence of her father's chamber. His valet was there, tidying up after a visit from the surgeon, putting away all the medicinal paraphernalia.

"My dear, here is Venetia to see you," Catherine breathed, in that reverent voice which people reserve for the sickroom. She poised herself nervously at the bedside; while able to manage her babies and household duties beautifully, any disruption of the daily round disorientated her.

Exhausted by the doctor's ministrations, he lay with his hands on the embroidered coverlet, every vein distinct on the brown flesh. He looked shrunken, so different from the hale, robust squire whom Venetia remembered; now he was woman-controlled because he was helpless, far too tidy, scrubbed, tucked in neatly, his head resting on an unwrinkled pillow of virgin whiteness.

"What is this strange instinct in women which urges them to do this to their men?" Venetia wondered.

Her father's hair, showing a great deal of grey, was carefully brushed, but it had lost some of its curl. Venetia's throat felt swollen with unshed tears. He opened his lids and sighed, trying to grasp at the tattered edges of his wandering thoughts.

"Oh, father." She pressed his hand in real distress. "Is it very bad? Will the wound mend?"

Catherine hurriedly answered for him, raking at the dying embers of hope. "The surgeon has given us good comfort. He thinks 'twill heal apace now that he is home, where we can tend him."

"The cause——" His tongue slipped across his dry lips and he framed the question in a whisper. "How fares the cause?"

She could not find it in her heart to tell him the truth about the gradual dissolution of the party for which he had fought so long and served so faithfully. "The Prince and King are friends once more," she said instead.

He nodded, pleased. "That is good. A wild young man, but a great soldier." There was a long pause while he

315

made the effort necessary to go on speaking, "And you, child? Will you not marry Michael?"

In his eyes she read all those sane reasons for this request, and her own gave answer, begging him to understand and forgive. "I cannot, Father. I love Prince Rupert."

The room was insufferably hot, the fire blazing halfway up the chimney. Venetia felt faint, her stomach rising at the odor of his wound, which was suppurating, soaking through the bandages.

She could not tell if he heard her any more, as he sank again into that dark wilderness which might soon swallow him forever. She so much wanted him to think well of her still, and conquered the nausea to lean closer and whisper against his ear:

"There has been no one else, Father—I swear it. I have never been a whore. But I adore him—he is my life —my very soul." And she put her cheek against his hot forehead; even if he could not forgive her, she still loved him.

She returned to headquarters through the twilight, very sobered by her stay in that sad household. Rupert was right—this war must be stopped.

Damaris had insisted that she find Venetia a personal maid, saying, scandalized: "No lady of fashion can be expected to dress her own hair! You have a station in life now, my girl, and must live up to it!"

No point in making a half-hearted reminder that she had survived on the various treks with Rupert, or stressing the shortage of funds—as it was, supporting the "family" was ferociously expensive. Damaris promised to pay the girl's wages.

She selected, from her own staff, a bright wench called Emily. The arrangement worked very well, Emily became devoted to her new mistress and Venetia, growing increasingly heavy, and easily tired, welcomed her attention. She appreciated being pampered these days; Pierre was especially good to her whenever she sat foot in the kitchen, plying her with tasty morsels which she ate, more to please him than with much appetite.

While Venetia changed, she remembered Rupert's interest in the baby and how, only last night as they lay in bed, his hand had come to rest on her pumpkin of a stomach, feeling the strong thrusting movements of the tiny limbs within her. He had pushed back the covers and hey had laughed to watch the bizarre movements distorting her stretched flesh. She was getting large, and the child was very active—Rupert seemed convinced that it was a fine boy.

Emily helped her out of her cloak and gown and untied he waist strings so that she could step out of her three crisply starched petticoats. Always more enthusiastic than methodical, she rooted through the wardrobe in a flurry of gowns, skirts, and Rupert's doublets, searching for Venetia's flowing lacy dressing-robe.

She unpinned Venetia's hair, then they heard Rupert below, returning with the hunters. He sounded in a fine mood, his rich baritone voice ringing out in some rollicking ditty as he clattered up the stairs. Exercise and forest air worked wonders on him. He came gusting in, full of animal vitality and not a little brandy, transforming the room from a lady's boudoir to a soldier's quarters, teasing Emily about Gallois, soon having her blushing furiously, glad to bend over his boots and pull them off, to hide her red face.

Venetia was sitting at the dressing-table, and his head and shoulders appeared in the mirror behind her. He watched her for a moment, his face growing serious, then bent, one hand sweeping the hair from her neck, brushing his lips over her skin. She shivered as he turned her about and, with infinite gentleness, lifted her with an arm under her knees and another beneath her shoulders, carrying her effortlessly over to the bed, dismissing the round-eyed maidservant with a jerk of his head.

Venetia was able to tell him about her father, to cry against his shoulder and feel better. He was comforting and sympathetic. "I'll send my own surgeon to see him. Don't let them bleed him too freely. I cannot believe this treatment is right. If a man has already lost a deal of blood, it seems to me the worst kind of folly to rob him of more!"

"It is done to release the ill-humors, surely?" She had already heard his unorthodox views on medicine, and pitied the doctor who would attend should he ever ail!

"You must not fret, *liebchen,*" his voice was tender. "You will upset Hans-in-the-cellar!" And he smiled as he used the term in which the Dutch coyly referred to an expected baby.

"How do you know that it is 'Hans'?" She was delighted, as always, when he spoke of it.

He laughed softly, running careful hands over her breasts and belly. "Of course it will be a boy!" Then his face sombered again, eyes filled with compassion and remorse. "It is a barbarous process, is it not, darling? You will suffer to give my child life."

She was not afraid though it was a great hazard. Many women died in childbed, but she loved Rupert so much and wanted the baby with such a passionate intensity that she could not believe God would be so cruel as to let anything go wrong. She burst out with:

"Oh, how I wish I had been the first woman who ever made love to you?" And she ignored his laughter, rising on one elbow, staring down into his eyes. "Who was it? You have never told me!"

He was looking at her with a trace of amusement. It made her bridle; that tacit assumption that because she was a woman she was not to be taken seriously, and treated almost as a pretty toy.

"Why d'you want to torment yourself?" He was unwilling to hurt her, but she put a hand on his arm insistently, so he shrugged and gave in. "You know that I joined the army at thirteen, campaigning with the Stadholder. Charles Louis and I went together, and it was a successful venture, resulting in the capture of Rhynberg. The Stadholder celebrated with a tournament held at the Hague. Mother was there to watch us, and we dressed up as Moors, and did very well. I carried off the palm, and, I suppose, it was my first great day."

Venetia remembered Pierre telling her something about this. He had added that the women spectators had been enchanted by the gallant boy's grace and beauty and had made themselves quite ridiculous over him.

"It happened then?" she accused, her lower lip rolled out, wanting to know but dreading his answer.

He laughed, and kissed her fingers lightly clasped in his. "What! With my eagle-eyed mamma so concerned over my morals!—no, *liebling*—it was later, when I was serving in the Stadholder's Lifeguard. My fellow soldiers, detailed to keep an eye on me, took it upon themselves to see that my education went beyond simple warfare. They took me along to one of the camp *hurweibles* of our well-organized Netherland army. She was a motherly girl, much older than I, and skilled in her trade. I was all eager confusion, my strict Calvinist upbringing had not helped —but she soon put me at ease. My mother heard of these

318

new activities, and hurriedly recalled me to her side, fearing that I was being corrupted!"

The whole episode seemed to amuse him now, but Venetia was not finding it very funny.

"Oh, the row we had!" he went on, eyes sparkling as he recalled the explosive scene between him and the Queen. "How I stormed and sulked! Hating her for treating me like a child! I missed the army life, the fighting, the excitement, and made so much noise that she had to allow me to go back. The whore was good for me. Later, I saw to it that Maurice visited her."

All very fine to make brave assurances that she was mature enough to accept this confession. Venetia sat there striving to shut out the painful pictures which his words conjured, managing to ask, with what she fondly hoped was an air of sophisticated panache: "And when you were in England, that first time, did the Court beauties lie with you?"

"*Ach Gott!* Those dainty damosels expected too much in return." Rupert tried to make a joke of it, not a whit deceived. "I preferred the accommodating brothel wenches."

There was a grain of comfort in the fact that he had been in prison for three years, shut away from all female company—except Suzanne Kuffstein.

"And Suzanne?" She had to say it, now that he was in such a confidential mood—there was still so much that she did not know about him.

"Ah, Suzanne——" Venetia did not like the way his voice softened. "She could have helped me, of course, without the risk of getting with child, but she was so innocent—I did not like to suggest it. We were friends, nothing more."

"And later—those women in Vienna who made such a fuss of you when you were released—and in England, after the war started?" Her hands were moving over him possessively, as if to erase the memory of any other.

"Whores only."

She was so glad that Rupert never lied, but found it strange to understand. "Why, darling? All those lovelorn girls who have adored you—can this be true?"

"Professional lovers demand only money." He was thoughtfully stroking the narrow line of moustache which he had left after shaving his beard at Belvoir. "A very simple, uncomplicated exchange. Other women want emo-

319

tional entanglement. I have never been willing for that—until now."

Everything she had gone through for him already, and all that was bound to come in the future, seemed well worthwhile at that moment. She leaned over him and kissed him deeply.

"Did your whores ever kiss you like this, Highness?" she murmured against his mouth.

His eyes were glowing. "Harlots do not give their lips to customers, only to the men they love."

Venetia could see the logic of this; mouth to mouth contact could be such a revealing expression of tenderness, of affection, of friendship as well as passion. One kisses a child, a parent, a dear companion who is very close. Venetia traced the cleft in Rupert's chin with pensive fingers, and kissed him again.

TEN

Barney came streaking in from the West, making a typically theatrical entry into the High Street, pulling in his steed hard so that he plunged and reared outside Damaris' house.

"Barney!" She flung herself into his arms, while he laughed and kissed her and swung her off her feet. "Oh, Barney, 'tis so good to see you! What d'you mean by going off and deserting me so ungallantly?"

"Ah, Duchess, these troubled times make very sad brutes of us all. But now I am back, with my hand, heart's blood and guts at your service!"

"What devil's work have you been about?" Damaris rang for a servant and was soon pouring him sack while he flung cloak, sword and gauntlets onto the couch.

"The King's work, for the most part, but 'tis hopeless. Goring's command fell to Wentworth, one of the wildest of our wild boys! A man after my own heart—keeps a couple of painted madams and drinks in taverns till he can't stand! He carried on a running feud with Grenville

320

and his bullies. We were forever brawling with 'em over the best quarters!"

When Venetia came visiting later, he rose, stared at her in astonishment, and then bent to place a smacking kiss on the side of her cheek. One eyebrow shot up:

"Who did it? Michael—or His Highness?"

"Now Barney, don't twit her! You know full well that the poor creature is mad in love with Rupert. It is his child, and a mighty large one too, by the looks of her!" Damaris came to her rescue, drawing Barney back to the table and demanding that he continue with the account of his adventures.

" 'Sdeath! I've not had such good stuff in weeks! The ale in the West tastes of horse-piss, like to swell a man's belly like a sail—or yours, sweetheart!" He yelped with laughter, while Venetia wanted to hit him, touchy about her appearance, feeling a frump with her skirt hanging inches short in front. The only thing she resented about pregnancy was the loss of her figure, though she took comfort from the fact that Rupert did not seem to be revolted; far from it—he was proud of her.

"Have done, Barney!" Damaris buffeted him playfully, but he only grinned more widely, sticking out a knee and sitting her down on it.

"How now, sweeting? Have you missed me? I hear that you have been debauching the younger Prince."

Damaris smiled enigmatically, toying with his love-locks, making no objection when a hand disappeared into her bodice. Venetia often marvelled at the way in which she could so easily divide her favors. She said that she loved Maurice, yet this did not prevent her from enjoying other men, sometimes, incredibly, even persons that she had been criticizing and did not particularly admire, dismissing it with a shrug and a—"One may like the love and despise the lover, I hope!"

Such sophistry was not easy for Venetia to understand and, when she had mentioned this to him, Rupert had answered, quite sharply, that he was very glad that she could not!

"Did you know that Prince Charles has had to leave in a hurry, taking boat at Penzance and making for the Scilly Isles?" Barney asked.

Venetia wanted to weep for the King. What must he be feeling now that his son had left English soil? The next step would be exile in France.

"The Prince left in the nick of time." Barney's face clouded. "The men were deserting by the dozen to the enemy, officers and all! That didn't suit me! If we'd fought more and plundered less and patched up our quarrels, things might have gone differently." He shook his head but did not look in the least repentant.

"Some very jolly lads had joined us for sport, outcasts, rogues, great fighters! How the godly of the West-country hamlets hated and feared us! When we burst upon them, they'd gawk as if we'd just come from the moon, believing the tale that Satan had been seen disguised as a carrier, and had struck three of the wicked Cavaliers dead with a terrible stink of brimstone! Praise be to God!"

In his garish finery, with his sharp laughing eyes, the single earring which flashed against the fall of his bright hair, and his devil-may-care attitude, he was a wickedly attractive man.

There was no doubt that Barney enjoyed every minute of his ruffianly life. He was used to living on his wits; hardship and danger meant little to him. He was one of those adventurers who would latch on to any cause to cover their private crimes. He had thrown in his lot with the King, attracted by Rupert's reputation as a plunderer, a little disappointed to find that the Prince was among those Generals who strove to check the abuses of the hotheads. Goring had been much more lenient.

But now there was no genial General Goring, and Rupert had been cashiered. Many young men, like Barney, uprooted from their homes, unskilled at any trade, floundering, leaderless, were let loose on the country. At least the army had given them some sense of purpose, but now all they had was a thirst for adventure, a taste for violence, while looting had become a way of life.

Meanwhile, the King hovered between various courses of despair. Hope flared up again with the news that Lord Astley, that grizzled stalwart, had got together two thousand infantry in Wales and was now at Worcester, ready to come to Oxford. With this small army, the King insisted to Rupert, they might be able to postpone surrender until the French troops were ready, and the Vatican subsidies materialized. Montrose would, without doubt, conquer Scotland and, of course, the Irish troops were almost bound to arrive any day. Had not Digby been giving his valuable advice to Lord-Lieutenant Ormonde on this matter? Rupert said nothing.

Astley was defeated at Stow-on-the-Wold on March 21st. The Welsh, green boys with no experience, gave up easily, begging for quarter, and the cavalry fled to Oxford bringing their stories of the rout.

Venetia often found Rupert in the foundry, perfectly at home amidst the furnaces, the smoke-blackened vessels of iron, copper and glass, impervious to the noise, the heat and the fumes, his head bent in close consultation with some sweaty gunsmith with a newly-made firelock to be inspected. She knew that his brain was chockful of notions which he longed for the time and money to produce, setting down his ideas on paper in painstaking sectional drawings of cannons, showing the working parts. He was fascinated by the possibilities of smelting, his mind running ahead, visualizing the finished article, itching to produce efficient weapons, far in advance of the existing ones.

If he were not there, she would wander further afield, seeking him in the alchemist's laboratory, puffing up a tall tower with steep winding stairs, half afraid to enter that abode of mystery with its crucibles, astrolabes, and old, musty books, the queer substances smoldering in chafing-dishes sending up a sweet odor, redolent of green bracken on a very hot day. And Rupert, with some wrinkled graybeard, sifting through yellowing parchments, or again, down in the college libraries or street bookshops, his nose buried in a weighty tome. His intellect astounded and humbled her; his presence made all things wonderful. It was good to have this lull, with time to get to know him better.

When Rupert was really interested in a subject, he had endless patience to explain it, spending hours telling Venetia about the craft of engraving, which had been one of his occupations in Lintz.

She gazed enraptured at the drawings which he produced reluctantly for her perusal, flinging them across with an ungracious: "You may find something there to please you. Of course, Louise is the real artist of the family."

In spite of this modesty, he was childishly delighted by her praise. Even to her untutored eye, his work was good; such meticulously executed etchings must have taken him a very long time. Could his critics have seen them, would they still have dismissed him as a coarse, bloody-minded soldier of fortune?

He was far more at ease in the free, outspoken company

of the Oxford artists than with the Courtiers. Dobson wa
painting him and a number of sittings was required
Venetia always went along to watch.

While Dobson daubed, she listened to the flash an
sparkle of their talk, Rupert's wit keeping pace with his
The atmosphere was stimulating, filled with the earthy
smell of oil-paint, the room cluttered with the interesting
tools of his trade, and little personal touches, for he lived
as well as worked there. Stacks of canvasses leaned against
the walls among the draperies and props used to simulate
the fashionable classical backgrounds demanded by his
patrons. Pots of brushes, palettes splashed with vivid color
jostled on the table alongside dirty crocks, ringed glasses
and trays of food sent in from the cookshop next door.

Mallory and Michael had begged Rupert's permission to
go back to Woodstock which was being prepared for a
siege. They may as well swell Captain Fawcett's garrison
as sit in Oxford growing introspective. Michael came looking for Venetia just before he left. She was walking in
the garden, enjoying the spring sunshine, and looked up
expectantly on hearing his boots on the gravel, hoping i
was the Prince. The ensuing scene was very upsetting
leaving her drained and trembling; it was terrible to see a
grown man cry, especially one who was so brave in action
so cool under fire, and who had been such a good friend

He begged her to reconsider, perfectly willing to accept
the child if she would only marry him. "But what are you
going to do?" he kept repeating. "He'll not wed you—
you know that! And he will go back to Europe when this
is over."

Stubbornly, she was refusing to face this yet. Rupert
needed her now—the future must take care of itself. The
birth of her baby was her guiding star—the war, the King
everything except Rupert, paled into insignificance.

After the loss of Astley's force at Stow, even the King
could see that this must be the last battle. For some time
he had been considering the idea of taking refuge with the
Scottish army. He would not treat with the rebels; the
Scots were his own people, he would throw himself or
their mercy. Rupert thought the whole thing mad and said
so, when the King confided in him, his young, strong voice
hammering on, angry and despairing, as he tried to make
his uncle see the dangers. Yet even as he spoke, he knew
that it was useless; Charles had made up his mind, and
there was a sense of relief in having reached a decision

He was exhausted—let God do with him what He willed. At least no more of his subjects should shed blood for him.

"I hated myself for trying to bring him back from the sacrificial heights where he sees himself, down to the sordid depths, where it will undoubtedly end," Rupert said gloomily, as they walked past Christ Church on their way back from Dobson's.

Venetia hung on to his arm, looking up eagerly, trying to bring him comfort. They reached the portals of the church just as the King was coming out after service. Rupert stepped forward to bow, as he came slowly from under the great arches, attended by his gentlemen. The last notes of the organ were beating faintly into silence and, behind him, the magnificent edifice seemed very dim and peaceful. That peace was reflected in King Charles' face, as he fell into step beside his nephew, discoursing on the sermon, and not knowing what else to do, Venetia struggled up from her curtsey, and walked with them.

The King's scholarly voice rolled gently on, blending with the quiet of the paved cloister. He fitted in well here, much more so than when on the battlefield, or presiding over a quarrelsome War Council.

"He should have been a don," thought Venetia, "happy to spend hours pondering some involved theological question in the company of learned colleagues. Would it not have been a kindness to have taken the dreadful responsibility of a ruler from his narrow shoulders and given it to Rupert?"

They parted at the entrance to the Royal lodgings and his eyes rested on her. She shrank a little closer to Rupert, expecting condemnation, knowing how the King deplored immorality. But he said nothing, his look one of stately benevolence. A page held back the door and she saw him silhouetted upon the threshold, walking all golden from the glow of the dying day, which seemed to gather brightness about his covered head.

"I told you so," nodded Rupert, as they hurried away. "There is something about him, trying though he is. I cannot explain it."

He did not need to. Now that she had experienced that spine-chilling reverence, she understood. It was that sense of Kingship for which men were willing to lay down their lives.

Very late on a balmy night at the end of April, King

Charles slipped out of Oxford like a shadow, dressed as a servant, taking with him only his Chaplain Michael Hudson, and Jack Ashburnham. He rode away over Magdalen Bridge to meet his destiny, and, for once, the secret had been kept and few knew his intention.

Rupert had gone to see him off. When he came in, he went straight to the casement, drawing back the curtain and staring out, though there was no chance of seeing the fugitive any more.

"I made sure that he put it in writing that I had no part in this. I have been blamed enough for the misfortunes of this damned business!" His voice was low and bitter, and then he added: "I wanted to go with him, but he would not let me—he said my tallness would betray us."

He had given the King his last piece of good advice—not to go, yet his loyalty still insisted that he offer his service even against his own counselling.

Damaris was busying herself with arrangements for Venetia's *accouchement*.

"The household of His Highness is quite unused to this kind of thing," she said firmly. "I have instructed my maids to prepare a room for you here. Now don't argue. I have had three children myself and know what is needed. I have engaged the services of the best midwife in Oxford."

"But Rupert——" wailed Venetia, close to tears as she always was these days.

"Rupert? My dear, he may be an expert at delivering cities, but not, I trow, babies!" Damaris teased, then flung an arm about her, laughing: "Heyday, cheer up, my chicken! You shall not be parted from your knight-errant. Maurice will persuade him to be my guest. Come now, I have a present for you!"

In the lying-in chamber stood a hooded rocking-cradle. Venetia paused on the threshold, giving a gasp of pleasure, then ran in, exclaiming with delight.

It was fashioned of oak and the carpenter had followed Damaris' instructions implicitly, carving the Palatine arms on the hood, surmounted by the entwined initials of Rupert and Venetia. It was furnished with woollen blankets, feather pillows and a handsome coverlet which Damaris had embroidered herself.

It was true enough, and never ceased to thrill Venetia, that Prince Rupert's race was as illustrious as her-ld could desire, combining the Royal blood of Scotland and Denmark, with that of the Palatines of the Rhine.

"Your little love-child is going to be someone of importance, if I have anything to do with it." Damaris patted Venetia's stomach. "And I intend to have much say in its future, as godmother!"

She produced another surprise, an inlaid coffer of marquetry in holly and bog wood. When she lifted the lid, a delicious scent rose from the bags of musk and herbs laid between the layers of baby clothes.

"Oh, Damaris, you are so good to me." Venetia could hardly speak, wanting to rush away and tell the Prince; her first instinct was to share any joy with him.

For a long while they sat gloating over the fine gowns, petticoats, lace caps, binders, bibs, cuffs and miniature mittens, the small shirts with flaps to turn over on back and chest. And Venetia could not wait, aching for the baby to be born.

The King had just escaped from the closing trap in time. His Cavaliers were no longer able to get food for man or beast from the sullen country-folk around. Enemy patrols chased Rupert's cavalry when they galloped out to forage, sending them back cursing and empty-handed. Mallory and Michael came limping in from Woodstock. That brave manorhouse had been ruthlessly battered by Roundhead ordnance, but it had held on for over two weeks.

Rupert had already demanded of the Governor of Oxford, Sir Thomas Glenham, whether he should prepare to defend the town, but Glenham made it brutally clear that he had his orders from the Council and Rupert must not interfere. This put him in a glowering rage which he could not even work off in a good hard day's hunting.

Venetia woke slowly, in the small hours of May 11th, wondering what had disturbed her. She clambered awkwardly out of bed to visit the closet and found that her nightgown was stained with blood. The sensation which had awakened her returned, this time as a pain which tautened her stomach. Terror, hope and excitement flooded in.

"Rupert!" Frantically she prodded him in the back, "Highness, wake up. I'm in labor."

"*Sacrément!*" He was instantly alert, reaching for the

327

bell, clanging for De Faust, his one concern to get her to Damaris.

"Geliebte." He paused to hold her for a moment, eyes black with contrition. "Crodolph shall attend you. He has many potions which will help the pain."

She saw that he was afraid, this Devil Prince who had always taken such risks. Now it was she who had to comfort him. The pages arrived with candles and everything sprang into life. Emily came from the kitchen with a message of cheer and a steaming poset from Pierre.

"He sends his prayers for you, ma'am, and this caudle which he swears is very efficacious in childbirth."

Venetia sipped the scalding, scented liquid, while Emily bundled her into some clothes, and then Rupert was at the door, shouting that the coach was ready. He was unshaven, wild-eyed, without either shirt or doublet, his cloak flung on over his breeches, unprepared to stop for anything until she was safely installed with Damaris.

For Venetia, there were hours of dragging agony before her ordeal was over. People came and went, their faces hanging mistily above her while she writhed on the bed. The midwife arrived, bringing her helpers. She was brisk and confident, examining Venetia with cool, kind hands, turning to consult with Damaris.

She stood by the laboring girl, mouth pursed ruminatively. "Could we but have the church bells rung, 'twould aid her."

"No chance of that, I fear," Damaris replied. She was working hard, rubbing Venetia's back, for a pain was at its peak. "The town would be thrown into panic. They'd think the enemy had attacked!"

Michael called to see how Venetia fared, wearing such a look of acute anxiety that she might have found it touching had she not been in such torment. The kind-hearted Maurice hovered in the doorway once, before Damaris shooed him away, and Rupert was there most of the time, pouring sweat, seeming to suffer almost as much as she did, tossing back one straight brandy after another.

Mistress Bryant's phlegmatic calm reduced him to shouting frenzy as he listened to Venetia's groans. He rounded on the nurse. *"Mort dieu!* Can you not do something for her? Call yourself a midwife! Why is it taking so long? My mother was always delivered in less than an hour!"

"Not with the first, I'll warrant, Your Highness!"

328

Affronted by this challenge to her professionalism, Mistress Bryant stood her ground against the huge, furious young man. "Oh, you fathers are all the same! No patience! Nature cannot be hurried, sir, not even by you! And you would be well advised to remember the poor thing's anguish, and not have her repeat it in nine months' time!" she added tartly.

Venetia's cries rose to a muffled scream as she buried her face in the pillow. Rupert, turning white and very pinched about the nostrils, thundered out a tempest of rage of which she caught the sense but not the words, half of which were in German anyway.

"Highness, have done!" It was Damaris, fairly dancing with fury herself. "Have you taken leave of your senses? We must have peace here to do our work. Go and get drunk or ride off and beat hell out of a few Roundheads!" Then seeing his distraught look, she burst into laughter. 'I promise you that all will be well! Most women make a noise when in labor. You should have heard me! Shrieked like a thousand demons, did I not, Etienne?"

Her husband was seated in the most comfortable chair he could find, admiring the peach-like bloom of his fashionable boots propped high against an oaken clothes chest and watching the proceedings with calm detachment. *Sacré nom!* A thousand stuck pigs, more like," he drawled. "Fear not, *Pfalzgraf*, the more they howl the safer the birth, so 'tis said."

Rupert scowled, laughed and swore all in one, took their advice and stamped off to find his brother.

Venetia was getting very tired, convinced that this torture was a punishment for fornication and would go on forever. Tears of weakness and self-pity ran back across her temples and she moved restlessly in the short periods between pains, sure that she was going to die.

"Sweet Jesus!" Adrian mopped his brow, and leaned on Etienne for support. " 'Tis the only time that I am glad not to be a woman!"

Etienne had to take him out at the brisk instructions of the intimidating Mistress Bryant who feared that he might swoon and get in everyone's way.

The faces of the waiting women were haggard and strained. Damaris murmured encouragement, thrusting the looped bedcord into Venetia's hands. Emily had tied the other end securely around the thickly carved post at the foot.

"Here sweetheart, pull on this like the very devil when you get the next pain. It will help—really it will! I can see the baby's head, and it has black hair. Come, one more effort!"

"Pant, my dear—pant like a dog! Don't push!" Mistress Bryant was ordering on a note of urgency. "We don't want to tear you!"

Blindly, Venetia obeyed the stern command while the midwife, moisture greasing her face which was set in lines of concentration, worked on her. After what seemed a racking eternity, she was able to wrest from Venetia's agonized body, Rupert's black-eyed, dark-skinned son.

And Venetia, floating in some soft cloud-land of exquisite relief, heard him give a gasp, a sneeze and a loud, lusty cry.

"My God, what a little monster!" Damaris was exlaiming admiringly. "Look at the size of him! I swear he resembles a child three months old!"

"He is beautiful." Mistress Bryant's voice was full of proud achievement. "And he certainly bears out the stable adage that 'tis the sire that gives the coloring!"

Then Venetia opened her eyes and looked down, for they had laid her child on her flat naked belly, flesh to flesh, following their women's insight which told them that this was right; the newly-born should not be snatched away from close maternal contact at this critical moment. Venetia reached out and took one of the crumpled red fists in her hand.

Damaris brooded protectively over them both, her eyes full of happy tears. "Isn't he lovely, Venetia? Worth all the pain, eh, my dear? And the spitting image of his father!"

It was true. Later that striking resemblance might fade a little but, in the hour of his birth, her son was uncannily like the Prince.

The nurse wrapped him in an old piece of clean cloth which she had brought with her especially—princeling he might be, but she would not court ill-luck by using anything new. She went over to the fireplace and sat down with him on her lap, giving him, as his first drink in the world, a sip of water into which a red-hot cinder had been dropped. Every precaution must be taken to ensure his good fortune, to placate the fairies and protect him from witches!

His angry-sounding squalls filled the air as she washed

and dressed him, swaddled him in a blanket, and tucked him into the crook of Venetia's elbow. She smiled and watched him, quiet now, little hands folded on his chest, his crest of black hair fluffed up, and that delicious baby-smell crawled insidiously into her nostrils and captivated her.

The midwife, this part of her job concluded, swept up her *ménage* and departed to the rooms set aside for her. Only Damaris remained, knowing that Venetia would not sleep. At last came the noises for which she waited so eagerly. Damaris rushed to the door.

"Is it over?" he was shouting. "And Venetia——?"

"She is well, Your Highness," Damaris hurried to assure him. "But there is a young gentleman with her."

"Who?" he barked angrily.

"Your son, sir."

Rupert crossed the room swiftly. Maurice was just be-hind him, trying to tread quietly in his big boots. The Prince's glance went over Venetia anxiously as he came close, then he took one of her slack hands in his and raised it gently to his lips as he looked down at the baby. But her delight changed to horror—there was blood stain-ing the right sleeve of his doublet.

"What happened?" she croaked.

Rupert shook his head and shrugged, " 'Tis nothing. Don't worry."

He was smiling, gently pushing aside the blanket in order to see his son's face more clearly.

"We took Damaris' advice," Maurice gave a wry grim-ace, "gathered up some stout fellows and rode out to have a little sport with the Roundheads. About twenty of us charged three troops of horse. Holmes was slightly wounded——"

"Some saucy knave called Gerard, 'Capon-tail,' and challenged him!" Rupert's teeth flashed in an amused grin, though he seemed much more interested in poking a finger into the baby's clenched fist, fascinated to feel the grip of the tiny hand.

"Le Diable got a ball in the shoulder, didn't you, Rupert?"

"Aye, just as I was taking aim. It shook my hand so that I dropped by pistol and, as it fell, it went off, shoot-ing my attacker's horse."

"Oh, Rupert——" Venetia's own recent pain was for-gotten in terror for him.

"It is a flesh-wound, nothing more," Maurice hastened to add, knowing that Rupert would be furious if he upset her. "He's had it dressed, and the surgeon removed the bullet easily."

Poor Maurice! Venetia could guess how much this incident must have alarmed him. For the first time ever, Rupert had been injured. Odd that it had happened in such a small, unimportant engagement.

"He didn't even stop fighting—sent into town for more men—took up position near the marshes, bringing us all up together in front. The enemy shot off their carbines, and then we fell on 'em, and beat 'em, and a lot of their men fell into the bogs!"

They were both grinning now, delighted with this skirmish which had been sheer bravado, one last fight before Oxford surrendered.

Maurice leaned over Rupert's shoulder to view his nephew. He whistled in surprise. "Goddam, he's just like you, brother! Why, he's even inherited your big nose!"

Rupert's narrow, strong, aristocratic hands reached down and lifted his son very carefully, up to his chest. And the child lay against the steel of a breastplate, held in mailed arms, as he himself had been at his christening.

"*Teufel!* His face is very red!" Maurice remarked, taking him gingerly when Rupert held him out.

"So was yours, I'll wager!" The Prince would tolerate no criticism of this little miracle. "Don't drop him!"

"What a fuss," grumbled the amiable Maurice. "I am quite used to children. You forget that I spent far more time in the nursery with our siblings than ever you did."

"This one is different. He is my first-born."

"You've already baptized him. There's a smear of gunpowder on his face."

It was remarkable, and moving, to see these two strapping brothers handling the baby.

Rupert sat on the side of the bed and stroked Venetia's cheek. Although her face was drawn with prolonged agony and her eyes were sunk in dark circles, joy radiated from her, and he was almost overawed by that wonderful luminous quality. He did not say much, but when he did speak, his voice was soft and he used those foreign love-words with their subtle intonations which vibrated down her spine and heightened her intense happiness.

"You won't go away?" she whispered and, when he had

promised, she allowed the billowing waves of slumber to engulf her.

It was customary for a baby to be christened as soon as possible, and, within a few days, Venetia's son was made ready for the ceremony.

She sat up in bed and watched the preparations—unable to go herself. It would have been most irreligious, besides downright unlucky, to have set foot outside the house before she had been churched, and this was not to be done until a month after the confinement. Mistress Bryant and Emily, ignoring his indignant yells, dressed him in an ivory satin robe, covered his elongated head with a cap, lavishly embroidered in seed pearls and silver thread, and put minute gloves on his pink, curling fingers. They spread the crimson silk christening-pall across the end of the bed, needing somewhere to lay it out for it was five feet long and nearly as broad. The baby was swathed in it, the women carefully folding the edges, so that the fine gold lace trim showed to advantage. The nurse, whose proud duty it was to carry him, wore a pair of long dress-cuffs, the color and decoration of which matched the pall.

Damaris, smartly gowned, conscious of her important position as godmother, was bustling about, getting everything organized.

Rupert had seemed rather reluctant when she asked him if she might give the child his name. "Why not make it 'Robert?' " he suggested.

She shook her head, downcast, always alert for the smallest sign of rejection and, after a pause, he had agreed. "Very well. God knows, I can give him little else."

His expression was full of that Stuart sadness which always lay just below the surface with them all, the King, young Prince James, even the clever, subtle heir, at present captivating the enthusiastic people of Jersey. In repose, their features assumed a remote melancholy, and Venetia anxiously scanned the face of her small princeling, but he, far removed, as yet, from all care, was nuzzling contentedly at her breast.

"I'll so wrap him in love," she vowed silently, "that he will never have cause to despair."

So he was baptized with the name of "Rupert," like

his father before him in far-off Prague, twenty-six years before and;

"I wonder if his first words will be as yours were, spoken in Bohemian, 'Dobrorecte Hospondinu,'" speculated Maurice, when they sat around in Venetia's chamber, enjoying refreshments after the ceremony.

"'Praise the Lord!'" laughed Rupert. "Don't tell that to my Cavaliers or they will think I have turned Roundhead!"

The baby had been returned to the impatient arms of his mother. Stripped of his finery, he was wrapped in a plain length of white linen which she knew would be the chrisom-cloth. It denoted that he was now a Christian, but he looked no different to her—heathen or baptized, he was still her precious son and a chill knifed through her as she recalled the tradition. If he lived, the cloth would be returned to the parson by herself when she went to be churched, but if he died within a month of his christening then it would be his shroud.

This idea made Venetia utterly wretched. The room was very hot and noisy and the day's excitement had tired her out. She was feeling weepy and morbid; her breasts ached, engorged with milk, and she was so bruised and sore that sitting for any length of time was most irksome. Mistress Bryant breezily assured her that she would soon forget and laid a jolly wager that she would be needing her services again within a year! Venetia winced at the thought of conceiving, let alone bringing forth!

"Of course you will forget, darling!" Damaris swooped over to join in the conversation. "There's nothing like a real honest-to-goodness, knee-weakening fancying a man, to blind us poor susceptible females to aught else! And holding that sweet infant fans my maternal fires! I vow and declare, I cannot wait to see my children again. They will have quite forgotten me. Their grandmother writes to say that Hercule has grown so tall, a proper little man now, and the girls are as pretty as kittens."

She beamed at the Chevalier. "I should like to have another baby! What say you, Etienne, to a further fine young sprig for the House of d'Auvergue?"

The chatter, the laughter, were rising and falling—waves of heat laved Venetia till she was dizzy, and then Rupert appeared by the bed, angry to see the hectic flush, the sweat which beaded her brow—sending them all packing to continue the party elsewhere. Mistress Bryant received a chill, terse rebuke which left her considerably subdued, the baby was tucked into his crib, Emily given crisp orders to fetch cold water, and Holmes dispatched for Crodolph.

Rupert propped Venetia against his shoulder and turned the pillows, laying her back on the cool surface. He wrung out the compress and put it on her forehead, changing it repeatedly as it grew warm. He was alarmed by her feverish symptoms and disgusted at the carelessness of her attendants—he had learned to trust but few and to follow his intuition in the care of those he loved.

Crodolph mixed a nauseating draught which Venetia swallowed to please the Prince, content to lie there and follow him with her eyes, basking in the wonder of his concern. She slept and dreamed, waking light-headed to find it dusk and Rupert still watching over her, anticipating her every need. She wanted to tell him that he must rest and give his wound a chance to heal, but the words tripped her tongue and she surrendered to that soft insistent blackness again even as she struggled with them. Peace permeated her mind and soul; it was one of the happiest nights of her life.

By the time Venetia was well on the way to recovery, news had begun to come in about the King. He had reached Newark, and, before leaving for Newcastle, had ordered the Governor to surrender to the Roundheads. Everywhere garrisons were going down like ninepins— a few held on grimly, officered by desperate men, some driven still by their loyalty to a broken cause, others to gain what pleasure and profit could yet be squeezed from the situation.

Fairfax was negotiating with Sir Thomas Glenham for the rendition of Oxford. Disagreements followed, treaties were torn up, tempers became frayed, and to hurry matters along, the enemy cut off all the water supply to the city.

"This makes surrender inevitable, I suppose," Venetia looked across at Rupert. She was sitting on the low nursing chair, feeding the baby, in the bright June sunshine which came flooding through the windows."

He shrugged. "It was bound to happen soon. Now we shall renew the treaty. I intend to see that the Council put in a clause for the safety of Maurice and myself."

He was so prudent these days, leaving nothing to chance. Problems arose, not with Fairfax, but with Lord Southampton who, when the request came from the Palsgrave, made some slighting remark to the effect that "the Prince was in good company.' "

Rupert's eyes kindled. "He said something about 'rats deserting a sinking ship!' "

He sent Gerard to expostulate with the Earl, who scornfully offered no apology, giving an excuse that his words had been inaccurately reported.

"Go to him again, Gerard, and tell him that I expect to meet him with his sword in his hand at as early a date as possible, lest a duel be prevented."

He was staring angrily at his friend, who would, no doubt, be called upon to act as his second. And Venetia was thoroughly alarmed, running up to him, grabbing him by the arm, a flush beginning to spread from her throat to her cheeks for she was still weak from the confinement.

"Rupert, don't! I don't want you to fight! D'you hear me?"

Southampton cheerfully accepted the challenge, gave the time for next morning, and selected pistols as the weapons, openly admitting that he was no match for the Prince with the sword. Venetia spent a wretched night while Rupert slept solidly at her side. He rose early, dressed carefully, fussed with his pistols and finally, after a casual kiss, went out whistling, as if for a pleasant canter in the park.

Venetia sat holding the child, tears dripping onto his little lace-trimmed holland cap, certain that he would shortly be fatherless. Damaris and Etienne tried to soothe her. When had Rupert ever been worsted in a fight? Then there was the unbelievable, wonderful sound of the Prince's laughter, and hearty male voices ringing with good fellowship, and the door burst open to admit him, followed by a collection of gentlemen. He had his arm across Southampton's shoulders!

"Someone told the Council of our intent," he announced, smiling widely. "The gates were shut and the guards had been told to arrest us! So we had a scuffle with them instead and here we are!"

Southampton, who obviously had not yet recovered his wits, was overcome with astonishment, goggling to find himself in favor. Rupert slapped him on the back.

"Come over here, my lord. Did you ever see such a fine child? This is my son."

There was no surer way of earning Rupert's esteem than to accept a challenge from him, it seemed! Venetia felt faint with relief; the walls of the sunny room, the curtains of the big bed, all seemed to be folding in on her.

Rupert displayed his offspring to the speechless Earl. "Of course, I can trust your Lordship's discretion." He was looking him right in the eyes. "I do not want a breath of scandal smirching Mistress Denby. You understand?"

Southampton understood very well, still unable to credit his astounding good luck. He had no desire to risk facing that deadly aim again.

Rupert received word that the King had reached his destination, in spite of the fact that Parliament had published an edict that anyone found sheltering him would be immediately executed. What would now happen was anyone's guess. At Oxford, the treaty was concluded.

"We've been given surprisingly good terms," Rupert said, puzzled, consulting with Maurice. He had made demands which he had not expected to be so readily accepted. A special clause, by which both Princes were to have the benefit of all the other articles plus free leave to quit the country, had been inserted, and passed without quibble by Fairfax.

"D'you mean that we don't have to promise not to fight against 'em again, if we get the chance?" Maurice scratched his head, as mistrustful as his brother.

Rupert nodded, lips compressed as he reread the paper. "We can take all our servants with us, and stay in England for six months, providing we do not approach within twenty miles of London." His eyes narrowed, suspiciously. "What can they want of us?"

Parliament was offering a settlement to Royalists, allowing them to buy pardons by an outright payment reckoned on the value of their lands. The trickle of needy, despondent Cavaliers became a steady stream, as they pocketed their pride and accepted these conditions, bowing to the miserable necessity of salvaging something from the ruins.

Mallory had decided to go home to the Cotswolds. "I promised my father, before he died, that I would see my step-mother and the children settled," he said in justification.

"I could use your services abroad." The Palsgrave had no definite plans, yet both knew that somehow, somewhere, the struggle for King Charles would continue.

"If it please Your Highness, I will endeavor to come to you, when you send word."

Damaris wept to see him go, wringing from him a promise to join them in Paris, desolate at the loss of his love, vowing that she would miss even their bouts of high-spirited name-calling!

Meriel called to bless the little Rupert before he departed for France with the actors.

Intrigued by all that Meriel foretold for the baby's future, Venetia stood looking down at his sleeping face for a while after she was alone. He was tiny and helpless and utterly dependent on her for comfort and food, and also he was the one sure tie that bound her to Rupert. He was his child too, his blood was in his veins, he had his features, he moved, cried and existed because of him.

The Prince strolled in through the wide open doors which led out onto the terrace. He had been lying in the garden, soaking up the hot sunshine, his body turning a deep golden brown. He came across, and, with an arm round Venetia's waist, joined her in mutual admiration of their child.

When she told him of Meriel's prophecies, he playfully tweaked her hair, giving a smile and saying: "Let her not bewilder you with too much star-gazing. We must conquer our stars!"

He was eager to be away, leaving Oxford a couple of days before the Counsellors, the officials, the attendants and their ladies, all that was left of the King's wartime court. On Monday, June 22nd, everything was ready.

The horses leaned into the straps, the spokes creaked, iron-bound wheels grated over cobble-stones, armed escorts curvetted on each side amidst shouts and the cracking of whips. Prince Rupert headed the long, straggling line, leading his baggage-train out of Oxford for the last time.

ELEVEN

"At least Baby Rupert will have the distinction of staying in one of the great houses built by Henry VIII," said his godmother, pulling back the coach curtains to view their new home. The palace of Oatlands, not far from Weybridge, was certainly impressive.

The journey had been trying, first to Wickham, then to Maidenhead, jolting over the rusty, rutted roads eventually to rumble along the curving drive to the broad flight of stone steps which swept up to this majestic frontage.

Gone were the days when Venetia simply saddled-up and rode beside the Prince, taking life as it came. Now the baby's welfare was top priority, and she must always be on call to suckle him, a benefit which he demanded loudly and frequently. When they pulled in for the night, suitable lodgings must be found, damp-free, clean and wholesome, not only for him, but also for the nursemaids, hired to cope with the endless round of rocking, changing, washing and soothing.

Before they left Oxford the question had come up. Where were they to reside? And, more important, who was going to pay? Rupert exchanged letters with Fairfax. Oatlands was suggested as being unoccupied. True, it was within the forbidden distance of the capital, but it was urgently necessary for the brothers to meet the Elector to discuss their future, and particularly their embarrassing financial position. Fairfax gave them leave to proceed to the palace.

It was good to step down from the stuffy, cramped confines of the carriage, to know that there was plenty of servants to engage in the tedious chore of unloading, and to take Rupert by the hand, leading him off in exploration of the nooks and crannies of the old house.

They wandered down pleached walks, between box-edges of yew, where sharp contrast of sun and shade splashed their faces, finding hidden avenues and summer-houses, aviaries and beehives, sundials and naked statuary and always the twisting paths brought them back to view of the palace, framed by swaying branch or rose clustered pergola.

" 'Tis all monstrously overdone," averred the Prince staring across the lush velvet-smooth lawn, eye half shut, visualizing it as an etching. "Every classical element has been distorted, columns which look like giant corkscrews writhing upward, all aswarm with carved garlands or buried in great coarse leaves. Very vulgar! Inigo Jones' architecture is much more pleasing, simple, perfectly proportioned."

His expression flickered and changed. "Did you know that Cromwell's men stripped him and turned him out in the night, covered only by a blanket, when they took Basing House? An old man of seventy——"

Venetia was glad that she had not already expressed her delight in the florid, outrageous grandeur, where no surface, inside or out, was left unadorned. She was trying hard to adopt Rupert's standards and taste, wanting no jarring notes in their relationship. Damaris had been explaining to her the meaning of a morganatic marriage; a timid hope had struck root.

As both Mistress Bryant and Damaris had promised her desire for Rupert had brought about that amnesia cunningly designed by nature. On the very night that she had returned from being churched she had wanted him tormented by the disturbing fragrance of his hair and the texture of it beneath her fingers.

"Liebchen," he had whispered, his mouth somewhere in the region of her ear. "I should not touch you again. shall give you another child, and you said, after the delivery, 'Never again!' do you remember?"

"No, I don't remember!" she had answered fiercely, breath quickening in delicious anticipation. Then she had tried to be practical, very difficult when his hand was exploring the convolutions of her spine through the thin linen of her nightgown. "Damaris says, that while I continue to suckle the babe, I shall not conceive again."

He had lifted an eyebrow sceptically, but her mouth blindly seeking, had slid across his cheek, finding his lips and fastening hungrily, putting an abrupt end to further discussion.

Venetia took heart from this new crest of passion, confident that she had never been more beautiful, slender again after the months of heaviness, but with an added poise and ripeness, the attraction of experience and maturity. She kept a firm hold on her adoration of her baby —Rupert must not feel ousted by this tiny, tyrannical rival for her love. He was turned over to his nurses when his father wanted her undivided attention.

Two idyllic days passed in the peace of Oatlands and then the authorities clamped down. Fairfax had, apparently, moved out of turn in showing the Palatines special favor, and it had created an uproar in Parliament. Rupert was thrown into a justifiable rage for it was declared that they had broken the articles and must leave the country immediately on pain of being treated as prisoners. Charles Louis, although written for, had not yet turned up, and this added to the storm.

Maurice was able to calm him down and together they composed a letter, answering the charge meekly enough Maurice's influence) and saying that they had acted in good faith, thinking the General's pass sufficient, and that in coming to Oatlands they had been more concerned at the convenience of the house than the distance from London, "of which we had no doubt at all."

Parliament refused to be placated and returned a reply insiting that the Princes depart within ten days. A brisk interchange of correspondence followed; Rupert kept his secretary very busy with letters to the Committee, relating chiefly to passes for various servants.

De Gomme and La Roche, the engineers who had been with Rupert from the start, were of the company, and there were, of course, Crodolph, De Faust and Gallois, the steward Powell, and Pierre with his scullions. It was no inconsiderable establishment for two young Princes about to seek their subsistence abroad, and worry about money aggravated Rupert's irritability.

Venetia's father had left her five hundred pounds, which should have been her dowry. She insisted that the Prince take half, and, not knowing where else to turn, he reluctantly agreed, but the question of her own future still yawned between them; she was afraid to broach it, unsure if his silence stemmed from a foregone conclusion that she would remain with him, or was sheer male cowardice in wishing to avoid a painful scene.

Michael proved an invaluable prop at this time, helping Venetia in little unobtrusive ways, following her with love-sick eyes. It was his intention to redeem his estate, and he

asked her to marry him once again, managing to trap her
in a secluded corner of the garden.

It was warm there, the biege stones sending back the
heat, the breeze hardly stirring the leaves of the peach
trees trained along the trellis.

Venetia tried to withdraw her imprisoned hand without
offending him. "Michael, please don't. I won't, and there
is an end on't."

"Are you going with him?" He looked as if he had
not slept properly for a long time. Helplessly, she shook
her head, and his forehead rucked. "D'you mean to tell
me that you've not asked him yet?"

No, she had not asked, afraid to admit, even to herself,
that she dreaded the answer. Yet, daily, Rupert seemed
to grow more fond of the child, which delighted her, for
she had half expected him to be an indifferent father, and
he could often be found in the nursery, carrying the wide-
eyed infant, talking to him very seriously, and holding up
interesting bright objects, like his pocket-watch, to capture
the wandering gaze. Venetia nourished her struggling hope
on these crumbs.

"Promise me, that if you ever need help, you will let me
know," Michael sounded stilted with emotion. "Wherever
you are, love, I will come to you."

She was sad and sorry, but her overlying feeling was
one of regret that it was not the Prince speaking thus to
her.

On the last night at Oatlands, they gathered in the
gallery; a narrow, ornate room which ran the length of
the first floor. Golden evening light flooded in through the
windows stretching along one wall. It was the finest room
in this house of lovely chambers and, collected there, were
rare treasures; cabinets filled with curios, paintings glowing against the panelling, foreign glass, chiming clocks,
delicate china vases. A spinet stood beside the wide fireplace and Adrian lifted the painted lid, running expert
fingers over the yellow keys, the sharp, staccato tinkle of
a galliard piercing the flow of chatter and laughter.

It stabbed Venetia with sadness. How long would this
beauty remain unspoiled? she wondered. Would it be
turned over to the rebel soldiers soon, to be carted away
and sold, like the riches of Basing House?

The talk veered to the war, an endless topic of gloomy
speculation.

"I never thought that it would end like this." Whil

Michael spoke, his eyes were on Venetia and he was not referring to the conflict.

"Tut-tut, comrade! Enough of this mumpish humor! Fill up your glass, my blood, I'm already ahead of you by a dish of claret or two!" Barney was practicing with his dice, his eyes on Adrian's rings, no doubt he would lure him into playing hazard before the night was through.

"Did any of us think to see this sad outcome?" he asked, pulling out a chair for the Chevalier who was already placing a pile of coins on the table. "I recall well how I left my village full of brave hopes. What a send off! The bells ringing, people hollering, dogs barking, and my mother crying! God rest her soul!"

No one was under any illusions about Barney's plans. He would call himself "Captain," draw about him a band of followers and join the new *élite* of the underworld. From the wreck of the King's army was born the English highwayman, sparkish in dress, witty and mannered, gallant to ladies.

Barney was already well experienced in this field. "I'll wager that I was one of the first!" he stated proudly, discussing it with the Prince. "Rest assured, Your Highness, I shall waylay Roundhead coaches only. It will be a proof of my loyalty to the Crown!"

If fortune smiled on him, he might avoid being caught and getting his neck stretched, for a few months.

After supper, Rupert and Venetia sauntered, arm in arm, on the paved terrace, and she told him about Michael. "Why do you not do as he wishes?" he said quietly, not looking at her.

"D'you want to be rid of me?" Even as her lips framed the question, she shook her head in denial. "Would you have another man rear your son?"

The light was quenched from Rupert's face. "I shall have little opportunity to do so myself. For once in my life, I am trying to be unselfish. I can give you nothing."

So much for her hopes of even that lowly style of matrimony where she would remain in her former station, and her children make no claim to his title or possessions.

Venetia shivered and pressed her face against Rupert's slashed sleeve.

"Oh, Highness, please let me come with you——" She could say no more for the strangling in her throat and knew that Damaris would be cross with her because she was not playing the scene as they had planned.

Urging her to get some decision from him, Damaris had worked out every move and, at her prompting, Venetia was wearing a dress which she knew Rupert liked, in thin summer silk of pale lilac, cut very low, with a wide square neck, and puffed sleeves ending in a rich fall of lace. She moved in a cloud of seductive perfume, which had an exotic smell, like incense, sprayed on generously by Damaris. This weeping, these inelegant gusty sobs which ruined her paint and shattered her veneer of calm, had not been part of the design.

He was watching her in a way which made her arms and back tingle. With a mournful wail, she threw herself against him, pounding on his chest with small, desperate blows. The familiar feel of his hard muscles, the scent of his skin, made her cry harder, with the sharp reminder of all she had to lose. For a moment he did not move, his arms slack at his sides; then he spat out an impatient curse and pulled her close to him roughly.

"Holy God!" he groaned out. "One day I shall have to leave you behind, *liebling!* You know that I must be free——"

"But not yet, my Prince—not yet." Venetia's tears dried on her face as his mouth came down to crush hers with an angry urgency, and she slid her arms tightly around his body beneath the scarlet doublet.

"I shall travel to St. Germains," continued Rupert much later that night and Venetia, rousing to look at him, did not much like the expression in his eyes, guessing what he had in mind. Digby would be there with Queen Henrietta and Goirng, Wilmot and Percy, all very busy blackening his reputation, each skilled at spreading calumnies.

"Damaris says that I can stay with her." She must not let him think her a burden. "You will be welcome there also."

He was brooding, pensive. "I know not what I shall do, I must work, for I am penniless. A commission in the French army for a while, mayhap, until we can reorganize the Cavaliers."

Venetia could see little through her daze of happiness —her mind filled with one joy only—she was to accompany him overseas.

Rupert's cavalcade moved on in the direction of the coast, and their first stop was Guildford. Fairfax's passes were proving essential for their safety. For the first time

344

they were facing towns which had been militantly Puritan from the start. Rupert's repute preceded him everywhere, and his reception was hostile, civil only because of that scrap of paper bearing the signature of "Fiery Tom."

The atmosphere of cold, angry suspicion would have dampened the most hardened Royalist. Even if there were sympathizers, under this new régime they hardly dared to express it, although the landlord of the sizeable tavern where the Prince lodged, could not conceal his pleasure, ordering the best suite of rooms to be prepared for his Royal guests, bobbing and ducking, running ahead of then, unlocking doors, standing back, bowing.

"Oh, sirs—Your Royal Highnesses! Such a privilege, such an honor!" He whipped out a kerchief and applied it to his brow. "But I must be discreet—you understand? I have to go on here after you have departed—you'll not doubt my loyalty, I trust—but I am a poor man, sirs, I have to live—there is my wife, you see—and six hungry brats! Those Roundhead knaves!" He spat to show his disgust. "But what can we do? It is as well you go abroad, life is almighty dreary now. They have put a stop to all jollity. No cards, no dice, no plays, no dancing! 'Tis all long faces and praying."

The apartment consisted of a parlor and two bedchambers, and the valets were soon moving about unpacking their masters' things. Across the landing, the nursery staff were taking up residence. When Venetia left them to join Rupert, she found him leaning against one of the windows which faced out onto the gallery. His face was moody and displeased as he frowned at the dusty rider standing before him.

"This is typical of him, isn't it?" Rupert was saying to Maurice, holding out the letter. "We send for him to come to us at Oatlands and he takes no damned notice. Now, when he wants us to do something for him, he announces that he will visit us here!"

"Shall we tell him what he can do with his message?" suggested Maurice helpfully.

Rupert dismissed the man to wait, while he considered his reply. "I would not lift a finger to help him get his Goddamned country back, but there are the rest of the family to consider. All those girls needing husbands and marriage portions! Not that I entertain any illusions regarding Charles Louis. I doubt much that any will benefit —saving himself!"

The war which had raged for nearly thirty years on the Continent was now drawing to a close. A treaty, which might restore Charles Louis to the Palatinate, was already under consideration, but the Elector could not make terms with the Emperor without the consent of all his brothers.

"Shall I absent myself while you see him?" Venetia wanted to know, getting ready for bed that night, presenting her back to Rupert to have him unlace her dress. They had sat up late, deep in discussion, and all the maids were asleep.

"'Sdeath! He'll have no right to censure me, he has mistresses aplenty in London," the Prince growled. He was concentrating on the lacing, but at last got it undone and released her with a light slap on the backside. "Stay, and you will. Indeed, 'twill be a proof that he is not the only one of the Queen's sons who knows how to please the ladies."

Venetia gave him a sharp look, unpinning her hair so that it tumbled down. Did that old snub of his mother's still rankle? She took off the rest of her clothes slowly—she often lost Rupert these days, unable to follow him into his thoughts which dwelt more and more on the land across the Channel.

Listening to the brothers talking over breakfast next day made her all the more conscious that there were vast areas of his life of which she knew absolutely nothing. She could piece together fragments from Pierre and Etienne——Holmes filled in some of the gaps and, lately, De Faust, who had ceased to frown upon her now he had taken the baby to his heart.

It was obvious that they were looking forward to going home. Their conversation turned much less on the fortunes of England. Much as they disliked Charles Louis, his anticipated arrival brought memories surging up.

Heidelberg! A great deal of the talk hinged on that dream city, which, to the young Palatines, had been a promised land, flowing with milk and honey! None of them could remember it——all but the four eldest had been born after their parents had lost everything in that mad gamble for the Bohemian throne. But their mother had fond recollections of it, she had been happy there a a bride, loved by the people, indulged by her adoring husband. Stolid Holland had been their adopted home and the kindly Dutch had rather liked having this lively bunch of young princes and princesses in their midst.

"Not so the English Puritans, even in those days," Maurice remarked. "D'you recall how a deputation came to mother with godly condolences once, and retired deeply disgusted by the songs, dances, hallooing and general carrying-on of our family?"

"And now they will all be grown. They'll have changed so much in four and a half years."

"And we also shall appear much altered to them." Maurice, clattering boisterously among the serving dishes, did not notice the cloud settling over his brother's face.

"We shall soon have opportunity for observing Charles Louis," he grated. "For my part, I have not set eyes on him since he ran off and left me to my fate on the battlefield of Vlotho, and that must be all of eight years ago."

"Rupert was captured when he went to the rescue of a Cornet who was struggling in a crowd of Imperial troopers," Maurice was explaining earnestly to Venetia, always happy to repeat this tale. "He fought hard till overpowered by impossible numbers, did you not, Rupert? Tell her what happened!"

The Palsgrave scowled—Maurice's hero-worship frequently embarrassed him, but he yielded to her additional pleas. "When the Austrians closed around me, I tried to escape, by clearing the enclosure, but my horse was tired and refused the jump. Colonel Lippe caught at my bridle, but I beat him off. Lord Craven and Count Ferentz rushed to my aid in vain—we were all three taken and I rendered myself to Lippe. He struck up my visor, demanding to know who I was. I was furious and shouted that I was a Colonel. *'Sacrément!'* says he, *'ein juger oberst!'* meaning, 'it is a young one!' "

The Elector arrived at Guildford on Wednesday, and the delay had not sweetened Rupert's temper. He did not want to see him, and was irked by having to hang about; now that his mind was made up, he longed to shake the dust of England from his feet.

Charles Louis expected, and kept, some sort of state (at Parliament's expense) and it was an imposing posse which accompanied him. Rupert disdained to add to the Elector's already inflated opinion of himself by any kind of show. He was taking his ease in a padded armchair, his feet on the table, and he hesitated just that fraction too long when Maurice led their brother through the wide doors, then he swung his legs down lazily, and stood to give the bow which he could not avoid according to the head of his House.

Their formal greeting remarks were spoken in French, and Venetia hoped that the whole interview was not going to be conducted in that language, but, in courtesy to her (and possibly to annoy the Elector), Rupert changed to English, leading her by the hand to be introduced. She swept into a low, graceful curtsey, disturbed by the boorish manner which Rupert had adopted at the sight of his brother. It was as if he chose to appear the brutish mercenary which Charles Louis had been naming him all through the war.

Two years older than Rupert, the Elector was another handsome Palatine, although his hair was fair and he had cold, pale, guarded eyes. He was not quite as tall as his brothers, but big enough to be striking, carrying his inches rather pompously.

The atmosphere was electric. Charles Louis looked into Rupert's savage eyes and then slid hurriedly away to Maurice's. He tried out a tight smile which brought no response from either. "Well, sirs, it has been a long time."

"Indeed it has," Rupert said with meaningful inflection which brought the rout of Vlotho right into the room. "And you have had a very good war, I believe, living in our uncle's palace at Whitehall!"

The years rolled back—it was as if they merely resumed the old arguments, bad feeling and jealousy of pre-war England, of Leyden—of the nursery.

"And you, dear brother, have probably spent it in a manner much to your liking—engaged in pillage and rape." Charles Louis attempted a sneer which did not quite come off. No one was as adept at sneering as Rupert.

Maurice's thick dark brows drew down as he ran a worried glance over both faces, anticipating trouble.

"At least my robbery was done in the open," Rupert answered loftily. "I did not deliberately set out to steal from a man who had shown me nothing but friendship!" There was a nervous flickering of jaw muscles under his smooth tanned skin and his hands were clenched into fists.

Charles Louis was not burdened with that overdose of pride which made life so difficult for Rupert. As heir to the Palatinate he had kept his eye on the main chance—he was well-versed in letting slights and insults pass over him, when it suited his purpose. Now he needed the help

348

of this objectionable soldier to recover his position in Westphalia.

While this family conclave was in progress, Venetia sat quietly, observing them, watching the play of emotions between these three Princes. The Elector gave a restrained, enigmatic smile, seating himself in the box-chair, drawing off his fringed gloves and coiling slim brocade-covered thighs. He was a dapper figure, not exactly Puritan, but strictly neutral; the outward display of a man who prefers to keep a foot in either camp. He was looking at Venetia with unconcealed interest and curiosity; obviously he shared the male Palatines' penchant for pretty women.

"Much as I would enjoy the company of your charming companion, Rupert," he said with heavy jocosity, "as these are somewhat private matters which we must discuss, would it not be better if we were alone?"

"There is nothing which cannot be said before Venetia," Rupert snapped back. "She is entirely loyal to me."

"Ah, yes." The Elector tapped the toe of his fawn leather boot meditatively with the tip of his silver-headed crop. "This must be the young lady of whom I have heard. Prince Rupert's light-o'-love, eh? There is talk of her in London." He smiled faintly, amused by her discomposure. "Well, you know your own business best, Rupert, but I trow, I'd not talk of anything significant before my lady friends."

"Knowing the drabs that you are wont to pick, this does not surprise me," Rupert replied with blistering scorn. "Venetia is different."

"Is she?" The disbelief in Charles Louis's voice was the final insult. "And what do you suppose the Queen our mother will have to say about her, and her bastard?"

This brought Rupert forward to tower over him, making him wish that he had kept to his feet instead of posing in attempted nonchalance. Of course, Rupert should have ignored him; he remembered too late how this was a game which the elder brother had loved to play in the past, knowing exactly how to flick at Le Diable's raw temper with his clever, spiteful mockery.

"You did not come here to discuss my mistress!" The Prince shouted. "You wanted my consent to talk terms with the Emperor. Well, you have it. There is nothing further for us to say!"

With a great effort, he restrained his impulse to pick up the Elector bodily and hurl him down the gallery stairs.

He caught the urgent appeal in Maurice's eyes and seated himself on the edge of the table, well away from temptation. Charles Louis tried to cover his fright with an exaggerated calm, as befitted a prospective ruler.

"My thanks for your co-operation, Rupert—but, by your leave, there are other domestic matters which concern us——"

"What matters? Has someone else turned Papist? Or that saucy minx Sophia been up to mischief and had her bears boxed again? News has trickled through to me, you know, even in my low camp-quarters and outlaw garrisons!" Rupert answered acidly.

The superior smirk returned to lift Charles Louis's features, his voice running on with that slightly patronizing note. "Nay, 'tis something of much greater import, brother —though, I mind me, it may be to your advantage in some ways. Mayhap, our mother will be more indulgent toward your liaison now."

Never had the Elector's prevarications been more irritating.

"What the devil are you driving at?" Rupert, who had been glowering and gnawing at the side of his thumb-nail, now grew still and menacing.

Charles Louis was in his element; he had caught the attention of these annoying louts at last! Now they could not brush him aside with their scorn, their damned unity, their sheer alarming physical size which turned him into a non-entity so that they had never shown him the respect which he felt to be his due.

"Then you've not heard about d'Epinay?"

"For the love of God, get on with it, Timon!" In his concern, Rupert forgot his rancor, and called him by that old childish nickname. "Who the hell is he?"

"Lieutenant Colonel Jacques de l'Epinay, Sieur de Vaux." Charles Louis pronounced the title with relish, only too happy to bring them up to date with the latest scandal now buzzing around the Continental Courts. Rupert's face had grown darker, almost as if he guessed what was coming.

"He was a young French exile known to be something of a lady-killer. The length and frequency of his visits to the Wassenaer Hof were beginning to set tongues wagging. They were asking just which Royal lady was the attraction, Princess Louise—or the Queen of Bohemia!"

"But she is nearly fifty!" Maurice broke in with all the

350

blank incredulity of the young man never sees his mother as a woman at all, and cannot believe that she might still desire—and indeed, be desirable!

"My dear fellow, have you not heard it said that women of that age often lose their heads over handsome boys?"

"What are you suggesting?" Rupert said, and the Elector should have been warned by that smooth, purring tone, used when he was at his most dangerous.

" 'Tis not what I am suggesting—it was on everyone's lips!" The Elector sounded huffy; d'Epinay had threatened his hold over the Winter Queen, causing him twinges of jealousy. "It was quite extraordinary. You know as well as I, that she doesn't usually have much time for Frenchmen, but this lad had such an insinuating manner and she could see nothing amiss with him, shutting her ears to all rumors that his reputation was unsavory. I took exception to the sight of her walking in the Lange Voorhout attended by him. He had not even bothered to remove his hat. I went up and knocked it off!"

"Well done!" There was grudging admiration in Rupert's voice and Venetia, fascinated by this unforeseen chink in the armor of the Queen, felt the change in the air; in pack-instinct, they automatically united against any outsiders.

"Phillip took action next——he is nearly nineteen, and grown into a fine lad. He told d'Epinay to stop hanging around our house. The scoundrel retorted-that he would do so when the Queen asked him to desist."

Rupert's hand was at his sword-hilt, his face flushing and that deadly glitter in his eyes. "Was there no one to defend her honor?"

"She did not want it defended!" Charles Louis shouted with a savage satisfaction in sending Rupert's idealized concept of her crashing. "She was infatuated with him!"

"What!" It was the roar of an animal in pain. Rupert was borne on a wave of disgust. The Queen, their vital, laughing mother, with her hunting and her hounds and her bevy of faithful followers—but always as untouchable as a goddess. The thought of her mooning after some foppish French dandy, luring him into her bed, made him sick with shame.

"That cannot be!" Maurice exploded, but much less violently. He had never felt the need for Elizabeth which Rupert had always had. "Why, she is the kind of person

351

who would rather hear her dog bark than a man swea
he loves her! She makes fun of them. I've often heard he
declare that as soon as one fool left her, there was an
other to take his place! Oh, I know they have alway
adored her, and been ready to die for her, but as a grea
Queen, that is all!"

Charles Louis raised his silk-clad shoulders in a shrug
"Women do strange things in their middle years. Perhap
she wanted to feel young again. Who knows!"

"God's blood! You sit there talking as if it were noth
ing! Why the devil did you not do something about it?"
Rupert was beside himself with fury. "Is there no fait
or honor left anywhere in the Goddamn world? But o
course, I was forgetting, you were too busy cultivating th
King's enemies. You would have no time to concern you
self about our mother's good name."

Charles Louis drew himself up to his full height, very
offended. "The matter has been settled."

"By whom? Answer, damn you!"

Rupert was acting like a wronged lover. Without bein
in the least aware of it, he was madly jealous. His mother
so niggardly with her love toward her children, had beer
able to pour it out on a good-looking young man. He
sympathies were suddenly with the Queen. What right ha
these domineering sons of hers to interfere with her hap
piness?

"Phillip did it." The Elector's voice was filled with prid
in the youngest brother. "There was a duel in the Bosc
one night. He came into collision with d'Epinay and thre
of his friends. A brawl ensued, but the watch put
stop to it. Next evening, as he was riding through th
Palace d'Armes, he caught sight of the fellow again. D
l'Epinay had time to draw and received Phillip on th
point of his sword, wounding him in the side. Phillip pulle
out his hunting knife and struck him in the throat."

"He killed him!" Rupert rapped out. "What a boy! H
should have been fighting with me in the war!"

"The family honor has been avenged," said the Electo
piously.

"And Phillip?"

"Had the presence of mind to get to horse and ride lik
hell for the Spanish Netherlands frontier."

"And our mother?" Rupert was looking down at hi
hands, flexing them.

"There has been an almighty storm. She has curse

352

Phillip, vowing that she will never look on his face again, but all the others are on his side, except perhaps that troublesome jade, Louise. She cares not a jot for what is said about us. It was partially her doing, the whole sordid affair, she encouraged him in the first place."

"What action have you taken, sir?" Maurice asked, seeing that Rupert had gone off into one of his moods when there was no knowing what turn he might take.

"I have written to Her Majesty, warmly espousing Phillip's cause. I expect she will get over it—in time."

"I shall write also," Rupert roused himself, adding darkly. "I can see that it is high time we went home."

"Are you quite sure that is what you want to do?" Charles Louis was watching Rupert carefully, and Venetia had the feeling that he was leading up to the real reason why he had ridden to Guildford.

It was his nature to be devious, and even now he went rambling into a welter of details of his hopes for help from Parliament, and the work he had put in over the years to make them lend a favorable ear to the Palatine cause. No one had made him an outright offer of the English Crown, so now he was content to settle for the substance of his father's lands in Germany, rather than wait longer for a shadow. But he saw no reason why it should not be kept in the family if possible.

Rupert's eyes sharpened into attention when he caught the drift of his brother's hints and suggestions.

"You see, Rupert"—he was going on, uneasy under the younger man's unwinking gaze—"some Members of the House are not at all opposed to the notion." He dried up, cleared his throat and tried again. "Fairfax, in particular, seems to have taken a fancy to you. Many are saying, in London, that they would sooner deal with you than King Charles. You've given them some stiff fighting, but they know where they are with you."

"What Timon says is true, Rupert," Maurice broke in eagerly, resurrecting his hopes, shooting a look at Venetia to see how she was taking it. "I've heard the Roundhead prisoners say the same thing."

Encouraged, the Elector continued more confidently. "Why do you think they gave you such good terms at Oxford? And why were you allowed to go to Oatlands? Fairfax had it in mind that he would be able to contact you easily there. It was only after Cromwell found out and started trouble in the Commons about it that he had to rescind the order. But it is not too late—I can carry a message to those who favor you——"

Rupert paced up and down with his long, fluid strides, passing Maurice, avoiding the eager pleading in his eyes, ignoring Venetia who struggled to remain expressionless.

"To put it plainly, brother——" The Elector took a deep breath and then said, in a rush: "There are those who want to make you King!"

The words rang in Venetia's ears like a call of trumpets, and she saw the instant response in Maurice. But Rupert's face colored to the brow and then grew pale. He wheeled on Charles Louis with such a look of white fury that he flinched.

"Have you done?" he snarled.

The Elector recovered his poise quickly when he saw that he was not going to hit him. He tried a supercilious curl of the lip. "Oh come, you cannot pretend that you have not thought of it—and wanted it. You have the army right behind you, every damn man of them! The masses must be led; if their natural leaders neglect them they will follow base fellows! The New Model controls England now and their chief is Cromwell—he is the only man who counts for much any more. Would you have England ruled by him?"

"If you have finished—get out!"

Charles Louis gathered together the tattered shreds of his dignity. "Very well, Rupert, if you are determined. But it won't help King Charles, you know. He is finished. He'll never rule again—they won't let him. The Scots will sell him to his enemies—you'll see. And if you won't govern England, then Cromwell will!"

"At least I shan't have betrayed the man I pledged myself to serve!"

"A lost cause, Rupert." The Elector picked up his hat from the table, smoothing the feather before he put it on.

"Then I shall fight for his son."

The elder brother paused at the door. "From all that I hear about Cousin Charles, you will receive little thanks from him for your pains."

Rupert's eyes focused on him; he seemed surprised at such a statement. "I am not seeking thanks," he said.

Dover was as busy as an ant-hill, the air fresh with the tang of salt and pitch, the sea as solid and calm as a sheet f lead, but Rupert viewed it with mixed feelings from the window of the inn on the wharf-side.

Sea travel always made him extremely ill, until he became used to the motion, yet he was impatient to be off and had found a small ship which was due to cross to Calais on next morning's tide. Maurice awaited shipping to Holland. His health was still poor.

"He is going home to mamma to recuperate, are you not, my pet?" Damaris teased, making a kissing mouth at him.

" 'Till Rupert has need of me," he maintained stoutly. "And I pray God that will not be long. Those sisters of ours will drive me mad. I shall be penned in a house of cackling women! *Mort Dieu!*"

"Do not worry, Twin," Rupert assured him cheerfully, "I'll soon have you out of it and back into action!"

He was leaning on the casement, cool and easy with his shirt unfastened, a tankard in his hand, exhilarated by the spicy smells borne on the wind. It was wonderful to see how his spirits had revived when they rode into Dover. He stood on the threshold of fresh experience—doors were closing behind him, but new ones opened ahead. The germ of an idea was formulating, suggested by the sight of the tall-masted ships, which swung gracefully in the bay. The sea—this could be the battleground for the King's Cavaliers! They would be pouring into France and Holland in droves soon—destitute, desperate, seeking honorable employment. He would lead them to fight on the high seas—forming a fleet of privateers and attacking the Parliamentarian shipping on the trade routes! He had always wanted to sail, eager to explore the coast of Africa—to see America—and Venetia grew quiet as he talked of this. She dreaded such ideas, they would take him from her.

Supposing he were to tire of her? She would be alone in a strange country, then, catching Damaris' encouraging smile, she put panic firmly in its place—that kindly woman had sworn to help her, and Meriel had given her an address where she could be found. There would be Michael, waiting in England—and Rupert could not possibly desert her!

But he was leaving her temporarily tomorrow, stating firmly: "There will be a more suitable ship sailing later in the week. You will travel on it with my staff and horses. Maurice will be here to look after things till then."

355

Then she resented her baby for the first time. For rea
sons of his own, Rupert was impatient to leave at once o
this small vessel with its limited accommodation. Had i
not been for that tiny, utterly dependent tyrant, she coul
have donned boy's clothing and endured the cramped un
comfortable conditions. The tie she had taken on was a
binding, as demanding, as her love for the Prince. It unite
them, but brought inevitable separation too.

"Maybe the *Pfalzgraf* does not want you to see him lai
low with seasickness," suggested the flippant Damaris whe
she had listened to Venetia's complaints for at least te
minutes. She was kneeling on the window-seat, throwin
pellets of bread to the noisy, quarrelsome gulls. " 'Slife
no one can cut an impressive figure in that sorry condi
tion. Fret not, my child, we shall join him anon at S
Germains. I, for one, cannot wait to get there! Quee
Henrietta has set up Court and it will be aswarm with th
most interesting people. Just think, in a few days I sha
be in the arms of someone I haven't even met yet! Eng
land is not much fun any more."

They grew silent under the spell of the fine summe
evening, washed in pink light as the sun, a crimson orb
drowned on the rim of the blood-tinted sea. Their thought
were with the ravaged country which they would soon b
leaving, their cause defeated, the King's brave champion
slain or exiled or imprisoned. Now the grim-faced soldier
of the New Model kept tight control. All persons comin
from Oxford or from any other Royalist garrison were for
bidden to wear arms or to be out after nine o'clock a
night. The Cavaliers, after their long, vain strife, foun
themselves in the degrading position of a beaten enemy.

They lingered over supper in nostalgic mood. The win
dows were flung wide, giving a view of the harbor, wher
the evening star, bright Hesperus, was shining, lying lo
on the horizon. Soon it would be just a memory—soo
they would be saying: "Do you remember, when we wer
in England——?"

Venetia wanted to cry, more than a little drunk, leanin
her head against Rupert's shoulder, while he patted he
and understood and longed to break down himself becaus
it had begun with such high hopes and had ended like thi

The reminiscences seemed to have already begu
Maurice said: "Remember that morning, Rupert, whe
news came through of a Roundhead party close by, an

356

you were in the middle of shaving and rushed out to fight with one side of your jaw covered in soap?"

There was answering amusement in the lean face close to Venetia's. "I licked 'em, too, and then went back to complete my toilet!"

Venetia had never understood how Rupert had been able to disguise himself for these escapades. He said that the home-theatricals had helped, he had learned there to hunch his shoulders and stoop; clad in old clothes, with an assumed, bucolic accent, he had fooled the enemy several times.

Rupert's last night in England. Venetia lay in his arms and listened to the waves and knew how he was feeling. She longed to say something, but was unable to find the right words, her mind heavy with boundless sorrow. Instead, she squeezed his hand, glad of the returning response on his fingers.

"You'll come back soon, darling," she whispered. "There must be a way to help the King to his own again."

But she did not believe it any more than he, oppressed by this sense of dark tragedy. He said nothing, thinking of the friends who had died and wondering why he had been spared—it was he who had once wanted to leave his bones in England.

De Faust roused them early, Rupert shaved, and dressed in a rigorously masculine suit, which yet carried no hint of Puritanism, all dark, rich colors with a mere edging of lace at neck and sleeves.

Rupert spent some time holding the baby, reluctant to part from him, and Venetia put on her clothes with that lump swelling in her throat and the sick, empty feeling clawing at her. The minutes slid by, gathering speed, rushing everything into readiness so that in no time at all they were standing on the wharf where the white mist was thinning. It was going to be a cloudless, hot day, and Rupert would not be there to share it with her.

The last of his boxes had been stowed, and those awkward farewells had to be said. He was moving restlessly, eager to be gone, hating this painful parting. The vessel swung lazily on its moorings, its captain glancing up at the sky, sniffing the wind, standing ready to welcome his famous passenger.

"You'll be able to bring Venetia to see mother," Maurice joked, one among the ring of faces around the Prince.

357

He threw him a quenching look, shouting to Damaris: "Keep him in order whilst I am away from him."

More laughter, with her promising, and everyone being determinedly jolly. Venetia knew that if he did not go soon, she would not be able to suppress the huge sob which was gathering like a rain-squall somewhere in the region of her chest.

He turned and drew her into his arms, ignoring the interested sailors who dawdled at the ship's side, risking the bosun's rope-end to stare at the lovely woman and arrestingly handsome man locked in a close embrace on the quayside.

"Oh, why can't I come with you now? Why?" she began in anger and despair—but stopped abruptly, knowing it to be useless.

She clung desperately, till he bent swiftly to kiss her once more, then took hold of her arms, forcing them down from his neck. Almost before she knew it, he had gone, crossing the gangway in rapid strides.

Venetia felt a touch at her elbow. It was Maurice, and he too was gazing up at the tall figure of his brother, engaged in talk with the captain, while the seamen hauled at the plank. In his eyes was the same wan expression of loss, the same anxiety.

"He will be all right, Venetia," he said in a rough attempt at comfort. "We shall be with him very soon and you earlier than I, for I must to Holland first."

The ship shuddered into life, with the creak and rattle of anchor chains and the men singing at the capstan. The sails caught the breeze as the first fingers of sunlight rent the mist, glinting on gold leaf and scarlet paint and the flag just starting to flutter.

They ran to the water's edge. Venetia gave a mournful little wave, then her hand flew to her mouth and she bit down hard on the flesh; she would not cry yet—nothing must film her eyes until the ship was an indistinct silver flash riding the shimmering waves. Somehow, she would get through the days—there was the baby, and she ached to hold him tightly against this fierce pain in her heart. Rupert's "family" would need to be organized, these tasks would keep her busy, but within she would be dead——all feeling, all joy suspended, to throb back in to life only when she saw Rupert again.

Her future stretched before her very clearly at that moment. He would be off adventuring—such a man as he

358

must be free—yet, as surely as the tides which rose and fell, so he must return, be it after months or even years, and she would wait at whatever base or headquarters they called home, as she had waited for him so often during the King's war.

BIBLIOGRAPHY

Ashley, Maurice: *Life in Stuart England* (1964)

Bund, J. W. W.: *The Civil War in Worcestershire* (1905)

Burton, Elizabeth: *The Jacobeans at Home* (1962)

Burne, A. H. and Young, P.: *The Great Civil War, 1642–46* (1959)

Cattermole, R.: *The Great Civil War of Charles I and the Parliament* (1941)

Chapman, Hester W.: *The Tragedy of Charles II* (1964)

Clarendon, Earl of: *The History of the Great Rebellion* (1819)

Coate, Mary: *Cornwall in the Great Civil War and Interregnum, 1642–60* (1930)

Edgar, F. T. R.: *Sir Ralph Hopton. The King's Man in the West* (1968)

Farrow, W. J.: *The Great Civil War in Shropshire* (1926)

Ferguson, B.: *Rupert of the Rhine* (1952)

Firth, C. H.: *The Journal of Prince Rupert's Marches, September 1642–July 1946* (1898)

Granville, R.: *The King's General in the West. The Life of Sir Richard Granville* (1908)

Hibbert, Christopher: *Charles I* (1968)

Hole, Christina: *The English Housewife of the 17th Century* (1953)

Lattimer, J.: *Annals of Bristol* (1908)

McChesney, Dora Greenwell: *Rupert, by the Grace of God*—(1899)

Nagel, Lawson C.: *Prince Rupert's Bluecoats. The Story of a Civil War Regiment* (1973)

Oman, Carola: *Elizabeth of Bohemia* (1938)

Robinson, Derek: *A Shocking History of Bristol* (1973)

Rowsell, M. C.: *The Life-story of Charlotte de la Tremoille, Countess of Derby* (1905)

Scott, Eva: *Rupert, Prince Palatine* (1900)

Shelmerdine, J. M.: *Introduction to Woodstock* (1971)

mith, G. R.: *Without Touch of Dishonour. Life of Sir Henry Slingsby* (1968)

oynbee, Margaret and Young, P.: *Cropredy Bridge. The Campaign and Battle* (1970)

ucker, John and Winstock, L. S.: *The English Civil War. A Military Handbook* (1972)

arley, F. J.: *The Siege of Oxford, 1642–46* (1932)

Varburton, E.: *Memoirs of Prince Rupert and the Cavaliers* (1849)

Vatson, D. R.: *The Life and Times of Charles* I (1972)

Veb, J.: *Memorials of the Civil War in Herefordshire* (1879)

Vedgewod, C. V.: *The King's War, 1614–47* (1958)

Venham, P.: *The Great and Close Siege of York* (1970)

Vilkinson, Clennel: *Prince Rupert the Cavalier* (1934)

Vinstock, L. S.: *Songs and Marches of the Roundheads and Cavaliers* (1971)

Voolrych, Austin: *Battles of the English Civil War* (1961)

Vroughton, John: *The Civil War in Bath and North Somerset* (1973)

oung, P. and Tucker, N.: *The Civil War. Richard Atkyns and John Gwyn* (1967)

oung, P.: *Edgehill 1642. The Campaign and the Battle* (1967)

oung, P.: *Marston Moor 1644. The Campaign and the Battle* (1970)

oung, P.: *The English Civil War Armies* (1973)

Venetia could feel herself dissolving,

wanting only to be devoured; she rejoiced that she was no inexperienced virgin. Michael had schooled her well. Rupert pressed her back against the tree, his body hard and demanding, his kisses hot on her face and neck and on her shoulders where he had pushed her bodice aside. He was fully roused, desperate for relief, as if he had not had a woman for a long time. This was what she had wanted since the first moment she had seen him, towering and godlike, in the meadow; his wildness, his roughness, and his need were so exciting that she was sliding rapidly toward surrender and had no inclination to stop.

But it must not happen here!

Books by Joan Hunter

The Cavalier's Woman
Roxanna
Under the Raging Moon

Published by POCKET BOOKS

 *Are there paperbound books you want
but cannot find in your retail stores?*